THE SILENCE OF BONES

THE
SILENCE
OF
BONES

JUNE HUR

Feiwel and Friends
New York

A FEIWEL AND FRIENDS BOOK
An imprint of Macmillan Publishing Group, LLC
120 Broadway, New York, NY 10271

Our books may be purchased in bulk for promotional, educational, or business use.
Please contact your local bookseller or the Macmillan Corporate and Premium Sales
Department at (800) 221-7945 ext. 5442 or by email at
MacmillanSpecialMarkets@macmillan.com.

Names: Hur, June, author.
Title: The silence of bones / June Hur.
Description: First edition. | New York : Feiwel and Friends, 2020. | Summary:
In Joseon Dynasty-era Korea, sixteen-year-old Seol, an indentured servant
within the police bureau, becomes entangled in a politically-charged
investigation into the murder of a noblewoman.
Identifiers: LCCN 2019018300| ISBN 9781250229557 (hardcover) |
ISBN 9781250229564 (eBook)
Subjects: | CYAC: Police—Fiction. | Indentured servants—Fiction. |
Murder—Fiction. | Brothers and sisters—Fiction. | Catholics—Fiction. |
Persecution—Fiction. | Korea—History—Chosæon dynasty,
1392–1910—Fiction. | Mystery and detective stories.
Classification: LCC PZ7.1.H8645 Sil 2020 | DDC [Fic]—dc23
LC record available at https://lccn.loc.gov/2019018300

BOOK DESIGN BY KATIE KLIMOWICZ

Feiwel and Friends logo designed by Filomena Tuosto
First edition, 2020

1   3   5   7   9   10   8   6   4   2
fiercereads.com

To Eomma and Abba—thank you for offering me the freedom and encouragement to pursue my love of writing.

THE SILENCE OF BONES

ONE

THE CAPITAL LAY deep in stillness.

By morning the dirt road usually clamored with life outside Changdeok Palace: women crowding fish stalls, farmers carrying produce, scholars garbed in silk robes, and monks with prayer beads strung around their necks. And there would always be a mob of children, faces burnt and glistening in the sticky heat, chasing one another down the street. But not today.

"Do you suppose the rumors are true, Officer Kyŏn?" Rain pitter-pattered against black tiled roofs as I lowered the satgat over my face, allowing the drops to dribble down from the pointed top and off the wide straw brim. "Whispers that the king was assassinated."

Mud squelched under boots as police officers trudged ahead.

Officer Kyŏn, the last officer in line and youngest of all, sent me a fierce look over his shoulder. "Watch what you say. The capital is nothing like your countryside."

He was referring to Inchon Prefecture. A few months had passed since I'd left home, brought to the capital to be trained as a police damo, an indentured servant-of-all-work.

"But, eh, I'll tell you this much." Officer Kyŏn eyed our gray surroundings as he adjusted the sash belt over his black robe. "When King Chŏngjo died, there came a terrible noise of weeping from Mount Samgak, and rays of sunlight collided, then burst into sparks."

"An omen?" I whispered.

"A bad omen. The old order has passed and the new will come with a river of blood."

The king was dead, and our lives were going to change. I had learned this while serving wine to police officers, eavesdropping into the accounts of politics and treachery that oftentimes left me over-excited. It was all I could think of, even as we were journeying to a crime scene, summoned there by the inspector.

"Let me tell you something about the capital, newcomer. The one thing everyone wants is power. To gain it or to stabilize it." He clucked his tongue and waved me away. "What use has a damo to know such things? No woman should talk as much as you."

Annoyance pinched at me as I followed in his shadow. He was right, of course—though I did not yet consider myself a woman. I was only sixteen. Still, I'd learned that among the seven sins a woman could commit, one was talking excessively. A man could even divorce his wife because of her chattiness.

I blamed Older Sister for my longing to know more. She was unusually learned for a servant, with vast knowledge of Buddhist and Confucian verses; she would always try to hide it from me and the villagers. I would tug at her long sleeve, asking her to tell me more, but she would pull away and say, "It is better for you not to know these things. Do not stand out, do not be so curious, then you will have a long life, Seol." I had resented her for this, though now I understood her better. The longing for knowledge only got me into trouble these days.

"You there."

I looked ahead. Inspector Han stood in the near distance, watching me from beneath the wide brim of his black police hat. The string of beads threaded on the chin strap trembled in the gusty rain. Behind him was his team of men, who must have arrived at the scene before us: two officers, a coroner's assistant, a legal clerk, and a police artist. I hurried toward the inspector while the six officers who had traveled with me exchanged information among themselves, murmuring in my periphery:

"Found by a watchman."

"When?"

"He was patrolling the South Gate, and at the end of his watch, there she was."

I gathered my hands before me and bowed to Inspector Han, deeper than was necessary. He was one of the few worthy enough to see the top of my head. He was to me the great spotted leopard from my village: the speedy and well-muscled hunter who excelled at climbing and jumping, and in slipping silently through the grass with scarcely a ripple.

"You called for me, Inspector," I said.

"Have a look at her."

He gestured at a lump a few paces away. I walked into the vast shadow of the wall that enclosed Hanyang, the capital of Joseon. Its height blocked out the sight of mountains, and it was so thick that an invader might take a thousand years to chip through the massive stones. Yet dangerous as the world outside the fortress was, clearly danger lurked within as well.

My stomach turned to water as I stood before a young woman. She lay sprawled, drenched in rain, her face turned to the ground. Her long dress and jacket of a silky ramie cloth, the hem and sleeves richly embroidered with floral patterns, marked her as a noble.

"Roll her over," Inspector Han ordered. "We have yet to see her wound."

I stepped over the corpse, crouched, and grabbed her shoulder. This was why the Capital Police Bureau kept female servants like me: I was an extension of the officers, my hands used by them to arrest female criminals and to examine female victims. An inconvenience for the police, and yet men were forbidden from touching women who were not directly related to them. It was the law, Confucius's law.

As I flipped the corpse around, her voluminous skirt whispered and I almost jumped back when her long, soggy hair clung to my sleeve. *Don't yelp.*

I closed my eyes, panic thrumming in my chest. Never had I touched a murdered corpse before, having worked at the police bureau for only a few months. I sucked in a deep breath and peeled the damp strands off me, then forced my gaze down again. Blood stained her white collar. A deep gash with puckered edges stretched across her pale throat. A cloudy film covered her eyes. And a bloody cavern was dug into her face, a staring hole like that of a skeleton where her nose once was.

"Stabbed in the neck," Inspector Han said. He gestured to the tassel-like ornament tied to the victim's skirt. "No one has stolen the norigae, and the jewel pin is still in her hair. This is no robbery. What is that under her left shoulder?"

I lifted the shoulder. A small, bloody knife with a silver handle . . .

I looked back at the norigae hanging from the victim. Upon closer examination, I noticed there was a silver paedo ornamentally knotted to the norigae, and it was missing a knife. My hands moved of their own accord, taking the murder weapon and slipping it into the turquoise stone-encrusted sheath.

"It belonged to her," the inspector whispered, a frown in his voice. "Give that to the clerk."

I did so, stunned that the victim's own decorative knife had resulted in her death.

"Now, look for her identification tag."

"Neh." I patted the corpse, buried my hand into her skirt, and discovered a yellow tag of poplar wood. By law, everyone in the Joseon kingdom had to carry one. There were characters engraved onto the wood, likely indicating the bearer's name, place of birth, status, and residence—but I couldn't say for sure, for to me words were brushstrokes with no meaning. It was likely Hanja, classical Chinese writing, the official script of our kingdom, for what else could it be? Our native script, Hangul, seemed to have more circles and straight lines.

Placing the tag in the inspector's outstretched hand, I looked up, wanting to see his reaction to whatever name was written. But my gaze only managed to reach his chin, for I knew not to hold the stare of my superior. I still didn't even know the color of Inspector Han's eyes.

"Lady O, daughter of the Cabinet Minister O, and only nineteen years old."

A murmur rose among the officers. "Pity, gone at such a young age," someone said. "I'll wager her father's enemy killed her. Members of the Southerner faction like him have one too many rivals . . ."

As they shared their low-voiced speculations, I dragged the corpse toward Officers Kyŏn and Goh, who were holding a wooden stretcher, waiting for me. No one else but I, the damo girl, was permitted to move the female corpse.

I clenched my teeth against the ache in my chest. In the past few days, an unusually high number of corpses had been carted in, the bodies of servants and peasants. Officers had looked upon their deaths as casually as they would butchered meat. But it was different now. The blood of a noble shocked them.

Another tug, and the sickly-sweet odor of death drifted into my nostrils. A smell that shouldn't have surprised me. I'd hunted rabbits and birds before with an arrow. I'd helped skin them too. But this, this odor seemed half mold, half animal. With one last heave, I pulled the woman onto the stretcher, and at once I shrank away from the horrible odor.

"Senior Officer Shim, take Kyŏn, question the watchmen." Inspector Han's voice resounded through the beating of rain. "The rest of you will go to all the inns, then all the houses. This cannot have been without witnesses . . ." He paused, and then called out, "You there."

I got to my feet, knees mud-damp. "Me, sir?"

Inspector Han cast a glance my way as he mounted his horse. "Yes, you. Follow me."

I hurried alongside, the horse's powerful hooves striking the ground, splashing more dirt onto my skirt and sleeves. The peasants must have heard the tramping, for they dropped to the ground, bowing head-to-mud as was protocol. Inspector Han was not only an aristocrat, but he was a military official of the fifth rank—a rank very few noblemen achieved in their lifetime. No one would dare refuse to bow to a man such as he.

But me?

I was born a servant and thus belonged to the palchŏn, the "eight meanest groups of people." Our lowborn class was crowded with monks, shamans, clowns, butchers, and the like. All of us, in one way or another, were considered polluted.

Still, I imagined they were bowing to me.

●

Older Sister always scolded me for having the airs of a Chinese empress. Growing up, I would always clamor after attention, convinced that I deserved much more—more love, more appreciation, more kindness. How could a servant have had such thoughts?

Life as a servant should have taught me that the world was cruel, and that I did not deserve anything better. Before I'd even learned to walk, I had learned of death. Father was said to have died from starvation, and while I could not remember this, from what I'd been told, I often dreamed that I was counting his ribs. Years later, Mother had tried to leap off a cliff into the sea, only to shatter upon the craggy shore. Then, at the age of seven, I had found Young Lady Euna of the Nam household, whom I had thought of as my playmate (though really, I was her family servant), cold and motionless under a silk blanket. But somehow my "Chinese empress" air had stuck to me like a spiky burr, until three months ago.

A patrolman had caught me trying to run away from the police bureau. Amid the chaotic shuffle of arms and feet and high-pitched screams, I'd tried to escape him as well. For on that day—the fourth day of my indenture—I had received news about Older Sister's deteriorating health, and my need to fulfill a certain promise to her had sharpened. But how foolish I'd been to think I could get away, and the police had made sure to teach me a lesson. They had scarred me with a hot iron, a punishment from the ancient times, branding my left cheek with a Hanja character: *bi*. Female servant.

I touched my left cheek, the skin thick and rough where the wound had healed. The memory chafed at me as I followed Inspector Han, the memory of wanting to die, not knowing how to endure the humiliation. The intensity of my death wish had passed quickly, though. So long as I had a purpose—to fulfill Older Sister's request—my life still had meaning.

Stay in Hanyang, she had begged. *Find your brother Inho's grave.*

We were both convinced of his death, for he had sworn on Mother's grave that he would write to me, no matter where I might end up in the kingdom. And I had believed him, for I *knew* him. My brother always kept his word. Yet twelve years had gone by without a letter from him. He had to be dead.

To help with my search for him, Older Sister had given me a sketch of our brother on the day of my departure to the capital. A sketch so faded and badly drawn that it had warped my own memory of him. Still, I had never left the bureau without it, making sure to keep it safely tucked inside my uniform. I had promised to find my older brother, and like him, I always kept my word.

Gradually the memory faded, my mind distracted by the labyrinth coiled at the center of the capital—of dirt paths and alleys, cluttered by huts made of cheap wood and thatch. Peasants crumpled in fear as we passed them by. The atmosphere changed when we ventured into the Northern District, the residential quarter of high-ranking officials, nestled between Changdeok Palace to the east and Gyeongbok Palace to the west. We were surrounded no longer by desperation but by the patterned stone walls and dark-tiled roofs of neighboring mansions. The rainfall had lightened, and in the clearing air, the eight peaks that surrounded Hanyang's basin cut the sky like teeth.

"Stop here," Inspector Han said as we arrived before the gate of a walled mansion. "What was your name again?"

"It is Seol, sir," I whispered.

A pause, and then he asked, "Well?"

I hurried forward, tied the rein to a post, then knocked on the massive wooden doors. In the silence that followed, I wondered why the inspector had failed to recall my name. Was I that forgettable? I straightened my raven-black hair, ran a hand over my uniform. The reflection in the shimmering puddle below revealed a small face with wide lips, and what I liked to think of as eyes shaped like petals. Not "Little Tiny Eyes" as my sister called them. My chest, tightly bound, and my frame—too tall, too lanky—made me look more like a boy wearing a skirt than a woman. There really seemed to be nothing remarkable about me.

The doors creaked open, startling me into attention. A gatekeeper peeked out and looked at me from head to toe; then his gaze slammed into Inspector Han. At once he lowered his head with humility. "Inspector!"

"I have come to speak with Lord O."

"H-he left the capital a month ago."

"Then who is home?"

"His wife, Matron Kim. But you will have to come another time. She is ill, you see."

"It is a matter of great urgency."

The gatekeeper hesitated, wringing his hands, then stepped back and let us into the compound. The maid who escorted us also looked uneasy. Following her deeper into the strained silence, we traveled across the courtyard toward the guest hall: a long hanok building lined with fourteen hanji screened doors all the way to the end, heavy beams supporting the tiled roof, which flared on either side like dragon whiskers. A few paces away from this pavilion stood a gate, likely leading to another courtyard, for mansions usually had five quarters, divided by stone walls and linked together by narrow passageways.

Inspector Han paused in his steps, and I nearly walked into him. "Interview Lady O's personal maid and report everything back to me."

"Yes, sir." Pushing back the brim of my straw hat, I watched him walk off until his robe of midnight blue disappeared. Not too long after, a servant passed by with a bucket of water.

"Excuse me." I hurried over to her. "Where might I find Lady O's personal maid?"

The woman turned her head quickly toward me. Her lips moved, but instead of words, she made a low moaning sound. I thought she meant for me to follow, so I did. She scuttled along, water sloshing out onto the wet ground. She set the bucket down under the eaves and led me through the gate beyond the pavilion, into the mansion's inner courtyard. It was a space only women could enter, forbidden to all men save for the most immediate male family members. The air certainly felt different here—heavier and filled with a sacred stillness.

At last, the servant woman tugged at my sleeve and pointed at a girl with plaited hair. She was pacing the grounds under the open sky, the rain now completely stopped.

"She's the one?"

The woman nodded.

"Thank you." I turned to face the girl, and our eyes met. I noticed immediately that she was extremely pale, strands of wet hair clinging to her temples. Sick, perhaps . . . or anxious. Afraid.

She too looked me up and down, took in the sight of my uniform—the light gray kwaeja vest worn over a dark gray dress, the blue collar and cuffs, the sash belt. Her eye caught on the scar branded into my cheek. "You're a police damo."

My face burned as I arranged my hair over the mark. "Yes."

"What do you want?"

"I come bearing bad news . . ." I wondered how I might inform her gently, but there was no gentle way to share that someone had sliced her lady's throat. "Your mistress is dead."

I waited for her trembling and tears, but the closer I studied her, the more she left me confused. I couldn't tell whether she was sad or not, whether she was too shocked to show emotions, or whether her emotions were too detached to register on her face.

"Dead," she said, her voice flat.

"I'm sorry." I explained the circumstance of her death as I understood it. Then I paused, wondering how to proceed. "You are the personal maid, so . . . so no matters regarding her could have escaped your attention. Tell me when the mistress left the house."

"I don't know. I woke up early to see if she had a good night's sleep, but I could not find her anywhere, so I raised the alarm."

"I see . . . And did she have any enemies?"

Her silence stretched on for too long. "I broke the rule."

I had begun my questioning only because Inspector Han had ordered me, but now interest raced through me like fire over hot oil. Curiosity was the one thing I couldn't resist. "The rule?"

"The rule taught to all servants."

That I knew too well. *I have a mouth, but I mustn't speak; ears, but I mustn't hear; eyes, but I mustn't see.*

"You heard something," I said. "Or saw?"

"I saw. Something I shouldn't have seen."

"What was it?"

I waited a long time for her answer. She stared and tucked a strand of hair behind her ear as she thought. "One night, without thinking, I opened my mistress's door and looked in . . . there was someone else there. It was dark and I couldn't make out the figure, but I knew it was a man. He jumped up and ran out through the back door. I was so embarrassed I ran away myself."

"When did this happen?"

"A week ago," she said. "And there was a letter."

My thoughts swung around. "You read?"

"My mistress taught me."

"And you were willing?" Not many indentured servants would be willing to learn, even if they had the opportunity. What was the point in becoming literate if the skill could never be put to use?

I studied the way she held her chin high and said, half to myself, "You don't wish to be a servant."

"I was satisfied with my position, but my mistress . . ." She hesitated again.

"You may tell me."

"My mistress said, 'I do not believe anyone is born to be an indentured servant. I look at you and I see a sister.'" The slightest tremor shook her lips, her eyes locked on mine. "Why are we talking of this? You came to investigate her death."

I cleared my throat, curiosity still bubbling in my mind. A literate servant was unheard of. Even scandalous. "The letter. What did it say?"

"It was short. I remember it well."

I waited. "So . . . what did it say?"

Her gaze did not waver from me, as though she'd summoned all her will not to look away. And in the steadiest voice, she recounted the words as though she'd recited it countless times. "It read, 'Dearest, My loyalty to you is as solid as stone, and my love for you still unshakable. Never doubt it. Tonight, when it is the Hour of the Rat, come to me at our usual place.' This is the letter she received yesterday morning before . . .'"

In the silence, I finished her words. "Her death."

"Yes." She straightened her shoulders. "Please, if there is no more, I'd like to be alone."

"I understand," I said. Then, unable to stop myself, I asked, "What is your name?"

"Soyi," she replied, giving me a long stare. Her eyes were like black pools that I didn't want to look at, feeling as though something lurked beneath the stillness.

"Thank you, Soyi." I shifted away, ready to find my way back. Yet I felt her behind me, as if we were not yet finished. I turned and asked, "Where is the letter?"

She didn't look at me this time, speaking instead to the rain-wet ground. "The letter ended with a request. 'Burn this.'"

●

Under the gathered clouds, I followed Inspector Han down the muddy street, reporting to him my interview with Maid Soyi. Or rather, not to *him*, but to his shoulders. They were like ancient rocks smoothed by blue silk. He was only twenty-seven years of age, yet something about his presence made him seem much older and wiser.

"And last, she shared with me a letter written to Lady O. A letter written by the lover," I said, and recited the letter word for word. When I finished, I added, "I wondered how it was that Maid Soyi knew how to read, and she explained that Lady O had personally taught her. After that, we parted."

"It is true, you do have a good memory," Inspector Han said. "You will be expected to assist more often in collecting information from women."

"Of course, sir," I replied, barely able to contain my thrill. To be of use to a man like him! "How can you tell, sir, if someone isn't telling you the full truth?"

"Why do you wish to know?"

"I'm curious, sir."

"Curious."

A single, curt word, and he said no more. His silence stretched, and a ball of nausea sank into the pit of my stomach. *Do not speak to your superior without permission, Seol. How difficult is that?* my sister had reprimanded me several times. I had felt the same knots of tension when in her presence; a weighty quietude packed with secret thoughts.

Our tense journey finally ended when we arrived before the Capital Police Bureau, an intimidating establishment I'd mistaken for the palace itself when I first laid eyes on it, with its elaborate pagoda gate, wooden beams painted red, and tiled rooftops.

"When you tell a lie, Damo Seol, how do you feel?" Inspector Han said unexpectedly.

It took me a moment to realize he expected a reply. "Extremely nervous, sir." *Just as I felt a moment ago.*

"Anxiety is a potent trigger. It leaves clues all over you. The pattern of your speech, the color of your cheeks, the movement of your hands."

I remembered Maid Soyi's eyes, those black, unknowable pools. I dared myself to ask a last question. "What about the eyes, sir?"

"They break away sometimes. Hiding secrets makes an individual flighty."

"What if they stare intensely at you in a very unusual way?"

He swung his leg over the saddle, and for a man of his height and build, he landed on the ground with the lightest *crunch*. "There is a special breed of liars who will lock their eyes on you. They are those who know how to manipulate and control."

Before I could say anything more, he handed the reins over to a manservant, then strode into the bureau. I paused before it and felt myself fold up; my head lowering, my shoulders drawing in, one hand hiding under the other. I shrank into my shell every time I beheld the invisible warning on the gate: *Be careful. Cross no one. Obey always.*

Cautiously, I passed through the gate. Everyone was bustling about the courtyard. A servant boy with a dirty face pushed a cart, its wooden wheels whining; a line of maids passed him by, holding trays of side dishes, neatly arranged; two men appeared—Officers Goh and Kyŏn—carrying a wooden stretcher with a corpse hidden beneath a straw mat.

"Inspector Han! You have arrived!" Kyŏn said with a simpering air.

"What is it?"

"The commander wishes us to move Lady O to the examination room."

"Do so." Then Inspector Han looked over his shoulder. "Seol, assist them."

I stared at the stretcher, at the sight of lifeless gray fingertips left uncovered. *Keep it away from me,* I wanted to say. But I kept silent before Inspector Han. His waiting gaze upon me, I wrung my hands as the odor of death reached my nose again, and at last dragged my feet forward, if only to show him my obedience.

I followed the officers into the drafty room filled with the scent of vinegar and decay. On a stand was an open book, an illustration of the human body. Next to it, a table with tools: knife, ruler, bowl, needle, a silver pin. My attention lingered on the pin. The last time I was in this room, a corpse had been brought in with witnesses claiming he'd died from drinking poison. I had watched the coroner's assistant inserting the pin into the corpse's mouth, then the anus. Apparently, the pin turned black in the case of poisoning.

"Servant!" Kyŏn called out. "Lift this corpse onto the table. The head needs to point south and the feet to the north."

The moment I grabbed and lifted the stiff corpse, my skin crawled. I had carried people before, like when I'd piggybacked my friend while playing, but her weight had felt different. She had felt alive. A corpse was nothing but a slab of meat. Death was heavier. When at last I dragged her onto the wooden table, I stepped back and waited for my stomach to settle.

"Get used to it."

I looked over my shoulder and found that I was alone with Officer Kyŏn, the other man gone. "Neh? Get used to what, sir?" I spoke to him in honorific, using the polite form of the language, as if he were a venerable soldier. But he was a low-ranking police officer, hardly two years older than me.

"You saw all those corpses this week." He picked the book off the stand and flipped through the pages of calligraphy and human body illustrations, stopping at the drawing of organs. "Commander Yi moved most of the corpses to another region to avoid autopsy. The rest were buried in surrounding hills, their killers acquitted or lightly punished. Do you know why?"

This was no trick question. I was always observant, watching everything from the corner of my eye. "The victims were all lowborn."

He snapped the book shut, sending a cloud of dust into a ray of blue-gray light. "Come closer, and I'll tell you a secret," he said. I took a few hesitant steps toward him, and because he was taller than me, I had to tilt my head as he whispered close, "They were all Catholics."

The hair on my neck rose. "Catholics . . ." I kept my voice as low as his, the word sounding too treacherous. They were followers of the Western teaching, and any teachings from the West were forbidden and could result in an execution.

"The victims were all Catholics, so no one in the bureau cared. But the killing of Lady O, now . . ." Officer Kyŏn shook his head, and a humorless chuckle escaped him. "You will suddenly find Inspector Han no longer so indifferent."

I turned to Lady O, her unblinking gaze fixed upward, along with the staring hole in her face. Someone had killed her in the wide open, so close to the patrolling guards. This someone could have immediately run away to avoid any chance of capture, but instead had crouched before the corpse and had taken the time to cut off her nose. I took a step back.

I had hoped that Lady O would be the first and last murder victim I'd have to touch. But after what Kyŏn had said . . . Gods, would I have to handle more corpses?

TWO

THE NEXT DAY, on my errand to deliver a letter for a police clerk, I took the long way around until I found what I was looking for. It was still there, the wanted poster of Priest Zhou Wenmo pasted onto the clay wall of an inn. Straw roof thatching cast a shadow over his thin face and eyes drooped down at the corners.

Only two months ago, the drawing of him had portrayed a man with a pair of much smaller ears and a rounder face. His changing appearance was like a man's trembling reflection on a puddle, never the same. No one knew how he truly looked, the artists who painted him guided only by floating rumors.

But his eyes had always stayed their same shape, the saddest eyes I had ever seen.

Now I could no longer look at the priest's silent gaze without recalling the dead bodies of Catholics. Since the king's passing, I had watched death swell and push its way through the gates of the bureau, and it had seemingly failed to shock Commander Yi. As though he had expected these killings to occur.

Two siblings starved to death, locked up in a storage hut by their own father. A drowned servant, pushed into his watery grave by his master. A missing girl, last seen collecting water from the well, only to be found lying lifeless under a thornbush, killed by her aunt. Following that, seven burned corpses piled in a cart, recovered from a hut that had burned down, right after the doors had been locked by the orders of an upper-class woman.

"To execute any person is a grave matter for the kingdom," Commander Yi had said while interrogating the noblewoman in the police bureau. "Even if your servants were Catholic rebels, the fact that they are the ruler's subjects should have prevented you from harming them carelessly." Her case had moved up into the hands of the Ministry of Justice for a final appeal, yet I'd heard whispers of the already-made decision: the execution of the Catholic rebels had been necessary for the good of the kingdom.

What was it about this teaching called Catholicism that terrorized the culprits enough to kill their own servants, their own children?

After delivering the police clerk's letter to a government office on Yukjo Street, near Gyeongbok Palace, I hurried back to the bureau to finish sweeping the main pavilion as the chief maid had instructed me. But once I retrieved my broom, I paused on the way and hid by the examination room door. I'd wanted to know more about the cause of Lady O's death since yesterday, but police protocols and the state-mandated mourning period for the king had pushed the examination to today.

Once it seemed safe enough, I inched closer, then peered through the crack in the door, drawn to look inside by the sound of solemn voices.

I shouldn't be here, I thought, but curiosity anchored me to the spot, as did the question: Was Lady O's death related to the other murders? Had heresy from the West killed her too?

"The crown and the left side of the head look normal," Damo Hyeyeon observed aloud, speaking to the men, who stood with their backs turned. She was their eyes, the only method they possessed to examine the naked victim. "There is an old scar a little behind the right side of the head, beanlike in shape . . ."

Hyeyeon explained every detail, however trivial, and the men trusted her observations. Unlike me, Hyeyeon and the other damos were educated girls, possessing vast medical knowledge and skills.

Rigorously trained to become palace nurses, but having failed to achieve good grades, they had been demoted to the position of damo and would remain in this low position until they successfully passed the medical exam.

A harsh punishment indeed for bad grades.

But if Hyeyeon ever thought this unfair, not a ripple of irritation ever disturbed the surface of her countenance. Her cheeks hadn't even flushed with anger when Kyŏn called her "a pretty face ruined by too-big ears." At eighteen, she had the grace and maturity of those highly respected palace nurses who served the queen herself.

"There is a single knife wound across the throat, with no hesitation marks." So calm was her voice, always so calm. "The nose has been cut off with a blade." With a ruler, she measured along the wounds and offered the lacerations' depths and widths in the measurements of ch'on and p'un.

"The knife wound was deep enough to be fatal," the coroner's assistant murmured.

"Based on the condition of the victim, and other factors like the rain and the late summer's heat," Hyeyeon explained, "Lady O's death occurred around midnight. By morning, she would have been dead for several hours already."

"Hmm. Then the murder occurred during the curfew hours," the coroner's assistant remarked, referring to the period that began an hour before midnight and ended at dawn. "Watchmen would have been patrolling nearby, yet the killer took the time to cut off her nose. Why do you think he did this, sir?"

He turned to a gigantic man standing in the room, who wore a wide-brimmed police hat that cast a deep shadow over his eyes. Only his long purple scar was visible, rippling down his red cheek, inflamed by a rash. It was Commander Yi.

"The murder was surely committed by someone with a deep grudge," the commander said. "Let me see what it was she was clutching."

My brows crinkled. *What?* She had been clutching something? I only remembered her fist, but had not looked closely.

A clerk presented Commander Yi with a wooden tray. A string the length of a man's arm lay coiled there. As he examined it, I craned my neck to have a better look.

"One can see it was knotted," Commander Yi said. "Inspector Han suspects it was a necklace, perhaps pulled off by the killer. I have officers searching the area for its ornament, if there was one."

A restlessness rippled through my limbs. I wanted to run out and search for the ornament, which might identify the killer, but before curiosity could pull me away, I saw Hyeyeon spray lees and vinegar on the corpse. My lips parted as I watched the way the flesh reacted. Something in the substance made all the injuries more visible, making patches of purple and yellow and red blossom all over. I clutched the doorframe.

"There is a bruise around her mouth, purple in color, the shape of a hand," Hyeyeon said.

"Someone tried to muffle her cries," Commander Yi observed.

Since my first day at the bureau, life had turned strange. I didn't know where I was heading, where I would end up, and I often walked around the capital without purpose. Each day ended like an unresolved case. While I could find no solution to my life, the tangle of frustration in me loosened as I watched Hyeyeon take the strangeness out of the corpse. There was a story behind every bruise and gash, evidence that—when pieced together—would surely return life back to normal.

I strained my ears, trying to better hear their low-voiced

conversation. Then a flush burned up my chest and spread across my face as Hyeyeon examined the private parts. I spun around, hearing her declare, "She is not a virgin," only to find myself standing before Inspector Han.

"What are you doing here?"

The tips of my ears burned. "I was j-just looking. Curious, sir."

"Curiosity seems to be your perpetual state of being. Where exactly is the end of it?"

I hesitated to answer. "I never reached the end myself, sir, so I do not know."

The slightest smile twitched at the corner of his lips. "Tell me, damo investigator, based on all that you've observed, what do you think led to her death?"

"I . . . don't know, sir."

He nodded. After a moment, he said, "There are usually only three causes for murder: lust, greed, or vengeance. Among these three, vengeance is the most common."

"I never knew that," I admitted quietly.

"No, you would not have. I wouldn't be surprised if she was killed by her family or an intimate partner. I have worked for so long at the police bureau that I find very few things to be surprising or new." Expelling a weary sigh, Inspector Han gestured to the door. "Announce me and go."

I announced his presence to Hyeyeon, who temporarily covered the corpse with a straw mat, and once alone, I made my way toward the main pavilion, still blushing. There, I swept the vast floor, and the repetitive swishing of the broom allowed my thoughts to drift back to Lady O. So she wasn't a virgin; she must indeed have had a lover. *Perhaps,* I thought, *a lover with a dagger.*

I stopped sweeping and covered the end of the bamboo handle

with both hands, resting my chin there. Fog that hid the morning sun rolled in through the open gates and swam in the courtyard, leaving a sheen of dew on the massive wooden pillars and the cold, gray stones. It was as though the bureau had plunged into the deep and livid sea, a boundless space between myself and the world.

I wondered if the underworld might look like this. The home now to Lady O, and the home to my father, my mother, my brother . . .

"Hurry! Faster!"

My thoughts scrambled as voices echoed from the distance. I saw shadows, shapeless lumps behind the fog. The shadows grew larger and more distinct. It was two officers, their black robes flapping behind them as they entered the bureau through the main gate. "You there!" one of them called out. "Where is Inspector Han?"

"In the examination room."

They ran past me, disappearing into the southern courtyard.

A complaint must have arrived. Perhaps another loose woman like Lady O, slashed to death for the sake of family honor, a crime I was coming to learn was quite frequent. Honor was everything here in the capital, more important than life itself to these nobles. I'd heard a bizarre story of a woman who had hacked her shoulder with an ax simply because a male stranger had touched it.

My thoughts wandered as I swept here and there, though mostly pulling the broom along, leaving large spaces untouched. I rarely put my whole heart into domestic chores, especially when it came to sweeping. There were more important things to do with my life than to chase after dust.

More important things? I could almost hear the chief maid's rebuke. *Such as what, Damo Seol?*

We damos were prone to avoiding our chores or doing them half-heartedly. Once, the chief maid had sent Damo Aejung to prepare tea, only to find her sleeping in the yard outside the kitchen with a medicine book open on her lap. She had lashed Aejung's calves as punishment, and did so with every other damo who shirked their duties. But it was the wrath of the police officers that we feared most.

When the space looked decent enough to keep me out of trouble, I dragged the broom along the courtyard toward the storage room, but I paused, hearing hurried footsteps behind me.

It was Officer Kyŏn. "What are you doing just standing around?"

"Sir, I was told to sweep—"

He tossed me a coil of rope made of five braided strings, used to arrest criminals. "You're to come with us. A woman is needed."

"Where?"

He replied under his breath, so quietly I barely heard him. "Mount Inwang."

I licked my dry lips, my throat suddenly parched. Now I noticed his bow and quiver full of arrows. Mount Inwang was a place I had dreaded since I'd first heard of it as a child, the home of white tigers.

I tapped my finger against the bamboo broom handle, trying to distance myself from panic. "What is on Mount Inwang?"

He might have reprimanded me for speaking out of turn. Instead, Kyŏn said, "Maid Soyi has fled."

●

The fog thickened by the time we rode out that afternoon, but Inspector Han had a keen sense of direction, easily leading the twenty officers and myself through Hanyang. The five-day mourning period issued by the royal court had ended, so shops were open again, vendors yelling out from their stalls as men and women streamed up and down the street.

With all this bustling of life, the capital ought to have felt less like a ghost village, but death was still heavy in the air. Everywhere around us were pale and solemn faces, and everyone was clad in pure white, the color of grief. The king had died. It was like the deadly frost of winter had already kissed the capital. Only the urchins seemed free from this spell, running through the crowd without a care.

We rode out of the fortress through the West Gate, and the road wound through a village of thatched-roof huts, then an overflowing grassland. Mount Inwang was only a half hour's journey away, but already keeping up was no easy feat. I rode on a pony named Terror, notorious for her many vices: she was a self-willed, quarrelsome, and tough little beast. Seeing her more glorious and quicker brothers charging ahead, she seemed determined to fling me off, the load slowing her down. I clung desperately to her and fixed my eyes on the officers, not wanting to lose them in the fog.

So focused as I was, I hardly noticed my surroundings. Faraway mountains unfolded, layer upon misty layer. The gentleness of the distant trees lasted only for a few paces, and all of a sudden, the forest grew tall and thick, trapping us in darkness like a cave of cruel and violent dreams. I pinched color into my cheeks, hoping no one would notice my blood-drained face.

"Search until the gong is struck, then return here," Inspector Han's voice resounded from the front. "Now spread out!"

The torchbearers rode ahead and led us deep into the wooded base of the mountain. We combed slowly through trees and clear streams, thorns and bushes. The mist floated around us, sometimes leaping from craggy rocks. I gasped more than once. And one officer, startled, grabbed for his arrow only to see the mist drop and drag away.

The longer we spent in the forest, the farther we fanned out, and the more the isolation swallowed me up. My mind conjured growls everywhere—in the murmuring of water, in the very rushing of blood in my ears.

What had driven Maid Soyi into such a fearful place? What did she have to hide? Or perhaps she was simply more frightened of the inquisition than she was of tigers. Witnesses—*innocent* people who had the misfortune of knowing a victim or suspect—were often imprisoned for months, beaten sometimes to death to obtain evidence.

"She's probably cowering in a cave somewhere," Officer Kyŏn said.

I rode closer to him. The first time I'd laid eyes on Officer Kyŏn, he'd reminded me of legendary royal investigators from tales I'd grown up listening to. Young men secretly sent out by the king to faraway villages to solve great injustices. He certainly looked the part: his black hair tied into the perfect topknot, revealing his chiseled face, strong jaw, distinctively edged full lips, and his athletic figure, rippling with lean muscles—all of which seemed to tell a story of bravery and honor.

I knew better now. If there was one thing Officer Kyŏn had taught me, it was that brute strength was not a measure of a man's courage. He could have muscles made of steel and yet a backbone made of mother's milk—the only thing occupying his heart was love for no one other than himself.

As the swimming mist darkened to blue, reflecting the dimming sky, I felt no safer with Kyŏn close by my side as we ascended the mountain slope. "It's growing late," I observed, hoping he would hear my silent question: *Should we not head back?*

"Didn't you hear the inspector's order? We search until the gong is struck."

It looked like we were nearing the Hour of the Rat, though. Any later and we would be stuck outside, the fortress gates slammed shut on us. "But how are we—"

A twig cracked somewhere too close to us. Fear punched my chest as I stared to the side. "Did you hear that?" I whispered. My mind pictured Maid Soyi in the underbrush, but my heart saw only lurking teeth and claws.

Officer Kyŏn gripped his bow tighter. "Lead on."

We rode toward the sound, through countless trees, then around a large, moss-covered rock. My pounding heart slackened; it was only a deer. The creature watched us from behind the bushes, as still as a stone.

"Damn it," Kyŏn hissed, jerking the horse around. "She couldn't have gone far. Royal guards always make their patrols around this mountain. She *has* to be nearby."

"But why is the inspector so determined to find Maid Soyi?"

"She's a suspect. Witnesses saw her leaving the mansion around the time Lady O ran out."

That surprised me. I could hardly picture meek Soyi holding a kitchen knife, let alone carving the nose from the face of her mistress.

"I *will* find that bitch. No doubt I will. I've already arrested over fifty scoundrels while serving in the bureau. Almost as many as Inspector Han."

I bit my lower lip to keep myself from grimacing.

"What is your life's goal?" he asked, his voice tinged with amusement. "Let me tell you. You'll get married, have babies, and keep on doing what you're good at doing: serving. Serving your master, your husband, your children." He tapped his head. "I know these things."

"I don't wish to do any of that, sir."

"But you will serve. That is fact, that is your fate."

Fate. A shackle as solid as truth—unchangeable, unmovable. On the day of my departure, my sister had told me how long I was bound by the government to serve in the police bureau, away from home, from family. *For one generation,* she'd whispered.

My entire life.

That is, I would be free by the age of forty-one, as old as death itself.

A thunder of fluttering wings filled the sky in all directions, the birds overhead taken to flight. A shriek in the distance pierced the air; a terrified horse. Officer Kyŏn charged ahead, while it took me a scrambling moment to realize what was happening. I jabbed my heels into Terror's side and followed him through the thicket, over the protruding roots, branches hitting my face.

Then we reached a glade and my heart stopped. Across the stream stood Inspector Han, his sleeve blood-soaked, his hand inching toward the sword at his side. A matter of paces away prowled a tiger, a deep growl rumbling from its white-and-black-striped chest. Powerful paws with sharp claws. The beast looked as large as Inspector Han himself.

"Do not move," he said, though not to us. Past the thick cluster of leaves was a horse struggling on the ground, shaking its head as blood continued to ooze from its wounded side. And hunkered down behind the creature was Maid Soyi.

Unable to look away from the scene, I hissed to Kyŏn, "Shoot it!"

A muscle worked in Officer Kyŏn's jaw. Clearly he was incensed at an order from a girl, but he drew out an arrow and nocked it to his bow. As he aimed, the iron point trembled. What resolve he had, I watched falter and crumble.

"I'll do it." I snatched the weapon from him and rode out into the glade for a better aim. My motion caught the tiger's attention. *Good.* My fear had reached its climax, and another sensation flooded in, a powerful longing that churned within me: the desire to matter.

Don't think too much about your target, my sister's husband had taught me on our hunts for birds and rabbits. *Don't rattle your mind with possibilities. Focus on what you want and shoot it.*

In one smooth motion, I aimed and released.

The arrow whistled and flew into the tiger's side with an audible thud. It let out a roar, startling me—and startling Terror even more. The shaggy pony nearly knocked me off as she jolted, then raced into the woods. The tiger charged after us, its snarling roar shaking my bones. Despite the wound, it was fast, quickly closing the distance between us. I could almost feel fangs sinking into my shoulder.

I dropped the bow and kicked Terror's side. *Faster. Please go faster.*

Suddenly, Terror rose on her front legs, tossing me into the air. Then I was rolling down sloping ground, wrapped in a whirl of green and brown. A sharp edge sliced me. My head struck something hard and pain burst. I fell into darkness.

●

Shadows swam in my head.

I was in a boat, floating on black waters under the night sky. My hands scrubbed, my neatly braided hair tied with a yellow cloth strip, I sat across from my brother and sister on a wooden seat.

"When will we be home?" My questions were endless. My brother's patience with me always impressed people, the calm way a boy so young would answer, weighing the inquiries of his younger four-year-old sister with solemnity.

"When we finish crossing the sea."

"Why is there so much water?"

"Because ten thousand rivers are flowing through."

"That's a lot of rivers." I looked out onto the vastness ahead, and all I saw was a lonely stretch of darkness punctuated by a single moon.

"Listen." My brother, my orabeoni, leaned out from the edge of the boat. "Do you hear that?"

"Hear what?" I asked.

"A heartbeat in the sea."

I strained my ear against the lapping waves, and I watched the foam crashing. "What is down there, orabeoni?"

"Turtles, jellyfish, shrimp. Many creatures."

"Are they kind?"

"Yes, they are."

I dipped my fingers into the waves, and gradually, I saw the land so close and yet so far away, illuminated by the moon and the glow of lanterns. Home appeared to me like an unreachable land of fairy maidens. And when I turned to tell my brother this, he was gone.

●

A breeze woke me. Bits of soil clung to my lashes, falling into my eyes when I blinked up at the sky. It was night, and I was alone and surrounded by ancient trees, hundreds of them. I struggled to my feet and all my bones cried out in protest. Knife-sharp pain sliced my head, and as I waited for it to ease, I glanced around.

Right, left, front, back. Each direction looked the same—rocks, branches, and rustling leaves.

I needed to escape this mountain. Low twigs and thorns caught my skirt as I stumbled, and in the wind, the swaying shadows of trees grasped for me. Desperate, I scrambled down the slope like an ant— tiny, insignificant, lost in a world of giants.

The slope led me to a stream and I pushed through the icy water, climbing over broken granite slabs and trying to keep my skirt from getting soaked. Then my feet slipped. My knees and hands landed on the slimy rocks, sending forth an explosion of icy water. I remained on all fours, too stunned to move, and slowly, as the cold bit into me, a feeling of helplessness pierced deep.

Was everything I had thought about myself—that I mattered—nothing more than a story in my head?

There's no time for sulking. Move on, Seol. I was good at doing that.

I took off my sandals and stepped barefoot from rock to rock, but the tears burning my eyes made it difficult to see clearly. I jumped too far, my feet slipping off the edge, and I was down again. The river ripped the sandals out from my grasp. "No!" I cried as they rushed away in the black current, sandals woven for me by my sister. The only thing I had to remember her by.

Move on.

My teeth were chattering and my lips blue by the time I reached dry land. I pushed into the trees again, twigs and stones pricking my bare feet, and the raw weather rattled my bones. I needed a fire. I pictured how I'd seen other servants spark them with rocks, not a skill I'd ever learned. All the while, thoughts of the tiger stalked through my mind. The wind through the trees was its breath, the crunching forest floor the scrape of its claws. Its growls rolled from streambeds.

The mountain was a tiger, and it was hungry.

I went on that way, not knowing the hour or direction. What felt like an eternity later, I saw light—the flicker of torches. I halted, keeping low as the figures moved among the trees, while behind them an ox pulled a wagon laden with crates. The torchbearers were quick-footed, five in all, big, lean men in dusty cotton clothing. In their midst was a gentleman on horseback, in a silk robe and a tall black hat. Beads of nobility were strapped around his chin.

All the men held clubs and swords. Guards, I considered . . . or bandits.

I slowly rose to run, but a twig snapped beneath my step. Holding my breath, I watched one man turn in my direction, then gesture quickly. Without warning, a shadow of another man I hadn't noticed charged toward me, and his rough hand grabbed my arm, hard fingers digging deep as if to snap bone. The man dragged me over to the group. I could barely walk, and when he released me, I fell to the ground, prostrating myself before the gentleman on horseback. "Have mercy, sir!"

The gentleman slid off his horse, and as my head was lowered, I only saw his leather boots close to my hand.

"Do get up."

The tone made me look up. Under the starlight, I saw a long face, a strong jaw, and high cheekbones. The face of a woman.

"Now," she said, "what are you doing out here all alone?"

I was at a loss for words. What was *she* doing disguised as a man?

"You shouldn't venture onto this mountain alone. Come, we will accompany you to the main road."

I followed them, feeling much safer than wandering about alone—a group of people and a woman. A *woman*.

"You look at me strangely." She must have felt my stare on her disguise. "When I go on a long journey, I prefer to dress as a man. It is safer and draws less unwanted attention."

My lips formed into a silent, "Oh."

When we reached the road, I looked ahead, the capital waiting for me somewhere in the dark distance.

"Where is your destination?" the lady asked, standing still, waiting for my answer as her servants led the ox away from Hanyang.

It did not take me long to think of where I wanted to be. *Home.* The quaint hut I'd come to live in after escaping our first master and his plague-ridden household. The place Older Sister, her husband, and

I had lived for nearly a decade afterward as napgong nobi, outside-resident servants. We'd lived in relative freedom, except for when our second master pestered us for our annual tribute payment, so most of my days had been spent in freedom. I remembered those days so vividly, so fondly: the bright blue sky, the *mem-mem-mem* of the clear-toned cicadas. And sleeping without the fear of being rudely wakened, safe in the shadow of Older Sister's back turned to me. Sometimes in the winter when snow fell, she would discreetly turn and tuck the straw mat closer around me. But in Hanyang, I felt like a slave, and as dispensable as one. No one cared for me; they had left me for dead on the mountain of tigers.

"You are running away, aren't you."

A coldness blew right through me. "No, I would not dare, mistress!"

"We passed by officers earlier on the mountain, though they are likely now long gone. They said one of their damos had gone missing. And by the mark on your face, and from your uniform, you must be she."

I touched my scarred cheek, which burned with the memory of the glowing red iron, the sizzling of my skin.

"Go on. Run," she said. "Do not stay if that is not what you wish."

Her words left me stunned. "Why would you let me go, mistress?"

"Because I do not believe in indentured servitude. Your lower class was created by those who wish to oppress."

I nearly tripped over my own feet. Someone else had said this too. Before I could remember, the ox let out a loud groan and suddenly the wagon tilted. Boxes crashed to the ground, and one splintered open. Rolls of silk spilled out, and from them, square parcels that tumbled in the dark. *Books?*

I moved to help collect them, but the woman called in a sharp voice, "Just stay where you are."

I froze as the servants lifted the materials back onto the wagon. "Just a rut, my lady," one man said. "Nothing is damaged."

Yet I felt the eyes of the men on me. Their knuckles white, clubs tightly clutched as they shifted toward me. But the lady raised her hand, and they backed away, just as tigers might withdraw from fire.

"What did you see?" she said to me.

For a moment I fought confusion. Just books, meaningless to me. But I felt the test in her voice.

"I saw nothing at all," I said.

She nodded, her approval gentle. "You may go on your way now."

I wondered if this was a trap, for I couldn't understand why a noblewoman would be so kind. I crafted my response carefully. "I cannot run. There is nowhere for me to go."

"You have a home."

"Home is the first place slave hunters are sent," I said. And it was far from my brother's grave. My promise had to be kept. "So I have no home now. I must be what I was bred to be."

"And what is that?"

"A servant. I belong to the police bureau, so I should return. I will be obedient," I assured her.

"A servant, you say. Look at your wrists; I see no master chained to them."

"I am branded."

"Old scars can be burned off."

My heart beat, low and strong. Her talk was dangerous, rebellious, yet sweet as honey. "Burned off?"

"No one's fate is written in stone, child." She accompanied me farther down the road, which cut through a field of grass swaying in the breeze. Soon she would return to her servants and I'd have to walk this path alone. "Slave Jang Yeongsil, he knew this and ascended to officialdom as a renowned engineer in the time of King Sejong. Even in ancient times, many slaves rose up to become generals because of their courage. No one was *born* into their glorious position, just as no one is born to be a slave."

Who was this woman? I watched as she moved to tuck something back into her robe. A beaded necklace bearing an odd ornament: two wooden pieces crossing one over the other. A crooked and misshapen cross.

THREE

I SAT ON the edge of the pavilion veranda, surrounded by the familiar high walls of the police bureau. The clouds above me hid the stars and the sliver of moon, the midnight sky pitch-black, while the trilling of a lone bird echoed somewhere in the east.

My entire body burned with pain, but my head ached the most, half my hair crusted with blood. But Hyeyeon said that I'd be fine, that she'd bring her medical supplies to clean and stitch it up. So I waited for her with a cloth pressed against the wound.

I couldn't move even if I'd wanted to. The weight of those last hours—when I'd woken up alone in the forest and journeyed all the way back to the bureau, barefooted, with the mysterious lady—pinned me to my spot.

"So she came back," an officer said as he passed by, slowing down to glance at me. "Thought she'd run away, like last time."

"You should have seen her return, Officer," the chief maid replied, walking alongside him with a rattling tray of cups. "Her hair was hanging by her face, and her dress—her dress!—it was soaked and torn like a beggar's."

"Aigoo." The officer sounded hardly interested.

Trying to block out their voices, I pressed the cloth and my hand against my ears. But I could still hear them, distant though they were now.

"Look at her, she is likely furious. Left behind for dead, she was—"

"Hush!"

The cause of their sudden silence, I could sense, was a few steps away from me. My pulse leaped at the sight of Inspector Han taking a seat on the edge of the veranda, though not right next to me. He sat far enough for two people to sit between us. Then he spoke, his voice as deep and quiet as the night. "You weren't left behind."

I looked at his dusty leather boots, unable to form a response.

"I sent out men to look for you but called them back just now. I would never abandon one of my officers or damos."

The weight in my chest lifted, just a bit. "Thank you, sir," I said timidly to his boots.

Silence hung between us, and when I peeked up, I saw his head turned to me. But I couldn't tell whether he was looking at me, for the shadow cast by his police hat made it impossible for me to see his eyes. "I had a little sister," he murmured. "She would have been your age if she hadn't died."

I silently mouthed a word of gratitude to the dead girl, for reminding her brother of my life. Perhaps he would have left me behind otherwise. To most aristocrats, I was a mere servant, easily disposable.

"I'm indebted to you," he said.

I blinked. "For what, sir?"

"I might not have lived if not for you."

"It was my honor to serve you, sir. If only I had come earlier, then you would not have been wounded."

"It was not my blood. It belonged to my horse."

I recalled the horse struggling on the ground, its head nodding up and down. "Oh . . ."

"Come closer," he said.

Surprise lit in me. Inspector Han had always kept his distance from all, officers and damos alike. I slid across the veranda, and once I was close enough, I wondered if he could feel the heat of my nervousness.

"Hold out your palm."

I reached out and spread my fingers. He pressed a solid and cold object into my hand: a tasseled ornament, a norigae, like the one tied to Lady O's dress—but much different in color and shape. This one was an amber carving of a terrapin, attached to a long tassel of blue silk strings.

"This was a gift I wanted to give my sister on her birthday, but never got to. Hold on to it until I fulfill my promise to you."

"Promise, sir?"

"Tell me. What is it you most desire?" he asked. "And I promise it will be yours."

Still staring at the ornament, unable to believe my eyes, the truth slipped out of me before I could weigh its full implication. "*Home.*" His gaze drifted to the brand on my cheek, and I opened my mouth to quickly erase that request. "I mean—"

"Then when the investigation is over, I will return it to you."

"Sir?"

"Your home. I will send you back."

I froze, and as his words sank in, my heart rocked back and forth in shock. He would send me home . . . The place that whispered to me through the familiar smiles, the familiar scenes, the familiar patterns of each day: *you belong here.*

Brother had once told me that when you long for something too badly, and for too long, it begins to feel like a faraway, unreachable dream. That was how home had begun to feel to me. But Inspector Han had just reached out and placed that hope, a solid promise, into my hands.

Real. So real.

"You are not a palace nurse sent here because of low grades," he observed. "So how did you end up in the bureau?"

It took me time to collect my thoughts, scattered in dozens of directions. At length, I spoke, my voice cracking. "I was a nobi servant, a property of my master, Lord Paek. I was different from other servants who were only bound to their masters by a contract; Lord Paek *owned* me. So when he decided to sell me to a nearby police bureau in Inchon, I had no choice but to go. Then . . . then my sister overheard an officer telling his superior something."

"What was that?" he prompted.

"The officer said, 'You might regain Commander Yi's favor if you sent the servant girl. She is strong, and the police bureau needs strong damos.' And so they transferred me to the capital." I worried my lower lip, wondering if Inspector Han could truly keep his promise. "I am indentured for one generation."

"There are ways to end the indenture sooner."

"With money? It would take me too long to earn enough, sir."

"Freedom can also be received through government favor. I will make sure that you return home by the new year. Until then, keep that norigae safe."

"Of course, sir," I whispered, believing him. "With my life!"

Quietly, we sat side by side, staring ahead at the sky above the police bureau walls. The clouds had moved, revealing a splinter of the moon that glowed skeletal white.

●

All night, I couldn't sleep and just listened to the *drip, drip, drip* of water falling into the rain catchers. My heart full and able to think of little else, I repeated the scene of me shooting the tiger in my mind so many times that the memory itself began to fade, like a sketch folded and opened once too often. The memory of the Mount Inwang incident was irresistible. Of Inspector Han, his eyes widening at the sight of me, his eyes seeing something in me no one else had seen before: the empress in me, rising, holding her bow steady. Perhaps he had felt a sense of indebtedness mixed with admiration. Perhaps this had led to his realization that I deserved more kindness? That I deserved a reward—to be returned home?

When the morning arrived, my mind whirled, filled with crashing waves of nervous excitement and exhaustion. It took me a while to recognize that people were conversing inside the servants' quarter.

"It has begun!"

"What has?"

"Commander Yi ordered Maid Soyi's beating for running away, and now Inspector Han is interrogating her. Come quick!"

I wanted to know too, why Soyi had run, what had scared her. I changed out of my nightgown and bound my breasts; the hanbok uniform required the waistband of the skirt to go around my upper chest. Then I donned a long kwaeja vest over my garments, securing it with a sash belt. Once presentable, I followed the distant sound of Inspector Han's voice to its source, the main courtyard.

I walked around the crowd of civilian spectators and dove into the flock of people, elbowing my way to the front. No one blocked me now, so I had a clear view of Inspector Han; he paced before Maid Soyi, who was tied to a chair.

I observed the dark shadows beneath her eyes and the blood staining her pale lips from biting down too hard. I frowned as the sight of her probed at something in me, something important that I had forgotten. Then a memory swept into my mind.

I do not believe in indentured servitude.

Was it a coincidence that Soyi's mistress shared the same rebellious idea as the mysterious woman? More pressing, if Soyi had indeed murdered Lady O, why kill the woman who had offered her the gift of equality?

Inspector Han's commanding voice broke into my thoughts. "Do you know why you are here?"

"Because I am Lady O's personal servant, sir."

"She had many personal servants—but only one who blatantly lied." After a beat, he folded his arms and took a step closer. "You informed a damo that you'd woken up early to see if your mistress had had a good night's sleep before raising the alarm. But you knew of her disappearance long before then, didn't you? A witness saw you leaving the mansion soon after Lady O's disappearance."

"I . . . I was asked to keep an eye on her."

"Asked by whom?"

"Lady O's mother."

"For what reason?"

"It is indecent to say—"

"This is a murder investigation, Maid Soyi. Do not withhold anything from me."

Her gaze flicked to me, as though she had sensed my arrival from the start. "As I told the damo, my mistress had a lover. And when I saw her sneaking out at night, sir, I followed. She had mentioned Mount Nam often, so I wondered if she had gone there."

"Tell us what you saw."

"I was walking down the street. It was the curfew hours, so everyone was asleep. I took the long way around to search as many alleys as possible, and walked toward Mount Nam—" She stopped. Though tied to a chair, she managed to sit straighter. A sudden clarity lit her eyes as she looked up. "I remember now. I saw someone."

Everyone fell still, no longer whispering and speculating among themselves, and the silence amplified the sound of a young nobleman fanning himself. He stood with his manservant near the front, garbed in a robe of violet that glowed in the sunlight. He had shining jet-black eyes, arched brows, and a seemingly perpetual smirk; conde-scension seemed carved into his face.

"What did this person look like?" Inspector Han asked. "Answer me and do not leave anything out."

"It was a man on a horse. He was wearing a blue robe. There was something suspicious about him, seeing him roaming at curfew. But it was too dark to see his face clearly, and he rode off before I could approach him."

There was an intake of breath among the spectators, and everyone but the young noble frowned. He was still fanning himself, and the corner of his lips rose higher.

"And what time was it when you saw this man?"

"A little before dawn," Soyi answered.

"Why were you still on the streets so long after midnight?"

"I searched for my mistress, and when I couldn't find her, I returned to the mansion. But then I thought of how furious Matron Kim would be at me. She *had* ordered me to watch over her daughter. I grew so fearful that I went out again, to look for my mistress one more time. I was determined to even search Mount Nam."

Inspector Han arched a brow. "You could have easily shared this. Instead, you ran away. Only two types of people run: children and the guilty."

"I heard someone had seen me leave the house, and I was afraid." Her once neatly plaited hair now hung loose, and through the black strands, she peered up at the inspector. "My mother was executed for a crime she didn't commit. I was afraid the same would happen to me."

"So that is your reason. And you would say you were on good terms with your mistress?"

"I . . ." She paused for the briefest moment. "I was."

"Then is there any reason as to why Lady O would have specifically referenced you? Why she expressed anger toward you in her diary?"

My hand leapt to my throat. Diary? The police had never discovered Lady O's diary. The inspector was bluffing, but Soyi seemed to believe it. The whites of her widening eyes made her pupils look even blacker. "She . . . she wrote about me?"

"She did, but about what?"

"I . . . I don't know."

Time slowed as I clutched my collar, wanting to know the truth—and yet frightened of it. Could I have read a person so wrong that I'd looked a murderer in the eye without even sensing it?

"As bad as things are," he whispered, "you could make them less so by telling the truth. But once I find the truth, no one will believe anything you say. Take control before it is too late. Think about what I have told you."

Soyi looked sideways and locked her gaze on me, her eyes bright and feverish. "I swear, I would never hurt her."

●

Soyi's gaze haunted me as I watched the damos untie her wrists and legs, then drag her back to the prison block. Her bound state flooded me with a sense of pity and almost guilt. I would be returning home soon, while she might never leave this place.

The interrogation now over, the spectators dispersed, looks of disapproval or pity etched into the lines of their faces. I was ordered to clean the blood off the interrogation chair. Soyi's blood. As I did, I noticed the young noble still lingering.

Our gazes met across the police courtyard.

He did not look much older than me. Nineteen, perhaps. He was handsome in a too-perfect and hostile way, like the beauty of a winter's night: moonlit snow, gleaming icicles as sharp as fangs, and a bone-chilling stillness.

With a gasp, I ducked my head and rigorously scrubbed at the splattered blood. Even when the redness rubbed off, I continued wiping at it, all my attention centered on the footsteps approaching me. On the shadow looming over me.

Swallowing hard, I peeked up. My heart slammed against my chest when I saw the young noble towering above me.

"Are you Damo Seol?"

Immediately I jumped to my feet, held my hands together, and bowed. "Neh."

"You are the damo assisting with Lady O's case, I hear."

"I am, sir."

"You must have seen her corpse." He gazed down at me with an air of too-sweet friendliness, and his left cheek twitched. "What did she look like?"

I blinked, caught off guard by his question.

"Is it true?" he pressed. "The rumor that she was a great beauty?"

"I—I cannot say, sir."

He arched his brow. "It is not a tricky question, girl."

His prompting lifted the dead woman out from a pool of memory. Her bluish face surfaced, the staring eyes, the purple bruise over her gaping mouth, the dark hole where her nose ought to have been. Death had drained Lady O of every ounce of beauty. It was impossible to imagine who she had once been when all I could think of was what had happened to her—sliced, stabbed, murdered.

"Sir," I whispered. "I cannot imagine what she looked like before she was . . . killed."

Before he could ask any more questions, Senior Officer Shim stalked over, and I had to withhold a breath of relief.

"Finally!" The young noble's voice pierced the air. "I *did* want to speak with you, Officer Shim!"

The much older Officer Shim looked like a stray dog that had to fight daily for food. Tall, seemingly scrawny, his face emaciated. Yet he possessed surprising strength and was far more streetwise than even Inspector Han himself. I took a step back and hid behind him.

"Young Master Ch'oi Jinyeop." An uneasy edge slid into Officer Shim's voice. "Why are you still here?"

"You look as though you have not slept in days." The young master snapped his fan shut, then held his hands behind his back. "I hear that once a murder occurs, police officers do not return home for weeks, too absorbed in the investigation to rest."

Officer Shim kept quiet, still waiting for an answer.

The young master let out a breathy laugh. "You dislike small talk as usual. Very well. I came to inquire if it was true, the rumors of her affair."

"I am not permitted to share information freely."

"Inspector Han's order, I suppose? You obey everything he says. If the rumor is true, perhaps Lady O deserved to die. A woman who cannot be honorable . . . it is better that she die than live and bring dishonor to her family."

"Your father must be ashamed to have a son like you."

Officer Shim's remark startled me, but what surprised me more was the young master's calmness. Amusement glinted in his eyes. "What irony, hearing such an insult from a seoja, a bastard abandoned by his own father."

A muscle worked in Shim's jaw. "Whether the victim was deserving of death is not up to anyone to decide. No man or woman, noble or slave, ought to be killed without the sanction of the ruler."

The young master's gaze shifted to the space behind Shim, and

I followed his gaze and saw Inspector Han passing by, too occupied to notice us.

"There goes your master, Officer Shim." With one smooth motion, he flicked open his fan, airing his manicured face again, and under his breath he said with a smile, "Only dogs and horses long for a master."

The young master strode away with long and measured steps, his manservant scrambling behind him. Once he was far enough away, I said quietly to Officer Shim, "He asked me about Lady O's beauty, but I told him nothing, sir."

"Good."

I waited, and when he said no more, my curiosity got the better of me. "Who is he?"

"The son of Third State Councillor Ch'oi. A philandering drunkard, I hear."

"Begging your pardon, sir, but why does he care so much about Lady O?"

Officer Shim looked at me. At once, my eyes dropped below his chin to avoid his gaze, and I ended up staring at the braided scar across his neck. Some whispered he'd tried to hang himself, though most claimed that a criminal had tried to strangle him.

"Inspector Han told me you had the curiosity of a magpie. I see that now," he said, warmth in his voice. "The young master was betrothed to Lady O when they were children. They never saw each other's faces. Perhaps that is why."

"He must have been infuriated when he learned of the affair."

"Indeed. His side ended the engagement two months ago after hearing the rumor."

I knew people like the young master, namely Kyŏn. Men who thought so highly of themselves, men who rarely experienced humiliation, and when they did, drew out their swords with vengeance in their hearts, unable to let the slightest slander pass them by.

"Inspector Han interviewed him earlier today," Officer Shim continued. "Apparently, he was at the House of Bright Flowers when the murder occurred, and he named five people who could vouch that he never left the house that night. Sons of government officials."

The impossibility of the investigation sank into me. "Wealth and power must make a man untouchable, sir."

"You were raised by servants, so of course, you must see aristocrats as gods," Officer Shim said, as kindly as an older brother. "But wealth and power also make a man err in his arrogance. That is what Inspector Han said. If he was indeed involved, we will find a careless trail of evidence, Seol."

⬤

The small entrance of the prison block, monitored by two guards, waited ahead as I approached with a tray at noon, bearing a bowl of water and a cloth. It was my duty to keep beaten prisoners alive, though sometimes Commander Yi instructed that witnesses be left unattended to, that the fear of death might wring the truth out of them.

"Who are you here for?" one of the guards asked.

"Maid Soyi."

"Follow," he said, opening the gate, then disappearing inside.

I tried to balance the tray with both hands as I stumbled through the drafty darkness. Water sloshed out from the bowl. As my eyes adjusted, I saw the narrow passage, the ground layered with dried mud crumbled into dust. On either side of me was a line of cells built of logs, with planks nailed vertically to keep prisoners from escaping, and tiny barred windows that offered a glimpse of skylight.

At last, the guard stopped. Keys jangled, then the cell gate creaked open. "Call for me when you're done." And he locked me in.

Soyi was too weak to acknowledge my presence, resting her back against the wall, her legs stretched out before her. Her bloody hands lay almost lifelessly by her sides, palms out. Like me, she had been punished for trying to escape, except with a less permanent wound than my own. Not a branding of the cheek, but the common beating of the legs, with a stick that a flogger had swung with the force of an ax.

"I'm here to clean your wounds." I crouched before her and lifted her skirt slowly. The blood must have crusted onto the fabric, for her lips fell open in pain, as though I were peeling off her skin. I managed to hike her skirt up around her waist. The torn undergarment revealed ripped skin, a sight that left me nauseated.

"This might hurt just a bit." I soaked the cloth and wiped her wounds, and immediately she turned as pale as death. Beads of sweat formed along her temple, and biting her pale lips, she swallowed her scream.

"Endure it," I urged, holding her trembling leg down to clean around the torn skin rolled up along the gashes. If I didn't clean her well in this damp weather, I knew her wound would rot, and its smell would fill the whole prison. "Endure, and stay alive."

"Stay alive," she whispered. Faint. As though the pain had reached an unbearable level. "I'm going to die here, I know it."

"You don't know the future."

"The future. One needn't be a shaman to know it."

I continued to press the cloth against her, my fingers gleaming red.

"Mother told me this, that even dogs become troubled before a storm arrives. They sense the rumbling of a faraway thunder, and I can feel it too." Her eyes turned glassy as her brows puckered together. "The trembling of the earth."

I wanted to ease her despair somehow. But I also knew that if she had committed murder—no matter how much I might sympathize with her—she was deserving of punishment.

"You never know," I said. "Perhaps the storm will come, then pass by."

Soyi shook her head, and while she had hesitated before Inspector Han, she opened to me, as easily as a clam in hot water. "Why do I have to be me? Why couldn't I have been born a lady?" she said, emotions infusing her voice with color. "I am one mere servant among ten thousand of them. The worst part is . . . the police can kill me and it will make no difference."

Not knowing how to ease her fear, I quietly dipped the cloth into the bowl and squeezed out the blood, a smoke of red unfurling in the water.

"But perhaps I am a killer."

My hand stilled in midair, the cloth dripping red water onto my skirt.

"My mistress told me that hate is like murder. And I despised her."

I squeezed the cloth one last time, then set it aside on the tray.

"She called me her sister, her equal. So I thought she would understand my longing to be free." A tremor shook her solemn voice. "She said she wanted to keep me by her side because she cherished me. I, her equal? I wept every night after dressing her and brushing her hair—sad each time she refused my request, terrified when she criticized me for this longing to be mistress over my own life."

"Is this why your mistress wrote about you?" I said, playing along with the inspector's bluff about finding Lady O's journal. "Is this why you fought with her?"

"I asked for my nobi deed," Soyi said, her confession slipping so easily out of her lips, unaware that I was recording every word in my memory. "I had asked her before, but this time I was determined. I wanted my nobi deed, to end our mistress-and-servant contract. But she wouldn't give it to me."

"But why *would* she give it to you?"

"She promised to return it to me on my eighteenth birthday."

A question that had burned at the corner of my mind now resurfaced. "You said Lady O doesn't believe in indentured servitude. Is that a common idea here in the capital?"

"Common? No."

"What kind of people believe it?"

Her dark gaze steadied on me, as though suspicious.

"You are a lowborn, but a noblewoman called your status manmade," I explained. "I don't understand why she would say so." I bound her wounds with a fresh strip of cloth. "Please, tell me."

"Lady O was a Catholic rogue. Converted two years ago. She told her mother that she valued this teaching over blood relation."

"Catholic?" The teaching that was prohibited and punishable by death, knowledge smuggled in from the West. "And you didn't think to tell the police?"

"It had nothing to do with her murder. You must swear not to tell this to anyone, or Matron Kim will sell me off like a dog as soon as the inquisition is over. I'm sure that Lady O's lover killed her. It is *him* you need to find." Dragging her skirt down, she whispered, "So many questions from you."

"I am just curious."

"No, it is more than curiosity."

Her words crept into me like a deep chill, and it took a moment for me to realize that she was right.

"Mere curiosity, truly," I repeated, rising to my feet and slowly dusting off the strands of straw, my thoughts drifting away until I found myself staring at the deep pool of my past. A pool I was frightened to reach into and touch—afraid of smoothing my fingers around the edges of something awful.

FOUR

"SST!"

I stepped out of the police bureau after taking my midday meal, ordered by the chief maid to shop for her. It was then that I saw a bright-eyed girl with a tiny face and an even tinier pair of lips. Her dress was elegant, yet the colors were subdued, not brilliant like a noblewoman's. Likely a servant of a wealthy household. Seeing no one else around, I pointed at my chest. *Me?*

"Yes, you. My mistress has summoned you."

I held the market basket between us. "How do you know who I am?"

She pointed at her cheek, where my own face was marked. "It's impossible not to know who you are."

"And who is your mistress?"

The tiny lips emitted a high, cheerful voice. "My mistress said you journeyed with her from Mount Inwang to the fortress gate."

I nearly dropped the basket. The mysterious noblewoman. Why did she wish to see me? I remembered the books that had spilled out, the men on edge. It would be wise to turn away, yet even as I thought this, my feet followed the maid.

"I am called Woorim." She faltered in her steps, glancing over her shoulder. "Are you permitted to leave freely? I can wait for you outside if you wish to tell your superior."

"I'm not imprisoned in the police bureau," I said. "So long as I finish my duties."

"I suppose so. I see damos wandering in and out of the bureau as they please. I, too, am free to wander and explore the capital. My mistress permits me."

I remembered the lady disguised as a man, her cart full of secret books. "What kind of person is your mistress?" I asked.

"A benevolent one," she said. "The anchor cable can measure the depth of the four seas, but nothing can measure the depth of my lady's kindness!"

She had a flair for language, words from a scholar's brush, not usual for such a servant. My own mouth was filled with eloquent words, but only because I'd stolen them from Older Sister. Whom had Woorim stolen her words from?

"Do you know how to read?" I asked.

"Omo, how did you know?"

"Your mistress taught you, I suppose."

Woorim's eyes turned even rounder. The dainty lips smiled. "Not just me."

I wasn't surprised to hear this anymore, but the philosophy felt dangerous now. What better way to defy the role of servants than to teach them how to read and write? To equip them with the same knowledge and power as their own masters and mistresses?

My stream of thoughts was interrupted by a servant calling out, "Make way, make way for Councillor Ch'oi!"

Woorim and I dropped to our knees at once and pressed our foreheads to the dirt, listening as the servant continued to call out, "Make way for the Third State Councillor!"

I shifted my head just enough to catch a glance. Four bearers carried a sedan chair, in it a middle-aged man with a short black beard and a forehead wrinkled from years of strife. Despite his beaten appearance, he was handsome, with his high nose, squared jaw, and intelligent eyes. He was all shoulders and straight back, holding himself regally, not a limb in his body slouching.

Councillor Ch'oi, father of Young Master Ch'oi Jinyeop. They could not have seemed more alike and yet different.

As the sedan was lowered before the police bureau, someone tugged at my collar. I looked and saw Woorim already on her feet. As was everyone else. I jumped up and dusted off my skirt and palms. The sight of Councillor Ch'oi sharpened my attention on the questions floating around my mind as loose as cobwebs—about his son's broken engagement to Lady O, her Catholic past, the last letter she'd received before her death. Were there any connections?

"How well do you know the nobles in Hanyang?" I asked.

Woorim's eyes surveyed our surroundings, then stopped before a massive merchant shop, famous for its Chinese silk. Rolls of fabric glowed like seashells in the skylight. "Look there," she said, pointing at a noblewoman whose face was veiled by sheer gauze hanging from her headdress, hidden from foreign men. The lady was examining the fabric and asking the shop assistant for a price.

"That is Lady Rhee," Woorim said as she beckoned me to walk closer. "A shallow woman who only talks of fashion and men." She cast a bragging smile my way. "I know almost *all* the noblewomen in the capital."

"Then you knew Lady O."

"Of course. She took tea with my mistress a few times. She seemed very sweet and cheerful."

"But you must have heard the rumor that she had a lover," I said. "Did you see Lady O in the company of a man?"

"Besides her father and younger brother, no. An unmarried lady like her isn't permitted outside. You should know that. When she did go out, it was always hidden deep inside a palanquin."

"Lady O could have snuck out alone." As she had on the night of her murder.

Woorim shook her head. "I cannot imagine her dishonoring her family."

I was talking in circles, getting nowhere. What would Inspector Han say to uncover what he wished?

"Councillor Ch'oi and his son have ties to Lady O's household, do they not?"

"Oh yes," Woorim replied. "The young master was betrothed to Lady O. That's *hardly* a secret."

"And if it were a secret," I said slowly, "I suppose you would know it."

A small, quick smile. "Perhaps."

"And if you did not?"

She paused to think, then pointed down the road in the direction of Mount Inwang. "Keep walking that way until you see an inn with a red lantern. The innkeeper was once a gisaeng, a female entertainer favored by Councillor Ch'oi. Their love was the talk of Hanyang many years ago. Her name is Madam Song, and everyone calls her the storehouse of information."

I'd seen that inn before, on the day I had run from the bureau. I'd learned from an acquaintance visiting Hanyang that Older Sister had fallen deathly ill, that her last words before passing out had been, *I cannot die in peace without seeing my brother Inho*. So, desperate to comfort her, I'd run and had spent an entire day traveling from shop to shop, showing people the sketch of my brother. It was by the day's end that I'd finally reasoned that an innkeeper would know roads and towns . . . and where the dead were buried on the road from Inchon.

And now, in the street, the weight of my brother's unfound grave hung around my neck. Older Sister, fortunately, had recovered and my promise to her remained. In my robe, even the folded paper bearing his sketched face felt heavy, unbearably so. I carefully withdrew it and held it out for her to see.

"You said you know many people," I said. "Have you ever seen this person?"

Woorim puckered her lips. "The sketch is so faded I can hardly see how he looks. Don't you have another picture of him?"

"No, this is all I have." I looked down at the drawing of him, and I wondered if he still looked as he had more than a decade ago, when he had been only a boy with the pudginess of childhood still clinging to his face. A face as round as the glowing moon, framed by long hair tied loosely at the back, and his puffy eyes filled with a youthful innocence. "He doesn't seem familiar at all?"

Woorim shook her head. "There are some even I do not know."

I fell quiet. The sketch of my brother always opened me up to a world filled with echoes, like a faraway stranger calling to me from a mountaintop. I missed his stories about home, a home I had been too young to remember, a home filled with the intensity of affectionate words and the texture of comforting arms around me. Those tales had vanished and had left me feeling hollow, as though I were a wandering spirit.

"So . . ." Woorim's voice filled the silence that had opened between us. "How old are you anyway?"

"Sixteen."

"I am, too!" She grinned. "Since we're the same age, shall we lower our words?"

To lower our words meant to speak in banmal, "half words," rather than in formal speech.

"If you'd like," I said.

Her smile faltered. "Seol-ah, you know that feeling you get, when your skin goes all bumpy like chicken skin, because you sense some-one is watching you?"

"Eung. I know that feeling."

"I feel watched sometimes. No, not sometimes. All the time; whenever I leave the mansion."

"By whom?"

"I don't know, but I feel it." Then the concern flew off her face like a flighty bird. Her lips popped into a grin. "Maybe it is a ghost!"

Our conversation ended when we arrived at the residence, a stately mansion on the far edge of the Northern District. The spark of concern I'd felt for Woorim dissipated as I followed her across the courtyard and up stone steps, then took off my sandals.

Standing close to the hanji doors, Woorim called, "Lady Kang, the damo is here to see you."

A smooth-soft voice replied, "Send her in."

I stepped into the guest hall, and through my lashes I observed a vast and airy chamber. Blue-gray light shone through the translucent paper panels, framed by wood and used as sliding doors and room dividers. A few steps closer, and I smelled the lady before I even saw her: the warm and sweet scent of clove buds. The scent of nobility. I didn't look up, yet I could feel her gaze as I prostrated myself.

"Lady Kang," I said. "I am honored by—"

"Lift your head. I cannot hear you."

I lifted my eyes, just high enough to see a low-legged table, drag-ons inlaid and lacquered. Behind the table, a full skirt of crimson silk.

"Let us speak face-to-face."

I picked myself up—my shoulders and back, then my hands, which I rested neatly in my lap. At last, I saw her, and she looked different today. She had thick, lustrous black hair, braided and coiled neatly at her nape, decorated with pins and ornaments.

"You must wonder why I summoned you," she said.

"Yes, mistress."

She placed her elbow on the table and locked her eyes on mine. *It is rude to stare at your superiors,* my sister's warning whispered into my ear. I looked away, but the lady's gaze beckoned me to meet her eyes again. As I did, the heat of my anxiety left me sweating.

"I wish to know if you informed your inspector about those books."

Books, mere books. "I did not."

She studied my face so intently, I almost wanted to see my reflection, to see whether my thoughts were somehow written upon my face. Finally, she bowed her head. "I believe you. And your name, what is it?"

"My name is Seol."

"You have not asked me, Seol, why those books were hidden. Are you not curious?"

"I am, mistress." I rubbed clammy palms against my skirt as I remained kneeling on the floor, my eyes fixed on her. "But it would be improper to ask, and so . . ."

"They are all copies of one book, a book that turns life's bitter and unbearable taste of pain into sweet and delicious pleasure."

She was speaking in riddles, though riddles I'd heard before from Maid Soyi. Perhaps this was why Catholic women educated their servants, so that they might read these illegal books on their own and understand.

"Pain into something sweet . . . ," I said. "How is it possible, mistress?"

She paused with consideration, then opened a drawer and pulled out a long, thin pipe made of precious silver. "Come closer. Help me light this."

I shuffled forward, and with practiced movements, I accepted tobacco from her and added it into the tiny bowl, then used a tinderbox to light it.

"Have you ever believed in something before?"

"Yes, I have, mistress," I said quietly.

"Such as what?"

"I believe . . . I believe my family is waiting for me."

"Then have you ever had a conviction?" she asked, and when I paused, unable to differentiate the two words, she explained, "When we believe, we hold on to what we think is true. But when we have a conviction, that truth holds on to us."

"Oh," I whispered, still not understanding anything.

"I am convinced, Seol, that I am passionately loved by our Heavenly Father, and that my life is in his good hands. So though pain and sorrow press in around me, conviction holds on to me and strengthens me. It makes my yoke lighter to carry."

Conviction. Whoever this Heavenly Father was, Lady Kang trusted in his character, enough that she'd let nothing in life shake that trust. I rubbed the spot over my vest where I'd hidden the norigae ornament, tying the tassel to the strap beneath the layers. I felt the same way about Inspector Han.

Perhaps it was the tobacco fragrance—woody warm, with earthy undertones—rising in white clouds that returned my focus to the task at hand and calmed my nerves enough for me to grasp onto a fistful of boldness. Or perhaps it was the memory of Inspector Han that coaxed the words from me.

"Mistress, would you permit me another question?"

She made a gesture. *Do so.*

"Begging your pardon, but did you hear of Lady O's death?"

"I did." Wisps of smoke curled from her lips. "I was not well acquainted with the lady, but I knew her to be a kind and virtuous woman who died from no sin of her own."

I considered carefully, afraid I would offend her with my presumption. I forced myself to think of Inspector Han again, brave before the tiger. "There is a rumor that the victim had a lover."

Lady Kang remained quiet. At length, she said, "It is as you say, a rumor."

"But they examined her, and she was not a—a virgin. So she must have had a lover, though none know of him."

"Why do you ask me?"

I looked up at her. *Because you are a Catholic as she was.*

Catholic, like the murdered servants and peasants.

"Woorim said you are aware of the goings-on here in Hanyang," I lied, but did not feel that my guess was untrue. "That is why I ask you, mistress, and I beg your pardon for being so forward."

Lady Kang lowered her pipe and sighed. "Perhaps Lady O did have a lover, yet she is of such a gentle temperament. No man could have despised her enough to have harmed her."

But what if the reason behind the violence had its root in Catholicism? I didn't know where to begin to unclutter this question. All I could do was dig and dig. "I have one last thing to ask, mistress. On the week of Lady O's passing, there were many deaths among Catholics of low origin."

A shadow passed over Lady Kang's countenance, and a chill jabbed into my chest. I had crossed a line; *this* question, I ought not to have asked. Yet I could not think of anyone more knowledgeable. She might have even worshipped the Western God together with the victims.

I pressed on. "Do you know why such tragedies occurred all of a sudden?"

"All those corpses found recently . . ." She lowered her voice, as though straining against a harsh weight. "They were the corpses of those who refused to apostatize this foreign learning. You see, Seol, it is dangerous to be different here in Joseon. Queen Regent Jeongsun is preparing the magistrates to reinforce the ogatong chi pŏp."

I frowned, not understanding.

"It will be peaceful for the next five months, the formal mourning period before the elder king's burial. But afterward, every five households will be grouped into a unit. If a Catholic is found in any one of them, all five are to be found guilty of treason in the New Year."

"Oh . . ."

"But I believe the persecution is a double-edged sword. It will wipe out the Catholics, whom the kingdom despises for being different. But it will be the queen regent's means of wiping out her opposing faction as well."

"The Southerners," I whispered, and withheld myself from adding, *the faction to which Lady O's father belongs.* Yet another question rose to my lips—and I knew I'd already asked one too many, but Lady Kang's willingness to talk encouraged me to speak on. "What connection does this faction have to Catholicism, mistress?"

"That is a very important question." She sucked on her pipe. A string of smoke twirled into the air as she breathed out and answered, "Southerner scholar-officials were among the first to spread Catholicism when it was smuggled in. They spread it in the name of reform, but the regent believes it is nothing more than their attempt to regain power in the government."

Lowering my gaze, I played with a loose thread on my sleeve. Masters and mistresses, lowborn parents and relatives—all were killing heretics out of fear for their own lives. And soon the fear and panic would reach their sharp fingers deep into the imperial court itself. Perhaps the lover had killed Lady O because he knew her heretical ways might endanger him or someone he cherished far more. Or perhaps Lady O's mother had killed her. Honor killing was common in the capital.

"You care about this case." Lady Kang's solemn voice lifted my attention back to her dark eyes, steadied on me. The uneasiness in her composure from moments ago was gone. "You are free to suspect, but do not jump to conclusions. Do not fixate on only one possibility. Wait until you have thoroughly examined all angles of the case."

"I am a servant, mistress," I reminded her. "A servant's conclusion could never matter."

"All who are involved in an investigation are responsible in taking care of a life. Each decision you make, you will look back to it one day and you'll realize that it took something out of you, never to be replaced. So tread with care, Damo Seol . . . great care."

The thought that my decisions were of importance filled me with a free-falling sensation, as if I were a bird released from a cage, thrown into a world of endless sky. Yet I couldn't help fearing that I was being tempted. She'd said so herself: it was dangerous to be different.

"I understand," I whispered.

The creak of footsteps brought our conversation to a hold. The silhouette of a maid bowed outside the screened door. The tranquil voice said, "Mistress, Scholar Hwang is here to speak with you."

"So he has arrived . . ." Lady Kang puffed on her pipe, turning back to me. "Because you are so curious, I will tell you this: since I was a child, I've had a certain peculiarity. I have known things that others did not. I would study the face of a man or woman, and right away, I could tell much about them. I said once, 'This marriage is bad,' and they ended up divorced later. Even as a child, I was called 'the Matchmaker.'" A smile tugged at her lips. "It may seem incredible, but in truth, you can know a person's character by the direction of their emotions, actions, words—as you might know the direction of the wind by studying a magpie's nest."

I waited in silence, daring no interruption. She could tell much about a man or woman, and seemed to know much about me, yet to me she was mysterious and unknowable. I could not understand why a woman such as she—wealthy and privileged, wanting nothing—had chosen to risk everything for heresy.

"I was informed that you saved your inspector."

"Yes, mistress," I whispered.

"You have courage, that is clear. You are also intelligent and possess a good heart—and incredible curiosity. Cunning, yet honest too. There is too much empathy in you, though, and it will burn you out." Her gaze remained fixed, as though peering into the wilderness of my future. "A darkness will fall on you. But never let fear stop you from doing good, Damo Seol. Everyone dies; what is difficult is a meaningful death."

I sat straight as a hollowing sensation expanded in my chest. "What do you mean, mistress?"

She didn't answer, and instead said, "When you are in trouble, do not forget. Come to me for help."

●

A flash of subdued robes the color of Woorim's hanbok caught my eye as I slipped on my sandals outside the guest hall. Woorim, just disappearing through a courtyard gate. I followed, keeping my steps quiet. If I could not find answers with Lady Kang, perhaps it was time to consult the maid again.

I emerged into another quiet courtyard, the women's quarter. A paulownia tree stood by the stone wall, and I kept under the shadow of its huge, heart-shaped leaves. A few paces away, Woorim set a tray down and crept up to the middle pavilion. She peeked through a crack in the papered screen. Only for a moment, as if she was afraid of being spied upon, then withdrew and hurried along her way. The tray remained.

My heart thrumming, I walked quietly over to the pavilion. My warm breath rushed against the paper screen as I drew closer to the gap. Within, a middle-aged gentleman sat cross-legged. His eyes were downcast and his dark hair tied back, revealing a broad face covered with small scars.

A man was not to linger in the women's quarter. Fathers and brothers might visit, but never for long. This man was concealed, away from searching eyes . . .

Away, perhaps, from the eyes of an investigator.

The hairs on my skin rose. I tried pushing the thought aside, shocked by the leap my mind had made. Yet, once there, the thought could not be undone.

I slipped from the courtyard as quietly as I'd come and collected the still-empty market basket. Speaking to no one, I hurried from the mansion, the secrets of Lady Kang burning inside me.

FIVE

THE DEEP RUMBLE of the great bell had already echoed through every street and alley, announcing the start of curfew. The time of total silence. Occasionally footsteps hurried across, followed by a patrolman's call of "Arrest him!"

I had spent the entire next morning and afternoon trying to appease the chief maid's fury. After all, I'd left the bureau for *far* too long the day before to visit Lady Kang. So I'd made sure to catch up on all my chores until every limb in my body ached in protest.

Now the sky had finally darkened, and it was nearly time to retire for the night—but not yet.

I stood by the courtyard gate with a lantern, waiting for Damo Aejung. Iron cauldrons, ablaze with smoky light, cast moving shadows against the curve of rooftops, reminding me of the midnight waves of my childhood, crashing against the cliffs, then withdrawing. I had watched their dance from the door of our hut. A dance that reached for the moon.

The moon had fascinated me: how alone it looked, how locked up within darkness. My brother had told me its story. *To escape a hungry tiger, two children climbed a rope to the sky. The brother became the sun. And the sister became the moon. "I am scared of the night," said the sister, and so the brother replied, "I will be the moon for you instead." So the brother became the moon, and the sister became the sun.*

I opened my eyes to the flooding light. It was never pitch-dark in the capital, especially in the police bureau, the place that never slept. Prisoners groaned in the eastern courtyard. A servant ran with eyes to the ground, his torch going *whoosh, whoosh* as he searched for something lost. Though most of the gwanbi—the local office servants—had returned to their homes for the night, the damos were ibyeok, live-in servants, so we had no families to go to. The police bureau was our home.

Lanterns hanging from eaves illuminated the main pavilion; our superiors got little rest when a murder occurred.

This hanok building was divided into three quarters: the office of the commander, the meeting hall, and the guest room. The paper-screened doors of the office stood open to allow in the late summer breeze. Two gentlemen knelt inside. Inspector Han sat in a position of subordination, and the commander sat at the head of the table with the paneled screen behind him, the position of honor. Their voices were faint but audible, like the rustling of faraway trees.

"Councillor Ch'oi visited you, I hear," the commander was saying.

"He did, yeonggam. His Lordship reminded me of his friendship with"—Inspector Han cleared his throat—"my father. He asked that I help him for the sake of old ties."

"With what?"

"He fears the regent's offensive to purge the Southerners."

"Of course. He must be counting down the remaining days of his life."

"Indeed. Without King Chŏngjo's protection, Councillor Ch'oi fears the Old Doctrine will come for him. He wants protection."

"And what could you possibly do for him?"

"Assist in the capturing of Priest Zhou Wenmo."

Silence pooled. I could feel the rippling tension. *Priest Zhou Wenmo.* There were wanted posters of him all over the capital, all over my hometown, and likely all over the kingdom. The only priest of Joseon.

Inspector Han continued, "If Councillor Ch'oi can claim to have had a hand in the priest's capture, it will shield His Lordship from being swept along with his fellow Southerners. But you may rest assured, I have no intention of assisting him."

A shiver trembled down my spine as a thought crept into my mind. Councillor Ch'oi feared that the link between his faction and Catholicism would lead to his death, *and* the councillor's son resented the Catholic Lady O for humiliating him. A connecting thread gleamed.

"Aigoo, aigoo. Always eavesdropping, you." It was Aejung, arriving with a tray of bottles of wine and bowls for officers staying at the bureau tonight. Even though she was a year older than I was, she was a head shorter. In fact, I was taller than most damos here. "One day, you will learn something you should not know and it will kill you."

"They will never find out," I said. "I'm invisible."

As we passed by the pavilion, I noticed someone whom I hadn't seen earlier. Senior Officer Shim was standing next to a pillar, hidden in the shadow. Though he must have seen us, his head didn't turn as we passed. His gaze was locked in the direction of Commander Yi and Inspector Han, and his normally stern brows had weakened. I think there was despair in his eyes.

It seemed the bureau would drain the joy out of all of us until we were only shells.

●

"Seol! Hold the lantern higher."

Aejung struggled to balance the clinking bottles as we walked through a small gate and stepped into the western courtyard. She kept her voice low as she said, "Officer Kyŏn is also inside. He hasn't forgiven you for stealing his bow."

I felt as though I'd swallowed a steaming cup of hot water. I had almost forgotten that incident, but now it returned with a fury that burned through me.

"You may think he's a lowly officer, but how do you suppose Officer Kyŏn got his position despite his poor military skills? His family was once nobility and still has old ties to powerful families."

"I know, I know," I murmured.

"Senior Officer Shim"—Aejung glanced over her shoulder, as though to ensure he was not following us—"he is quite the opposite. His status is lower than Kyŏn's."

"Eh? He's not a nobleman?"

"He's a seoja, a bastard. He was prohibited from taking the exams because of his impure blood."

I frowned, confused. Police officers were selected through the mugwa military examination, and all men were allowed to take them except for illegitimate sons. A seoja was as helpless to rise in the ranks as the most ignorant peasant. "So how did he become a military officer?" I asked.

"Inspector Han. He appealed to the commander that great talent would be wasted. You know Inspector Han's closeness to the commander, like son and father, so how could our chief—Seol! Lantern!"

I raised it high again, the flame bright through the rice paper.

"I once overheard Officer Shim say his father has no legitimate son," Aejung continued. "And instead of making Shim his heir, he adopted a nephew. Common enough, but still . . . can you imagine the pain of being denied by your own father? 'Tis no wonder he is so quiet. He keeps his gaze lowered even when speaking to us!"

He bore a mark like me, I realized. An invisible one that flared across his forehead: *son of a concubine.*

I should be kinder to him, I thought. *Another outsider, like me.*

"Officer Kyŏn is free to take the military exam as often as he wishes." Aejung grunted. "He just doesn't have the talent to pass it. He's not very good at *anything*."

"Except being a rat. I think he's a rat reincarnated into human form," I said, and when Aejung spit out a laugh, I added, "But unfortunately, he does not look like one."

Aejung laughed harder, and I joined her, the two of us filling the empty courtyard with our conspiratorial giggling. But we immediately fell silent when we arrived at the low steps that led up to a long wooden building, the officers' quarter, illuminated by two burning cauldrons. After climbing, I set the lantern down on the veranda and slid open the door, wood rumbling against wood. There officers lounged, legs crossed, all occupied—talking, reading, or mending uniforms. Thick cotton bedding lay sloppily folded in a corner, stacked one over the other. Black police hats hung by their silk chin straps on wooden nails.

As I helped Aejung set up the low-legged tables, I sensed Officer Kyŏn's presence, just as I might hear the whining of a barely visible mosquito. I tried to ignore him, ducking my head and staring at the bottles and bowls, but a question drew my eyes upward: Was he still angry at me?

He watched me with a tight, displeased smile that strained across his teeth.

I bit my lower lip hard, remembering how I'd snatched the bow from him as though he were a foolish boy. I wished the earth would open and swallow me up. Honor was like life to a man, and I had taken that from him. I had shamed him before all his fellow officers.

"Impudence!" An older officer's bellow startled me. "How dare you stare into the face of your superior?"

With just the right amount of remorse in my voice, I apologized, then ducked my head again and continued to pour wine into bowls.

"That is fine," Kyŏn said, low-voiced.

"No, sir. I won't allow her to treat you with such disrespect." The older officer's voice groveled at the feet of the far younger Officer

Kyŏn. "Seol is still being trained, so one must discipline her more harshly from the start, or she'll never learn how to conduct herself properly."

"This creature is so thickheaded she'll never learn." Kyŏn emptied the bowl with a few gulps. "Pour me some more."

I did so carefully, cautiously. But before I could move away, with a snap of his wrist, Kyŏn threw the liquid onto my face. Anger exploded in my chest, but I sat still, wine streaming down my forehead, my cheeks, dripping onto my hands folded around the bottle. *A servant mustn't express emotions,* I told myself as I gritted my teeth tighter. *Hide it until you're alone. Cry and yell only when all are asleep.*

As though nothing had happened, he said in a smooth voice, "I hear that Matron Kim is infuriated."

The officers did not respond to Kyŏn and instead stared at my shame-soaked face. After a beat, the older officer asked, "The mother of that noseless victim?"

"The same. She thought she would be summoned for the corpse's examination, but proper protocol was not observed. She has ordered a servant sent from Inspector Han's household to receive his punishment." Kyŏn scratched at his chin as if in deep thought. As if he were capable of it. "Perhaps I will speak with Inspector Han. I'll suggest a servant who might be willing to save his life yet again . . ."

His eyes rested on me, and as they did, a thought raced through my mind. *Inspector Han would not dare hurt me.*

"What are you smiling about?" he demanded.

"Neh?" I asked, confused. "I'm not smiling, sir."

"Yes, you are."

"I am not!"

He was still for all of a second, and then he lunged forward. It all happened too quickly for me to scramble away. He grabbed my collar and dragged me, tugging so hard the fabric turned into a noose around my neck, squeezing my throat shut as I stumbled across the floor. A moment later, I was in the air, crashing down the steps and rolling onto the courtyard. Saliva tinged with coppery blood rolled in my mouth as I tried to reorient myself.

"Who do you think you are, inyeona?" Kyŏn spoke with deadly calm. He had called me many nasty things in the past, but never this, never a bitch. He was standing near the burning cauldron, his face pale with murderous rage. "Do you think that you are more than a slave just because you impressed the inspector that one time?"

My stomach sank with his every step toward me. His boots crunched, crunched across the dirt, and everything in me coiled tight, waiting for him to kick me. Instead, he crouched before me and craned his neck so that we were eye to eye.

"Learn your *place*." His hand smacked me across the back of my head, so hard I saw white spots. "It is serving *tea*"—another smack. And he went on this way, as though trying to shove a lesson into my skull. "Not solving *crime*." *Smack*. "Aigoo, aigoo. Look at you. So proud and *arrogant*!" *Smack*. "Who do you think you are, little *girl*?"

I remained on all fours, breathing shallowly as I swayed against the pressure of each strike. The back of my head burned with humiliation, and my eyes stung with tears, with an emotion I'd never felt before: hatred. If my brother were here, or even the inspector, they would have put Kyŏn in his place. But they were not here, only officers who had stepped out of the building to watch and gloat. I had no one but myself.

Officer Kyŏn raised his hand to smack my head again, but I ducked, then scrambled to my feet. "Who do I think I am?" I echoed, my voice sounding like steel, and yet my knees were knocking against each other. "I am a girl who knows how to hold an arrow steady. Don't blame me for your inability to shoot one properly."

He stared at me, his eyes blazing with disbelief as he stood up. "Say that again, inyeona!" he snarled, spittle flying from his mouth.

"Inspector Han said that I could ask him for anything, for saving his life. Perhaps I will ask him to send you out of the bureau."

"Hah!" Something like madness drifted into his large eyes, each as large as a mouth ready to devour me whole. "You think he'll give me up for *you*?"

"Do what you wish with me then, if you don't believe it. Shame me. Beat me. Slap me." I fumbled with my uniform, then pulled out the norigae ornament and held it up to the torchlight. The amber terrapin gleamed, the tassel of blue strings swaying. "Inspector Han gave this to me, and he is a man of his word. Everyone knows that. So whether he wishes it or not, I swear to you—if you lay a hand on me, I will ruin you."

Officer Kyŏn took a step back, then another. "There is an old saying: 'Ilsan bulyong iho.' 'One mountain cannot abide two tigers.'" The words trembled out of his lips, repressed fury infused into a whisper. "You and I, Seol, one of us must go. And it will not be me."

His gaze darted around at his spectators, all embarrassed for him. They all knew that no servant would make such a large threat if it were a lie. When he turned to me again, something shifted in the pools of his eyes.

"I was going to let it go, for Inspector Han's sake. But now I think he doesn't deserve my loyalty at all." A new light burned in his eyes as he grinned. "I was in charge of collecting more testimonies and found my way to a drunkard at the inn who saw it all."

I stood my ground, still clutching the norigae, my only source of safety. I *was* safe, I convinced myself. Inspector Han would take my side—

"Inspector Han was the blue-robed man who crossed paths with Maid Soyi. Isn't it strange that he didn't mention this encounter? Like he had something to hide?"

My pulse beat faster, a franticness dizzying me. "Y-you don't know what you're talking about."

"*You* think you know something?" he hissed. "Everything's in your head, it's all an illusion. And I'll make sure to smash it for you. It'll do you good."

A plump raindrop splattered onto the earth, and Kyŏn must not have thought me worth getting drenched for; he at once slithered away for shelter. It was then that Aejung rushed to my side, gingerly touching my elbow as she whispered, "Seol-ah, let's go." But I stood still. More drops splashed against my neck. Then the rain came in gusts, pounding the earth. The flaming torches hissed and threw my world into darkness.

SIX

GRAY CLOUDS LURKED in the sky, the streets muddy from yesterday's rainfall. Furnace-hot humidity left me so sweaty that everything stuck to my skin—dirt, strands of hair, my dress, more dirt. The heart-pumping anxiety made it worse. I spent the entire morning looking over both shoulders. Kyŏn's gang of police officers followed me with their eyes, their stares prickling my shoulders, tugging at the hair on my skin.

Inspector Han was the blue-robed man. Officer Kyŏn's words rattled in my head. *He crossed paths with Maid Soyi.*

A drunkard at the inn saw it all.

"The inn," I whispered. Even Woorim, my new friend, had pointed to the inn as the crossroad of information. Maid Soyi must have run to Madam Song to ask if she or her customers had seen her mistress.

"Always daydreaming, never working." The chief maid's voice startled me out of my thoughts. "Do you need another beating? Go on, now! The damos are all searching for you. It is time for Commander Yi's afternoon tea with his guest."

A few moments later, despite the weight of reluctance rolling in my chest, I traveled through the courtyard as quietly as a passing shadow, following behind the other damos. Each of us carried a tray, and mine held side dishes neatly arranged: thinly sliced marinated pork, finely cut fruit, soft persimmons, and spice-mixed stir-fried vegetables. The dishes rattled as I tapped my finger impatiently against the side of the tray. The answers proving Kyŏn a liar were out there somewhere, answers that'd prove that Inspector Han had nothing to do with the blue-robed man who crossed paths with Maid Soyi. Yet here I was, bound to my role as a tea server.

Still, my steps remained quiet as we entered the guest room, filled with the low rumbling of male voices.

Commander Yi sat with legs crossed, the folding screen behind him. His dark beard hung from his chin, long and stringy. Eyebrows slashed across his face, flaring up at the ends. He would have appeared intimidating even without his purple scar.

The commander's guest was not handsome, but striking in appearance. He had slender, willow-leaf brows, and his fox eyes peeked from a face of sharp angles, reminding me of a poet of sorts. He was certainly dressed to suggest a life of leisure, clad in a lightweight and sleeveless outercoat of jade green, worn over a long robe of white ramie, a thin blue cord tied around the waist.

We served the gentlemen, and then the other damos and I withdrew to kneel by the wall, our heads bowed. We were invisible. We usually heard everything, but today their conversation slid off me, like rain rolling off the eaves of a roof.

Only two things I remembered:

First, the guest's name was Scholar Ahn. He was twenty-one winters old, and he was a tutor to the Lady O's little brother.

Second, Ahn had asked a thousand questions, and those thousand questions had all been about the murdered Lady O. As a family friend, he was most concerned about the progress of the investigation.

Once we were dismissed, we waited outside the guest room on the veranda, in case the commander or his guest needed anything else. We also made sure, as the chief maid had instructed us, to be out of hearing distance, and to stand as still as a table or a chair, our heads bent in a position that said, *We dare not be noticed.*

But my mind refused to stay still. I was already planning out the route I would take to the inn.

●

I never quite knew to whom I was begging, but urgency drew a prayer to my lips. *Please let there be answers here.*

I stood wringing my hands before the inn, a thatched-roof building enclosed by a low brushwood gate. People sat on the platform in the yard, fanning themselves and smoking pipes. This place was both an inn and a tavern. Per custom, lodging and stables were free, money exchanged only for food and drinks.

"Jumo! Jumo!" a man called out for the tavern owner, shaking an empty bottle, and when no one answered, he yelled in a melodic voice, "Madam So-o-o-ong!"

A middle-aged woman appeared with a tray of wine bottles, her hair braided into a coil secured by a pin, decorated with red glass that winked at me. As she served her guests, I tried to examine her more closely. I'd met Madam Song once before when I'd gone around showing strangers the sketch of my brother; I'd be able to recognize her. But before I could catch a better look, she disappeared into the backyard kitchen. I sat down on the platform in the yard and craned my neck from side to side, hoping to see her return soon.

"Are you here from the police bureau?" a voice called out.

I turned to find the drunks and wastrels watching me, the lone girl sitting on the platform cluttered with low-legged tables, cups and bottles of rice wine, and bowls of either steaming rice or stew. An aged man in a dusty white garment waved, his hair tied in a topknot, his long beard a tangle of gray and yellow-stained white. He was sitting cross-legged behind a table to my left. "Pour me a drink and I will tell you whatever you wish to know. You may have seen me before. I was a clown famous for my storytelling. Unfortunately," he added with a dramatic sigh, a rush of alcoholic breath sweeping into my nostrils, "I got kicked out of my traveling troupe of performers."

For drinking too much? I thought as I slid around so that I sat before the low-legged table. Even closer to him now, I had to hold my breath as I picked up a bottle and poured him another drink. "I came because I hear Madam Song knows everything about the goings-on here in the capital."

"Oh, she does know many things. Everything except for a certain man's heart." His lips twitched as though they were itchy—perhaps to gossip.

"Councillor Ch'oi, you mean," I said.

"So you have heard the rumor!"

"Not really."

"Well, well, well. Let me tell you a story, a tale of passion and betrayal—"

"Thank you, but a quick summary will do." I looked around the courtyard, hoping to spot Madam Song. "I can't stay long, sir."

He swatted my request aside, as if it were a fly. "As I was saying, this is a love story between a high official and a gisaeng who never smiled. He was a competitive man, Councillor Ch'oi, and when he learned of all the men who had tried and failed to make her smile, he took hold of the challenge with the determination of a general bent on conquering a kingdom. After months and months of sharing with her all the jests he could think of, he fell in love with her, slowly but surely. Then one day, unable to withhold his feelings anymore, he confessed his love to her."

"And that was when she smiled?" I guessed.

"No, she never did smile. Instead, he made her cry enough to fill the entire sea. They love each other still, even after twenty years. I see the councillor riding by, now and then, just to ask about her health, about her day. And I see such passionate longing in his eyes. But she was the one to end their affair, all to become an innkeeper's wife." He snorted. "What a prize this place must be, eh?"

"So she loved the innkeeper more than the councillor," I observed.

"*Aigoo,* she loves no one more than Councillor Ch'oi. After she left the House of Bright Flowers, too old to stay there and too stubborn to ask the councillor for help, she simply had nowhere to go."

"No family?"

"Her family sold her to a gisaeng school when she was a child."

"Oh . . ." I'd heard of gisaeng schools, places where girls as young as eight were taught to sing, dance, play music, read, and write. They grew up without mothers or fathers, their tears wiped away with promises of gigantic mansions filled with servants—but only if they could become the mistress of a rich man's heart.

"I don't understand," I said. "If Madam Song and the councillor love each other, why did she choose to become an innkeeper?"

"She was too pretty for her own good," he mused, not answering me. I wondered if I was speaking to a man or the dozen empty bottles littered around him. "It's a good thing that *you* aren't pretty."

I kept my expression blank, pretending not to feel stung. "Will you answer me or not? Why are Madam Song and the councillor not together now, ajusshi?"

"Ajusshi?" He barked out a laugh. "I have not been a middle-aged man in a long, long time. I'm old enough to be your grandfather!"

"*Ajusshi!*" I pressed, growing annoyed.

Finally, he answered. "There was another woman—*Jumo!*" he yelled out, shaking the empty wine bottle to catch the owner's attention.

I wanted to reach out and yank the rest of the story from him, but before I could, Madam Song appeared. She had a broad forehead and pointed chin, full lips, and heavy-lidded, dreamy eyes. Eyes that watched me. I curled my lips into my mouth, hoping she wouldn't see the taint of gossip glistening on them.

After setting a new bottle on the man's table, Madam Song's gaze drifted to one corner of my face. Her knitted brows straightened.

"What did you do?" she asked.

I blinked. "Pardon?"

She tapped the side of her face. It was then that I became aware of the hot summer's air brushing my branded cheek. I loosened short strands of hair from my braid, letting them fall over the ugly mark. "I looked for my brother. When I couldn't find his grave, I tried to run home," I mumbled. "I was caught. That is all."

"Home . . . ," she said in a steady voice. A series of emotions flowed through her dark eyes. "So my guess was right: we did meet before. You are the girl with the drawing. Have you found your brother's burial ground yet?"

"Not yet, madam."

"Let us see the sketch of him if you have it still," the drunkard called out. "Perhaps I've seen him."

"Yes," Madam Song said, "let me see him again."

"My brother?"

"That is why you have come, is it not?"

"It is, madam." I fumbled for the sketch and thought to myself that this was a good way to continue my conversation with Madam Song. I doubted she would be pleased to know that I'd come for the sole purpose of learning more about a killing. Once I handed the drawing to her, I tensed as she studied my brother's face.

"A fragile-looking young man," she observed as she sat down on the edge of the platform, and I scooted over to sit next to her.

A moment later, the drunkard also joined and looked over both our shoulders. "He traveled to the capital all on his own, you say . . . No, I never did see him."

The drunkard chimed in, "Neither have I," and returned to his drinking, finally leaving us to sit quietly together.

"I would remember a face like his. Does he have any other recognizable features?"

I often recalled my brother's voice, his words and stories a clear echo in my ears, but the image of him had faded into a blur. I looked over Madam Song's shoulder at the blank sky, trying to remember the last time I'd seen him. On a boat, surrounded by misty waters. A glimpse of his brown eyes, so light that it had seemed almost amber. The apple of his throat that had amused me, the way it would rise and fall with each uttered word. As my mind's eye surveyed him, I frowned at a detail I had forgotten until now. On his lower right arm, a wound—a large patch of raw red.

"He had a burn on his arm," I said, my thoughts still twelve years in the past. "A very bad burn."

Madam Song nodded. "Then it would have left a scar. And do you know of any relatives here in Hanyang?"

"No, madam." I knew very little about the details of my past. Older Brother and Sister had made sure of that, always speaking about our parents and relatives in whispers whenever I was around. As though stories about our family were a great and terrible secret.

"Was your brother clever?"

I nodded. "Neh."

"Then he must have come to the capital knowing there was someone here," she said. "When we first met months ago, you referred to your brother as someone who was dead. But he may be alive—and quite well."

I lowered my head to avoid Madam Song's gaze. She was wrong, and there was no point in considering a thought so preposterous. My brother had to be dead; I could feel this truth bone deep, this feeling that ties had been severed.

"Ajumma!" a maid yelled out, fracturing my thoughts. People called crude and tough middle-aged women "ajumma," not queenly ladies like Madam Song. "Ajumma, a letter for you has arrived!"

Madam Song moved to leave, and at once, I remembered why I had come to the inn—to investigate. I threw out a question, letting it cling to her. "Madam, one last thing! Four nights ago, did you notice anything odd?"

"You mean the night of that young lady's murder."

"Yes, madam."

Madam Song clucked her tongue. "An officer was pestering all my customers about that incident. He pestered me too, but I told him to leave."

"Who was the officer?"

"A handsome one," she answered, and when I stared blankly at her, she added, "Very obnoxious and arrogant."

"Officer Kyŏn," I whispered. "*Did* you see anything that night, madam? He claims that one of your customers saw something."

"Hmm. I remember seeing a young maid, running into the inn to ask my customers if they had seen her mistress. Everyone said no, so she came to me next. She was so pale, the blood drained from her face, her lips nearly blue."

"And what did you say, madam?"

"I told her no as well. It is busiest at night here at the Red Lantern. I hardly notice my own hunger as I'm too occupied tending to the needs of others."

"And after that?"

"After that, she left, and I saw her hesitating before a drunk man on horseback. He was slumped forward, slightly swaying on his saddle. So I was worried for the young maid. A drunk man can trample a girl with his horse."

The clamoring and yelling around me fell silent, as though someone had placed Madam Song and me under a bowl. So silent that I could hear the blood pulsing in my ears, and the long "hmm" that hummed out from between her lips.

"It was too dark to see him," Madam Song noted. "He was wearing a hat, so it cast a shadow over his entire face."

"What else was he wearing?"

"He was passing by a lamp . . ." Her eyes narrowed on a scene somewhere in the past. "I saw the color—blue. And the silver emblem of something. A tiger, I think."

Inspector Han's uniform, I thought. Everything Officer Kyŏn had told me matched with Madam Song's testimony, only I'd learned something new. Something crucial he had not noticed, or had left out. The inspector had not remembered Soyi because he had been too intoxicated to notice anything. *That* was the reason for his silence. Not because he was hiding his memory of her. Not because he had a secret.

Relief rushed through me, melting every tense knot, making me want to lie flat on the platform. After Madam Song excused herself, I examined every corner of her statement again and again. Inspector Han had nothing to do with the murder, and I felt foolish for having even harbored a shred of doubt. Officer Kyŏn had surely intended this to happen and would likely laugh if he knew I'd come all the way to the inn to confirm his words.

But this meant the killer was still out there. Once the annoyance pinching my chest eased, I followed the gleaming thread of coincidences, and it led me back to Councillor Ch'oi.

Twisting around, I looked at the drunkard pouring himself another bowl of rice wine. "Ajusshi, you said their relationship ended because of another woman. How do you know?"

"Everyone knows," he slurred, the alcohol finally unwinding his tongue, and flushing his face and eyes red. "She left the councillor 'cause of a necklace. Another woman's gift to him."

"A mere necklace?"

He gulped down the wine, and wiping his lips with his sleeve, he let out a dry laugh. "My wife still wears a jade ring from her former sweetheart. Why am I so envious?" Through all his layers of ridiculousness, I caught a glimpse of a wound, and it slipped a hoarseness into his whisper. "The dead are gone, yet we live in their shadows."

A necklace, I thought. Lady O had died clutching one in her fist.

●

In the western courtyard, a hanok building stood at the center, flared eaves offering shade to the raised wooden veranda surrounding it. Never had I requested Inspector Han's audience before, but here I was. Inside, I knelt on the floor before him. He was in half-dress: hat off, his sword resting by the wall, his hair in a topknot and a silk band tied around his head. Seated behind a low-legged table, he rested his hands on his knees and watched me. Wondering, perhaps, what a girl like me had to say.

Sweat dampened my armpits, and I realized with a shock of horror that there was mud splattered on my skirt. Perhaps even on my face. My mind too occupied, I had forgotten to clean myself.

On my way to the police bureau from the inn, I'd come to the thatch huts and towering trees near the southern fortress wall. With a sturdy branch, I'd pushed at the mud around the crime scene. Nothing. A fallen pendant could have washed away into the gutters in the heavy rain. It could be anywhere.

Still, at least I'd returned with one certainty—a sliver of Inspector Han's story. Kyŏn had forced his suspicion onto an innocent man. Wanting to lay before the inspector the secrets I'd withheld from him, I whispered, "Inspector, may I have permission to speak?"

"Speak."

I clutched my hands tightly and stared at the sword by his side. "The man Maid Soyi saw that night was—was—" *Do not be afraid,* I reminded myself, *Inspector Han is an honorable officer.* "She saw *you* on the night of her mistress's disappearance."

Inspector Han's expression remained as blank as paper. "I was returning home after having drinks with Senior Officer Shim Jaedeok," he replied slowly. "I believe I did encounter one woman, but I did not know it was Maid Soyi. I had one too many drinks to remember clearly."

"Oh, I see . . . I'm sorry, sir."

"For what?" A note of surprise edged his voice.

"For not going straight to you after what Officer Kyŏn told me."

"And why did you not?"

"I was afraid, sir."

"You were afraid of me, and you are sorry for having questioned me." He had taken the vagueness out of my words and laid the truth before us. "Do you know what it means to be a true detective, Seol?"

"No, sir."

"A true detective should not have feelings involved when investigating a crime. The truth is far more important, and that is what you pursued. The truth. So do not be sorry."

I bowed my head, hiding my flushed cheeks. I still couldn't believe that Kyŏn had managed to slip a thorn of doubt into me. Scheming and petty Kyŏn, the last person I should have listened to.

"Is there anything else you wish to ask? Or tell me?"

"No, sir." Then a memory splashed me with a cold reminder. "Actually, one more thing, sir. Soyi confided in me that Lady O was a Catholic."

His expression turned to rock. "What?"

Had I done wrong? In panic, I babbled, "Lady O became a Catholic two years ago. She told her mother that she valued this teaching over blood relation. I learned of this because Maid Soyi had mentioned before that the lowborn class was man-made. When I questioned her, she confessed the truth, about how this remark was inspired by her mistress's Catholic learning."

"A Catholic . . ." In the inspector's voice, the word alone carried the weight of iron. "Damo Seol, do you know why your discovery changes everything?"

"No, sir," I replied breathlessly.

"With Catholicism comes rumors that a thousand foreign ships will dock along the coast between Bupyeong and Inchon Prefecture. Do you wish for our kingdom to be invaded by foreigners from the West?"

I did not know much about the West; all I knew was that I disliked change. "Absolutely not, sir."

"Neither do I. For more than a hundred years, we have held our seclusion against Japanese warlords and encroaching Western powers, though now I am left to wonder whether it was all for naught." He was only twenty-seven winters old, yet the graying hair behind his ear made him look a decade older, a decade wearier. "Lady O is the daughter of a Southerner, so I suppose I oughtn't be surprised that she was a heretic."

"From what I've heard, sir, the Southerners are the ones who first spread this learning. Is that true?"

"It is. And there is a reason why being the daughter of a Southerner attracts danger. You are a girl, so you may be unaware of politics—the controversy surrounding the Indong Revolt."

"I know of it, sir," I rushed to answer.

"Do you?" Interest lit his voice. "Tell me what you know."

Ever since Lady Kang had shared with me the reason behind the pending Catholic persecution, my eavesdropping ears had grown sensitive to rumors about the revolt that had occurred a week ago. I drew from the well of stolen knowledge and shared all that I'd learned.

"Members of the Southerner faction, believing the king poisoned by the Old Doctrine with the help of the Queen Regent Jeongsun, raided the Indong administrative office in outrage. The regent executed all those involved. Now no one dares slander the new ruler."

"You are correct. And the execution is a sign of a massive political offensive in the works; the regent intends to finally wipe out the Southerner faction after all these years."

I pieced together his words. "So you think it possible, sir, that a political enemy killed Lady O?"

"I will need to further investigate, but what you shared does indeed complicate the case. It would help to search through her belongings. Yet only in cases of treason are we permitted a warrant to search a noblewoman's home . . ."

As silence fell between us, I looked at my surroundings. It was my first time in the inspector's office; his tea was always served to him by Hyeyeon and no one else, so I'd never had a reason to step inside. The office was small and clean. On either side of us were narrow shelves filled with scrolls and side-stitched books, as well as a black-lacquered document box with gold-painted decoration, the only pretty item in the stern office. There was also a folding screen behind the inspector, and on each panel, calligraphy of Chinese characters flowed down.

Inspector Han must have noticed my gaze, for he asked, "Can you read those words?"

"No, sir."

"*Hyo, che, ch'ung, shin, yae, ŭi, yŏm,* and *chi.*" He read aloud the Hanja characters and then translated them into Hangul for me. Filial piety, brotherly love, loyalty, trust, propriety, justice, integrity, and a sense of shame.

"These are the highest Confucian virtues." His eyes roved around my face, as though he were weighing and measuring my character. "Which virtues do you possess, Damo Seol?"

I bit my lower lip, then answered, "Loyalty. I may waver, but I always fight to return to it. And you, sir?"

It started raining, droplets tapping against the hanji screened window. I could hear the birds twittering and the splattering of mud as servants made their rounds.

"My sense of shame," Inspector Han answered at length. "That I have in abundance."

SEVEN

THE LONG HOURS of training were woven into my muscles as I knelt on the floor the next day like a butterfly would perch on a leaf. My heart felt lighter, the weight of Kyŏn's lie lifted from me. I straightened my back as I poured tea into Commander Yi's bowl, then stepped back slowly with my head stooped, never showing him my back.

I knelt by the screen wall with the other two damos. Commander Yi had invited Senior Officer Shim to take tea with him. They spoke about the weather, and of Councillor Ch'oi and his son, but the discussion then slowed to a halt around one name: Inspector Han Dohyun.

"You are so much the same." Commander Yi's voice usually reminded me of thunder, but today he sounded more like a weary old man. "Save for that Han clings to the past, while you are trying to escape yours."

"And didn't quite make it," Officer Shim added.

"Double your efforts then and make something of yourself. Time waits for no man."

Commander Yi made a gesture to drink. Officer Shim gulped down the tea, and my insides writhed in pain for him, knowing how hot the tea was. He seemed too nervous to notice, for all that he seemed composed.

"How old are you now, Officer?"

"Thirty," Shim replied.

"Older than Inspector Han by three years. As an older brother to a younger brother, keep an eye on him. Make sure he does not act recklessly."

"Of course, yeonggam."

The air fell so still, the silence so complete, that I heard Aejung gulp down saliva. She must have noticed the tension, for her cheeks flushed. Then the blush only continued to burn brighter, until her face looked as red as a goji berry. It took me a moment to feel it as well, a pair of eyes watching us all. Commander Yi had stopped conversing with Officer Shim and had turned his attention our way. I slid my gaze back to the floor, holding my breath, my own cheeks stinging now.

"Pour us another bowl, then leave. All of you," Commander Yi ordered.

I did so quickly, then shuffled backward to retreat from the room. But the commander's deep, rumbling voice stilled me. "Except you, Damo Seol. You are to stay."

Me? Dread balled into something tight, pounding sharp behind my left eye. The other damos, who normally obeyed immediately, remained petrified for a moment. Then they were gone, leaving me alone.

I couldn't understand why he wanted me to stay. The sight of Commander Yi's trembling hands further unsettled me, the reflection in the tea bowl he held rippling as he picked it up, then set it down, as though he feared it wouldn't make it to his lips. The tremor moved into his voice.

"Inspector Han came to me today with his testimony. Apparently Damo Seol collected a secret from Kyŏn and Maid Soyi. I hope she did not share this detail with anyone else."

I rushed to answer. "I did not, sir. Only with Inspector Han."

Both men stared at me, the meddler in police affairs. The heat in my cheeks moved up to my brows, up to the tips of my ears. Sweat beaded along my hairline. At last, Officer Shim cleared his throat, lifting the knife's tip of their attention away from me.

"The person who spread this information, yeonggam, was Kyŏn, not Seol," he said. "He shouted about the inspector's whereabouts on the night of the killing before an audience of officers."

"I was not made aware of this. Now word will spread throughout the capital, and there are people——" Commander Yi lowered his voice. "There are people who have never trusted the inspector, no matter how many times he has proved himself. This incident has stirred the past awake."

"That is why I wished to speak with you, yeonggam," Officer Shim replied. "I was with Inspector Han at the House of Bright Flowers when the murder occurred. When he first arrived, by his mourning robe and manner, I knew he was grieving deeply for his father. You know, Commander, that his father passed away over a decade ago on that very night. That is why he drank more than usual."

A tense silence followed. My legs had grown numb, the slightest movement shooting an unbearable tingle up my knees. But Officer Shim's response left me more uncomfortable, and I couldn't understand why.

"For how long were you with him?"

"From curfew until nearly dawn. Madam Yeonok was with us," Shim said, and the name he mentioned bloomed with shades of pink in my mind. *Yeonok.* I'd heard of her, a gisaeng known for her beauty and intellect, who entertained powerful men in the mansion nestled at the foot of Mount Nam. "We were deep in our cups and conversed for most of the night. I remained longer at the House of Bright Flowers, and the inspector left first. He must have encountered Maid Soyi on his way home."

"But he didn't return home." Commander Yi's voice sank. "At dawn, Inspector Han left the House of Bright Flowers, as you claim. He passed by Maid Soyi—but he did not return home. That is what I learned. So where did he go?"

Officer Shim stayed silent.

I stayed silent.

The question seemed to have thrown both of us into a whirl of disorientation.

Then Commander Yi, surprisingly, turned to me. "What do you think, Damo Seol?"

I licked my dry lips, my mouth filled with stammers and hesitation. I only knew how to be invisible before Commander Yi. In a bare whisper, I answered. But he told me to speak louder, more clearly.

"Wherever it is that the inspector went," I repeated, "he left long after the murder occurred."

"That is so . . . That is so . . ." With each moment, the shadows clouding Commander Yi's brows seemed to clear, and certainty returned to his voice. "That is indeed so."

Officer Shim looked over my way, a slight smile on his lips. I returned it, two comrades serving the same officer, recognizing each other from afar.

●

Dismissed, I picked up my tray and stepped out of the guest room into the vast shadow cast by the pavilion. *We'll soon find out who Lady O's lover was,* I thought, gripping the tray tighter as I traveled from courtyard to courtyard. *He murdered her. Inspector Han had nothing to do with it.*

The moment I walked into the kitchen, two pairs of curious eyes fixed on me. Hyeyeon's and Aejung's gazes followed me as I set the tray aside and reached for a wooden cup. My throat scratched with dryness, my tongue stuck to the roof of my mouth. Anxiety did that to me. I dipped the cup into a water bucket, filling it to the brim, and then emptied it in a few swallows.

"Well?" came Hyeyeon's voice, smooth and calm. "What happened inside?"

The thought crossed my mind that what I knew was confidential, yet Commander Yi had not warned me to keep silent, and so I told her bits and pieces of what had occurred, about Soyi's confession, about Inspector Han's testimony.

"I found it strange," I added. "Commander Yi mentioned that Inspector Han's rivals might use this testimony to ruin his reputation somehow."

"I can think of only one rival Inspector Han has, and it's someone close to this case. Someone whose name starts with an *R*."

"Do you mean . . ." I paused, remembering a name mentioned by Commander Yi at one point. "Kyŏn?"

Hyeyeon arched a brow. "I said, starting with the letter *R*. I forget you don't know your Hangul characters. But yes, I was referring to the same person. Kyŏn, the Rat."

"I'll wager it is him," Aejung hurried to say. "I've seen him sneaking in and out of the bureau often these days. Like today, I overheard him tell an officer that he's going to get his hands on something that will bring Inspector Han down. He mentioned 'false accusation,' but by then he was too far for me to hear the rest."

"I don't understand," I said. "Why is he suddenly going against the inspector?"

"It's because he's jealous," Hyeyeon said.

"Of who?"

"He is jealous of you."

"Me?"

"Kyŏn is only two years older than you, Seol-ah. He despises you for discrediting him, and he despises the inspector for rewarding you when you saved his life by stealing Kyŏn's arrow. But above all, he cannot stand you because you are a *girl* who did all these things."

"Because I'm a girl," I repeated. A sickening sensation rolled out from those words, and in that moment, the gravity of his hatred became real before my eyes. A hatred that did not wallow as a mere emotion, but toughened into a blade that would make skin bleed.

Aejung's face drained of color, too. "Do you think we should actually be worried for the inspector?" she whispered.

"Inspector Han has an alibi. He has someone to prove that he was elsewhere during the time of Lady O's killing." There was a solidness to Hyeyeon's voice, leaving no room for doubt. "He had nothing to do with the killing, so we needn't worry. Kyŏn can stir up lies, but in the end, the truth will remain."

I'd always prided myself on my sense of loyalty; I'd had the best of friends at home in Inchon Prefecture because of it. Yet compared to Hyeyeon's, mine seemed watery.

My voice sounded too light as I asked, "Then who do you think the killer is?"

"Someone *without* an alibi."

●

False accusation.

The term had blown by me when Aejung had mentioned it, yet now it was all I could think about. Those were the words Officer Kyŏn had uttered in the same breath as his claim that he'd discovered something that might ruin Inspector Han.

I had once been too young to understand this term, but it had stuck to me, and with passing years it had grown in meaning. Hidden truth—injustice, the victim hurting while the criminal went unpunished—a veil of lies and misunderstandings that needed to be torn down. *False accusation.* Those two words had turned into a sharp bone caught in my throat, digging and piercing, refusing to go down no matter how hard I swallowed.

Whatever Officer Kyŏn was up to, I needed to know. Everywhere he went, I tried to follow. Sweeping the verandas, mopping floors, carrying trays in and out of quarters, delivering letters for clerks and officers. I did anything that would keep me close to him. As invincible as Inspector Han seemed, I knew he was human, his life as fragile as my mother's. And how easily her life had shattered into splintered bones upon the rocks. Lies could easily topple the inspector off the edge, too.

"I'm convinced of it," Officer Kyŏn was telling his gang of officers. "This year, I will pass the *mugwa* examination. I've failed getting in each time, because it's not about skills, it's about whether you know the right people . . ."

Nothing about Kyŏn's behavior seemed out of the ordinary, until evening approached that same day, hours since Aejung had shared Kyŏn's plan to falsely accuse the inspector.

The purple sky deepened into midnight black. A darkness so deep and quiet, swamped in slumbering silence, that Kyŏn must have thought himself sneaky. But in the western courtyard where I crouched, hiding beyond the screen of blue fog, my eyes widened at the sight of him. He snuck out of the officers' sleeping quarter and now stood on the pavilion veranda. Sneaking around like the rat that he was. A creaking step forward, stop, another step, pause. He glanced in all directions, except at the shadowy area to his side, where I was hiding. At last, he pulled open the sliding door, then disappeared into the Office of the Inspector.

My straw sandals muted my steps as I hurried along the veranda toward the edge of the stone steps. I opened the door slightly and peered through the slit. Officer Kyŏn took out what seemed to be a tinderbox, and light sparked to life, too bright in the dark office. He seemed aware of this, for his movements quickened, as though time was running out. He rifled through papers inside a box-shaped object and took one. A longer look, and familiarity struck. It was the black-lacquered document box, the pretty one I'd seen sitting on Inspector Han's shelf.

Officer Kyŏn quickly folded the sheet he'd stolen and inserted it into his robe. He blew out the candle, and at once I withdrew back into the shadows as he rushed out of the office and out of the court-yard.

For a moment I stayed still, my hands and legs trembling. I had to wait for Inspector Han to report what had happened. But then an impulse leapt into my bones.

Follow him.

•

Outside the torch-lit bureau was absolute darkness. The silence, too, was absolute: not a hum, shuffle, or gurgle. Occasionally patrolmen passed me in pairs, and even then, the only sound was of their boot heels. And the rush of my nervous breathing.

Officer Kyŏn was quick, darting from shadow to shadow down an alley, throwing a glance over his shoulder as though he sensed me. Each time he did, I ducked behind a wall or crouched as small as I could. My heart fluttered liked a trapped bird in my chest, so fast I felt light-headed, the exact way I'd felt months ago when I'd tried to run away.

On a night exactly like this one.

Only, I had tried to escape while half-blind, my eyes too puffy from crying all day after hearing the news of Older Sister's illness.

I'd wanted two things in that moment—to find our brother for my dying sister and to run to her side. But a few days after my capture and branding, she'd sent me a note, which Aejung had read to me. A request that I remember my promise to her.

The promise to find our brother's lost grave.

A promise that had kept my feet tied from running away again. But now something else kept me here.

Damo Seol. The memory of Inspector Han's voice drew close to me, deep and fortifying. *Do you know why your discovery changes everything?*

My discovery had mattered to Inspector Han.

I had made a difference.

Suddenly, a strand of cloud blocked the half moon, throwing me into a swamp of darkness. I groped my way through the alley, patting the damp clay wall and the patches of shredded wanted posters, until I saw a dim opening. The cloud rolled away and moonlight shone onto a stone bridge arched over the trickling Cheonggye Stream. By it, a gigantic willow tree stood hunched over, its tresses a pale green-gray in the mist.

It took another glance to notice two shadows beyond the leafy veil.

One was Officer Kyŏn. The second wore a tall black gentleman's hat and a silk dopo robe. His brows and eyes were angled like a fox's. I held in a gasp at the sight of Scholar Ahn, the tutor of Lady O's little brother. The one who had visited the commander, asking him a thousand questions about the dead young lady, much too curious about her case.

Blood pulsed in my ears as I edged along the bed of flowers bordering the river until I could hide behind the bridge, close enough to the willow tree.

"Hyung," came Officer Kyŏn's voice, a harsh whisper I could barely hear over the trickling water. "What are we to do with her, hyung?"

A frown crinkled my brows. *Hyung?* This was not only the word a younger man called an older man by, but a word that suggested intimacy. An intimacy bound by blood, or in this instance, perhaps by friendship.

"We will do nothing," Scholar Ahn replied.

"What? Why not?"

"Behind that girl is Inspector Han, and behind him is an entire police force. I do not move or fight unless I see an advantage, and I see nothing to be gained in whatever scheme you're devising."

"If you're not going to move, I will. *Seol!*" Officer Kyŏn hissed, stalking out.

My heart leapt into my throat. The next thing I knew, he was grabbing my arm and dragging me through the swaying leaves, under the willow tree, where shadows swam and moonlight speckled the ground. He threw me down, so suddenly my head nearly snapped back as I landed on all fours before Scholar Ahn's feet.

"So you'll do nothing? She was following me! That means she saw *everything.*" The roar in Kyŏn's voice strained into a whisper, scraping his throat raw. "I'll lose my position if she tells the inspector!"

"If she tells, then he'll be exposed prematurely. Why would anyone punish you, Kyŏn, for seeking the truth?"

Neither man could speak above a whisper with the patrolmen nearby. I myself didn't want them to be arrested. Not yet. I had too many questions racing in my mind.

"Scholar Ahn," I said, avoiding Officer Kyŏn, who seemed incapable of a levelheaded conversation. "What he did was wrong. He went into Inspector Han's office and stole a document."

"This?" Scholar Ahn held up a sheet of paper. The moonlight

glowing through it exposed the vertical lines of Hangul characters. He folded it and slipped it inside his robe. "This letter confirms my suspicion that Inspector Han does indeed have vengeance in his heart toward Catholics. Coincidentally, a Catholic woman ended up dead, a woman who had information he may have wanted."

"What do you mean?" Incredulity prickled through me, then flashed into heat that raised my voice a notch higher. "He had no reason to kill!"

"Ah, 'reason.' That is a word I like. I have read many detective tales in my lifetime, and often 'motive' paves the path to the 'who.'" He drew his hands behind his back, gazing down at me in solemn consideration. Perhaps he was a cruel man—he had to be to conspire with Kyŏn—yet along with his meanness were brushstrokes of sincerity. "I once asked your inspector how he knew so much about Catholicism. He quoted Sun Tzu to me: 'Know thy enemy.' He knew his enemy too well, had spent five years trying to catch a priest whom no one had seen before."

Motive. Catholicism. Inspector Han's past. Loose strands whirled in my mind, a chaos I couldn't make sense of.

Scholar Ahn seemed to notice my confusion, for he said, "What I am saying is this: if you understood the inspector's hatred for Catholicism, you would understand that the man you think to be so honorable and kind is the darkest book in the human library. And you *will* find it odd that on the night Inspector Han was roaming the capital, a night he coincidentally was too drunk to remember, a Catholic girl ended up dead."

I shook my head. Perhaps Inspector Han was filled with contempt for Catholics, but so were hundreds of others. Scholar Ahn had leapt from Inspector Han's personal hatred to his actually being involved in a killing. A ridiculous connection.

"And you, sir, are a family friend of Lady O's. Where were you on the night of the incident?" I demanded.

Scholar Ahn's lips parted, then shut, hesitation flickering clear in his face. "I was studying at home."

"Can someone vouch for your whereabouts?"

"Unfortunately not. My wife was ill, and so all the servants were tending to her."

"Then you have no alibi."

Officer Kyŏn, who had stood quietly by the trunk, now approached. His black uniform pooled around him as he crouched before me. I waited for his display of brute strength, a slap across the head, a tug at my collar until the seams ripped. Instead, he whispered, "Don't fill your head with useless speculations. You'll see, Inspector Han will soon be out of power."

He leaned closer until I could see my reflection in the moonlit irises of his beetle-black eyes, so close that his breath disturbed the tendrils of my hair, the very depths of my soul.

"No one will be by his side in the end," he whispered, "not even you."

"You are wrong," I said, trying to keep my voice steady. "I will always be loyal to Inspector Han."

The corner of his lips rose. "You are naive, Seol. There is no such thing as always. Loyal, you mean, until one of you dies."

EIGHT

THE FOLLOWING DAY, my search for an excuse to leave the bureau, to get far away from Officer Kyŏn, arrived in the form of the chief maid's order that I deliver a note for her. I gladly complied, and after delivering the message, I was in no hurry to return to the bureau. I wandered the capital, then paused to watch a deolmi puppet play at the marketplace, appreciating that I could have a moment where I didn't need to worry about Kyŏn's threat.

But I slowly realized: I was no safer here than in Kyŏn's presence.

Deolmi puppet plays were always about resistance, but this, this one was the story about Queen Regent Jeongsun's hunger for power and her bloodthirsty ways. To perform it so openly, in public—it was suicidal.

I took a step back, then another, until I was outside the crowd. Easier to run should soldiers raid the performance.

"Are you enjoying the play?"

A familiar male voice scattered my thoughts into a million pieces. I whirled around and my heart lurched into my throat when I found myself standing face-to-face with a man. By the silver tiger embroidering his blue uniform, I knew it to be Inspector Han. Yet the fierce sun behind him made it impossible to see his face, so I couldn't tell whether he was looking through me or at me. Moments like this, I felt it was true, that between a nobleman and a slave was the distance between heaven and earth.

"Come away before the soldiers arrive," he advised, "while you still can."

I clasped my hands together and quickly followed, walking a step behind Inspector Han in silence.

"I've been meaning to speak with you," he said after a moment. "Last night, when I left to meet briefly with Officer Shim, someone entered my office and took something. I'm sure of it, for all the contents had been there earlier."

I pressed my lips tight together. Officer Kyŏn had warned me that there would be consequences if I told, that it would expose whatever "evidence" he and Scholar Ahn had against Inspector Han. I didn't know whether to believe him.

"A servant said he saw you lurking around the pavilion at night."

"Me?" My pulse quickened, as did my words. "I can explain everything, sir. I didn't go inside. It's not what you think."

"Do not look so alarmed. I trust you. That is why I wish to know your side of the story."

Whatever reserve I'd felt moments ago flew away. I rushed forward to walk alongside the inspector and told him everything, from Aejung's suspicion that Kyŏn was up to something, to catching Kyŏn in the act myself, and finally to our argument under the willow tree with Scholar Ahn, as well as their accusation against him.

I waited for the fury, the outburst, but instead a muscle worked in his jaw as he muttered, "Why am I not surprised?" Then he looked at me. "You are a very unlucky girl, to be thrown into such dangerous circumstances."

My brows lifted. "Begging your pardon, sir, but I was not thrown into anything. I chose."

"You chose," he said quietly. His steps slowed as he paused to consider me for a moment. A second look, the way a general might pause to reconsider a candidate for the army. "For me?"

"Remember, sir, loyalty is my greatest virtue."

"Are you pledging your loyalty to me?" There was a hint of warmth to his voice.

"I am, sir."

He smiled, but it was a sad smile. It was as though, all along, he'd considered me too young to understand the weight of loyalty. Too young to understand the terrible weight of my promise. But I understood, and I would prove it to him.

I had to ask, though, "What was stolen, sir?"

A dark shade deepened the panes of his cheek. The inspector's face remained stoic, yet the burning told me, warned me, never to ask about this box again.

"Do not concern yourself. It was a letter, and I'll make sure to retrieve it." Quietly, and filling his words with misty vagueness, he said, "Ahn is bent on proving his theory correct—that Lady O's death is somehow connected to me, because of her Catholic beliefs. And because of my past. He knew before all of us that she was a heretic."

Willing myself to stop wondering about the black-lacquered box, I asked, "How, sir?"

"He confessed to Commander Yi recently that he'd overheard Lady O's parents discussing her heretical beliefs. So in the end, he reported it anonymously to the police bureau, delivered the note through a street urchin. It was sent on the seventeenth day of the sixth lunar month."

I swallowed a gasp. That was a full four days before Lady O's death . . .

"Commander Yi never received that note. And so Scholar Ahn's theory is that I intercepted it. He thinks, knowing of Lady O's Catholic beliefs, I somehow became involved in ending her life."

"But you were at the House of Bright Flowers. You have an alibi."

Inspector Han grunted. "Ahn's imagination is creative and preposterous."

"Everyone seems suspicious, sir." I let out a little sigh and peeked up at him, at his furrowed brows. "How do you untangle this confusing web?"

"You collect more stories until a pattern solidifies," he said, and suddenly he walked in longer strides again, as though remembering something. "Come with me. I spoke with Matron Kim earlier. She would not tell me the full truth, but I know someone who might. So I've been meaning to request your assistance."

My heartbeat quickened as I followed him into the bureau, across the connecting courtyards.

"Fear persuades most people to speak," he said quietly, "but Maid Soyi withdraws deeper into silence with every interrogation. My patience is running thin."

"What would you like me to find out, sir?"

"What she used to blackmail Matron Kim."

Blackmail? It caught me off guard, as if a rough hand had shoved me. I could not imagine Maid Soyi to be capable of such a thing. "I don't understand. Are you certain, sir?"

"If I were absolutely certain," he said, "I wouldn't have asked you to come. Thus, your task is to learn what all of us cannot. Can you do it?"

I couldn't help but feel a spark of pride at the question, glowing brighter and brighter with each step. His favor was almost too much for me. But I wanted it—the feeling that I was part of something so much greater than myself.

"I can, sir. I will."

●

Inspector Han waited outside the prison block as I followed a guard deep into the darkness, thick with the rancid smell of blood and rotting wounds. The surprise I'd felt at the inspector's accusation vanished when we arrived before her cell. How could I feel anything but pity? Soyi cowered against the wall, terrified of the guard. The jangling of keys had become the sound of another round of interrogation.

"It's only me," I said.

Her shoulders slumped from relief. "Only you."

I sat next to her, against the wooden wall. The straw pallet rustled beneath my skirt. As my eyes adjusted to the darkness, I saw that the bedding was bloodstained. Soyi sat, unable to keep her head raised. Fear twisted in my stomach. It was entirely possible that she might die in this cell.

"Why have you come?" she whispered.

"To give you advice." I took hold of her limp hand. "I don't think you killed your mistress, but your silence hurts you. The officers have no choice but to break you. All they know is that you tried to run."

Soyi stared in blank exhaustion.

"There is much you could say," I suggested calmly. "You know things others would not wish to have discovered. For instance . . . Matron Kim."

Again, only silence. But I was not a police officer to her; I was not someone who would hurt her. A life among servants had taught me that no human being *wished* to remain silent and misunderstood.

"You must have overheard Inspector Han," Soyi finally said.

"Yes, I overheard," I lied, surprised by how honest I sounded. "You know how curious I am."

"His commander is determined to beat me to death for the details."

I sought something, anything to bring out her words. Then Inspector Han's voice whispered to me, *There is always a weakness.*

"It is too late. Matron Kim spoke long of your blackmail," I said. "She is trying to push all suspicion onto you."

Shadows of anger clouded Soyi's eyes.

"Matron Kim wishes you to seem darker than herself. She said that blackmail is vile, enough that you might be capable of much worse—such as murder."

Soyi turned to me, her breath sickly hot. "She told Inspector Han everything?"

"He seemed shocked. When I heard this, I was just as disappointed . . ." I rubbed my eyebrows. The weight of my lies was making me falter. I didn't know how Inspector Han did it with such ease. "But I realized you must have your own reason. Won't you tell me your truth?"

Silence stretched, a moment of tangled thoughts, thick with hesitation. At last she licked her crusted lips. "Never liked me, Matron Kim. She wanted to dismiss me. But three years ago my young mistress ran away at night, returning the next day. No one knew but Matron and me."

"That is what she confessed," I said, withdrawing my hand so she wouldn't feel the heat of my guilt. "You told Matron Kim you would gossip if she dismissed you, didn't you?"

"Yes, but it was to survive."

"I see . . ." There was little left to ask, but I knew I could not be done yet. The inspector wouldn't have been. I rummaged through my thoughts. "Did she leave to meet a man?"

Soyi nodded, so slightly I barely noticed.

"The same man she went to on the night of her murder?"

"I do not know, but both times, she was going to meet a lover, that is for certain." I let her pause to collect her memories. "A few months after her escape, I discovered her pregnant. Her mother sent us away to a temple, to hide her from family, acquaintances, everyone."

Soyi turned her stare onto me. "I know Matron Kim wouldn't have confessed it. You will tell the inspector, won't you?"

"Do you wish me to?"

"You must tell him all that I said." Eagerness gleamed in her eyes, as though she'd caught sight of a crack through which escape might be possible. In her excitement, her voice strained into a rasp. "Don't let him believe that Matron Kim is an honest woman. *She* could be the killer, for all I know. She gave Lady O a paedo, a suicide knife."

"What did it look like?"

"It was silver and encrusted with turquoise stones."

"The murder weapon," I whispered, remembering the sharp blade found beneath Lady O's bloody corpse. Still, this meant nothing. It was common to gift young ladies with suicide knives, morbid ornaments dangling from their norigae pendant.

Shaking my head, I continued with my line of questioning. "And how long were you in the temple?"

"Months. It was at Yongjusa Temple in Suwon. My mistress wouldn't tell me who the father was, but she did confess . . . Do you have water?"

"I'll bring some soon. Go on."

She licked her lips again. "She'd met the gentleman innocently. She'd wanted to see the Harvest Festival, and he had offered to accompany her. But it rained and they took shelter at an inn . . ." Soyi's voice drifted off as a faraway look glazed her eyes, as though she were peering into her mistress's intimate encounter. Then something like a laugh escaped her. "Everyone thinks Lady O was gentle and obedient, but those like her are the most rebellious. Whatever the case, she gave birth to a healthy and strong boy, whom we left in the care of the monks, yet after we returned to the capital, a few days later, Matron Kim told us the boy had died. Smallpox. My mistress mourned for a long time, until she met Lady Kang and was converted."

I frowned. Lady Kang had told me she hadn't known Lady O well.

"Examine her diary," Soyi said. "It will be there. And other things too."

I shifted uneasily. Inspector Han had obviously bluffed about having Lady O's diary, to make Soyi confess. Hesitantly I replied, "We don't have it."

It was Soyi's turn to frown. "Your inspector never read her diary? She wrote her every thought in it."

"The police aren't allowed to search her chamber."

Soyi tilted her head to stare past the window's wooden bars, out into the bright sky. The hope I'd seen there was gone now, replaced by empty submission. "I should have kept quiet."

"Soyi, I shouldn't have told you—"

"So you've got what you came for," she said. "Since I've talked now, I suppose one secret is no different from another, and I still have one. Matron Kim would never reveal it even if you tortured her a hundred times."

Soyi's voice, now eerily devoid of emotion, filled me with a slow, quiet dread. Taking in a breath, I whispered, "I would hear it, if you would tell me."

Soyi nodded. "Matron Kim never knew I returned to the temple a year ago, sent there by her daughter to perform gravesite rituals, but I found no burial site. The monks were surprised that I'd come looking for one, because the son of Lady O had not died. And on my return, when I told my mistress, she looked furious enough to kill someone."

●

"So she does have a diary," Inspector Han said after I finished speaking.

I had reported everything in a matter of minutes, and for a long moment afterward, he'd remained silent. I stared at the lone bird twirling above the tiled police bureau walls, deep in thought as

I tried to guess the identity of the child's father. Young Master Ch'oi Jinyeop, perhaps . . .

"What is your next move, sir?" I said.

"For now, let us go to the temple. If the father of the boy ever visited, we'll learn it there."

Us. Thrill and anticipation tingled down my spine, which only doubled when he added, "You are proving to be quite useful, Damo Seol."

He walked away, his hands clasped behind his back, and then cast a look over his shoulder. "Keep this between us. No one but Commander Yi is to know where we are going, especially not Kyŏn."

Even the mere sound of Kyŏn's name made my stomach twist. "What will you do with him, sir?"

"Transfer him out of the bureau, but not yet. For now we must focus on Yongjusa Temple."

"And Officer Shim?" I asked. "Will you tell him what we learned?"

"Of course." A faint smile passed over his lips. "I trust that man with my life."

I bowed my head, holding back the words, *And you can trust me with your life too.*

NINE

THE FOLLOWING MORNING, I bound my breasts with practiced quickness, tighter than was necessary to hide the slight fullness. The sign of womanhood, of vulnerability. I had seen the way some officers and visiting gentlemen stared at the maids, some even groping and stealing kisses.

I wanted to be noticed, but not in *that* way.

Once I finished dressing, I picked up an iron club, which had a rope hanging from its gilt-brass handle. I tied this onto my sash belt, then looked around the room, hoping to find a reason to linger a moment longer. My eyes strayed to the door, and reluctance gnawed at me. At the far corner of my mind, a thought had burned for days, and now it surfaced, looming dark beyond the door. The answers waiting for us might turn out to be ones we wished we'd never discovered . . .

The deep, rumbling boom of the great bell fractured the early morning stillness. Snatching my satgat off the hook and donning it, I stepped out and hurried through the courtyards. Inspector Han had instructed me to wait by the main gate when the curfew was lifted.

"Seol!"

A male voice startled me as I stepped out onto the street. I turned and saw a stable boy pulling a shaggy white pony my way. It was Terror, the beast that had tried to save us from the tiger on Mount Inwang.

"I was told to bring this troublemaker out." He transferred the reins into my hand. "I hear you're leaving the capital. Going with the inspector?"

"We're heading to Suwon."

"That is not far. The Fox Mountain Pass is halfway there—I think that's him."

He looked to a gentleman on horseback, his face shadowed by the wide brim of his hat. His military robe was of forest-green silk, and a pleated skirt swathed his trousers. Silver tigers embroidered his sleeves. I could tell it was Inspector Han only by the sword he wore, its black scabbard encrusted with seven gold dots for the Seven Stars Spirit, an ancient deity of fortune. Not that the inspector was a man of superstition; a true Confucian did not believe in ghosts and spirits, only the here and now.

As he drew up to me, I noticed the manservant riding behind—a tanned young man in a sleeveless gray robe over a white tunic. I had seen him at the bureau a few times before in passing. He couldn't have been much older than me. Inspector Han told him to fetch a scroll on the writing table of his office. With the speed of a quick-footed deer, the servant leapt off his horse and sped into the bureau, and within a few blinks of my eyes, he returned, proffering the scroll to his master with two hands.

Inspector Han tucked the scroll into his robe, then steered his sleek horse around. "Are you ready, Damo Seol?"

"Yes, sir." I climbed onto Terror, my stomach clenching. I feared she would toss me off her saddle again, but to my relief, she was unusually calm as we rode down the streets of Hanyang, past the stalls and shops.

By now, I knew my way around the capital well enough that I could easily point people in the direction they wanted to go. Looking for brassware? At the intersection of Jongno Street turn north, past the silk shop to your right. Looking for honey, rice, and fruits? You will find it at the far west end. Or perhaps you are looking for an expensive gift? Visit the jewelers at the southeast corner of the intersection, or travel farther east to the silver and jade merchant shops.

I had come to know the capital so well, yet it grew more frightening to me day by day.

"What's your name?"

I glanced at the young servant, now riding alongside me. I wasn't in the mood to talk, but I also wasn't good at ignoring people. "Seol."

"As in snowflake?"

"As in storyteller."

"My name's Ryun, and it means 'one who is kindhearted.'"

We crossed over the Cheonggye Stream, where women gathered, ladling water into pails and rolling laundry into hard bundles, which they pounded with heavy sticks on stones. As we passed, I returned my attention to "kindhearted" Ryun.

"Have you worked for your master long?"

He looked over, holding the reins with one hand. "Nine years, since I was a child."

Inspector Han was near—but not close enough to hear if I asked quietly. "Do you know Officer Kyŏn?"

The corner of his lips twitched. "I do."

"Officer Kyŏn is trying to make others suspicious of your master. It is worrisome."

"And he received a good beating for it last night." Ryun clucked his tongue. "Who does he think he is, daring to go up against a military official? All because of a horse."

"A horse?"

"My master's horse was found roaming alone near the Northern District, days ago. Had deep cuts on his shoulder and stomach, the legs too. An unbalanced rider might make an unbalanced horse, and my master was deep in his cups that night. Officer Kyŏn discovered the bloody horse and brought him to my master's stable boy, who told Kyŏn the inspector never made it home. After that, Kyŏn went harassing people for answers. He seemed convinced that the blood did not belong entirely to the animal."

"So the horse had deep cuts . . . He must have fallen?" I said, "And when the horse fell, Inspector Han had no means to return home. I assume he found shelter at an inn—"

"Not an inn. My master went back to the House of Bright Flowers. In the morning he sent a maid from there to fetch me. He was still in his mourning robe and needed another uniform."

So this was the "evidence" Kyŏn and Scholar Ahn had against Inspector Han? I pressed my lips tight, holding in a laugh.

●

We rode across a stone bridge that arched over the Han River, which flowed around the capital, then into the East Sea. According to my brother, it had received its name "Han" because it meant "great and sacred," and during the ancient times, the Three Kingdoms of Baekje, Goguryeo, and Silla had all fought to control it.

Once we reached the other side of the long bridge, the crowd thinned, and we rode like coursing water, rushing through a field of vivid green grass. My spirit had so lightened that I flowed along. Following a dirt road that snaked upward through a large valley, I watched the land rise higher and the wind grow fiercer, whipping my skirt and sleeves, throwing loose strands of my hair into my smiling face.

I looked behind to see how far we'd come and was greeted by a sweeping view of the capital. Its main road ran both ways, east and west, through the sea of black-tiled and thatch rooftops. There was the Defunct Palace to the south, the residence of the executed Prince Sado's illegitimate male survivors, along with those that had married into the bloodline, like Princess Song and her daughter-in-law,

Princess Sin. To the north was the true royal residence, the sprawling Changdeok Palace, with its lotus pond and pavilions, green lawns and various audience halls.

"Seol!" Ryun called out. He and Inspector Han were far ahead of me.

Bending low over Terror's neck, I urged her forward and rode into what looked like the Fox Mountain Pass. On either side of the narrow path were mountains, shadowy giants rising alone, so far from the merry flowers carpeting the valley around us. "Gosan" meant lonely mountain, a fitting word for this scenery. It was also Inspector Han's nickname, apparently, for he always kept his distance from everyone. He seemed to prefer silence from those around him if what they had to say was irrelevant to his investigations.

Except with me.

I dared to close the distance to Inspector Han. Sensing my intrusion, he turned his face to me, just barely. Only a crescent of his countenance was visible; his straight nose, his high cheek, the elegant curve of his firm lips. Unbidden memories flickered, glowing images from a decade ago. A boy with amber eyes and a radiant smile. I blinked, and the images vanished.

"Do you know why I'm involving you in this case, Seol?" he asked me.

It took me a moment to collect my thoughts. "No, sir."

"Who would you say you are?"

"A servant?" I answered. He kept silent, waiting. I bit my lower lip in thought, then frowned up at the sky, a gradation of light to bright azure blue. "They say that between the servant and yang-ban aristocrat is the distance between heaven and earth. I am the earth, sir."

Inspector Han chuckled, a quiet rumble from deep within his chest. "Is that what you think?"

"I don't know, sir. I'm always changing my mind."

"They say many things here in the capital . . ." He paused, as though weighing whether to speak on. In a too-light voice, he said, "When I was young, they called me the sun, the great burning star, but when my father's sin besmirched me, I became lower than dirt."

My lips formed into a silent O as I looked at him closely. The golden light illuminated his face, allowing me to see details I hadn't noticed before: the strain around his eyes, the oppressive stillness of his gaze, the small scars littered across his right hand. I knew little about his past, and this glimpse into it revealed a world filled with humiliation.

Silence continued to hang over us, intensified by the whistling chirrup of a lone sandgrouse, and at length Inspector Han said, "Whether you are the sun, the earth, or the moon, you are a capable girl. To me. Your mind, somehow, can grasp the chaotic threads of this case. There aren't too many like you, Damo Seol. Man or woman."

I sat still on my horse, fingers weakening around the reins. For the first time since my brother had disappeared, I felt seen.

●

It was past noon when we arrived before the fortress surrounding Suwon. The four-hour-long journey had filled my heart with one prayer—a prayer so immense, it felt as though I'd swallowed a heap of cloud. In my next life, I wanted to *be* Inspector Han.

Look at how tall he sits on his horse! I wanted to call out to the crowd bustling outside Hwaseong Fortress. *Look at how the peasants kowtow before him, trembling. Look at how he spares them nary a glance.*

This was *my* master, and I was his extension.

At the fortress gate, Inspector Han presented his identification tag to the guard, and at once we were permitted entrance. Never would I have imagined that by becoming a lowly damo I would be traveling around the kingdom, seeing places I'd never have visited while living with my sister back home.

The town of Suwon was a crowd of shops and people, a labyrinth of streets and alleys. Bristling along the walls were intimidating block-houses, observation towers, bastions, and other military facilities built to fortify the defense of our capital a short distance away.

As we rode through town, Ryun reached into the sack tied onto his saddle and pulled out a ball of rice. "Here. It'll keep you full for a while, Seol."

I lifted it to take a bite, which was when I noticed Inspector Han's light brown eyes again. They looked almost golden in the sunlight.

"You will stare a hole through Inspector Han," Ryun's voice broke into my thought, "watching him so fiercely like that."

I took a bite into the rice ball, chewing on the sweet and slightly undercooked rice, the grain sticky on the outside but hard in the center. "I wonder, if someone dies and is reborn again, would they look alike?"

"I don't know," Ryun replied. "But I think you would feel a tug . . . a feeling of affinity. Why?"

I only offered him a smile, his question disappearing into the silence. The similar hue of my brother and the inspector's eyes comforted me. It was as though Older Brother had sent his spirit and had lodged it in the eyes of another. But besides the color and the warmth of spirit, their similarities ended there.

I took another bite, but this time I tasted nothing, lost in memories of the past.

Older Brother had always been fragile, more of a sensitive and deeply feeling poet than a fierce military official. Most of my memories of my brother were of him sitting before a table, studying and memorizing Confucian classics. And while Inspector Han was capable of shooting two hundred arrows a day in rain, snow, or sleet, I couldn't remember my brother hunting down any of the wild dogs roaming Heuksan island.

But similar or not, my brother was dead, and it was my sister's fault.

I once asked her why Brother had run away, and her only response had been that they'd had a dreadful fight. One thing she didn't know was that I had seen everything: her throwing at him an earthenware pot filled with boiling tea, her yelling, "Go to the capital then, that place of terror. We are not family. We are finished." Older Brother had run away and had died alone because of her, and I knew that he was dead, for he had never written home.

●

The thought of Older Brother dampened my spirit, but life in the capital had taught me not to dwell on sad things. Do not dwell on being branded on the cheek, everyone watching and clucking their tongues at you. Do not dwell on your dead brother. For when grief swells around you like the sea, you must swim and keep your head above it. Do not drown in it.

I locked the memories of him in a box, to be opened only when I was alone. I didn't want Inspector Han to see a sulking, homesick girl; I wanted to impress him. Straightening my shoulders again, I readjusted myself in the saddle.

"Curse this heat," Ryun muttered. Dark patches of sweat blotted his attire as the sun pulsed overhead.

"You look about to faint," I said, my voice strong again.

Ryun waved my words away weakly, wiping his brow. "Don't talk to me. I have no energy to reply."

We traversed through the town and rode out of it, passed by different landscapes, rice and cornfields appearing, then receding. At last, the road branched out into little paths, with one disappearing up the slope of Mount Hwa. The stifling heat eased as we traveled deeper into the woodland shade, and before long, I saw the sweeping rooftops of Yongjusa Temple.

Most temples were in ruins, Buddhism having lost favor with the imperial court long ago, but Yongjusa was a rare jewel. "King Chŏngjo agonized that his father, the murdered Prince Sado, was wandering near hell," my brother had told me, "and so His Majesty resurrected Yongjusa and moved the tomb nearby, that the temple might protect his father and grant him eternal peace."

After tethering our horses, we climbed up the granite steps, which led us to the main gate. Four statues with bulging eyes glowered down at me, and one held a sword as though prepared to kill anyone with a wicked spirit. Quickening my steps, I hurried past the monstrous figures. We passed by two more gates, drawing closer to the chanting and steady beating of wooden handbells. But not a single human soul appeared as we searched through the smoky mist. The sound of chanting hummed on without a tangible source. It was as though we'd stepped into a deserted village filled only with ghosts.

At last we reached what seemed to be the main temple, with a heavily tiled roof supported upon towering pillars, the eaves richly carved and painted in blue, red, and green. Inside the open hall, monks with shaved heads sat on the floor, chanting the Heart Sutra, and at the far end was a child in a gray robe, sitting cross-legged and dozing off.

"Come, let us not disturb them," Inspector Han said.

We had not traveled far when a voice spoke out from the stillness. "Don't get lost in the mist." We turned, and on the veranda built around a smaller hanok building stood a monk with a string of beads around his neck. "Have you come from afar?"

Ryun hurried up to the veranda and bowed to the monk. "We traveled here from the capital," he announced, "and my master would like to make a few inquiries."

The monk examined Inspector Han, and after a pause, said, "Why don't you all come in and rest?" He pulled at a brass handle, sliding the door open onto a dark and drafty room. "I will prepare a tea table for your master."

"No need, sunim," Inspector Han intervened. "We will not be staying long."

The monk bowed his head. "What is it you came all this way to ask, sir?"

Inspector Han joined the monk on the veranda, while Ryun and I waited in the courtyard. "Women often come here to pray and burn incense, do they not?"

"They do."

"And when they flee to the temple to escape trouble, is it usual to take them in?"

"It is the way of Buddha to be compassionate to all."

"Is that so?"

"Each new encounter is the result of karma; everything has its cause and effect. It would therefore be unwise to turn the desperate away." The monk's billowing sleeves engulfed his arms and hands as he crossed them at his waist. "It would worsen the karmic link and create future enmity rather than affinity. So Buddha's way is to treat each new encounter with respect and consideration."

"Might I ask then," Inspector Han said in a low voice, "whether a woman by the name of Lady O Eunju ever came here for shelter?"

"The name is not familiar, sir."

"Then do you have under your care a boy around the age of three?"

The corners of his lips tightened, though the rest of his expression remained pleasant and composed. "We do."

"Would it be considered a liberty, sunim, to ask for information about this boy?"

"Not at all. Unfortunately, I really don't know what to say about him, except that he is an orphan."

"Any information will do. Where he came from, or anything concerning him, which might offer us a hint as to his connections."

"I assure you," said the monk, "that I know no more about where he came from than I know—"

"Why his mother left him here?" suggested the inspector, and the slightest look of surprise registered on the monk's face. "Out of shame, perhaps. The truth that an unmarried young lady bore a child would surely ruin her family's good name."

"You know the mother?"

"She died several days ago."

A pause. "Died?"

"Murdered."

The monk's brows pressed together. "Murdered!"

"We are trying to find out possible connections to her death."

"You are her family? Or the police?" The monk's intelligent eyes took him in. "Ah, yes, you must be the police. You look it."

"Did any forgotten points occur to you just now?"

The monk hesitated a moment, then confessed, "Something *did* occur to me, now that you mention it."

A lump formed in my chest, a single emotion that whispered, *Amazing*. As I followed them down the veranda, which wrapped around the pavilion, I thought about how skillfully Inspector Han had fished the secret out of the monk's mouth, and whether I could one day be this good.

From where we now stood, I could see across the courtyard the boy sitting in the main temple. He looked ready to tilt forward in his sleep, but then an elderly monk poked him. The boy sat straight and looked up, his face round and bright.

Pop. I startled at the sudden sound—above on the tiled roof, faint, something hard and loose, rolling and rolling. Something tiny dropped from the eaves and tapped down against the stone. Leaving Ryun's side, I picked up what I found to be a pebble. I stepped back to stare up at the rooftop. Nothing but green foliage.

"About three years ago, to the best of my belief," the monk said, "was when the pregnant young lady first came to the temple."

"Do you happen to remember her maid's name?"

"Her name . . . Her name was . . . Yeoli? Chobi? Something like that."

"Soyi, perhaps?"

"Yes, Soyi, I believe."

Throughout the dialogue, Inspector Han stood aloof, with his hands behind him. To all appearances, he looked removed from the things pulling at my own attention—the twitching flesh beneath the monk's eyes; the suspicious sprinkle of dirt falling off the eaves; a young novice sweeping the courtyard, staring our way. Inspector Han's face remained inexpressive and unaffected. Was he even thinking? He revealed nothing of what was going on in his mind.

Then he spoke at last. "And has a man asked for the child during the past three years?"

The monk looked at the young novice and gestured at him to come over. "Well, sir. One afternoon only a few days ago I left to visit Hanyang—I know it is forbidden for a monk to enter the capital," he quickly amended, "but my mother was ill."

Inspector Han bowed his head, brushing the issue aside.

"When I returned the next day, I learned about a strange visit," he said as the young novice walked over, dragging his bamboo broom. "Tell them, Uchan, about the visit. About the strange man who spoke with our little Minho. Go on, tell them."

The novice, who had a sparse mustache above his upper lip, rubbed his nose. "I was just cleaning the temple that day"—his voice crackled, as though not knowing whether to dip low or high—"when a gentleman came in and asked for Minho. The child isn't partial to strangers, but the gentleman still held him in his arms, telling him things."

"What was being said?"

"I forget things easily so do not remember too much, but I do recall one thing he said. 'Remember my name, never forget it.'"

"What did he say his name was?"

The novice rubbed his nose again. "*Eummmm.* I haven't a good ear for names."

I heaved out a sigh, and Inspector Han gave me a warning glance. He calmly proceeded to ask, "Do you recall anything unique about his appearance?"

"His eyes were curved at the end—like a phoenix's eyes."

"And his speech? What dialect did he use?"

"He was using the correct capital speech."

"And his height?"

"Not very tall. I can't remember too well, though."

"What was he wearing?"

"He wore a bright yellow dopo."

The slightest frown flitted across Inspector Han's brows. A dopo was the overcoat robe of high scholars, or sometimes government officials on private business. No commoner could have worn such a garment. If this was Lady O's lover, he most certainly belonged to aristocracy.

"If you saw his face," Inspector Han continued, pulling a scroll out from his robe, "do you think you would recognize him?"

The young novice paused a moment. "Yes, sir."

The paper unrolled, Inspector Han turned it toward him. "Do you recognize this face?"

"Him . . . ," the novice whispered, and his mouth fell open. "Hah! It was him!"

"You are certain?"

"I am! I swear upon my mother's grave!"

I walked around to see for myself. The charcoal sketch was of a young man with an angular face, delicate brows, and eyes ever so slightly tilted at the corners. A chill prickled through me, raising the hair on my skin. I had served tea to this man before.

It was the tutor of Lady O's brother. Scholar Ahn.

●

"How did you know, Inspector," I asked as we stepped out of the temple, with Ryun going ahead of us to retrieve our horses, "that it was Scholar Ahn?"

"It was natural to suspect him," he replied. "Think, Damo Seol. The life of an unmarried lady and the life of a peasant girl . . . what is the difference?"

I rarely saw an unmarried lady leave her residence—alas, this was the answer. "One is kept within the mansion walls, and the other is permitted to freely roam?"

"Kept within the women's quarter, an unmarried lady would hardly be acquainted with many men."

I understood. "Scholar Ahn was a frequent visitor."

"Several years ago, Lord O invited Scholar Ahn for tea, impressed by his grade in the state examination. This was before Ahn was offered a tutoring position. He was invited again on the week of the Harvest Festival."

I remembered Soyi's account of how Lady O had been tempted by a gentleman's innocent proposal. "That was the same week Lady O ran away for the first time."

"The following week, he married another woman."

My heart plummeted, though I couldn't understand why. It wasn't *my* love story. "He didn't care for Lady O?"

"Whether he did or not, Ahn wasn't in the position to marry her. He was an impoverished gentleman in those days, waiting for a post, and forbidden by etiquette from taking on any occupation other than a government or tutorial position. In such a circumstance, to break his engagement to the daughter of a powerful family would have besmirched the only thing to his name: his honor."

Honor . . . Never had the word sounded more shallow and cowardly to my ears.

"A few months after the wedding," Inspector Han continued, though he had no obligation to explain anything to me, "Ahn followed his father-in-law as an envoy to China and fell ill there. It took him a year to fully recover, and on his return to Joseon, Lord O hired him as a tutor for his youngest son. That is when Ahn was likely reunited with Lady O."

"And then he killed her?"

"As for that, I do not know yet—"

"Master! Master!" Ryun came running back, his face blanched. "They are gone."

"What are?"

"The horses."

We arrived at the tree where we had tethered them, now bare. Not only had we lost a fortune, for a single horse was as expensive as two to three servants, but we had lost our only means of transport. I was prepared to run around the forest in search of them, but instead, Inspector Han crouched with a controlled calmness and touched the ground.

"They were led northeast," he said.

We accompanied the inspector deeper into the forest, following a trail of evidence that only he noticed. Each time he stooped down to touch or pick something up, I stopped to examine it myself, wanting to see what he saw. What he noticed were things in nature disturbed: broken twigs, trampled grass, crushed leaves, an overturned stone. Hoofprints.

"At least we're not too far from the fortress," Ryun said to me. "I saw a police bureau there. They will help us, I'm sure. My master has this bronze medallion that only important military people have, and he can use it at any police bureau in the kingdom to mobilize horses."

Inspector Han stretched out his hand, quieting us. We froze in our steps. Silence pooled around us, not a ripple of noise, and then I heard what sounded like the distant clopping of hooves. Inspector Han walked ahead.

"Ryun, come with me," he whispered. When I took a step forward to join them, he snapped, "Seol, do not leave this place."

"But—"

"Promise me."

Reluctance gnawed at me, but his waiting stare forced the words out. "I promise, sir."

And with that, he and Ryun disappeared through the thicket.

I stood still and strained my ears to hear whatever was going on beyond the cluster of trees and leaves.

A bird chirped.

A rabbit scrambled through the leaves.

Then I heard the echo of Inspector Han's voice. "Stop where you are!"

My promise to him wrapped tightly around my ankle, as though roots had shot out from the earth to keep me from running. But when I heard his threatening voice again, I shook myself free and ran from tree to tree, wanting a better view. Trouble was near. I could feel it brushing against the raised hair on my skin. Pushing past the branches, I saw Inspector Han standing behind a fourteen- or fifteen-year-old boy, our horses nearby. When I looked closer, I noted the boy was missing an ear.

"You were spying on us. In the temple," Inspector Han said.

"N-no, not I," the boy replied. His eyes darted around, as though searching for help.

"Who sent you?"

The boy glanced at the horse to his right, weighing his chances of escape, but Inspector Han was easily close enough to grab him. The boy remained still.

"Don't make me repeat myself," Inspector Han warned, his voice so sharp the boy flinched. "Tell me who sent you."

"I—I truly do not know wh-what you are talking about, sir."

A quick and forceful flick of thumb, and sword rushed out from scabbard, its ring so high-pitched that I felt it like a pulse. The boy's legs buckled and he was on his knees, trembling.

"Ryun, tether the horses." Inspector Han walked around the boy, then pressed the blade against his quivering chest. "Who sent you here?"

"P-please, do not hurt me." The boy breathed hard, sucking air in and out, in and out. In a barely audible whisper, he said, "Young Master Ch'oi . . ."

There, for once, I saw Inspector Han's visage break, if only for a moment. A flash of anger . . . and something barely recognizable on his face. Confusion.

"Speak quickly," he said.

"The young master. He . . . there were men he sent after you."

"And he ordered you to take our horses?"

"No . . . Our l-leader wanted to sell th-them."

"Fool. The stolen horses led me right to you. And what did the young master want you to find out? Did he say anything that—"

A twig snapped under my feet. Inspector Han heard it too, shooting a glance my way. I was so startled I staggered two steps back to hide, only to trip over a raised root.

"Seol!" The inspector's voice rumbled with fury, rage vicious enough to gash my heart and leave me trembling. "I told you to stay where you were—!"

The one-eared boy grabbed a fistful of earth and sprayed Inspector Han, blinding him. Then he scrambled for a fallen tree branch splintered by lightning. Grabbing it, he charged as the inspector struggled to clear his eyes. Rather than swing in any direction, the inspector pulled his sword behind him, pointing the tip to the ground, leaving himself defenseless.

Oh gods, what had I done? I pulled the club free from my sash belt and raced forward.

In that moment, a high-pitched whistle pierced the sky and sent a rustling throughout the forest. Men stepped from behind trees, faces obscured by scarves, swinging planks and knives. They were so bony and burnt they looked more like starved farmers than fierce bandits. One man gestured and yelled, "Tie them up!"

The circle of eight rogues swept in upon us like a fierce wave about to suck a vessel under.

Hands grabbed for me, but I dove and slid across the ground, then leapt over squirming bodies. The one-eared boy moved fast. He raised his wooden weapon, ready to split it over the inspector's head—

Steel flashed white in the sunlight, impossibly fast. Blood splashed out as though the boy's stomach had burst. Bit by bit he fell; his hand dropped, the plank thudded to the dirt, his knees buckled, head craning until he stared up at Inspector Han. A choke, a gurgle, a single stream of blood slid down the side of his lips.

All fell still. Every man among the bandits flinched as the blade was pulled out. Life sprayed crimson onto the inspector's robe as Missing Ear folded to the ground.

Vomit lurched to my throat. I tore my gaze away from the dead boy and looked at the inspector again, and he was changed. He seemed unable to drag his gaze away from his bloody hands, and as though the forest floor were tilting beneath his feet, he stumbled. Sweat glistened on his temple.

Seeing Ryun sprinting to his master, I grabbed ahold of myself and ran. I kicked one bandit between his legs, and as he buckled forward, I raised my leg high and struck down with my heel. His head slammed to the ground as Ryun punched and rolled and grabbed hair. Inspector Han swung his sword at the bandits as a drunkard might swing a torch to frighten off a tiger, no direction or balance to his movements.

A large hand suddenly gripped my arm, and a coldness touched my neck. I had not heard the approaching man, and now my life centered around a sharp, cutting sting digging into my skin.

"Drop your sword, Inspector," my captor yelled, "or I'll kill her!"

My heart pounded. Inspector Han blinked, as if haziness clouded his vision. He struggled to look at us. I held my breath.

"I'm not fooling around!" The bandit pressed the blade deeper, but not yet through my skin. "I'll kill her!"

Silence. A grimace darkened Inspector Han's face. "Go ahead."

My stomach dropped.

"What?" The captor gaped. "Do you not value your servant?"

Pain clamped my heart as Inspector Han swayed, then stabbed the blade into the earth to support himself. "I have no need for a damo who gets in the way of my investigation."

Disbelief weakened my knees. I'd made one mistake, a small mistake—wanting to see what the inspector was seeing. I had never meant for any of this to happen. Yet Inspector Han was finished with me. Just like that.

The ache of betrayal jabbed at the underside of my ribs, more painful than the blade pressed against my throat.

Little Sister, my brother's voice whispered into the burning cavern of my chest. His voice steadied me, as it always steadied me. *No one in this entire kingdom can care for you as deeply as family.*

The words coursed through my body. The bones of my brother wept in the cold earth. No burial mound, no eulogy, no flowers. All alone. As alone as I felt now, though I was surrounded by grimy faces.

I could not die like this.

Ten thousand rivers run unceasingly into the sea, yet it never overflows. That is the measurement of our love for you. Mother, Sister, and I. Our love is the sea—a deep sea.

I still had family. I had to live for her.

With all my might, I crushed my heel into the bandit's foot, and the knife jolted away from my neck. Grabbing the blade with my bare hand, I bit his wrist hard, my teeth clinging to his very bones as he grabbed my hair and tried to wrench me off.

"Master!" Ryun's frantic voice cried.

Ahead of me, Inspector Han fell to one knee. No one had struck him, or even touched him. Yet he swayed, then lost his grip on the sword and collapsed to the side.

"This is heaven's sign!" a bandit called out. "Collect our wounded men! We need to retreat, now!"

My captor tried shaking me off, but when I continued to cling to the blade, a growl rumbled deep within his chest. The hilt struck my face and stars exploded before my eyes. Blood rolled in my mouth as I found myself lying flat on the ground, staring up at the blur of dizzying green. I closed my eyes, sharp pain shooting up from my fingers and piercing my head, making my ears ache, and when I looked down at my hand I saw why. I'd cut my fingers open, my palm a puddle of fire-hot blood.

I curled into a ball and remembered what to do when the sight of blood terrified me. *Breathe slowly and deeply through your nose, then let it out,* Older Brother had taught me. *Listen to the whooshing sound.*

Whoosh, the waves upon the shore.

Whoosh, Mother falling off a cliff.

TEN

WHEN I WAS young, I could sleep long into the afternoon if no one woke me, drunk on dreams filled with sweetness and warmth. But on the night after the Mount Hwa incident, I closed my eyes and saw a dead boy with a sword in his stomach, just him and me in the silent forest. No matter how hard I tried to wake up, I could not escape the forest, and no matter how far I ran, the corpse always followed. Then at last I woke up, thrashing and entangled in a drenched blanket.

"You have a fever," Aejung told me, urging me to lie still. She placed a cloth on my forehead. "It is your wound. Infected."

It got worse, and I was thrown in and out of strange nightmares, unable to recall the time passing or whether the tall shadows around me were humans. Then the bitter taste of something herbal poured into my mouth. I choked and a cloth wiped my mouth.

Female voices consulted one another as they inserted thread-thin needles into my skin.

"Not there!" came a whisper. "When the head nurse trained me in acupuncture, she said the needle should go a little higher. Right here."

Was I dying?

Then the raging storm stilled, the freezing spray of sea-mist withdrew, and I was lying flat on my back, blinking up at the white ceiling. The world no longer twirled. A strange emotion crept into my chest as I continued to stare. It was as though the storm had blown out the light that had danced around in the swaying grass of immortal green, leaving a dark cavern in me.

I flinched at a sudden noise, the screen door sliding open. Aejung stepped in and knelt before my sleeping mat. She touched my forehead and inspected my wounds before rewrapping it.

"How long was I sick for?" I asked.

"Five days."

Five days. It had felt more like a single night.

"During the first three days we worried you wouldn't make it, but then you started recovering on the fourth." She helped me up onto my feet, peeled me out of my nightgown, stale with dried sweat. My frail and ghostly pale body gave us both pause.

"For five days," I murmured as she assisted me into a clean dress. "So much must have happened."

"So much has happened indeed. Inspector Han is preparing an arrest warrant for Young Master Ch'oi Jinyeop."

Just as Aejung finished securing the sash around my dress, Hyeyeon entered with a table bearing a bowl of gruel and side dishes of pickled cabbage and radish.

"You're awake." She set it down before me. "Eat and strengthen yourself again."

I sat down and picked up a wooden spoon, stirred my meal, and blew the steam away. Tucking an oily strand of hair behind my ear, I took a bite. Surprise lit my stomach at how tasty it was. The finely ground rice swam with pine nuts. The pickled vegetables offered a tasty zing and crunchiness to the soft, bittersweet meal.

"I heard—overheard—that Inspector Han killed a man," Hyeyeon said.

The spoon stilled in my hand. Unable to look up, I spoke to the bowl. "Is he to be punished?"

"The inspector is a military official," she replied, and did not elaborate.

"I suppose the higher authorities will overlook it," I whispered, no longer hungry. "A guilty person was killed—"

"No one would have died had you followed a simple order to stay still. Inspector Han hates blood, but you made him kill a boy."

I shifted on my knees, wishing the floor would open and swallow me whole.

"A little favor from the inspector, and look what happened to you. Your head grew too big with pride and you forgot your place as a servant." Hyeyeon clucked her tongue at me. Then she rose to her feet and slid a stare over her shoulder. Our eyes met. "This is what happens when a foolish girl thinks she can be someone of consequence. She creates chaos, utter chaos."

●

A few hours spent outside the servants' quarter was enough to leave me dripping in cold, panicky sweat.

It was as though a storm had swept through the police bureau, flipping over tables and trays, knocking down shelves and chairs. Hyeyeon was right, I had caused chaos. Inspector Han had threatened to transfer Kyŏn out of the bureau for his insubordinate behavior, and everyone knew it was because I had "tattled" on Kyŏn. And with the inspector's threats, speculation spread fast—about Inspector Han's whereabouts on the night of the killing, about his horse covered in blood.

"Inspector Han killed a boy and is now trying to silence an officer," some whispered. "A man threatens when he feels endangered."

Utter chaos, and everyone blamed me for it.

This weight grew heavier when Inspector Han summoned me. I dragged myself toward the western courtyard, and there he stood, alone, his uniform of dark blue flowing in the windy afternoon. The blood seemed to drain from me, leaving every part of my body cold. I clasped my hands before me, carefully, so as not to disturb the wounds. And then I bowed to him.

"Did you call for me, sir?" My voice sounded detached.

"Do you have anything to say to me?"

"I do not, sir."

Silence beat between us. Then, ever so quietly, he said, "You are still young, and so do not understand your position in life. Though I value you and admire your cleverness, never forget this, Seol. My investigation comes first, and I will not let anything get in the way. When I order you to do something, you will listen."

"I understand, sir." I stared at the ground, hurt flaring up in my chest. And the pain of it, along with my torn skin, made it impossible to keep silent. "You said you had a little sister, sir. Would you have dropped your sword for her, if it had been her and"—voice wavering, I paused to regain composure—"and not me?"

"My sister is dead because of me," Inspector Han said, his face stoic and his voice steady. Yet his reddened eyes betrayed him. "And if she were alive, she would have told you the same. Never get in my way."

Saying no more, he walked forward and bade me follow behind him. For once I was grateful for this. I didn't want anyone to look at me right now, as searing thoughts and emotions blew into me from the east and west, colliding and conflicting.

I could not un-remember the truth about him, which not even sympathy could melt away: Inspector Han was not so very kind, not so very honest, and not so very just.

Once he took off his boots and stepped onto the veranda encircling the Office of the Inspector, I struggled with my wounded hand

and neatly arranged his shoes, even as wetness stung the corners of my eyes.

"A guest will be joining me," Inspector Han said. "Sit in silence until I give you further instructions."

Following him into the office, I knelt by the wall, far away from where he sat. The silence continued, cramped with all the things unsaid, and I sat there, grinding my teeth, which sounded like trees creaking in the night.

"Inspector," a voice called from outside the office, "he is arrived."

"Let him in."

The doors slid open onto a gentleman clad in shimmering silk. His face glowed with health in the skylight, and if rumors were true, he had washed his face with the freshest water, fetched all the way from the peaks of a mountain. It was Young Master Ch'oi. "How gracious of you to invite me to your office."

"Do you know why I asked for an audience with you?"

The young master flipped back the tail of his robe and sat down on the mat before Inspector Han, a low table between them. With a smile, he said, "I hear you are trying to arrest me."

"And yet you still came."

"Why should I be afraid of you?" he asked. "Already the queen regent has my life dangling from her fingers."

"So the rumors have frightened you. Her Majesty will uproot Catholicism, first with your family."

As the men exchanged cold words, I was reminded of the norigae ornament Inspector Han had given to me. I'd kept it safe within my personal chest for the past few days. But now the promise retained within the norigae seemed tainted, stained by the inspector's resentment toward me.

"Damo Seol," Inspector Han said, his voice stern.

Startled, I glanced up.

His gaze was on me, distant and indifferent. "Remove the bandage and show this gentleman your hand."

The cavern in my chest grew. *Just do what he tells you to do,* I thought. I unwrapped the bandage around my left hand, exposing bloody, scab-crusted wounds, that looked like someone had chopped my fingers off and sewn different ones on. Only Inspector Han looked away. Guilt bit into him, perhaps.

"And what kind of evidence is this?" the young master asked.

The inspector shook his head, as though trying to shake the redness of my blood from his vision. He returned his gaze to the rogue. "We were nearly killed by the men who tailed us."

"And what has that to do with me?"

"What do you think?"

The young master shrugged.

"Those rogues interfered with my investigation, and one of them mentioned your name," Inspector Han said. "How do you feel about that?"

"So you are convinced that I hired men to tail you."

"I am."

"Then I will not attempt to dissuade you. All I shall say is that, if I did indeed hire those men, I would not feel that I had done wrong."

"Please, elaborate."

"Vengeance is a common practice in our kingdom, Inspector. So what crime would I have committed in wanting to discover the truth about Lady O and her lover?"

"What do you mean, 'vengeance'?"

"A rat informed me that you were traveling to Suwon, following some information. That it was related to Lady O's death."

"What were you hoping to discover?"

"Perhaps I wanted to know the depth of Lady O's depravity, to expose it and to set right my reputation of having once been humiliated by a slut. I might have wanted to discover who her lover was too, to punish the man who tempted and killed her. Perhaps I wanted to wield justice my own way." He rested his elbow on the low-legged table, then leaned in toward the inspector. "I think you understand, more than anyone, what it means to hate. I hear you offered to spearhead the Catholic purge."

My heart recoiled, and perhaps the young master saw the disappointment crinkling my brows, for he made efforts to paint the inspector even blacker. "When the mourning period for King Chŏngjo ends," he said, "I hear you will execute or banish the Catholics. Men, women, and children alike will be put to death."

"Ch'oi Jinyeop," Inspector Han said, his voice low, his gaze unwavering, "I take no pleasure in harming others."

"But? There is always a 'but' with *honorable* men like you, sir."

"There are only two types of people. Those you protect and those you crush so that they can never rise up again."

"Not all—" The words slipped out of me, pushed out by the memory of Lady Kang. The only aristocrat who had ever been nice to me from the start. I bit my lips hard, punishing them.

"Please." The young master gestured. "Finish your sentence."

I swallowed. "I just . . . Surely they cannot *all* be so bad. Could they, Inspector?"

The corner of Inspector Han's lips twitched. "They are all bad. Their teaching encourages division. Father against the son, and the son against the father; the mother against the daughter, and the daughter against the mother."

In the most casual tone, the young master said, "Just as it divided your own family, Inspector?" His gaze slid to the black-lacquered document box resting on the shelf, the box Officer Kyŏn had stolen a letter from. I'd nearly forgotten about it.

"That is none of your concern," Inspector Han said.

"Well, then. It is almost time for my afternoon tea." The young master uncrossed his legs and rolled up onto his feet, shaking the wrinkles out from his robe.

"I am not done interviewing you." Irritation pricked Inspector Han's voice.

"You may interrogate me all you want once you obtain a warrant." The young master turned toward the door, and I weakly moved forward to open it. But then he stopped and looked over his shoulder at the inspector. "Allow me to make one thing clear, however. If I did hire those men, it was to avenge my reputation, not my heart. I never loved Lady O. I have never cared much for anyone."

●

All day, the young master's remark lurked in the back of my mind. He knew, everyone seemed to know, of Inspector Han's deep-rooted contempt for Catholics. But I couldn't see how his history connected to Lady O's death.

I sharpened a knife on the whetstone, for the chief maid had directed me to do so despite my condition. As I did, I lined the other suspects up in my mind; I longed for orderliness, the world outside me far too chaotic.

There was the cocky young master, who'd declared that a woman like Lady O deserved death. Surely a man who could declare such incriminating things assumed he was immune to police interference.

There was also his father, Councillor Ch'oi. The councillor belonged to the Southerner faction, which was endangered by its ties to Catholicism, and was soon to be wiped out by the queen regent. He needed to capture the priest to shield himself from the purge. And, coincidentally, a Catholic woman had turned up dead.

And Scholar Ahn. He had run away while I was sick—from what I'd overheard—perhaps to avoid interrogation and the punishment of having seduced the daughter of an aristocrat. Punishment for sexual deviance was severe in our kingdom, including floggings and imprisonment. It was understandable that Scholar Ahn would run away for this reason, but he could have also escaped to avoid being punished as the killer.

Another questionable person was the victim's mother, Matron Kim. She had given her daughter a suicide knife, the symbol of ultimate honor, which had been used as the murder weapon. Her daughter was not only a heretic, but an adulteress who'd borne a son out of wedlock. Violence could have resulted from an accumulation of shame and anger in the heart of a mother . . .

A scream ripped through the silence. Startled, I nearly dropped the knife. "What is that?" I asked a passing servant.

"Maid Soyi," she whispered. "She's been screaming at the guards to let her out."

"Why?"

"It is her turn again. Not yet, but in the afternoon. I think she knows . . . Inspector Han seems to be at his wits' end. He's using torture this time to interrogate her."

She whispered the terrifying technique that would be used. The juri-teulgi method, where one's knees, bound together, would be forced by sticks in opposite directions, again and again, until the leg bones curved. Blood drained from my head, leaving me dizzy as I steadied myself against the counter. I had to go speak with Soyi before it was too late.

Whatever had happened in the prison block, or within Soyi's mind, it had worn her out until she seemed as translucent as a ghost. The moment I stepped into the wooden cell, swamped in shadows, Soyi's lips would not stop moving.

"I dreamt of skeletons, and when I woke up, I heard the guards talking about graves, and then just yesterday, I felt something under the straw mat. Look, look what I found." Soyi opened her palm and showed me a tiny bone, perhaps belonging to a rat. "Isn't that strange? It is a cluster of coincidences, little links I see each day that somehow all seem to connect with one another, leading somewhere."

"Leading where?" I whispered.

"Gods, I don't know. Wherever it's going, I don't want to go there. I just want to be left alone." Her hands darted out and, grabbing my injured hand, she squeezed it.

My mouth dropped open, my face contorting with pain as I snatched my arm back. "Ow!" I yelled so loudly it seemed to wake her up from a spell. Something of her old self returned at the sight of my bloody, bound-up hand.

"So it is true," she whispered, her breathing slowing down. "I overheard everything."

I held my hand, cradling it. "Overheard what?"

"Your inspector is like every other aristocrat. His kindness is conditional. So long as you please your inspector, do what he tells you, he will treat you like his sister. But upset him, and you become again a mere slave to him."

Silence filled my mouth. No words rose in his defense, because Soyi was right.

Then the translucent, ghostly look returned to her eyes. "Don't let Inspector Han take advantage of your loyalty, as Lady O took advantage of mine," she hissed. "She made me *do* things I didn't wish to do. She promised to return my nobi deed and free me from servitude if I obeyed her."

I stilled, afraid that I might disturb this moment. "Like what?"

"She made me deliver letters to Scholar Ahn, and I'd go back and forth, terrified of being caught. I dreaded it, each time she asked me to sneak out for her—"

"Wait," I whispered. "You knew Scholar Ahn was the lover all this time?"

"I . . ." It dawned on Soyi what she had confessed. "I mean . . ."

Right then, the prison doors flew open. I gasped and turned around to see Hyeyeon barging in, grabbing the whimpering Soyi, and dragging her out. Inspector Han stood at the far corner of the prison block. Watching me. Steadily. Like he had been there in the shadows all this time. Like he had heard everything.

●

In the main police courtyard, Soyi's two knees were bound together, and two sticks passed between the legs, which two floggers pulled in contrary directions, forcing her bones to curve. Then the sticks eased, allowing the bones back into their natural position, and Soyi's scream crumpled into a whimper. I bit my lip to keep myself from yelling out, "Stop this!" It was too cruel.

"Why did you not confess earlier to me that you knew Scholar Ahn was the lover?" Inspector Han demanded. "You were already in trouble and might as well have revealed everything else."

"I . . . I did not wish for you to know that I was delivering the letters."

"But why? The letter delivery doesn't implicate you in the murder. It implicates Scholar Ahn."

"I was scared." Long strands of black hair fell over Soyi's blanched face. "That is all."

"Tell the truth and do not cause any more confusion."

Her eyes reddened. The vein along her temple bulged, and words ripped out from her chest. "That is the truth. What more do you want me to say?"

At the inspector's gesture, the floggers grabbed the sticks and pulled in opposite directions again, and I could see her legs bending into a terrifying curve, about to shatter. I held my hands over my ears to muffle her unbearable noise, and then all fell silent. Soyi's head swayed; she had fainted in her seat. With a callousness that I now recognized, Inspector Han took a bowl of water and splashed her face. He did not even have the mercy to allow her a moment's relief from the pain.

Soyi blinked and spit and cried, her hair dripping, streaming down her face like black ink.

"Any information that makes my duty easier will save you from further pain," he said with a menacing quietude. "In fact, I will have you released from the police bureau, immune from further harassment, if you tell me the truth in detail."

Soyi tilted her head far back and stared at the sky as a bird flew overhead. How she must long to fly away with it, over the walls of the police bureau. I saw a stream of tears run down from the corners of her eyes. All those days she had held it in, staying strong, but now she was broken.

She closed her eyes and spoke through shudders. "I wanted to protect him."

"Go on. Tell me. Scholar Ahn is beyond your power to protect now. Save yourself, at the least."

Bound as she was, Soyi rocked back and forth in her seat. "He promised," she whispered. "With Lady O dead, there was no one to protect me. Matron Kim would surely do something horrible to me. He promised me my freedom and . . ." The dark irises of her eyes gleamed with desperation. "And he said if I revealed his relationship with Lady O, he would make sure I was dragged down along with him. I feared for my life."

"And have you any idea where Scholar Ahn is now?" Inspector Han asked.

"I do not, sir. I swear it."

The inspector's pale-eyed stare did not waver from Soyi, and I followed his gaze to see what it was he saw in the maid. Another lie? All I saw was a shadow of a woman, not a fighting streak left in her. Perhaps the inspector saw what I saw, for he blinked and looked away, as though she had quenched his suspicion. He flicked his hand at her. "And is there something you also hid from the police, just as you hid your involvement in the affair?"

She lowered her head, her lips opening and closing, trying and yet unable to utter whatever she was hiding.

"You need to tell me everything, withholding nothing, or you will not leave this place alive."

Silence stretched, and then the truth came out, a timid stream of words, as if she were unsure how to proceed. "A man came up to me . . . and . . . and he said, 'Are you not the messenger for Lady O and Scholar Ahn?' I tried to deny it, but he had been watching my movements for too long, and he told me something frightening . . . He said that I shouldn't rely on my mistress any longer. Her days were numbered. Scholar Ahn had sent a note to the police, exposing her heretical beliefs and something about a priest. Indeed, she must have done something to upset Scholar Ahn, for they had stopped communicating in the previous few days . . ."

Inspector Han nodded his head, a gesture that he approved of

Soyi's confession, and that was when the truth came out in a flood. "I wondered how I would survive without her. How would I earn a living? What would I eat? Where would I stay? I worried about these things day and night. But the strange man offered me a handsome sum. He said there would be more if I did one favor for him."

"And what was that?"

"He gave me a letter and told me to give it to Lady O. He said to pretend it was from Scholar Ahn."

"Can you describe this man?"

"It is difficult to say. His face was covered with a scarf and his bamboo hat was lowered. He was wearing a black robe."

"And have you seen him again since that encounter?"

"No, sir."

"A witness claims that a man in a bamboo hat, garbed in black, was seen delivering a note to Scholar Ahn five days ago. Right after I'd left for Yongjusa temple in Suwon. You knew nothing of this?"

"I did not, sir, I swear it."

A moment of quiet observation passed, and finally Inspector Han asked, "That letter you received from the stranger. Did you read it before or after delivering it to your mistress?"

Soyi sat there as still as death. Then she whispered, "Before."

"A letter from a stranger that summoned your mistress to come out at night. Were you not worried for her safety? Did you not think she would be in harm's way?"

"I . . . I did . . ."

"Repeat what was written in the letter you received."

"He said his loyalty to her was as solid as stone . . . to meet him at their usual place . . . at the Hour of the Rat. He wished to tell her something."

A cold shiver ran down my spine as I stared at Soyi, the maid whose wounds I had cleansed, whom I had looked at with a heart brimming with pity. But had she deserved this pity? Soyi might not have killed her mistress, yet she had made the murder possible.

"I am done with her." Inspector Han summoned a legal clerk and said, "She ought to be punished for causing such chaos."

"No, no!" Soyi frantically shook her head, as though her hair were on fire and she were trying to douse it with the wind. "No, no, no—I want to be free!"

"You delivered a letter that ought never to have been delivered. You kept silent when you should have spoken. You knew beforehand that Lady O's life was in danger, yet permitted the stranger to lure her out, and all this resulted in her death. That is how this crime took place. Lock her up."

The damos unbound Soyi from the chair, dragged her to her feet. The noise that escaped from her was neither a scream nor a cry, but something in between man and beast that tore out from her chest and exploded in the air.

And not once did Inspector Han flinch.

ELEVEN

THE HORRIBLE NOISE Soyi had made continued to ring in my ears.

A month ago, I had felt a morbid interest in murder cases, enjoying the thrill of chasing the truth. But the thrill had vanished, replaced by a heaviness in my chest that made breathing difficult.

The truth seemed as tangled as a lie, and the darkness seemed to grow darker, with no promise of a bright morning.

Officer Kyŏn, for one, seemed pleased by the turn of events, sowing anxiety among the other officers, whispering, "This bamboo hat man, he has outsmarted Inspector Han."

For the next three days, I tried to visit Soyi to ask her questions about the man in the bamboo hat. I wanted to know whether he had told her anything else while persuading her to deliver his letter. I wanted to know even more, considering the same man had also delivered a letter to Scholar Ahn, who had disappeared soon after.

But I could not bring myself to enter the prison block. I feared her, and more than that, I didn't want to see the accusation in her eyes. In confiding in me, in trusting me, she had lost her last chance to escape the bureau.

Then, on the fourth day, I mustered up enough determination to face her. I got so far as the prison block only for my courage to vanish at the sight of a man in a worn-out tunic and trousers crouched down next to Senior Officer Shim. Plunging his hands into a bucket of water, the man washed his blood-speckled face, a dazed look in his eyes. I did not know his name, and no one really did, for we all called him simply the executioner.

"There was an execution today?" I asked.

Shim kept his eyes downcast, so the executioner spoke into the silence. "By the southern gate. Traitors."

Dread whooshed out of me, and I leaned against the prison-block wall, much relieved. A traitor had died, not Soyi. The fresh splattering of blood belonged to someone else . . . some other poor soul.

"So . . . what kind of treason did the rogue commit?" I asked.

"Gossiped about the queen regent. About the assassination by poison." His dialect was from the eastern coast. I could tell because of its tonal nature, rolling up and down like the mountain peaks and low valleys, so different from the mild and flat capital speech. "She ordered that they be punished as traitors."

"You will kill many more in the new year," Shim said to the crouching man. "Catholics."

Officer Shim continued to linger, his shadow stretching tall in the setting sun, and I wondered why he was here at all. No one got on friendly terms with baekjeongs like the executioner, for baekjeongs were the outcast group forced to live separate from the common people. Their communities were mostly left alone so long as they caused no disturbance, and they survived off money made from work others refused to do: the taking of life. They butchered, made leather, killed stray dogs. And they were the ones summoned by the police to execute criminals.

Then I realized why Shim might have more sympathy for the executioner. He was an outsider himself, a seoja, marked by shame since his illegitimate birth. For a moment, moved by pity, I almost forgot that Shim was the alibi of a cruel tyrant, Inspector Han.

"You were there for the execution too, sir?" I asked kindly.

"I always am," Shim replied.

Now I noticed Shim's police robe, red spots staining the white collar. He crouched and rested his hand on the executioner's trembling shoulders. Perhaps Officer Shim's words had troubled this baekjeong, a reminder of his inescapable fate: he would kill many more.

Death, it was so final. A finality that did not discriminate, stealing both the young and old, rich and poor.

"Officer," I whispered, "do you ever grow accustomed to death?"

Shim peered up at me, his eyes reddish-brown, as though he had witnessed so many executions that if he were to cry, blood would flow out instead of tears. "No, Damo Seol," he replied, his voice soft. As though he were a brother speaking to a little sister. "Seeing a dead person will continue to be difficult."

Was it difficult even for Lady O's killer? Surely no one could kill and hide the evidence so thoroughly as to evade Inspector Han's notice.

"How can you tell if someone has seen death, as you have?" I asked.

"Some cry, some are desperate for distraction, but most of us . . . most of us go mad."

●

In the early hours of the next day, when the morning dew soaked the ground, we were summoned to the central courtyard. Damos Aejung and Hyeyeon appeared, along with a group of officers. I examined each pale and tired face for a sign of madness, unable to forget what Officer Shim had said. Surely no human being could be so hardened and unfeeling as not to be affected by the murder of another person.

Inspector Han's commanding voice filled the courtyard. "We do not have a warrant yet, but we will make our way to Lord O's mansion and demand entry. I want a thorough search of the place. As for the women's quarter, the damos will search Lady O's chamber. Bring anything of interest to me or Senior Officer Shim, and keep your eyes open for her journal. I need that journal."

From beneath my lashes, I glanced up. Inspector Han's eyes were bloodshot from exhaustion, shadows smudged beneath; the face once shining with health was now gaunt and pale. The usual crispness of his robe had been replaced by wrinkles, and even from where I stood, a spot of crimson was visible on his sleeve, perhaps from a round of blood-splattering interrogation. Perhaps this was the appearance of an inspector gone mad.

Pain pulsated by my temple, growing stronger and stronger, until I felt my entire head vibrating, as though someone had struck me. I wanted this all to be over, I wanted to be done with this investigation, but I feared it never would be over.

●

Our journey did not take long; the sky was still a shade of purple-blue as we entered Lord O's mansion and gathered in the main courtyard. Inspector Han stepped forward and bowed, paying his respects to only Matron Kim, for her husband had returned to his governing post in Gwangju after briefly mourning for his daughter here.

She did not look pleased. Her hands were clasped within her wide sleeves, and she was garbed in a white mourning gown, not only for the king but also for her daughter, it seemed. Her black hair was twisted back into a braided coil so tight that the corners of her eyes were tugged dagger sharp.

"You are here again, Inspector," Matron Kim said, her voice brusque. "Why?"

"Forgive us for this intrusion. I have come to ask once again for permission to search Lady O's private chamber."

"My answer remains the same. You dishonored us by having my daughter examined without the presence of family. You will get nothing from me."

"The killer is still out there, mistress. The longer we wait, the more evidence will be lost."

Her lips tightened and her blank eyes showed remarkable restraint.

"Maid Soyi has confessed about your daughter's affair during the torture session—about the son born out of wedlock, too. Now the duty of a mother is no longer to protect the honor of the deceased, but to appease her grieving spirit. Do you not wish to know the truth behind her death?"

"No. All I wish," she said, her voice steady, "is for the police to stop harassing our family. I wish for no more reminders of the horror my daughter endured."

Inspector Han pressed on. "When murder is committed, grieving relatives of the victim will plead for sangmyŏng, 'requital for a life.' They appeal to us to redress the grievance suffered by the deceased with the sacrifice of another life, that of the perpetrator. Yet you do not ask for justice. Instead you ask that we forget it ever happened?"

Long shadows crept around us as the purple sky deepened, clouds gathering. There would be no sun today.

"It is because I am afraid," Matron Kim said. "I am afraid of what more I will discover about my daughter. What more she was hiding from me."

"Your daughter died alone on the cold ground, bleeding. Her nose was sliced off—"

"Must you remind me?" A tremor shook her voice.

"Her slender throat was slashed without hesitation or remorse, deep enough to sever her vocal cords, silencing her cries for help. How will you face your daughter in the afterlife when you have kept us from finding the truth? How will you look into her sad eyes?"

Matron Kim's eyes turned red-rimmed, and in that moment,

I remembered she was a mother. And I remembered my own mother's eyes, the last time I had seen her, red-rimmed like the matron's. My last warm memory of Mother was of a wooden bowl of rice prepared for us all. We had all eaten together, and Mother had looked at me with those red eyes. I hadn't known it was a farewell before she'd jumped off a cliff.

"This investigation is nothing more to you than a mere crime among the multitude." Matron Kim's upper lip curled slightly. "My daughter died on her birthday. I made a jeogori jacket for her as a gift, sewed the silk pieces together myself, and I knew the length and circumference of her arms, the length and breadth of her torso, all measured meticulously. I knew her. She was my daughter. And from the day of her death, all you saw was a crime to be solved. From that day, you disrespected my affection for my daughter, and even now, you speak to me with a cruel, impatient look in your eyes."

Inspector Han stood tall, not slumping forward in guilt as my own shoulders did. Never had I thought of the dead Lady O as someone who had been precious, as my own family was precious to me.

"I promise I will find the one who killed your daughter," Inspector Han replied. "Should I not live up to my promise, I shall bear the consequences."

She lifted her grieving eyes to him. "How?"

"I will submit a formal report and resign from my post."

Senior Officer Shim frowned. Everyone else exchanged wide-eyed glances. I could feel what they were thinking: Inspector Han was putting too much on the line, and they couldn't understand why.

"Do I have your word, Inspector?"

"You do."

Matron Kim nodded and the dagger in her eyes softened into a well of tears. "Everything in my daughter's chamber remains as is," she whispered. "I have not permitted anyone to disturb her room since her passing."

●

"The medical exam is in a few months," Aejung whispered as we entered the women's quarter. "I've hardly had any time to study. How are we expected to pass it and return to being palace nurses when half the time we're solving crimes?"

Hyeyeon shook her head. "You must sacrifice something to achieve your goal, Aejung. I sleep only three hours a day, so I only need to master *Injaejikjimaek* now. But you've mastered none of the five required texts."

"*That* is because I'm focusing on the investigation for now," Aejung retorted. "Inspector Han will be forced to resign otherwise."

"So it's true," I whispered. "He does mean to resign if he fails."

"Are there no such things as consequences in the countryside?" Hyeyeon asked. Her voice was elegant, yet her eyes sent me a cutting look. "*Someone* must take the blame."

With tension pressing in around us, we climbed up the steps to Lady O's chamber, where stale air loomed over us like a lost soul. At the far end was a folding screen with a calligraphy of butterflies and flowers painted onto the panels. Before it was a silk cushion and a low-legged writing table. Furniture lined either side of the room.

Hyeyeon searched the two-tiered wardrobe made of pagoda tree, pulling open the miniature doors that revealed folded fabrics. She pulled everything out, but found nothing. There were also four small drawers in the wardrobe's upper tier, all of which she examined, turning over every article. Again, nothing.

Aejung opened all the heavy chests, pulling out dusty books and pausing to read their contents. Her eyes flicked up and down, up and down, reading so quickly I watched with awe. "Verbose nonsense after verbose nonsense," she murmured.

As Hyeyeon made her way to a ground-to-ceiling bookcase, where side-stitched books rested in piles, I moved over to a lacquer cabinet, with elaborate mother-of-pearl inlaid scenes of strange creatures with fish tails, turtle shells, and the heads of mammals. Butterfly-shaped brass lock plates and hinges decorated the double doors. Opening each door, I discovered porcelain pots of color, hair ornaments, and a brush with strands of hair in it. Lady O's hair. I reached for one and the moment I pulled a strand free, it struck me how transient life was— one night a woman was brushing her hair, the next night she was dead.

I left the cabinet and checked behind the folding screen, then sat before the low-legged table, which had two drawers on either side. I tugged at the left drawer, and it slid open to reveal calligraphy brushes. I tugged at the next—

Surprise punched my chest. It was locked.

"Here, here!" I called out, excitement bubbling. "This drawer. It's locked!"

"It's locked?" Aejung threw the scrolls back into the chest and hurried over to me. She too tugged at the right drawer. Locked indeed. "I'll look around for the key. Must be here somewhere. It wasn't on her person when we found her."

"Couldn't we just break the desk?" I asked. "I have my club."

"No." Hyeyeon frowned at me from where she stood. "We were not given permission to sabotage. You are so thoughtless sometimes."

Her rebuke stung. Trying to ignore it, I pulled at the drawer with all my might, but in vain. All we could do was find the key, but after what seemed like ages, Aejung shook her head, her forehead glistening with sweat.

"I've looked everywhere!" she whined. Wiping her brows, she

glanced at Hyeyeon. "I'll go ask if we can use force . . . There's no other choice."

We both waited on Hyeyeon for permission, for she was our senior and we never did anything without her agreement. And yet Hyeyeon stood frozen before the bookcase. She was examining a book, then flipped it shut. "These books are all journals, and this seems to be the most recent one, though dated four years ago."

"There is nothing more recent?" Aejung asked.

"I have thoroughly inspected them all. This is still *something*." She tucked the book under her arm, ill-disguised thrill straining her countenance as she hurried out of the room. Aejung followed her.

I settled my attention on the lock again, leaning forward to peer into the hole. There was something inside that was forbidden to me, like so many of the secrets kept away from me growing up. All my curiosity about Lady O's death returned, though this time alone, no longer accompanied by my desire to please Inspector Han. I narrowed my eyes and squinted. In my childhood days, I had always wanted the skill of opening secrets. I would carry around a thin knife to see which locks would open and which would not. The cheap ones I'd managed to open quickly. The harder ones were the locks slammed onto expensive chests.

Remembering the lacquer cabinet from earlier, I crawled over to it and rummaged through the sparkling ornaments until I found the perfect hair accessory. It had a lotus attached to a steel pin, which was curved in order not to fall out when inserted into one's hair. Lady O was dead already, so I hesitated only a moment before bending the steel into a straight line. I returned to the table and inserted the pin into the lock, wiggling it around, scratching my knuckles in the attempt. No luck this time, but I kept trying. My fingers became bruised red as I pushed the pin this way and that, shaking and twisting it.

I heaved out a sigh, the curiosity so unbearable that it turned into physical pain. Surely, whatever Lady O had hidden, it would peel off the skin of lies and reveal what lay within. I was tired of chasing after an elusive truth, tired of being surrounded by suspicion and speculations, tired of this investigation that seemed to choke up in smoke everything it touched.

I exhaled another sigh and looked around the room. Blankets were strewn across the floor, shaken out during the inspection, and all the drawers were pulled open, as were the lids of every chest. Aejung had searched every nook and cranny, so there was no point searching again.

I tugged at the locked drawer in frustration, shaking the brass handle. Why couldn't it open smoothly like the other drawer? I wrenched at the handle of the left drawer, and the angry force sent the entire compartment flying to the ground. Brushes scattered everywhere. Then something hard struck a porcelain vase nearby, a high-pitched clinking sound.

I looked over my shoulder. An iron key rested on the floor.

I scrambled forward and grabbed the key, my hand trembling. Lady O must have hidden the key under the pile of brushes, perhaps in the far corner of the drawer. My heartbeat accelerated as I crawled back to the drawer. I took in a deep breath, then let it out, and at last inserted the key into the lock. I rotated it. *Click.* Swallowing a shout of excitement, I pulled open the drawer smoothly.

Piles of paper greeted me, but there was a lump in the way the sheets lay. I looked beneath and found a few sheets of folded paper tied together with a string. When I untied it and unfolded a page, I saw writing and ink blots. Could these be the letters from Scholar Ahn? They had to be. The one common thing all girls hid from their mothers were the boys they fancied.

The sound of distant footsteps reached my ear.

I clutched the letters against my frantic heartbeat. There was a feeling digging into me, sharp and persistent, as I stared down at the letters written on white mulberry paper. *White.* I dug through my mind, through the layers and layers, trying to pick out whatever was hidden in the whiteness. And I managed to draw out a sliver: Ryun. But I had no idea why.

I thought back to the day I had first talked at length with him, all the way to the moment when we had returned to the capital, bloody and bruised. I retraced each step, then returned to the beginning again, focusing on each detail about him, his every expression, our conversations—

My thoughts skittered to a halt. White. White meant mourning. Ryun had mentioned that he'd visited the House of Bright Flowers with a police uniform for Inspector Han, who had still been in his *white* mourning robe. Senior Officer Shim had also told the commander that Inspector Han had first arrived at the House dressed in a *white* robe. Yet in Maid Soyi's first testimony, she had mentioned that on the night of the murder she'd recognized a man (who had turned out to be Inspector Han) by his *blue* uniform.

Panic licked down my back, a hot trail of sweat. I realized why Shim's statement had bothered me from the beginning. He should have said, "Inspector Han arrived at the House dressed in his uniform," not in his mourning robe. For the inspector had been wearing his blue uniform when he'd first left the House, when he'd encountered Maid Soyi before drunkenly stumbling back to Madam Yeonok. She must have changed him out of his soaked and muddy blue uniform into a spare white robe.

So why, in Shim's memory, did he recall Inspector Han wearing only white?

Was it possible that Shim had only seen Inspector Han in the white robe? This meant he couldn't account for Inspector Han's presence at the House of Bright Flowers until dawn, long *after* the murder had occurred.

Then who could say Inspector Han had been present at the House just before midnight—the time of Lady O's death? The only possible witnesses were the gisaengs, the keepers of secrets.

Blue robe. White robe.

Perhaps these letters would prove my worst fears correct. Perhaps this was why Inspector Han was so determined to collect all evidence, so that he might burn it.

"No, no," I whispered to myself, trying to shake off the feeling that snaked around me. Suspicion. It had returned, and this time, it coiled around me in a death-tight grip. Even then, I wanted to believe, I wanted to give Inspector Han the benefit of the doubt. "Please, don't be involved."

My hands shaking, I skimmed through the opened letters and was bombarded by shapes I did not understand, and for the first time, I felt it deeply—the anger and frustration of not being able to read. The feeling of being kept away from the truth by an impenetrable wall called ignorance.

There was nothing I could do. For half a second, I considered setting the letters back down. I'd give them over to the inspector. He might be lying about his alibi, but surely he had his own reasons for making Officer Shim give a false testimony. I wavered, yet it was the memory of Inspector Han that held my wrist still.

The truth is far more important, he'd told me. *Do not have feelings involved when investigating a crime.*

I grabbed my sash belt and untied it, tugged at the collar of my uniform. A light breeze came in from the doors, which had been left open, tickling my bare collarbones as I tried to loosen my breast band, desperate to shove the letters inside. Letters that might shine a light on what Inspector Han was hiding, if he were indeed hiding anything at all. I'd find someone to read them for me.

"What are you doing?"

The letters fell from my grasp and slapped onto the floor. It was Hyeyeon, staring at me with an arched brow.

"I—I was—" I stammered, my mind racing. "A bug crept into my uniform."

●

The search was completed with my discovery, and Hyeyeon declared that there was nothing else of value to the investigation to be found.

Once we were all gathered in the courtyard of Matron Kim's mansion, Inspector Han opened the letters I'd discovered, four of them in total, positioned so that he could observe them all at once. "Three of the letters must have been written by Scholar Ahn. But this letter . . ." He briefly raised it up to Senior Officer Shim. "This last letter was the one Maid Soyi delivered to her mistress, which led to her death." He studied the letter again. "The writing style is certainly different."

As the inspector studied the letters, Hyeyeon walked forward and bowed her head. She said something to him under her breath. I couldn't hear anything. Whatever she said made him walk slowly down the line of officers and damos. He paused before me. I stood frozen. Inspector Han sized me up for long, agonizing moments. Then he moved on.

TWELVE

BLUE ROBE, WHITE ROBE.

My great fear was that Senior Officer Shim had lied for Inspector Han. He'd told the commander that he'd been with the inspector at the House of Bright Flowers before midnight—the time when the murder had occurred. But Shim had gotten the color of the inspector's robe wrong. This had to mean something.

Shim's possible lie filled my thoughts as I hid by the gate the following day, observing Inspector Han in his office. All the sliding doors were open, allowing the cool summer breeze in and out of the pavilion. I stood straighter, alert, as he looped strings around his ears, which secured over his eyes a pair of circular glasses framed by wood. Spectacles. I had heard about such contraptions before but had never seen them. They made him look peculiar.

Inspector Han then laid out on his desk four crinkly pages, which he flattened out by adding a stone weight to each corner. Then he leaned forward and observed the calligraphy, studying it closely. It must have been the letters we'd found in Lady O's chamber. Why did a frown wrinkle his brow?

Ever since the discovery of those letters, I had lost sleep wondering about them. No longer could I restrain my curiosity. I arrived by the steps that led up to the pavilion and bowed. "Excuse me, sir. But . . ." I reminded myself that I had the right to know. I had told Inspector Han about the Catholic connection to the murder. I had accompanied him on the journey to Mount Hwa, fighting off bandits for him. "Is it true that the last letter was not written by Scholar Ahn, but someone else?"

Silence.

I tried again, clutching my skirt, trying to hold on to my courage. "I heard that everyone's handwriting is unique. Will you be looking for someone with a similar handwriting, sir?"

"You have no business asking." He was still studying the letters, not bothering to give me his attention. He shifted the spectacles higher up the ridge of his aquiline nose. "For you have no business knowing."

"But, sir—"

He removed the spectacles and stared at me with his pale, spooky eyes. "Should you continue to meddle in my investigation, it will trouble me, and should I be troubled, you will get hurt. Your family would not wish that."

Surprise tightened my chest. I remembered Hyeyong whispering something to him. Perhaps she had told him that I'd tried to steal the letters . . .

"In fact, from what I have managed to quickly gather, your sister has no children, but one night she had a dream that she would have a son in the new year. If I want, I could learn far more about your sister—her weaknesses and fears, her darkest secrets. I am sure she would not wish this."

Everything in me went still and silent. For a moment, I couldn't even blink. "How do you know this?"

"I have people in different parts of the kingdom. Their business is to do my bidding." With unnerving calm, he rolled up his sleeve and reached for a calligraphy brush, which he then examined with the keenness of a soldier admiring a sharpened blade. "Everything has a consequence. With a stroke of this brush, I can determine your fate. But it is up to you to decide what I shall write."

Even when faced by suspicious evidence that pointed an ugly finger at Inspector Han, I had fought my way to maintain my loyalty. I had always tried to understand him. Yet how quickly, how easily, his own suspicion frosted over his trust in me.

I wanted to charge up the steps and slap the brush out of his grasp. Maybe grab him by the collars and shake him until every crooked secret fell out of him—

Then I saw it. A smooth, pinkish scar covering the side of his lower right arm.

"You are dismissed," Inspector Han said, but the sight of the wound pinned me down as a memory drew so near, almost graspable. As I turned and walked toward the gate, I couldn't stop frowning, the sensation still there. Beneath the murky waters of my present, a memory waited for me, its silver scales rippling, so close to my reach.

For a moment, I almost managed to forget the terror Inspector Han's threat had sent into my soul. The cost of curiosity would be not only my own life, but the lives of my family, and the little one that would one day grow in my sister's belly.

●

Later that day, rain rushed into the capital in a black cloud, pounding and drumming on the earth and rooftops, but it left almost as soon as it had arrived. It had been a sonagi, a quick shower. Silence returned to the servants' quarter, the stillness occasionally broken by a raindrop falling from the eaves. Silence, *spack*. More silence, *spack*.

"Hyeyeon has been watching you like a hawk," Aejung said when we were alone. "What happened yesterday at Lady O's mansion?"

The memory of Inspector Han stayed with me, a chill that bit deep into the bone. Yet my calm pretense surprised me. I continued to work on the police robe in my hands, pulling the thread in and out to mend a tear. My fingers were trembling, though. "I'm not certain myself."

"Inspector Han has changed too. The way he looks at you . . . it sends a chill of fear through me."

"He does not like anyone," I snapped. "That is why they call him Gosan, lone mountain—"

The needle pricked my finger, and the sudden pain startled a gasp from me. A crimson dewdrop formed. Sucking the blood away, I returned my attention to the torn fabric and said, "Inspector Han confides in no one else but Senior Officer Shim." I held myself back from adding, *Shim, the alibi, the maybe-liar.* "I wonder . . . how did Inspector Han and Shim become as close as brothers, despite their difference in status?"

Aejung, sitting before a low-legged table, ground a stick of ink into an inkstone. She paused, glancing at the screened door. "Do not tell anyone I told you this."

I laid the needle and thread down. "I promise." My voice sounded strangled, tension knotting my throat.

She returned to grinding the ink and said, "An uncle on his father's side tried to kill Inspector Han. The uncle had returned from exile, formerly condemned for a crime associated with the inspector's father. I hear the uncle lost everything: family, wealth, status. His mansion was burned down, too. So out of this long-held grudge, he attacked the inspector, but Shim protected him."

"That was why Inspector Han recruited Shim despite his seoja status?"

"I believe so, even though it went against regulations. Inspector Han is someone who will move heaven and earth for those loyal to him."

Except me. The thought came at me like a bitter stab. He had not tried to rescue *my* life from the bandit's dagger.

"No one knows much about Shim, and he does not talk about

his past at all," Aejung added. "I did hear rumors, though, that Shim's hometown is a village called Myeonmok, wherever that is."

Pushing down my bitterness, I maintained enough calm to ask, "How do you know all this?"

Aejung added water to the crushed ink, then spread out a sheet of paper on the table; she was always writing home to her family in the late afternoon. I had never felt the urge to ask someone to teach me how to read and write until yesterday, when I'd held the unreadable letters in my hands.

"I overheard Officer Kyŏn talk about it a year ago," Aejung explained. "He seemed to have a keen interest in Inspector Han's life, including those close to him like Officer Shim. And what I didn't learn from Kyŏn, I learned from local gossip."

She rolled her sleeves up to her elbow, her wrists moving with grace as she wrote.

I couldn't look away, and neither could I breathe, seeing a movement almost identical to that of earlier, when Inspector Han had rolled up his sleeve to write, exposing a part of his history. The side of his right arm, a burn from long ago, as though he had once tried blocking himself from scalding hot liquid.

Something in my mind clicked. I saw myself, a young girl, peering in through the cracks of our hut. Older Sister was hissing, "Go to the capital then, that place of terror. We are not family. We are *finished*." Her cruel hands tore our genealogy book, the history of our family. My brother slapped her face, shocking them both. But Sister was too proud and no one had dared hit her before, so she hurled at him words of hate, as well as a pot filled with boiling tea. He had tried blocking it with his arm.

The memory disappeared in a few seconds. And those seconds left me drenched in cold sweat.

"Are you not feeling well?" came Aejung's voice. "You look ill."

I looked up at Aejung. She was watching me, her hand still holding the calligraphy brush. Desperation ravaged me. I had to write to Older Sister, demand answers from her. She had withheld too many secrets from me.

Who is our brother? What made you scared?

I moved quickly to Aejung's side. "Is it very difficult to write?"

"No . . ." There was uneasiness in her voice, as though frightened by the gleam in my eyes. "It is so easy to learn that a fool can know it in a day."

"Could you teach me how to write? Then I can write to my sister as often as I need."

Aejung scratched a corner of her lips. "I wish I could help you . . . but I must study for the medical exam—"

"I'll do your chores, as many as I can. I'll sweep and mop, I'll sew, I'll do your laundry. Then you'll have plenty of time to study!"

She hesitated, and her long silence chipped away at my longing. *Not for me,* the voice said as it pulled me away. *Literacy is not for me. Knowledge is not for me.*

I pressed my fingers against my eyes until I saw stars. What madness had drifted into me? Was I truly suspecting that the blood flowing through Inspector Han flowed through me as well? I needed only approach the inspector to confirm that I was sick. Only a sick person would dare assume blood connection.

Whatever Aejung saw when she looked my way compelled her to change her mind. "Even if the chief maid asks me to bring water from the well," she said gently, as one would to a wounded bird, "you will go for me?"

I did not have the strength to answer, too stunned by the workings of my mind.

"Come, sit closer." With a sigh, she took out another fresh sheet of paper. "This is how I was taught when I was a girl." With long strokes, she drew a large square, dividing it into columns and rows, and in the boxes she drew shapes. I took this all in with a stare filled with tears, my mind still whirring.

"Fourteen consonant letters are on the vertical side; ten vowel letters are on the horizontal side. One must assemble the two together to create a word." She dipped the brush into the ink and dragged it across the paper, another black stroke across white. "And when you write, every brushstroke must be decisive, with no going back."

"It is like life," I said under my breath, as a warning prickle ran down my spine. "There is no going back."

●

The other damos were asleep by nightfall. I crept out of the servants' quarter, holding my breath. I dared not wake anyone. No one could know where I was going. The House of Bright Flowers, the place this entire investigation had circled back to yet again.

Once outside, I inspected the inside of my sleeve. It was still there, a blank paper folded into an envelope, which Aejung had given me to write home to my sister. Instead, I would find a servant at the House to bring me to Madam Yeonok and say that Inspector Han had sent me to personally deliver a letter to her. But hopefully, instead of her, I would be guided to her maid, from whom I might collect secrets more easily.

There is no going back, I reminded myself as I strode out of the police bureau. My heart pounded loud in my ears and my dress clung to my perspiring body as I passed by patrolmen prowling two by two, unmindful of the women who wandered the streets with their paper lanterns. For women were not considered threats to the capital, as men were, when darkness fell.

And I was a girl, and thus harmless in the eyes of the patrolmen.

Gods. They had no idea what I was about to do.

My sweat felt like ice water, the weather having cooled considerably. My limbs trembled by the time I crossed the stone bridge over the trickling Cheonggye Stream, closer to the wild and windy desolation of Mount Nam.

And yet the memory of Older Brother's radiant smile burned. The brightness of his memory chased after me like a ghost in flames as I ran down the muddy path, shadows of grass and trees swaying. Field crickets chirped and leaves rustled, and soon, the nocturnal hum gave way to woodwinds whining over the beating of a drum and the rumbling of laughter.

I saw the House of Bright Flowers. Its roof, illuminated by hundreds of hanging lanterns, rose into a peak, then curved into flared eaves, in harmony with the rolling slopes of Mount Nam in the background.

I repeated the words, gathering every ounce of courage in me, "There is no going back."

A true police officer would have come to this place determined to find evidence that would bring down the inspector, determined that an inspector who blackmailed truth seekers into silence ought to be brought down. Yet it was not so with me.

The desperate roots crawling through my soul longed for something more than justice. I wanted to know who Inspector Han was. And his story crouched hidden in the House of Bright Flowers, perhaps a story of anger accumulated over a decade. Or a perverse hunger that would reveal many dark deeds strung throughout his past. Or something about his family—who they were, where they lived, and why no one had mentioned their existence.

Wiping the sweat from my face, I walked along the wall, then stopped at the side gate. A maid entered through it, balancing buckets of water on a shoulder pole. I clutched my lantern tighter and followed her into the servants' courtyard.

Large brown pots lined the wall, filled with soy sauce, soybean paste, and pickles. Servants strode in and out of the kitchen, from which steam drifted, oiled with the scent of pork boiling in ginger and other herbs. Within, maids cut vegetables into piles of colorful slices—carrots, spinach, eggplants, cucumber, radishes, clumps of garlic cloves. Straw baskets lay piled with fried scallion and zucchini patties.

"Are you lost?"

I whirled to see a maid with graying hair along her temples, perhaps a senior-ranking servant. With tight lips, she held my gaze, and I could sense her refusing to look at the mark on my cheek. It often made other servants uncomfortable, reminding them we were property.

"My master sent me with a letter," I said. "I'm not sure where to go."

"Who are you looking for?"

"Madam Yeonok," I said. "But I realize now she must be occupied. Her maid will do."

She nodded. "Leave your lantern."

I was ushered into a large courtyard, crowded with men and women garbed in brightly colored dresses and robes, shimmering fabric and sweeping curves. Everyone looked in one direction. I followed their gaze toward a gisaeng sprawled at the center of the courtyard, her skirt hiked up, baring her white undergarment. I glanced at the old servant, wondering if such disorder was a usual occurrence here at the House.

Her lips were pressed into a thin line of displeasure.

Approaching the gisaeng, slowly and stealthily, was a man with his robe hanging off his bare shoulder, as though he had woken from a thrashing nightmare. His hair was tied into a topknot, and loose strands were kept from falling over his face by a silk headband embroidered with gold patterns. His sword gleamed in the lantern light. With each approaching step of his, the gisaeng scrambled farther back.

"Say it again, inyeona." His suave voice, filled with malicious humor, rang familiar—then I recognized his face. It was Young Master Ch'oi. "Say to my face what you whispered to others. I am not Ch'oi's *real* son but an imposter, you said. Repeat it!"

He raised the sword and I thought he was going to kill her, but another gentleman restrained him by holding on to his arms, and by the young master's stumbling gait it was obvious he was deep in his cups.

The old servant clucked her tongue and parted her lips as though wanting to spit out a sharp rebuke at the young master. But, changing her mind, she clucked her tongue again and said instead, "We mustn't stare, child. Come away now."

I followed her into the sprawling mansion through a side entrance, deep red pine beams and pillars against white walls, while my thoughts still lingered on the scene I'd left behind. With such pent-up fury behind his frosty smiles, surely Young Master Ch'oi must have harmed many others before that gossiping gisaeng.

For a moment, I wondered if I had made a grave error. Perhaps my suspicion toward Inspector Han and Officer Shim was all wrong. A ball of stress tightened in my chest. *Damn it,* I thought. *Am I suspecting the wrong person?*

But I did not have long to wrestle with this question. My concern withdrew to the far corner of my mind as the old servant led me farther down the hall. I expected to be shown to a maid, for surely the mistress was occupied at this hour, but instead I was led to sliding double doors. A maid stood on either side, their hands clasped and their heads bowed, as though they were waiting on the queen regent herself. The old servant whispered something to one of the maids, who then drew her face close to the paper screen and called out in a low voice, "Madam, a letter has arrived for you."

I startled a step back. This was not supposed to happen. "I do not wish to disturb the mistress herself," I whispered. "I can deliver it to the personal maid instead—"

"Enter," came a husky voice from within.

The doors slid open to reveal a lady whose beauty so stunned me that despite my turmoil, I could not help but admire her. She reminded me of a fairy maiden with her snow-white skin, perfectly red lips, and eyes as bright as black pearls. I felt like a wet rag in comparison, with the glaring mark on my burnt face.

"Come closer, girl."

Panic returned as I approached Madam Yeonok. She sat on the floor, garbed in a voluminous silk skirt of crimson and a jacket of a sheer black material that revealed her pale shoulders and arms. She had one leg propped up, and her elbow rested on her knee.

A maid was also present, slipping a jade pin into the mistress's mass of coiled braids. Once that was done, she scuttled over to me. I took the letter out from the inside of my sleeve, and as I gave it to her, our fingers touched. Her eyes bore curiously into mine. I wondered if I'd erred in coming here as the maid walked off and gave the letter to her mistress.

"Whom do you belong to?" Madam Yeonok asked.

I felt light-headed with terror as she slipped two fingers into the envelope.

"Go on, answer my mistress," the maid said, an impatient edge to her voice.

I licked my dry lips and stammered, "Inspector H-Han."

A humorless smile tugged at the corner of Madam Yeonok's lips. Paper whispered against envelope, and the folded sheet slid out a quarter of the way. She paused, a frown flickering, before she drew it out entirely. "What is the meaning of this?" she said, her words as cold as ice piercing through my chest. "Have you come to play a jest on me? This letter is blank."

"The truth is . . ." I floundered, straining to improvise, but I could find nothing but the truth. "I only came to fetch something."

Madam Yeonok fixed me with a stare. "What?"

"I was wondering if you knew anything about Lady O and her murder."

The maid gasped. The gisaeng kept silent, but she could not hide the blood draining from her face or the trembling of her fingers. A sheen of sweat glistened on her brow, betraying her through the mask of anger she put on.

"Impudent girl," Madam Yeonok said, and a spiteful laugh tinkled in the air. "Who do you think I am? I am a gisaeng, a keeper of secrets, and so is everyone in this house. Go before I have you flogged and reported to Inspector Han—"

"I have come here by Commander Yi's orders." The lie slipped from my lips. I'd rarely lied before, but now it was all I had. "He has set up a secret investigation. He wants to know what happened here the night of the killing."

The gisaeng arched her brow. "And he sent you, a mere damo?"

It was true, that was all I was. A mere damo. My name, my existence, was nothing but ashes and burnt bridges. I was already hated by Inspector Han, despised by all of Kyŏn's gang of officers.

"If you do not tell me the truth," I whispered as menacingly as I could, "Commander Yi will send his men to search every nook and cranny of this mansion. He will beat and he will tear until the truth comes out."

Madam Yeonok raised her chin as she examined me. A thousand thoughts flitted across her eyes, like the swift reflection of clouds over water. She had to know that for me to utter such an immense lie would be to put my life at risk. Surely, it made more sense to her that I was telling the truth.

At length, she slid her stare to the maid. "Go bring a manservant to deal with this damo, Misu-yah."

My bravado faltered, my courage crumbled. I couldn't risk causing a scene. "Madam, if you wish me to leave, I will leave. I have done my best to warn you."

She remained still, and I dared to take a step back, then another, and when I realized she had no intention of stopping me, I turned on my heel. The maids slid open the doors, and the moment I stepped out, the doors shut with a *clack*. Cold sweat clung to the back of my neck as I stared down the hall, trying to gather my thoughts. That was it? I had come all this way just to be scared off so soon?

"Misu-yah," came Madam Yeonok's lowered voice from beyond the paper screen. "*Burn it.*"

A gasp caught in my throat. The urgent fear in the madam's voice was undeniable.

"Now, mistress?"

"You should have burned it long ago."

Hearing Misu shuffling toward the entrance, I hurried down the hall and turned a corner, and right then I heard the doors slide open, followed by the sound of footsteps drawing near, closer to my hiding spot. I bit my lower lip, and as quick as I could without making a sound, I rushed forward and finally managed to escape into the main courtyard. I whirled behind a pillar and kept an eye on the front mansion entrance as Madam Yeonok's order pounded in my ears.

Burn it.

Soon enough, Misu's face, ghostly pale with terror, flashed down the veranda, disappearing through a connecting gate. And I followed. I wound my way through the crowd and didn't realize that I was only in my socks until I was running, but I had no time to run back to the side mansion entrance to retrieve my sandals. As soon as I passed through the gate, I hid behind a wooden beam, watching Misu scurry into what looked to be the servants' quarter with its dusty and run-down appearance. Whatever she'd been ordered to burn, I'd give her no time to do so. I raced forward, threw the door aside, and stormed in.

Misu was shoving fabric into a sack.

I grabbed it, a material so soft I knew it was silk, but she refused to let go.

"Hand it over," I ordered, and when she continued to cling, I opened my mouth wide and bit her wrist, my teeth digging into her skin as her shriek exploded in my ears. She dropped the fabric and scrambled away into the corner, clutching her hand to her chest. The whites of her eyes gleamed.

"Please," she begged, "don't look at it. There are things better left unknown. Leave, just leave."

The lantern light flooded in through the open door, illuminating the deep blue silk. I shook out the material until hanging before me was a man's robe. Silver tiger embroidery glinted in the light, the emblem worn by military officials. This was an inspector's uniform.

I stared at Misu, who rocked back and forth. "Whose robe is this?" I asked.

"Please go back. Please. I'm begging you."

"I have come here by Commander Yi's orders," I reminded her. "Tell me whose robe this is, and he will let you live."

Misu's eyes widened more, if that was even possible. I could almost see her mind jumping back and forth between *Tell her* and *Do not dare* as her gaze darted from the robe to me to the door then back to the robe again.

"The truth!" My voice sounded nearly frantic. "Tell me the truth!"

Silence fell, a few seconds too long. Then Misu whispered, "I should have burned it when she first told me to."

My heartbeat rammed against my chest. "Go on. You must tell me the truth, everything you know. It will save you. But if you hide something from me and the commander discovers it, you will be interrogated."

"What do you wish to know?" Misu whispered.

"When did Inspector Han arrive at the House?"

"An hour after midnight."

The inspector had no alibi . . . I could hardly breathe as I forced myself to ask the next question. "When did he leave the House?"

"I do not know, but I know he did not return to his residence that night. He returned here a little before dawn. One of the servants, she saw Inspector Han in poor condition and brought him to Madam Yeonok."

"Why did the servant bring Inspector Han to your mistress?"

"They are on close terms. I heard him call my mistress imja, 'dearest,' and he's known her since he came to the capital as an orphan. A little over a decade ago. And it is my mistress's dream, you see, to be bought and kept as his concubine."

The remark about Inspector Han's past tugged at me, yet my mind was already rolling in a different direction, too fast for me to stop. "You said a servant found Inspector Han in poor condition. What happened next?"

"The servant notified the mistress and had him smuggled into a private chamber for the sake of his dignity. It would look poorly for the public to see him so."

"How drunk was he?"

"Not drunk . . ." Her eyes remained fixed on her hands, which she was wringing together. "He was covered in blood."

I turned the blue robe around in the lantern light and finally saw dark stains. Dried blood crusted the sleeves and the hem, and it was smeared all over the torso area. "Blood," I whispered, and before accusation could settle in, I reminded myself of Ryun's statement about the horse accident. The blood belonged to the horse.

"I saw blood all over Inspector Han, and I thought it was because he was wounded. He looked like he was dying," Misu blurted, as though relieved to be finally telling someone. "He seemed unable to stand, and what is more, he was shivering violently as though he had a fever. Telling my mistress he couldn't feel his hands, and saying over and over again, 'She is dead.'"

She.

Ryun had referred to the inspector's wounded horse as a "he." Was I remembering wrong? I ran a hand over my face, cold with sweat, then rose to my feet again and paced around, trying to walk out the jitters. "And why did you try to hide this robe from me?"

"Madam Yeonok asked me to hide this robe and fetch a clean one. I ran around the House until I found spare attire."

"It was white?"

"Yes! Then my mistress told me to burn this uniform, but I told her, 'Who knows when you might need power?' She knew too that the inspector was losing interest in her. And what better way to bind herself to him than with his secret? So we kept the robe in here ever since."

"And Senior Officer Shim was there too? You didn't mention him."

"He arrived around dawn."

So Officer Shim had lied for the inspector—to hide what for him?

There were footsteps outside, and someone called, "Misu? Misuuuu."

Misu clamped her hands over her lips. "You need to go," she said in a harsh whisper. "And that robe, give it here!"

I clutched the robe tighter and strode out of the room, not daring to lift my face as I passed by whoever had been calling out Misu's name. I did not know where I was heading, everything shaking within me, but I continued to walk. One moment I was wandering through a deserted courtyard, and the next moment I was outside on the street, approaching the South Gate. Torchlight glowed high above, like a fallen star, as a watchman walked along the parapet. Then all at once my feet stopped in their tracks, and I found myself staring down at the spot where Lady O had lain.

I saw it now, the pieces fitting together too perfectly.

Shortly before dawn, Soyi had seen Inspector Han heading somewhere, not back home but—as I had learned—back to the House of Bright Flowers. The darkness so deep, the innkeeper and others had not seen the blood on him, and suspecting nothing, they had thought him drunk with wine rather than drunk with shock and terror.

She is dead, she is dead.

I covered my face with my hands. Only moments ago I had wished the inspector's downfall, if it meant that he would never lay a hand on my family. And now I had in my hands a weapon made of blue silk and blood. I could destroy this man. Me, a mere damo.

THIRTEEN

SECRETS. HOW HEAVY they are, Older Sister had once told me as she'd run her hand across her scalp, pulling free a fistful of hair. *They have ruined me.*

I had once tried to pry these secrets out from my sister's husband. Was my sister a criminal? A runaway adulteress? But he had replied, *She's trying to protect you from whatever is hiding in her past. Something made her scared.*

I ran my hand down my thick hair, wondering if this would happen to me too. Perhaps the secret would feel so much like death that strands would fall out, leaving bald patches of despair. I wasn't meant to keep the evidence to myself, yet I didn't know who to trust, who to confide in. Perhaps many secrets began like this, with fear.

I walked down Jongo Street with a yoke resting on my shoulders, water buckets dangling from either side. *I ought to have hidden the robe elsewhere,* I thought. Last night, I had shoved the bloodstained robe into the chest packed with my personal belongings, thinking it safest. Everything that was of any value to me went into that chest. But what if, today, someone decided to rummage through it?

I stopped, unable to take another step.

A curious hand needed only to flip the chest lid open and reach in to end my life. They would find a bloody robe, an inspector's robe, and it would be my turn in the interrogation chair. I quickened my steps, realizing my error. What a foolish place to hide such a secret! I could not run quickly enough. With each step, the image became more vivid, of Damo Hyeyeon holding up the robe in the police courtyard, surrounded by officers.

Water spilled out of the buckets, which were empty by the time I stumbled into the bureau.

There was a crowd. *Too late.* Inspector Han stood a few paces away, garbed in his flowing uniform of midnight blue, like the one hidden deep inside the wooden chest. He was at the head of the crowd, watching me. My heart pounded, each beat so knife-sharp. It was my first time seeing the inspector since I'd heard Misu's pale-faced confession.

Misu had referred to Inspector Han's past as an orphan, a comment I'd overlooked. But now I looked again and what I saw was not a harmless remark but a detail as hideous as an insect with a thousand tiny legs darting about in the shadows. He had come alone to the capital over a decade ago, just like my brother. The coincidences were piling up. *What if,* I thought. *What should I do if he is*— Not even my mind could finish the thought, as though it sensed danger lurking at the end of it.

Someone's cold fingers pinched my shoulder. I gasped back into the present. It was Hyeyeon, dragging me forward as she hissed, "What is wrong with you?"

"I'm s-sorry," I stammered. "I didn't know who to trust. I found it—"

"Hush!" she said, turning her attention to the crowd.

Inspector Han returned to speaking to a young peasant who had an A-frame jigae loaded on his back, piled high with firewood. *He* was the focus of the inspector's sharp gaze, I realized. Not me.

"Why did you go into the shed?" Inspector Han asked.

"I went up to collect brushwood and caught an odd smell," the peasant replied. "I looked in and saw it."

"Do you often venture onto Mount Nam to collect brushwood?"

"I do, Inspector."

"But you did not encounter the smell before?"

"I never went so far as the shed before."

"And why today?"

"The days have grown cold, and I wanted to collect as much wood as possible. Before the frost settles in."

While the questioning continued, I crept by and made my way to the empty kitchen. No one had discovered the robe. I was still safe. For now.

I rested my forehead against the wall and let my heart thunder as the image of Inspector Han filled my mind, his large shoulders and brute strength hidden under his silk robe, his calloused and veiny hands never too far from his sword, his almost lifeless eyes that had sunk into his face over the past few weeks, like a man so obsessed over a case that he always forgot to eat and rest.

I finally dared myself to wonder: *What if Inspector Han is my brother?*

I stepped back from the whirring emotions and observed the coincidences laid out before me. The similar amber eyes, the burn mark in a similar spot to my brother's, and the similarity in timeline— both orphans, both had come to Hanyang over a decade ago. But one crucial link to tie all the coincidences together was missing: I could not have simply ended up in the same region, the same police bureau, at the very same time as my brother, who had been missing for twelve years.

Besides, if Brother were alive and had lived this long, he would have kept his promise to me. That he would write to me, wherever I might end up in the kingdom. He was not one to break promises.

"Not my brother," I said aloud, and hearing those words comforted me. "Never my brother."

No one was outside the servants' quarter. Unlocking my personal chest, I opened the lid and saw two things. The inspector's blue robe was still there, the silk swimming in the darkness. I also saw the norigae pendant. The amber terrapin stared at me from the corner of its eye, and the long blue tassel of silk strings swayed as I picked it up. The colors around me—the white wallpaper, the yellow floor, the slice of pale blue sky outside the door—seemed to bleed together until everything was a blur, nothing vivid, except for the norigae dangling from my finger.

Whether you are the sun, the earth, or the moon, you are a capable girl. To me.

I wanted to shut out the echo of Inspector Han's voice. I threw the pendant back in, slammed the lid shut, but I knew it was still there. Whispering to me, condemning me. I walked out of the servants' quarter and returned with a dirty cloth from the backyard. It was large enough to fill the chest, so that if anyone opened the lid, they would be too repulsed to dig any deeper.

For now, this would do. I couldn't risk moving the robe in broad daylight.

I paused before shutting the lid. Reaching into the depths, past the fabric, my fingers smoothed themselves over the terrapin again. The moment I drew it out again, memories reached into my mind like beams of light that wrapped their arms around me, echoing with memories.

There aren't too many like you, Damo Seol. Man or woman.

I squeezed my fingers over the object and imagined throwing it into the rushing water. Or over a cliff. I must have imagined this scene over and over again, for by the time I blinked back to reality, the courtyard hummed with busy steps of servants returning for their midday meals.

"Seol."

I snatched the pendant close and slammed the lid shut. Slipping the norigae quickly into my uniform, I whirled around to see Aejung frowning at me.

"You look so sick!"

"What do you want?" I snapped.

She pursed her lips. "Why is everyone so unkind these days?" She turned to stalk off but stopped herself, remembering why she'd come for me. "You are summoned by Inspector Han to the main courtyard. Go, and don't dally around like you always do!"

Memories scorched my skin as I made my way back to the front of the bureau. I expected to see only Inspector Han, the man I dreaded most. Instead, I saw a team of legal clerks and officers gathered, as well as the coroner's assistant and the police artist. I was to accompany them.

Curiosity ought to have sparked in my mind with a question: *Where are we going?* But not today. The inside of my skull felt so bruised from the tsunami of one crashing thought after the other. All I wanted to do was hide under my blanket and sleep for an entire week. To be surrounded, for once, by nothing but silence.

My stare blank, I followed the team, leaving behind the filthy maze of streets and marching into desolation. The wilderness grew thick around us as we climbed up Mount Nam, trapping in the shadows and a creeping sense of uneasiness that woke me from my dazed spell. The past two times I'd ventured into the mountains, something dangerous had occurred. My wounded fingers tingled as though sensing the nearness of hostile spirits.

"Commander Yi spoke to me today." Officer Shim's voice drifted through the forest, somewhere ahead of the line. "He said you haven't been sleeping at all. You don't do well without sleep, sir . . ."

"Long few days," Inspector Han replied. "It would be easier to find rest if only I could see the sun, to feel its soothing warmth. All this darkness leaves me restless."

Physical exhaustion distracted me from the inspector's presence, and I was grateful for that. Twigs cracked and soil crumbled down the slope as the men climbed upward. We were not even halfway up the mountain, yet already officers were losing their breath.

Consequences, Inspector Han had said, threatening me for my meddling ways. I wished I could tell him that there were consequences, too, for those who threatened my family.

I looked around. No one was close in front of or behind me. I drew out the norigae, the inspector's gift to his dead sister. I was about to release my fingers and watch it drop, drop, drop down the mountainside until I could no longer see the terrapin, until I could no longer feel the ties connecting me to the old promises or to the new *what-if* fears.

But an ache in my chest stopped me.

I couldn't do it. It wasn't in me to punish. Not this way. I could not throw away Inspector Han's token of affection for his sister.

Cursing under my breath, I shoved the norigae back into my robe, and it was then that a light drizzle fell, like sea mist spraying through the leaves. The soil released a moist, earthy scent. Strands of my hair became plastered onto my face, and when I pushed them back, I saw that I was too far behind. Hiking up my skirt, I hurried up until I was close enough.

"Three months have not yet passed since the king's death . . ."

The legal clerk ahead of me spoke to another, his robe hanging from his slight figure and narrow shoulders, his black cap looking almost loose on his small head.

". . . and yet someone dared to kill a cow? Whoever did it, does he think to live?"

So we were heading over to investigate a slaughtered cow. I could already imagine what we would find inside.

As a child, I had once stumbled upon the scene of a butchering. An illegal one, for it was as forbidden to slaughter a healthy cow as it was to kill a human being. Cows were too precious to our farming kingdom. Careful to keep quiet, I'd watched the rogue strike the cow's head with a heavy iron hammer, and almost immediately, the creature had fallen over. In the next moment, the rogue had stripped the animal of its hide and had cut off its legs. What had terrified me most hadn't been the slaughtering, but the fact that throughout the brutal process, life had continued to hang on so desperately to the stumps quivering on the legless cow.

After climbing higher, there appeared a shed made of planks and logs, a thatch roof, and a brushwood door. The peasant's voice echoed ahead, and he was panting, "It was—it was this—this shed!"

Inspector Han crouched and observed the ground. "No hoofprints of the cow, but here are footprints, and the deep tracks in the mud suggest the men were carrying something heavy."

I joined the circle of officers gathered around Inspector Han, peering down to see the prints. Where the steps had halted was a large rectangular object printed into the mud.

"What do you think this print is, sir?" Officer Shim asked.

"It seems to be a palanquin."

"But a palanquin is not large enough to hold a cow," another officer said.

"But look here." Inspector Han pointed. "These vertical line prints look to be the handles."

The team studied the prints for moments longer, making room for the police artist, who began sketching the scene with charcoal. After a while, Inspector Han reached into his robe and pulled out a white handkerchief. Pressing it against his nose, he told me and the other officers to follow, then disappeared into the shed.

Not wanting to smell the stench either, I pressed my sleeve against my nose and stepped into the dark and drafty place. Blue light streamed in through the cracks between the plank walls, casting stripes of light onto the hay rotting beneath our steps. A few paces away reed blinds hung down from a wooden beam.

"There's something there," I whispered, seeing a shadow looming behind it.

Inspector Han moved the reed blinds aside with the hilt of his sword. Then he froze. "What?" he whispered.

I moved to see past him, and the moment I did, my legs buckled and I was sitting with my eyes locked onto a man hanging upside down, suspended midair by a rope tied around his ankle. I couldn't understand what I was staring at. A man, a dead man, hanging upside down.

"You said you saw a cow." Inspector Han's voice was flat and probing.

"I—I saw the shadow behind the blinds, and the s-s-smell," the peasant replied. "I thought surely a cow carcass. I've seen p-plenty of cow carcasses hanging, but never a human—" He never finished, running outside, and all we heard was him heaving out vomit.

An officer kicked down a plank with splintering force. An abundance of light poured into the shed. Someone gasped loudly; perhaps it was me. The corpse's wrists were tied. His nose was missing. And he looked familiar. He was hanging upside down, his face gray, so I couldn't say for sure—

My heart froze. "It's Scholar Ahn."

Total silence followed, then whispers of confusion. Inspector Han just stood there, staring.

Officer Shim frowned. Then he turned to the inspector and whispered, "So he is not the killer?"

"The bandits from Suwon," Inspector Han said in a subdued voice. "Do you have any information about them yet, Officer Shim?"

"No sighting of them, but a merchant said he'd seen an earless bandit before. He and the rest of the rogues caused trouble before in the Fox Mountain Pass, stealing from travelers. I had men comb through that area, but nothing."

Silence crept back in as we stared at the hanging corpse.

"Inspector . . . the nose," the legal clerk said. "Can this be connected to the first murder?"

"Perhaps."

"But why the nose?" Officer Shim leaned in closer to observe the cavity in the victim's face. "It reminds me of what occurred during the Imjin War."

"Go on," Inspector Han said.

"Hideyoshi wanted to take along with him the severed heads of our people, but there were simply too many. So he had their noses sliced off and pickled in salt instead. Maybe the killer took the noses of Ahn and O as a sort of memento. Much more portable and less suspicious than a head. And if that's the case, does it not mean he'll strike again? To collect more noses?"

"Hmm." Inspector Han did not sound convinced. "Or perhaps the severed nose is a kind of symbol."

"A symbol of what?"

"A symbol of the victim's guilt. Ui-hyung, a punishment in which the culprit's nose is cut off. Perhaps a mutilated nose is to the killer a justification for their death. To ease the killer's sense of shame."

The men nodded their heads, and I wondered what kind of killer this was. What kind of murderer understood shame?

Officer Shim tilted his head to the side as he frowned at the corpse. "But there is no sign of blood on him. No stab wounds. How did he die?"

"He drowned."

"How do you know, sir?" I could not stop myself from asking, and I hoped no one had heard the suspicion edging my voice.

"Look, there is froth at the mouth." Inspector Han took his white handkerchief and swabbed inside the mouth. "See this pinkish foam?" He raised the cloth to the stream of light. "It is tinged with blood."

The coroner's assistant approached. "Evidence of violent attempts to breathe," he added.

"But how could he have drowned when hung upside down?" Officer Shim asked.

"It's because he was upside down that his drowning was possible," Inspector Han explained. "Water would have been poured on his face, and with a constant stream, it would have effectually stopped his breathing."

Kyŏn, who stood in the shadows behind me, asked testily, "Might I ask how you know this, Inspector?"

Kyŏn and I were starting to sound eerily alike.

"It is a method of torture the aristocrats are known to use on servants, usually to obtain something—a confession, information, and so on," Inspector Han replied. "Less noisy than beating them." He paced around the corpse again, as though searching for other evidence. "Ahn and Lady O . . . they were lovers and shared secrets, which a third party wanted to know. Perhaps."

"It seems the young master was behind this all," Shim said. "He planned the Mount Hwa incident, and now this."

"Perhaps he was behind the Mount Hwa incident, but I am not so sure that he is the killer," the inspector replied. "He is not yet under house arrest, but I've had officers keep a close eye on him, and they claim he spent days in the House of Bright Flowers. It seems he is more distraught by Queen Regent Jeongsun's wrath than anything else."

I saw something twinkle in the blue light, winking at me from beneath the hay. I scrambled forward, right past Inspector Han, and picked up a necklace of lacquered brown beads. I might have mistaken it for one of those Buddhist rosaries, but the beads were smaller, and at the end hung a silver ornament like the one I'd seen hanging from Lady Kang's necklace. A cross shape.

The legal clerk snatched it from my hand and offered it to Inspector Han, who looked at it and swore under his breath. "The symbol worn by heretics."

"Catholics . . ." The legal clerk shook his head.

"I thought this was a case of a jealous lover." Officer Shim heaved out a sigh and ran a hand over his face. "Where do you begin to unravel this tangle?"

"At the beginning . . ." Inspector Han did well at hiding his feelings, by the stoic expression pinned to his face, by the silence that followed. Then he clicked his tongue and I realized he was afire with rage. His voice sank, and the words he uttered sounded as though they were being dragged through the mud of bitter defeat. "We will return to where it all began, and from there, we will find our way to the damn truth."

●

There was death under my nails. I had helped pull down the corpse, digging my fingers into Scholar Ahn's flesh, then used a knife to cut the rope. The corpse had thudded to the ground. Deep furrows marked his wrists and ankles, engraved by the restraints.

Rubbing my hand against my skirt, I walked quickly, jittering with the need to wash myself. Everyone, in fact, seemed eager to leave the shed, which now felt haunted with the mountain mist pouring in.

Inspector Han and a few officers remained at the scene of the crime, while the rest of us made our way back to the bureau, the corpse carried on a stretcher with a straw mat covering him from the prying eyes of passing pedestrians.

Kyŏn and another officer whispered ahead of me.

"Isn't it odd?" Kyŏn asked.

"What is?"

"You've read Ahn's letters to Lady O," Kyŏn said. The letters *I'd* found, the content of which Inspector Han had refused to share with me. I quickened my steps through the mud and puddles to hear better. "It was mostly them fighting, because O wanted to end their affair to join a 'Heretical Virgin Troupe.'"

"Virgin troupe," the other spat out. "Times are growing dark and *unnatural*. Why would a girl refuse her duty to marry and bear children?"

"Here is the odd thing," Kyŏn pressed. "How could Lady O join this virgin troupe if she wasn't a virgin?"

"Didn't you hear? Inspector Han said that in the letters, a man with the initials 'ZW' baptized her, then granted her absolution. And only one man in this heretical community is known to forgive sins. Priest Zhou Wenmo. As always, Inspector Han is a few steps ahead of you. You need to think quicker."

Kyŏn's prickly voice shot back in response, but I heard no more of this conversation. My mind withdrew, shuddering against the chill of new information. Were the deaths of Lady O and Scholar Ahn somehow connected to the most wanted criminal in our kingdom, the Catholic priest?

Why was this case becoming more tangled and hard to grasp? Why wasn't it getting any easier?

Right then, the straw mat shifted and I saw the gray face of Scholar Ahn, his eyes staring blankly up at the sky. I knew I'd never forget the sight.

●

The afternoon had grown cold, so the chief maid instructed me to light the ondol heating system of the main pavilion. She spoke with a tone of such casualness, as though nothing had happened this morning. As though I had not just returned from cutting down a hanging corpse.

Inside the under-floor furnace, a small space beneath the hanok structure, I crouched and fanned the flames. With enough kindling, the curls of woodsmoke would spread throughout the underground ducts and heat the stone plates laid under the floor of the building, warming the air inside as well. The fire crackled as I fanned, emphasizing the silence around me. A silence I did not want, for I kept thinking of the hanging corpse, his clouded eyes staring at me, as though he wanted to talk to me. *Who killed me? Why?*

A sound in the distance pulled me out of my thoughts, voices in the light rainfall.

I struggled out of the dark, cramped space and hid behind the beam that upheld the tiled pavilion roof, peering ahead. Officers, legal clerks, and servants stopped in their tracks to greet Commander Yi, who strode through the bowing crowd, seemingly oblivious to all, staring fixedly at the ground with his brows slammed low over his eyes. Behind him followed Officer Kyŏn.

A few steps more, then Commander Yi stopped and turned to address Kyŏn. "Clear yourself from my sight, and do not appear before me again until you have solid evidence," the commander said in a voice so low it was almost a whisper. "Do not make a single mistake."

The hairs on my skin rose, sensing that trouble was around the corner, and Kyŏn knew exactly what it was.

Once Kyŏn was alone, he rolled his shoulder once as he stalked across the courtyard like a predator about to pounce on his prey. I followed him, quickening my pace to catch up, until I was near enough to call out, "Officer!"

He paused in his step. A snarl slid into his voice. "Good afternoon, Damo Seol."

We stood alone in the narrow alley, the space that connected two courtyards. His lips stretched over his teeth into a grin, angry and sharp like fish bones. "So it has to come to this. My hyung is dead"—he took a step toward me, backing me up against the wall—"and you and I, I think we both know who killed him."

A pang of guilt hit my heart. Misu's terrified eyes watched me, her confession yawning around me like the grave. *She is dead, she is dead.* But Kyŏn was the last person I could trust with her testimony.

"I don't know what you're talking about," I said, keeping my expression blank.

"I think you do, and that is why you came after me." He tilted my chin up with his finger, his eyes peeling away my mask. "All I see is a face clouded with suspicion."

I jerked my chin away and slid along the wall until I was a few steps away from him. "What did Commander Yi mean by solid evidence?" I asked.

"Commander Yi wanted to know what I knew."

"Because you were close to Scholar Ahn."

"That, and because he took my suspicion seriously. When he read the letter, he could have dismissed me to cover up Inspector Han's sin, but instead he only punished me for breaking into the inspector's office. Cut my monthly stipend, he did, and that was it. The letter confirmed Inspector Han's guilt."

"What letter?"

"The letter you watched me steal nearly two weeks ago." Kyŏn closed the space between us again, making me feel his full towering height. "Whatever you know, you will tell me. Then I'll tell you everything you want to know. Or you can keep silent like a coward, and you will bear the weight of responsibility for the next person who dies. You're only sixteen, Seol, far too young to make important decisions. Just do as you are told." He tapped my chin, twice. "Think about it."

Once I was alone, I looked down at my fingernails, which had dug into Scholar Ahn's waxy skin. And Lady O's as well. Wind rolled through the narrow alley, laced with rain. Goose bumps rose as the breeze slithered up my skin. I didn't want to side with Kyŏn. I wanted nothing more to do with this investigation. But I knew too much now. The ghosts of the murdered returned, whispering into my ears, *There is no one but you.*

FOURTEEN

TWO WEEKS PASSED. As the rainy season stretched into autumn, when it ought to have ended long ago, and rumors overflowed that nature had lost its rhythm because a woman was regent, something peculiar began. I'd wake up drenched in sweat, dreaming of the dead again. The mountainous heap of burnt servants, the siblings starved into twigs and left to rot in the storage hut, the corpse sleeping under the bush . . . All Catholics. And last night, the woman who had visited my dreams most had turned her head to stare right at me, locking her eyes on mine.

Come find me, Lady O had called out in a singsong voice. *Come quick.*

All day I roamed the bureau with my skin pebbling at the thought that the time had come: I had to face Commander Yi. He needed to know the truth. But even though I knew this was the right thing to do, fear wrapped its icy fingers around me, its grip so strong that tears welled in my eyes. The *what-if* question would not let me go. What if—though I was certain this was not true—but what if Inspector Han and I were tied by blood? I wondered if I would still throw him into a den of hungry tigers, to be devoured in the name of justice.

My answer only a few months ago would have been no. But I had seen the puckering knife wound across a daughter's throat, a man flipped upside down and drowned. I was a hundred times less naive now, a hundred times less forgiving.

And of one thing I was certain: Older Brother had always told me, in a very stern voice, that it was better to die young than to live long and cause trouble. He would not have wished me to let him live the life of a killer.

I shook my head, unable to believe myself. Here I was brooding over a possibility that was not even based on a speck of hard evidence but my own imagination. There was only one sure truth: Inspector Han's alibi was a lie, and whatever had occurred on the night of the twenty-first had left him bloody and stammering in shock about a dead woman.

It was wicked and cowardly of me to keep silent. And should another victim die, all the guilt would be on my shoulders.

Gathering my thoughts on the dirt floor, I tried to spell out a question: *Will Commander Yi believe me?*

I erased it and tried again, for I sometimes got confused with certain letters. But besides the occasional mistake, brushstrokes no longer mystified me. Every night, too worried to sleep, I had rolled off my mat to study the Hangul chart by candlelight, recalling Aejung's teachings. The consonants were based on the drawing of one's mouth when pronouncing a sound. Whenever I wrote a character, I imagined dipping a calligraphy brush into ink and then following my voice as it curved off my tongue and hit my palate, or bounced off the front of my inner teeth, or circled around my throat, or hummed against my touching lips.

As for the vowels, they were easy to differentiate, created by three types of strokes: a horizontal line for the flat *earth*, a dot for the *sun* in the heavens, and a vertical line for the upright *human*.

Earth, sun, human. This was what made life, a simple sum of three. Yet life was not simple at all. It was a complicated web, a tangling thread of lies and deceit. I wondered, though, what the truth would look like if I followed the thread all the way to the heart of Inspector Han. Would the truth lying at the center of his being be as simple, a motivation rooted in the three most common causes for murder: lust, greed, or vengeance?

Tell Commander Yi, I wrote in the dirt.

A shadow stretched over me, as though a storm cloud had swept in, followed by a familiar voice. "How curious, a servant who knows how to write."

It was Young Master Ch'oi Jinyeop. His presence intensified the isolation of the kitchen backyard. His steps were heavy as he walked around, and I kept my eyes fixed on his shadow, growing larger and larger until at last the silk of his robe appeared in my periphery. He reached down and picked up a stray stick. Thinking he would strike me, I flinched.

"*Yi*, not *yeuh*," he said. "Your last stroke is wrong." With a flick of his wrist he corrected it, then threw the stick aside. I waited for him to walk off, but instead, he crouched so close to me that his quiet laugh moved the tendrils of my hair. "I see goose bumps along your neck. Are you frightened of me, young one?"

My muscles tensed.

"Perhaps you ought to be frightened, indeed. I might be the killer. Perhaps I did send the bandits after the inspector." He leaned even closer, and as he whispered, I caught the scent of alcohol on his breath. "I did indeed want to know who Lady O's lover was, and I did indeed want to punish him for humiliating me. What is your opinion? Am I the murderer?"

I dared to look at him, and what I saw took the fear away from me. I did not see a superior of mine whom I was helpless before, but a young man who needed to trample over others to feel better about himself. My lips parted, a thought sparking into a flame, and I had to look away to hide the beams of light in my eyes. He was not the real son, but rather a mere nephew adopted by Lord Ch'oi for no other reason than to fill the spot of a missing heir. The young master would be a man who'd have nothing but his title to guard his pride.

"Would Scholar Ahn's death have restored your reputation, sir?" I asked.

"Not at all."

Motives. I had no idea what Inspector Han's motive was, but the young master's was as clear as day. Perhaps he had indeed sent out the bandits, yet neither Lady O's nor Scholar Ahn's death seemed in his character to carry out. "You would have wanted Scholar Ahn alive, sir. Lady O, too. You would have wanted the entire kingdom to witness their public humiliation."

"It is true what they say . . . you are too clever for a servant. Too well-spoken."

I kept quiet. I didn't want to tell him about Older Sister, about how her suspiciously well-educated mind had rubbed off on me. I didn't want this young noble to know anything about my family.

"The missing nose has inspired a thought in me," he said. "Perhaps we are all being duped by someone very near to us. I'd very much like to know who the killer is." The roguish amusement dropped from his face, and a solemn young man watched me, annoyance gleaming in his eyes. "I was fooled once and shan't be fooled again. Tell your inspector this: follow the trail of shame."

My brows crinkled, not understanding.

"Do you know what shame does to a man?" he asked. "He becomes desperate to justify his guilt. He will slice off the noses of victims to remind himself and the world that they deserved to die." The young master stood up and straightened his black gauze hat. "There is one lesson all who enter the capital will learn: evil comes from the unfulfilled need for significance."

Before he could leave, I startled to my feet, unable to hold down my curiosity. "Why have you confided in one such as I?"

"Why, don't you know?" He looked at me and arched a single brow. "Everyone here in the bureau is too quick to judge, and it will end in the death of someone innocent. But you, you are an eavesdropper. The only person in this bureau who truly listens."

●

My nails were craggy and bleeding by the afternoon. I could not stop tearing off little corners, my mind tormented. Once Commander Yi heard my story, would he investigate thoroughly? Or would he be quick to execute Inspector Han?

I hid behind one of the pillars surrounding the main pavilion, a spot I often frequented these days. I watched Lord Seo of the Ministry of Punishment stalking away, clucking his tongue as he surveyed the police bureau. "Such incompetence," he muttered. "Absolutely incompetent." Nearby, Commander Yi stood still, yet his jaw was set, clenching back a violent emotion. He looked like an old man beaten by fierce gales.

"Commander Yi, I must make a confession," I recited under my breath. "I cannot hide it any longer. I must make a confession."

There was no more time for indecision. After a few moments, I pushed away from the pillar and hurried toward the sliding doors of the main pavilion, through which Commander Yi had retreated. How would he react to my words? I had not the faintest idea. My heart pounded loud in my ears and my uniform clung to my perspiring body. I clasped my hands together, preparing to prostrate myself before him.

Then an inhuman force snatched me back, away from what felt like the cliff's edge.

Are you completely certain? came my sister's voice, carried on the breeze. *Such recklessness. What if this inspector is your orabeoni? Will you be your brother's killer? For the commander will kill him, indeed.*

I shook my head, trying to clear out the whispers. I refused the possibility of having to carry the guilt of another murder victim, all because of my silence. Only the commander could stop the killer. He had the authority, the means, the intelligence. But with each step, I felt the weight of my sister's words, the weight of my hesitation.

"I found it!" Officer Goh cried as he came running into the bureau. "I found it!"

The sound of his voice froze me. Other officers hurried into the courtyard, blocking my path. With a crowd now gathered, so close to the pavilion, I lost my courage to face Commander Yi. One only needed to press their ear against the hanji screens to know that Damo Seol was a traitor, a servant handing her master over.

Another time, relief assured me. *There is no need to tell him today.*

After the trembling in me settled, I made my way over to Officer Goh, wondering what he had discovered. Peering past the other officers, I saw in Goh's hand a mud-covered wooden object.

"I found the missing ornament from Lady O's necklace," Officer Goh said, panting. "Look here, there is a hole at the top of this wooden pendant. It must be where the necklace string slipped through."

"Where did you find it?" Hyeyeon moved closer, her shoulder knocking into mine in the process. It was as though she had not seen me, though she clearly had.

"The area between Mount Nam and the South Gate."

She crossed her arms and arched her brow. "Who can say it was from the string we found in Lady O's hand? What if some random necklace broke during the past few weeks?"

Silence fell, watchful gazes turned in one direction. I looked to see Senior Officer Shim striding over. Everyone parted for him, heads bowed. He had lost more weight over the weeks, all bones tightly roped in muscle. He was the scrawny street dog that was always alert, flinching at sudden movements or sounds.

"What is all this commotion?" he asked.

Officer Goh stepped forward and reported his discovery. As Shim inspected the wooden pendant, I watched him carefully.

"Hmm." Shim used his thumb to break off the mud encrusting it, and then he fell still, so still that the crowd exchanged glances. "A horse-dragon pendant . . ."

"And what is the significance behind it, sir?" My voice cracked as I spoke, dry from disuse. I'd tried to keep quiet when among those close to Inspector Han, like a cat hoping she wouldn't be seen in the shadows, but this time my curiosity was slicing sharp. Would Shim try to dismiss the possible evidence? "For example, sir, the cross pendant signifies Catholicism."

"There is only one story behind the horse-dragon," Shim replied, unable to look away from the object. "It is a myth called the Agijangsu, The 'Mighty Infant.'"

"What is this myth about—" But before I could finish, Hyeyeon cut me off.

"Do you think this is evidence, sir? A month has passed since the murder, and thousands of people have trod the area around the South Gate."

Shim finally lifted his gaze, eyes red-rimmed and uncertain. At first, he seemed unable to speak. "It may be evidence," he said at length, his voice barely a whisper. "Take it away."

Commander Yi was occupied in the examination room, studying the horse-dragon ornament. It was not a good time to speak to him, I felt. Or perhaps this was another excuse to avoid the storm ahead. The wrath of the entire police bureau would be upon me, not just the commander's. They would call me the meddler, the girl who had recklessly ruined the inspector's life, and the other damos would spit into my drink before serving it to me.

Was I making a horrible mistake? Would I regret exposing Inspector Han? If only someone could tell me.

I took out Aejung's incense sticks, lighting each one. Smoke slowly curled into the air as I prostrated myself. One kowtow, two kowtow, three kowtow. By the hundredth time my knees hit the floor, sweat dripped into my eyes, and the sounds of my breathing and the showering rain were all that filled the shadowy servants' quarter.

I did not know to whom I was praying, or if my pleas had any weight, for I had no altar and no temple. But I continued. Hundred one kowtow, hundred two, hundred three . . .

My prayer rose silently from my lips. *If you want to protect Inspector Han, this is your last chance to stop me.*

Afterward, I lay on the bare floor, my knees throbbing. I watched the cloud of incense and wondered whose ears my prayers had reached, if the heavens even cared. Then I lifted my head, just a bit, as an unexpected image moved in the corner of my mind. Lady Kang and her tobacco.

I scrambled up to my feet. Suddenly, I could sense it—a deep knowledge—that she would help me out of the wilderness. The gods might ignore me, but she would not.

•

I donned my straw hat, wrapped myself in a straw cloak, and stepped out. Wet wind spit against me as I journeyed north. Mud splashed onto my skirt, brown speckles against gray cotton. I shouldered my way past the sparse crowd of mostly bareheaded peasants, then reached the outskirt of the Northern District. The weight of the rain pounding down on my hat eased up as I stepped into the shelter of the roofed gate.

I knocked on the door, waited, then knocked two more times. At last the door creaked open, revealing a pale-faced gatekeeper.

"I wish for private audience with Lady Kang," I said.

"*What?*"

The rain had drowned out my voice, so, loudly this time, I repeated, "I wish for private audience with Lady Kang! Tell her that my name is Seol!"

Soon I was following a servant through interlinking courtyards until we arrived before the main pavilion. The maid announced me in. The chamber was shadowy and dry, making me realize how drenched I was—my face, my sleeves, half my skirt. The gusting rain creaked the hanji-screened windows.

Lady Kang untied her gentleman's hat and placed it down on the low-legged table before her. Damp strands of her hair clung to her temple like dark seaweed washed onto the beach. I must have arrived at the mansion shortly after her return from some journey, dressed as a man like the first time we'd met. Perhaps transporting illegal books again?

"It has been so long since I last saw you, Seol."

"More than a month, mistress," I replied.

"I heard of Scholar Ahn's death."

I licked my lips, unnerved by the memory of the drowned man. "He was murdered."

"Was it the same killer, do you think?"

I bowed my head. The killer was still out there, his eyes fixed on the next target, and there was no one around me who could answer my questions—except perhaps for Lady Kang. There was no time for me to hesitate.

"I know you are . . ." I swallowed, then forced out the word, "*Catholic*."

The corner of her lips flinched. "You say the word 'Catholic' as one might say the word 'traitor.'"

"Begging your pardon, mistress," I whispered, my pulse hammering.

"It is not a secret. No need to look so frightened. I was imprisoned during the roundup of Catholics in 1791 but was soon released. After divorcing my husband, I moved here to Hanyang and began leading the Heretical Virgin Troupe. Another scandal. So you see, it is hard to keep my faith a secret."

Heretical Virgin Troupe. I didn't realize I was holding my breath until Lady Kang said, "Your face is red. And your lips are twitching, like you have more to say. What is it?"

"In a letter, Lady O expressed her desire to join this troupe. So you must have been close to her. Very close." My back stiffened as I rushed to add, "I won't tell anyone about this connection."

She laid her elbow on the table, and her eyes watched me with a shocking stillness. "I trust you. I do not wish to be involved in the investigation, Seol. I have enough troubles to keep me up at night."

"I understand . . ." I took in a deep, calming breath. "Mistress, do all Catholics wear a cross pendant?"

She withdrew her necklace. Hanging from the beaded string was a silver figure of a half-naked man pinned to a cross. "Not all wear this," she said. "But I wear it to remind myself that knowledge demands change. I cannot live as I used to live now that I have discovered the sacrificial love of our Heavenly Father."

"Scholar Ahn wore it. Do you know whether he was Catholic, mistress?"

"I saw him several times at Catholic gatherings. Sometimes I wondered if he had joined simply to be closer to Lady O, for he seemed disinterested in the teachings and was always stealing glances her way. But one day I noticed him treating Lady O with such coldness, and after that, he stopped attending the gatherings. So I was much surprised when I heard, quite recently, that he was Lady O's lover. *This* I did not know."

My brows furrowed as I tried to piece things together. If Scholar Ahn had used Catholicism to remain close to Lady O, and perhaps to even regain her trust after abandoning her for over a year, then Lady O might have confided in him about the priest—what he looked like, where he was hiding. Then, when Scholar Ahn had learned of her decision to join the Heretical Virgin Troupe, to end their affair, he must have exposed her secret Catholic belief and her ties with Priest Zhou Wenmo. A thought seized my mind. *It is the priest. The priest is the killer's main target.*

"Have you ever caught a glimpse of Priest Zhou Wenmo before?" I asked.

Her gaze flinched away from me as she slipped the necklace back into her robe. "I have not. Why do you ask?"

"The priest can roam our kingdom and no one would know, for I hear he looks like a Joseon person, speaks our language, and the police do not know what he looks like. But if the police caught him—say, someone like Inspector Han—the priest would surely be executed for spreading Catholicism, would he not?"

"Priest Zhou Wenmo is a subject of China, and so to kill him would be a terrible violation of our vassal relationship. Once he is caught, the police will deport him."

A sinking pit opened in my stomach. I had imagined a motive for all the suspects except for Inspector Han. But now I wondered, was Inspector Han searching for the priest in secret because he refused to deport the heretic and wanted to kill him instead? But *why*?

"This inspector of yours," Lady Kang said, raising an eyebrow. "I see you are concerned about him."

My breath quickened. "Neh?"

"It is odd. Why are you so involved in the case of Lady O's death?"

My lips opened and closed as I tried to figure out how to answer. I rubbed my hands down my skirt. At last, staring at the floor, I whispered, "I fear him, and I fear what he is capable of."

She slowly nodded her head, giving me a silent look, as though she had decided on something. "You, most of all, should fear what he would be willing to do to you."

I frowned up at her, and I remembered her warning, about the darkness that would fall upon me. Perhaps she had indeed seen into my future, or perhaps she had seen the sparks of trouble in my character. Overly curious. Cunning. Disobedient.

"How much shall I tell you about Inspector Han Dohyun?" she asked.

"Everything," I answered quickly. "Everything you know, mistress."

Silence filled the space. I had to remind myself to keep breathing.

"Inspector Han's father was executed for being a Catholic."

I blinked. This was my first time hearing this.

"After the execution, his entire family was banished to an island, guilty by association. They were stripped of their status and left to be slaves. But the late king shortened the banishment from ten years to three, and according to what Inspector Han shared with everyone, when the banishment was lifted, only he returned alive from the island. From which island, I do not know. Later, the inspector's distant uncle adopted him with much reluctance. Inspector Han's status as an aristocrat was also reinstated. Of course, this was only possible because the uncle was from his mother's side."

"You mean Lord Han, his uncle."

"Precisely. Your inspector severed his legal relationship with his father and took on Lord Han's surname."

"How do you know of all this?" I asked.

"I heard about the execution all the way in Tŏksan, my hometown. And when I came to the capital, I asked what had happened to the martyr's family. That is when I learned about Inspector Han's history."

Inspector Han had a Catholic past . . . This made his connection to the killing even stronger.

Now I knew why Officer Kyŏn seemed to think he could prove the inspector's guilt, and why Commander Yi had not rebuked Kyŏn's suspicion. Inspector Han had all the motive to avenge his family by killing a foreign priest, even if it meant angering China. "I never knew this . . ."

"No one likes talking about it. His past is as unspoken of as his own home—the one his family lived in before his father was executed. The new owner of it does not live there. He says it is haunted by the ghost of the original owner, Scholar Jeong."

The hair rose on my skin. *Jeong.* I mentally shook my head. Jeong was also my surname, but surely it was a common one. Another coincidence. I pressed my fingers into my eyes, trying to stop all the *what-if* questions from resurfacing.

Jeong Jeong-yun. That was my true name before Older Sister had changed my first name to Seol and had ordered me to never use our last name. All this she had done to protect me from our past. But she had never explained why we had to hide. "What past? What happened?" I'd ask, and she would only shake her head and walk away.

I also knew this: my surname Jeong meant loyalty, and the first word in my given name, Jeong-yun, also meant loyalty.

Jeong Jeong-yun! Older Brother's voice called out to me from a faraway memory in a teasing, loving voice. *Jeong Jeong-yun, what a girl full of loyalty.*

FIFTEEN

IT WAS RAINING still.

When I was a child, I would have found any excuse to run outside, to laugh and shake in the falling blue rain. But now my heart lay frozen in my chest as I stared at the paper-screened door, watching the sky turn from black to gray.

Jeong, Jeong, Jeong. The name from my past circled around my mind the way flies swarmed a carcass, attracted to the smell of death. Death was all there was in my past—the death of my given name, the death of my mother on the island of banishment.

Just like Inspector Han's family, my family had also been banished for ten years, which had been shortened to three years.

The coincidences left me nauseous, and there were too many similarities now to ignore.

Yesterday, after leaving Lady Kang, I'd asked Woorim to be my guide to Inspector Han's old house, and if she had not forgotten our agreement, she would be waiting for me outside Lady Kang's mansion gate.

My curiosity overwhelmed me in such a way that I felt out of control. I could not walk without colliding into walls. I could not will my hands to work. And so I stumbled out of the bureau with my uniform loose—not tightened with a sash belt—and my hair unplaited, hanging down the sides of my face.

In such a manner, I made my way to the mansion. It was like any other day, yet so different. Nothing seemed real anymore. Nothing made sense.

As Woorim had promised, she was waiting for me outside the

gate, rubbing her hands together against the early morning chill. The moment she saw me, her tiny lips popped open and she came running, her braided hair swinging from side to side. "You came at last. Are you frightened?"

I could only stare at her. *I'm terrified.*

"When I was younger, I would wander through the forest at night with my siblings and share ghost stories," she said, excitement animating her whisper. "My heart would race and all the hairs on my skin would rise! Then we would run home screaming. And now to go visit a haunted mansion this early in the morning? It is when spirits are most awake."

"I'm sure it is not haunted."

"Oh, but it is. All who enter that house start shivering, as though stepping into an icehouse."

We traveled together through the rain and the sleeping streets, wearing our straw cloaks and wooden clogs. She chatted on, but my thoughts were elsewhere. I remembered the first day I'd met Inspector Han. When I had first entered the police bureau, thrown before his feet, I'd heard his voice high above me ask, "Have we met before?"

I had looked him straight in the face, and on seeing a stranger, I'd ducked my head low again. "I'm sorry, sir. I do not think so." He had never asked that question again, likely thinking himself mistaken.

But now I wondered . . . *had* we met before?

Woorim and I kept close to the patterned stone walls lining the narrow dirt street the mansion was on, and the street rose with the upward slope of the land, the steepness dragging the breath out of us. We arrived at the end of the Northern District, and there stood before us a lonely mansion with a wooden gate covered in white bands of paper, charms sold by shamans to ward off evil spirits. A pigeon perched on the eaves of the gate, beady eyes staring down at us. *Coo-coo,* it sang, *coo-coo.*

Woorim walked over and shook the brass handle of the gate. "It's still locked. And I hear there are planks nailed to the other side of the gate to bar entry."

"How do you know this?"

"Yesterday, as I was passing by this side of the district, I thought to take a peek inside the mansion, but a stranger caught me trying to enter," she said, and when I frowned at her, she offered me an apologetic smile. "I didn't get in trouble, though. I *thought* I would, so I made up a tragic tale about a long-lost family member, and about family ghosts within that we needed to visit tomorrow as part of our ancestral worship, and he must have sympathized."

"What do you mean?"

"He said the only way in would be to climb the wall, but we can't do *that.*"

We had no choice. I took three steps back, then ran, grabbing hold of the lower point between the gate and the wall surrounding the compound. I used my elbows to lift myself higher and higher until I managed to hook my knee over the tiles, straddling the lower wall.

"This is madness!" Woorim whispered, but nevertheless she followed me into the compound, biting back a smile.

There was indeed no one living here. The place was a graveyard of cobwebs and weeds. The paper-screened doors lining the hanok building were torn, and some of the frames hung from hinges, punched down by the wind, perhaps.

A shadow haunted the extreme corner of my eyes, and I turned.

An old pine tree stood in the corner of the courtyard, bent into the shape of a river. I took a stumbling step back as a memory passed through me. I had seen this tree before, an old friend from another lifetime, a stranger and yet familiar.

"This is likely the most haunted mansion in this district." Woorim walked ahead, climbing onto the veranda, which creaked beneath her steps. She craned her head back to look around. "A place filled with so much *han*."

Han. This word meant many things—unresolved resentment, helplessness, acute pain, the urge to take revenge—and these many things were expressed within one word. *Han.*

Woorim spoke on. "The inspector's father was a Confucian scholar but was also a Catholic. After he was executed for possessing Western literature, his head was raised on a stick for days, guarded day and night so that no one could take it off."

"How do you know this?" I whispered.

"I heard the mistress telling you about the gentleman. So later, I begged her for details. She was reluctant at first."

"What more did she tell you?"

"When Inspector Han was a boy, he tried to bury his father's body, but the magistrate ordered the corpse to be taken and laid out in the open. After that, his entire family was banished."

I followed Woorim into the shadowy mansion, ripped wallpaper fluttering in the wind.

"None of his banished family but himself survived," Woorim continued. "His mother committed suicide because she hated all the accusations. People called her a Catholic demon. And as for his siblings, I heard they were taken as servants, but then they all died when a plague swept through the household."

A plague. I had barely escaped it before. Sister had voluntarily offered us to become nobi servants to the Nam household. There had been no other way to escape our crushing poverty, for the exile had

stripped us of our status, respect, and fortune. But the Nams had later
been forced into quarantine, for our master's daughter and a few servants had caught the illness. Young Lady Euna had turned blue in the
face, her skin shriveling, her eye sockets collapsing. Dead the next day.
That night, Older Sister had dragged me out from my sleep, and we
had run from the men posted around the residence to keep us within.

"Perhaps we will encounter their spirits here," Woorim whispered. "The ghosts of the inspector's dead siblings." She continued
to tell me about ghosts, and her voice sounded so far away, growing
fainter by the passing moment.

Look-look, the pigeon called out to me, *look-look.*

I turned and gazed out through the broken door into the courtyard, at the old pine tree. There was no one standing beneath it. And
yet there was someone: a woman. Her presence tugged at the stories
Older Brother had told me, and as though I'd stepped into one of
them, I could feel myself small enough to be held, lying in the arms of
the woman under the tree, staring up at the uncomfortable bright light
glaring down through green needles. The tree swayed, and I closed my
eyes. I caught the smell of fresh pine in the mountain breeze.

The smell of home.

A thunderbolt struck my core. This wasn't a scent that rose from
Brother's tales of our past, but I knew, deep down, that this memory belonged to me. Only me. Stunned into a deep trance, I floated
through the hall and out into the courtyard. I floated over the mansion wall and landed somehow. I felt more like a spirit than a body
until Woorim grabbed and shook me, her voice breaking into my
trance.

"Did you see him? Did you see the ghost?"

I think I said, "You need to go home, Woorim." Then my
knees buckled and the next thing I knew, I was holding my head,

locking my arms over it so that no one could intrude on my roiling thoughts.

"You saw something." Woorim crouched before me. "Don't worry. I am here with you. Open your eyes and look at me."

I opened my eyes, and at first all I saw was Woorim's face—round and kind. Then I saw a shadowy figure behind her. He wore a black robe. The lower half of his face was covered by a scarf. A bamboo hat shaded the remainder of his countenance.

"Behind," I whispered, panic creeping into me. "Behind you."

●

Woorim and I stood with our backs against the wall outside the mansion, holding hands.

"W-what do you want?" she stammered.

The stranger remained still and silent like a corpse.

"A-are you lost, sir?"

I could not see his eyes, but his head was turned toward Woorim. I heard myself wheezing, thinking of the stories about the man in the bamboo hat who had lured Lady O and Scholar Ahn to their deaths. My lungs filled with fear. No, surely not the same man. Thousands of men in our kingdom wore bamboo hats and black robes.

Taking a deep breath, I stood in front of Woorim, dread trickling into my chest and dripping into my stomach. My voice sounded braver than I felt. "You heard her. Go away. Leave us—"

His fist hammered into my chest. My head snapped back into the wall. Stars exploded in front of my eyes. Someone was whimpering. I blinked until my vision cleared and I found myself writhing on the ground, clutching my chest.

"No," came Woorim's quivering voice. "P-please no!"

I could not move, my limbs locked by white-hot pain; all I could see was what was before me. Woorim's skirt flapping around her ankles, her feet resisting the forward tug. Why was he taking Woorim and not me? This question flitted by, weightless compared to the desperation balled up in my throat.

"Help," was all I managed to say, barely a whisper. "H-help." This was a neighborhood of many ears. Rescue could not be far.

But no one came to help, and the stranger dragged Woorim far out of my periphery. Her distant voice continued begging, "No! Oh please, no-no-no!"

Her terror willed my legs to move. I rose and steadied myself against the wall.

The stranger had grabbed Woorim's hair, now wrenching her down the street as she half stumbled and half crawled on her knees. "No-no-no," she kept stammering, and then she saw something at the corner of the street that I could not see, for she began shaking her head furiously. "A p-palanquin? No! Don't put me in there! Please!"

In a desperate attempt, she pulled his wrist down and bit into it. Then she was on her feet again, running toward me. Just like when I had first seen her today, her braided hair swinging from side to side, her tiny lips calling out my name.

It all happened too quickly. One moment she was reaching out for me, the next moment I heard a *whoosh* noise as she went hurtling into the stone wall lining the street. There was the loudest thud, an impact so strong I thought I'd heard the cracking of her skull, the snapping of her bones. Then Woorim dropped and lay on the ground, mouth open, eyes staring at me. It came slowly, a stream of blood down from her temple, then all at once, pooling on the ground below her. Sticky blood glistened in her hair as she struggled and crawled toward me. She looked shocked. We were both shocked. We had only meant for this to be a simple excursion to a haunted mansion.

Footsteps echoed in the distance. Pedestrians. The man in the bamboo hat stared at me for a lingering moment, and then his out-stretched fingers seized Woorim's hair again. The veins in her forehead protruded, her eyes reddened as she grabbed both my hands. "Seol, please help me!"

I clutched tightly, and the more desperately I clung, the more the throbbing pain along my ribs and head intensified. And then she slipped away, leaving my hands empty. He dragged her for ten, fifteen, twenty paces. At the end of the stone walls, where the street branched out into different directions, they both vanished around the corner.

Woorim. Clenching my teeth, I lurched onto my feet again and staggered forward, my breath rushing in and out of me. Why was she so silent now? What was happening beyond this street, around the dark corner? I drew closer to it, then stopped.

"All done, sir," a male voice rasped, somewhere deep in the shad-ows. "I've secured her."

I took a step back, slack-jawed. There was more than one man in the alley, and even Bamboo Hat was already too strong for me. His fist had struck me like an iron ball hurled at my heart. I needed help, but when I listened over my shoulder, the neighborhood was silent. The footsteps I'd heard earlier had disappeared.

My skin prickled. Someone was watching me. Time slowed into a heavy twisting as I faced ahead and saw Bamboo Hat. Light gleamed from his hand.

A dagger, its blade reflecting flashes of red through my mind.

"H-help," my voice cracked. "Help, s-someone."

My knees wobbled in my attempt to run, and instead of a mighty sprint forward, I staggered and crawled in turns. *Pathetic,* a voice whispered. *This is how you'll die. Butchered alive.* Tears sprang to my eyes as I felt the shadow of death closing in on me. My skirt tangled around my stumbling feet, and gravity slammed me onto the road, knocking my breath out and scraping skin off. *Over, it is over.* I curled into a ball as his footsteps crunched behind me, growing louder.

Hands over head, coiling myself tighter, I braced myself.

Seol-ah.

My eyes were squeezed shut, but at the sound of the familiar voice, I blinked into the darkness of my shell. *Seol-ah, everyone dies,* Lady Kang reminded me. *What is difficult is a meaningful death.*

Her words flipped through pages of memories, of Woorim's eyes, lighting up as she gossiped, her colorful voice brimming with enthusiasm, with life. Woorim the first time we'd met, her waiting before the police bureau. *Sst.* Our eyes had met, and she had smiled, a warm hand of friendship extended.

This was all I'd needed. This was enough.

My fingers curled, digging into the ground, filling my palm. If I was going to die, then I would die without shame. The moment his footsteps were right behind me, I whipped myself around and flung out my hand. Dirt and pebbles sprayed at him, and I rushed to my feet again, running this time the way I'd raced the village boys: chin up, fingers arrow straight, the balls of my feet bouncing off the ground. A quick glance behind and I saw the man on all fours, his back turned, scrambling to tie the scarf back onto his face.

This was my last chance.

I dashed down paths, cutting through alleys, and unable to stop in time, slammed into the gate of Lady Kang's mansion. I clung to the door, waiting out the burning throb that pulsed throughout my body. At last I managed to collect myself. "Lady Kang!" I choked out, banging on the door. "Lady Kang!" I squeezed my eyes shut, and I couldn't unsee Woorim being dragged away by the hair, like she was nothing more than a slab of meat. Who could be this cruel? This *evil*?

A voice behind the door called out, "On my way!"

Hope flared up with an intensity that left me trembling. Lady Kang would help, she'd send forth an army of servants to rescue her. Woorim might live! I raised my fist to knock again—*faster, run faster, ajusshi!*—but my wrist caught onto something and would not budge. Someone's hand tightened around mine, and I froze in alarm, staring wide-eyed as the gate creaked open.

"Wh-what is happening here?" the gatekeeper asked.

"Return inside, ajusshi." It was a woman's voice coming from behind me, cold and commanding, and all too familiar. "You saw nothing."

"Yes, of c-c-course, of course."

The door shut at once, and from beyond, I could hear the thudding of wood as the gatekeeper locked the entrance with a beam. The hope I'd felt blew out, throwing me into darkness.

"I was right," the woman behind me spoke again. And this time I knew who it was. "You cannot be trusted."

My wrist thrown aside, I whirled around to see Hyeyeon, her expression so stoic that I would not have guessed her thoughts if not for the upward tilt of her chin, the unfriendly glint in her eyes as she stared up at me. Now I noticed her civilian dress, the uniform of a damo when out tracking criminals. The pedestrians behind her, lingering in the shadow of an alley, were not commoners at all, but familiar faces, officers also disguised. Their brows knitted, staring at me as one would a traitor—with anger, mixed with jolts of disbelief.

"You are spying on Lady Kang." My voice shook, the air around me suddenly wintry cold. "Why?"

"It is none of your business. Come, I'm taking you back to the bureau."

"*No*. You must release me. One of Lady Kang's servants was abducted, and I need to find her!"

Hyeyeon surveyed me with indifference, then flicked her chin forward, a gesture for me to walk. "You can go tell him yourself."

"Whom?"

"Inspector Han," she whispered, and I could hear the smile in her voice. "The one you would die for."

●

There was stillness in the early morning hour. The air was cold and moist with dew.

Guards holding sharp-tipped spears stepped aside, opening the gates of the bureau. An officer shoved me forward, his push so strong my head snapped back as I stumbled into the police courtyard, nearly tripping over my feet. Servants and officers stopped what they were doing to stare, their gazes following me, along with their whispers. *She tried to run home again? When will she learn?* Blood oozed down the back of my head, soaking my collar as I returned their stares.

"*Eoseo!*" Hyeyeon said, her voice a sharp slap.

I quickened my steps as ordered, through the connecting gate and into the western courtyard. The Office of the Inspector looked immense, like a dragon whose belly had swelled from devouring its kill. I let out my breath slowly, the sound of wind whistling through the bamboo trees. "Calm down," I whispered. Another deep breath, and I blew out through my lips. "Calm down."

But my hands still trembled, still ached with the memory of Woorim's hand in mine. She had disappeared, and with each passing minute, I was losing all chance of ever finding her.

Grabbing my collar, Hyeyeon dragged me up onto the veranda. We were alone, just the two of us, as the police officers had remained in the main courtyard. "Sir," she spoke to the screened door. "I am here to report an incident."

"Enter."

She pushed aside the door, which rumbled as it went. And I realized there was only one way that I could escape in time, only one way to run back at once to Lady Kang for help—pretend to submit. I licked my blood-crusted lips and ducked my head.

"Kneel," Hyeyeon ordered.

My knees buckled and slammed onto the ground with such a thud that Inspector Han glanced up, startled.

"What is it?" he asked.

"She was in front of Lady Kang's residence, calling out her name." Hyeyeon's eyes strayed to my hands, clenched together. "She is on close terms with Lady Kang. I'm sure of it, sir."

"Well?" His stare bore into me. "What do you say to that accusation?"

Accusation. Now I knew associating with Lady Kang was vile in the inspector's eyes. I parted my lips, then closed them. At last I whispered, "It is true, sir." I shot a glance at Hyeyeon before staring at the floor. A feverish hotness flared up my throat, leaving a sheen of sweat on my brow. "There is . . . there is something I must confess to you, sir."

Inspector Han sat forward, one elbow on the low table before him. "Speak."

I cast another look at Hyeyeon, then rocked back and forth, wringing my hands.

"Perhaps," the inspector said, "you would like to speak to me in private, Seol?"

I bowed my head.

"You are dismissed, Hyeyeon. Return to your post. No one must enter or leave Kang's residence without our knowing."

"But, sir—" Hesitation strangled her voice, but she swallowed her protest and was soon gone.

Only Inspector Han and I occupied the office now. Gray light glowed through the screens, illuminating the tall bookshelf, the black-lacquered document box, and the low-legged table, washing the folding screen behind him in a chilling hue.

My mind quickly drew out a plan: once I was certain of our isolation, I would escape this office and outrun everyone while they were caught unawares. The killer could already be carrying the palanquin up the mountain, to the shed, and what would happen to Woorim then? I could not linger here too long.

Raising my lashes, I meant to look up at Inspector Han's gaunt and bony face, but I remembered his skill at reading people. He might notice my scheming thoughts in the pools of my eyes. I watched his broad shoulders and neck instead, and it returned, another unwanted flickering of memory; me, pressing my ear against a boy's shoulder, warm as an ondol. The *thud-thud-thud* of the furnace pumping out smoke and heating the stone plates hidden beneath his coarse tunic. *Jeong-yun-ah* . . . Brother's voice as he turned to look at me with his pale-spooky eyes. His round, youthful face thinned into bones and sharp angles.

All the pores in my body opened, drenching me with cold sweat, and my heart pounded so fiercely. *Not my brother. Never my brother.* I didn't want to be in this man's presence right now. I couldn't even remember why I had come here, but then I looked down at my empty hands, and the image of Woorim's pleading gaze filled them.

"Well?" Inspector Han prompted me again. "What is it you wish to tell me?"

I could still hear Hyeyeon's voice outside the office. As I bit my lower lip, my mind raced. Perhaps I could save Woorim another way. For here I was before the man who'd had her kidnapped, and I was convinced of this for one reason. The bamboo hat man must have been spying on Woorim to have known that she'd be at the haunted mansion earlier today. Coincidentally, those under the inspector's direct order—Hyeyeon and three other police officers—had been spying on the house of Woorim's mistress. Perhaps the bamboo hat man was one of his spies as well, ordered to kidnap Woorim.

If this was the case, Inspector Han had the power to also change his mind and let her go. *I* would have to convince him. It would be a risk, one that might turn out horribly wrong, but I remembered what the inspector himself had taught me: find the person's weakness, and grab it.

"I found it," I whispered.

"Found what?"

"The robe you left in the House of Bright Flowers. The one covered in blood."

He froze as though someone had run a sword through him. "Have you told anyone of this?"

"No." I raised my chin, to show him I was a force to be reckoned with, though inside, every bone in me shook. "It was Lady O's blood, wasn't it?"

The corner of his lips curled, so slightly. "Where is the robe." It was not a question; it was a command.

With just enough steel in my voice, I said, "No one will know of this, sir, *if* you help Woorim."

"Woorim?" Inspector Han remained still, but I saw his fingers flinch. "What do you know about Maid Woorim?"

"Her mistress guided me safely down from Mount Inwang after the tiger incident. I promise you, sir, I will not dig any deeper."

"Dig deeper into what?"

"Into your past. If you return Woorim safely."

"Return her?" he asked, sounding surprised. "What do you mean, return her?"

"She won't say a word against you. I'll make sure of that."

"Me?" His voice sharpened. "Whatever makes you think I know where she is?"

"I'm sure you have your reason for what you are doing. I'll never tell anyone. Not about Ahn or Lady O, either. I promise."

"So this is what it was all about. You think I am involved," he said as I looked up into his eyes again. For a disturbing instant, I saw my own eyes staring back at me, and I had to look away. "You seem completely certain."

He stood up, so calmly, as though he were rising to collect another book from his shelf. He crossed the room and stopped before the sliding door. Without even looking at me, he said quietly, "Let me say this only once. Do not get in my way again, or I will knock you down—"

"I have your robe." I spoke to his turned back, the tremor in my voice threatening to betray my bravado. "You can make me disappear, but I've made sure to hide it well, and the world will learn of your dark ways. Even if you kill me, the world will find out." Then I held my breath, waiting to see if he would see through my bluff.

"Will they?" His voice was as cold as the snow-dusted peaks of Mount Taebaek. He looked over his shoulder, down at me, and his lips twisted into a smile, as though he found me grossly comical. "Tell the world your little secret; they will not believe. You're nothing more than a slip of a girl. No, less than that. A mere *damo*."

And just like that, he tore off my mask, so quick and painful my eyes watered. A blink, and the burning drop fell. I couldn't understand why I was crying. But as I stared at Inspector Han, the thoughts of Woorim drained away, and all I could think about was my brother. That brother was gone now. Dead. No, worse than dead: he had changed into an awful stranger.

This realization pushed me to my feet. Before I knew what was happening, I was running, then my fingers swung across Inspector Han's cheek, as though I were trying to peel off his mask. My heart thundered against my ribs, and yet I felt a growing sense of detachment as I finally stepped back. I saw a welt on his cheek, inflicted by my chipped nails, yet I did not care.

"Not my brother," I whispered to him, backing away. "*Never* my brother."

His hand remained over the bloody scratch, his eyes following me as I stumbled out of the room, across the courtyard. I wasn't certain where I was running to, but I knew what I was running from. I had committed a crime, assaulting a high official, and I had no time to rot in prison. Not now.

SIXTEEN

THE NEXT DAY, I stood on the dirt road wending through the field of reeds, their golden hair loosened to the wind. The sun pulsed in the seashore-blue sky, and with my hand, I shielded my eyes from the brightness as I looked around. *If not Inspector Han, then who took you away, Woorim?*

I had run toward Lady Kang's mansion immediately after escaping the police bureau, and while the undercover officers were rotating shifts, I'd run up to the entrance only to be denied. The fearful gatekeeper had answered that it was a bad time to visit, that the mistress was not even home. It was up to me to find Woorim. Yet no one had seen a man in a bamboo hat, especially not one accompanying a palanquin. Then an urchin had pointed her finger at the fortress gate, saying she had seen such a man leave the capital.

I had wandered all that day and evening searching for Woorim, imagining her nose sliced off. Not a trace of her called out to me in the streets and alleys outside the fortress, not even in the nearby mountains. No torn fabric dangling from a branch; no straw sandal left behind; no blood smears. An old woman found me stumbling down the road, half delirious from exhaustion, and had allowed me to stay the night at her hut. But sleep evaded me. All I could think about was Woorim. It was as though she had vanished from the earth.

And now I stared at the expanse spread out before me, and I understood what Older Sister had meant when I'd once heard her whisper, "The world looks so immense when you've lost someone."

I staggered back toward the fortress gate later in the morning, my legs weak with exhaustion. Ahead of me stretched a long line of people, mostly farmers with their wagons filled with produce. I waited for what felt like ages, then as I got closer to the gate, what appeared to be a red speck in the distance turned out to be a fierce-looking guard with a broad nose and curled lips, his robe vivid red. My heart beat low and heavy, the anxiety making it difficult to breathe. At any moment he might yell out, "Arrest her! She dared to strike an official!" The wiser thing to do would be to run as far as I could from the capital, but I couldn't leave Woorim behind. I couldn't live with that guilt.

At last I arrived before the guard. He towered two heads above me as he inspected my identification tag, then gestured at me to enter. "Next!" he bellowed. I walked into Hanyang and no one came to grab me. My nerves unraveled, tremors of relief running down my legs. I was safe for now.

Once I recovered a little, I picked my way down the road and stopped before different establishments: shops that sold black hats, silver, jade, and honey; tarped stalls where produce was laid out on straw mats; butcher shops reeking with the coppery scent of blood. I didn't want to give up on Woorim yet, so before each shopkeeper, I held up a drawing of her. I had sketched her myself last night, using an abandoned piece of charcoal and the back of my brother's sketch. I'd drawn her wide eyes, her round face, and her most unique feature—her small, small lips.

"Have you seen this girl?" I asked.

The answers never varied. *No.*

I stopped by a few more shops before arriving at the brushwood gate of the inn. A crowd of men and women were gathered on the spacious platform, eating and drinking, smoking their pipes. I had asked what felt like all the shopkeepers in the capital about Woorim but had not thought to visit the inn, so focused was I on the Northern and Eastern Districts. But here at the inn, there were travelers passing in and out of the capital; surely one of them had seen Woorim!

I entered the yard and interrupted the guests to show them the sketch. "Do you recognize this girl?" I studied each person, hoping to see someone's eyebrows shoot up with recognition, but there seemed to be no trace of Woorim in their memories.

I ran a hand over my face, frustrated and not knowing what to do. My cheeks were so numb from the cold morning of wandering that I could hardly feel the touch of my own fingers.

Madam Song approached with a tray of bottles. "You again." She served her customers, then turned to me, and her brows twitched as though in shock. "Look at the state of you." Her voice was so brusque I thought she would send me away at any moment, but then she said, "Come. I know what you need."

●

I sat down on the veranda at the rear of the kitchen, where huge crocks of soy sauce, soybean paste, and pickles were neatly arranged, and dried leaves that had blown down from the trees sat yellow against the glossy brown pots.

Madam Song soon returned with a small table that bore a bowl of fluffy white rice and a side bowl filled with doenjang stew. As she set the table before me, I saw my reflection in the irises of her eyes: my pale face and windswept hair. This woman pitied me.

"Eat up." She waved her hand. "You're twig-thin."

She wasn't wrong. A few days ago, when I'd had the rare opportunity to bathe, I had noticed my rib cage protruding enough that I'd managed to count each rib. My appetite had vanished ever since I had found the bloody robe. But as I stirred the stew, watching the tangle of zucchini, onions, mushrooms, and shellfish, my stomach growled with a hunger so fierce that the spoon shook in my hand.

"Go on, eat," Madam Song urged.

I dumped the rice into the stew, mixed it, then stuck the spoon into my mouth. I was too famished to savor the rich and full taste, wolfing the meal down.

"It seems they don't feed you at the police bureau," she remarked, and when I remained silent, too busy eating, she spoke under her breath, as though to herself. "Perhaps you know more about the rumor circulating . . ."

My mouth full, I managed to ask, "What rumor?"

"It is about an edict. Catholic rogues will be condemned to death as traitors."

I froze, my appetite disappearing.

"Have you heard of it? No? The police officers who stopped by here for drinks were sharing tricks on how to catch Catholics."

I set my spoon down. "Tricks?"

"I heard that when Catholics are frightened, they make this strange gesture—touching their forehead, their chest, then each side of their shoulders. They also spend much time chanting on their knees, so the fabric in that area might sometimes be dirtier or more wrinkled than the rest."

A frown crinkled my brows. Was it a coincidence that Woorim had disappeared the same week this rumor had spread?

"A sea of blood will flow if this rumor is true. It will be an especially difficult time for members of the Southerner Faction . . ." Her voice trailed off, and a faraway look of concern fogged her gaze. Perhaps she was thinking of Lord Ch'oi. She blinked, and the sharpness returned to her eyes. "On the day the edict is announced, you ought to return home. The capital will turn into a place of great disorder. No one will notice your absence."

At the word "home," a burning pain knotted my throat. I finally understood why my brother from years ago had sunk into a dark, grieving silence whenever the word "home" had been mentioned. Home, that place your soul longs for with an exhausting intensity, just as a bird might hurt for the sky, or as a flower might pine for the sun.

"Even if I had the chance, madam, I cannot leave," I whispered.

"You have nothing here."

"There is a friend here I promised to help . . . and I have responsibilities I cannot abandon." I needed to be strong a while longer, so I ate another spoonful of stew, forcing myself to chew and swallow.

Madam Song rested her hand on the table, tapping it in a contemplative motion. "Me, I wish I had left this place. I did not return home and now my parents have left me, gone to the netherworld. They did me wrong; still, they were family. My remorse never lightens." She glanced at me, as though to say that such would be the weight I'd carry if I didn't return home.

"Then why did you stay?" I asked.

She tapped her fingers some more. "The truth is . . . I thought it would be enough just to be near him."

I took another bite of my stew, slowly this time, allowing her words to sink in. She had loved Councillor Ch'oi deeply, yet she had still chosen to end the affair.

Her face tilted back, eyes squinting up at the sun. "I intoxicated Councillor Ch'oi one night so that he would tell me more about the pendant, which I knew he had been wearing for seventeen years. I wanted to know why he never took it off, why he always touched it whenever he was having his black moods. But perhaps I ought never to have asked . . . What I learned, I could not bear it. He spoke of a woman named Byeol, 'Star,' who had birthed his illegitimate child. He had not known of her pregnancy until thirteen years later, when she sent the necklace to him with a note. I can still remember it, for the words he recited to me were burned onto my heart."

When she fell silent, I gently prompted her, "What did the note say, madam?"

"It read: 'Since you left me, my mind was hopeless and I was resolved to die, yet was reluctant to commit the final act. There was my concern for our child's survival, but now I think it would have been better if he never lived at all. Now nothing prevents me from fulfilling my lifelong wish: to escape shame.'

"Councillor Ch'oi wept and wept," she continued, "calling out her name in front of me. That is the day I stopped receiving his visits. I couldn't continue loving a man whose heart had never stopped weeping for another woman." Her jaws locked as though she were biting back a rush of old feelings. "A man never forgets his first love, and I could not bear living in her shadow. How could I compete with her? The dead always look lovelier, warmer, and brighter. A living woman pales in comparison."

I watched her wipe the corners of her eyes, and I wondered what it must feel like to deeply love another human being, so much that even after a decade or more, the memories of him still hurt her. After allowing her a moment to compose herself, I asked, "What did the pendant look like?"

"It was a horse-dragon pendant."

I held back a gasp, my mind thrown into confusion. "Horse-dragon?" I repeated. The wooden pendant Officer Goh had found by the South Gate—also a horse-dragon pendant. "The pendant . . . it is made of wood?"

"It is made of jade."

There were two? Two pendants of the same mythical creature, one worn by Councillor Ch'oi for many years, and the other found at the crime scene . . .

"So why did his lover, Madam Byeol, send him a horse-dragon

pendant?" I whispered. "I heard that creature is from the 'Mighty Infant' legend."

"How did you know it was that particular legend?" Madam Song's brows knitted together as she stared at me. "I thought only I knew the story behind His Lordship's pendant. It took him three bottles of wine to get him to share that story with even *me*, his closest companion."

"Is there more than one legend about this creature?"

"There are many horse-dragon legends, and many are legends from Imperial China. But the 'Mighty Infant' myth is a tale that belongs to our kingdom."

"What does the story say?"

"It is about how a particular mountain in the town of Goyang derived its name, Yongma. This name is a combination of two Chinese characters: *yong* for 'dragon,' and *ma* for 'horse.'"

"Horse-dragon," I whispered.

She bowed her head. "You will find many stables in Goyang; ranchers set up businesses there, hoping the spirit of the yongma will descend upon their horses. Madam Byeol was also from this village; her father was said to be a rancher as well."

"But what does a mountain have to do with a 'Mighty Infant'?"

She sighed. "I have not told this tale in many years . . . ," she said, then shared with me the myth of "The Mighty Infant."

It was about an extraordinary child born into a lowly home. On the third day after the child's birth, the mother left for the kitchen to drink water, and on her return, the boy had disappeared. Surprised, the mother looked everywhere and finally found the child sitting atop a high shelf. She examined the child, wondering if he was hurt, and discovered a small pair of wings sprouting from his shoulders.

At once, she reported this discovery to her husband, who then told the entire village, causing a great commotion. The villagers debated fiercely, and once a consensus was reached, the chief elder declared, "A peculiar boy was born to a poor household, so when the boy grows up, he will most certainly not fit in and bring trouble to us instead. Perhaps he will become a dangerous rebel or a traitor, and then our village will not be able to avoid danger either. It is appropriate that we kill this boy."

The parents of this child, fearing for their own lives, later crushed the struggling child with a sack of millet. The moment the boy breathed his last, a strange creature appeared at the back of a mountain—half dragon, half horse. This beast, sensing that the Great Master who was to ride him had died, raced to the village well, jumped in, and drowned there. Concluding the story, Madam Song said, "The boy was different from the rest, and in this kingdom, one cannot survive being peculiar."

I couldn't understand why Madam Byeol thought the horse-dragon creature so significant to her relationship with Councillor Ch'oi that she had sent him a necklace depicting it before her death.

As though seeing my confusion, Madam Song said, "Don't you see? Byeol raised her child alone, the shame of the village. Her son was different from the rest, like the child in the legend, but in another way: he was fatherless and born out of wedlock. So she killed him, then killed herself."

Silence filled me. After a few moments, I asked, "They really died?"

"Councillor Ch'oi went to the village and learned that his mistress had thrown her thirteen-year-old son into a well, then hung herself," she whispered.

A loud male voice suddenly broke into our conversation. "There she is!"

Madam Song looked at someone over my shoulder, then frowned at me. "Are you in trouble?"

I looked behind and glimpsed a black hat with a hanging red tassel. A police hat. My eyes locked onto Officer Kyŏn's. He charged toward me with the swiftness of a dark storm cloud, prepared to swallow me.

●

The police whistle shrieked behind me no matter how fast I ran. Turning sharply, I bolted in between two shops and into Pimatgol Alley, the peasant's road that creased through the sea of shops. My legs burned, lit on fire as I pushed myself to run faster. But no matter how fast I ran, Officer Kyŏn was always close.

The row of rooftop eaves cast a shadow over me as I scrambled, looking for a hiding place. An alley appeared up ahead. Taking a chance, I rushed into the dark slit. Only a single ray of light reached in, illuminating a splintered wagon and a littering of fish bones. I ran deeper, but a sudden wall interrupted my flight.

A dead end.

I looked over my shoulder, cold sweat sliding down my cheek. I waited, but no one followed me in. A breath of relief rushed out of my mouth, and I pressed my forehead against the wall, my eyes closed. My hammering heart slackened into a deep and steady drumbeat. I was safe for now, but for how much longer? Where else could I run to? The longer I remained on the street, the more dangerous it would become, thick with the watchful presence of the police.

Lady Kang came to mind.

Hope sparked warmth in me. She must have returned home by now, and I would be safe with her. The law forbade the police from searching for me inside her home without permission, as noblewomen were immune to police attention. And more than anything, she needed me; I had witnessed Woorim's kidnapping.

My decision made, I whirled around, only to freeze in my steps. From the alley's entrance, a shadow prowled in, the dirt path crunching beneath his footsteps. It was Officer Kyŏn, his unsmiling face drenched in sweat and glistening in the dim ray of light. He carried a club in one hand and a coil of rope in another, the rope used to arrest criminals. His lips curled up into a sneer, revealing his chipped front teeth.

"Don't think to run again," he said.

I took a retreating step, only to back up against the wall. I was trapped with nothing—no weapon, nowhere else to run. All my effort to rescue Woorim and to find the truth behind the killings seemed to slip from my fingers. No one would listen to me; no one would believe me. They would lock me up and not care that a third victim was about to be killed. Just then, a memory of Inspector Han surfaced, like a chilling specter that sharpened my panicking mind. He'd said that one must grab a person by either their weakness or their desire. A method I was relying on more often these days.

Before Kyŏn could reach out to arrest me, I raised both hands in the air, palms out. "Wait!"

"Wait?" He grunted. "Wait for what?"

"I know what you need, and I can give it to you. E-evidence. I have it."

His sneer flattened and his eyes narrowed on me. "What evidence?"

"I will tell you if you let me go."

"Now you want to cooperate with me? Hah! First you tell me, then I'll consider letting you live, inyeona."

There was a surging opposition in me, an echo demanding that I remember the haunted house, the ghost under the pine tree. But I beat it down. My voice strained as I said, "There are personal chests inside the servants' quarter. Mine is the one with a loose bracket, and inside, I hid an inspector's robe. It is bloodstained."

A frown shot over his brows. "Bloodstained?"

"On the night of Lady O's murder, Inspector Han rode back to the House of Bright Flowers at dawn, and Maid Misu—"

"Who is Misu?"

"Madam Yeonok's personal maid. She heard him say, 'She is dead, she is dead.' He then changed into a white robe, and Madam Yeonok had the maid hide his uniform."

Silence filled the alley, so tangible that I could feel its weight press against my skin.

"So you are saying"—Kyŏn's voice dipped low—"that the blood might belong to Lady O? Inspector Han might have killed her and gotten her blood all over his uniform?"

Guilt closed in around my throat, making it impossible to talk.

Kyŏn's frown deepened as he rubbed his chin. "Inspector Han might claim that the blood belonged to his horse. An accident. He would say also that he had first left the House of Bright Flowers at around dawn, long after Lady O was murdered, which occurred around midnight. He had an alibi."

"He—" I stopped, my insides trembling.

"He what?"

"Inspector Han could have left earlier. Much earlier."

"What do you mean?"

"I think . . ." I hated how uncertain I sounded and wished to speak no more, but Kyŏn's eyes urged me to continue. "I think Senior Officer Shim was lying about being his alibi, so no one can account for the inspector's whereabouts around midnight."

"Why would you think that?"

"Shim told Commander Yi that the inspector was wearing a white robe when he first entered the House of Bright Flowers, when in fact, he had been wearing his uniform. Even Maid Soyi encountered him on the street when he was in uniform. But Officer Shim saw only the white robe, which the inspector had not changed into until around dawn. And . . ."

"And?"

"And Maid Misu also said she didn't see Officer Shim until around dawn."

"Which means Officer Shim was not present for the entire night . . ."

"But would this be enough to convince Commander Yi?" I whispered.

"Maid Misu's confession would be enough, along with something else I uncovered." He looked over his shoulder, then took a step closer to me. "Your suspicion is correct. You are always supposed to interrogate the alibi, make sure his testimony is certain, but no one thought to question Senior Officer Shim. I took it upon myself and asked around. I discovered that at midnight, when Shim claimed to have been with Inspector Han at the House of Bright Flowers, someone actually saw him returning to his residence. So Inspector Han likely made Shim lie about being the inspector's alibi."

"What? Someone saw Shim returning home?"

"It was the monsoon season, remember? Children were swept off the street and huts collapsed. His roof caved in under the torrent, and his neighbor looked in to see whether anyone was hurt. That was when he saw Shim return, and he had to hurry off."

"And this man . . . Why did he not tell the police? Lady O's death was so public . . . surely he must have heard that Shim was posing as Inspector Han's alibi?"

"Because he was afraid. He should not have been outside wandering the street at that hour. It was after curfew."

When no man was permitted to roam the streets except those in power—they were always an exception to the law.

"Maid Misu . . . she will be of use to me." Kyŏn nodded his head. "Yes, she is enough."

I clutched my hands together, tensing as the silence returned. "Have you . . . have you made up your mind, Officer? Will you let me go?"

"I have more than made up my mind. We ought to have been allies from the start. Here," he said, slipping his hand into his robe, then holding out a folded paper. "Remember. I told you that if you joined my side, I would let you see the inspector's letter. This letter confirmed my suspicion that Inspector Han was bent on killing the priest, and Scholar Ahn had told me that Lady O knew of the priest's whereabouts. Was it a coincidence that she ended up dead? I think not."

"And you have this letter with you?"

"Scholar Ahn gave it back to me, but everyone believes it disappeared with him. I've kept this close to me, ever since Damo Hyeyeon went through my belongings. Now, go find someone to read it for you."

I held the letter, the one I'd wondered about since late summer.

Kyŏn backed away, still facing me. "You see, Damo Seol. I was right all along. No one will be by Inspector Han's side in the end. No one."

I watched him leave the alley with long and hurried strides, as though he could not contain his eagerness to bring Inspector Han down. He ran and disappeared.

All my strength drained from me. I dropped to the ground and held my head, stared at the dirt pathway, at the letter I'd let fall onto the ground. Waiting for a thunder of emotions, of anger and grief, remorse and dread. Anything. But all I felt was a numbing cloud of fog filling me, and in the haze I saw a girl clinging to her brother's back, so that she wouldn't wash away down the slope with the mud. *T-t-t-t-t*, she'd imitated the sound of rain tapping her brother's straw cloak, *t-t-t-t-t*.

An immense weight sat on my chest, and I felt as though I'd suffocate. I thought I'd never change. Not me. But just as my brother had changed, from a delicate flower to a lone mountain—I too had become different.

I had become a traitor.

SEVENTEEN

INSPECTOR HAN'S LETTER TO THE DEAD

I was once told, Little Sister, that when the flower blossoms, the wind intervenes. When the moon is at its fullest, the clouds intervene. When do the affairs under heaven ever comply with human wishes? It is true. My life rarely goes as planned. But today I observed a change in the wind. Perhaps the cloud shrouding my path will roll away.

In the five years that have passed since Priest Zhou Wenmo illegally entered Joseon, I have never seen the priest's face before. I would more easily find a mouse in a reed field, for at least when it moves, the reeds twitch along with it. But when the priest moves, the Catholics around him remain silent and still.

But I have a new suspicion, and if it is correct, then the man in hiding is the one I have searched for all these years. I will find him, and not even Commander Yi can block my way, which he intends to do. It is better this way, that the priest should die early rather than live long and cause more trouble.

You must think this harsh, Little Sister, but it is because you were too young for me to tell you about Father. He was a traitor who was executed after months of beatings, interrogated for smuggling in and spreading copies of Catholic books, given to him by the priest. I could have prevented this, since I was the first to discover his heretical ways, but I kept quiet. Afraid. That is how our family was banished to Heuksan, the island of black mountains, covered with vines and thornbushes that left you cut and bruised.

Every so often, you would ask me if our exile was over yet. "Now can we go home?"

"No, little sister. We still have many more moons to count."

You were also too young to remember our home, and so home became to you the place I spoke so often about, a mansion with five quarters, all connected by courtyards. A tranquil garden and an old pine tree bent into the shape of a river. A place of togetherness. It must have become real in your mind.

The end of our banishment was when we traveled across the sea to build a new home for the three of us, but my fight with Older Sister resulted in us parting ways. As I walked away from the old life, I looked back to see you crying, your sister holding your hand. She would not let me take you. So you followed your sister, who chose the path of servitude, desperate as she was to escape our past. She preferred the life of anonymity to one of shame.

As for me, I chose the path that led to Commander Yi. He would later tell me of how he'd looked forward to my letters, and how, upon learning of my release from Heuksan, he had journeyed for three nights without sleep to meet me. Not only did he return me to the capital, but he urged our reluctant uncle on my mother's side to adopt me into his household, and since then, I've tried not to be a burden to him. I dared not ask my uncle for help. I dared not let him know that I was searching for you.

It took five years. I followed your trail from a slave market all the way north to Gyeongsang Province, and there I found you in a grassy hill. "It is a mass burial site, this place," an elder said. "The entire Nam household was wiped out by a plague long ago." No one survived, neither your sister nor you, Jeong-yun. Their servant girl.

Knowing that you are gone leaves me restless, and this life I wander seems to be stuck in perpetual dusk; neither the sun nor the moon are bright anymore. Yet it consoles me to write to you. You were my sister for too short a time. So read these pages in the afterworld, and when we greet each other again, remember to call me "Older Brother."

EIGHTEEN

I ARRIVED AT Lady Kang's gate, my eyes swollen from tears, hand pressed against my side to hold down the cramping pain. The last time I stood here, I'd had no idea betrayal would cost me a slice of my heart. One day—one single day of the sun rising and falling—had taken more from me than the past few years.

Knuckles white, I pounded on the door. This time I would push past the gatekeeper and force myself into the compound if I had to. But I heard only silence, and it persisted.

"Let me speak with the mistress, please!" I called out, desperation bursting in my voice. The silence went on for too long, leaving me drenched in sweat as I clenched and unclenched my hands, not knowing what to do. I couldn't risk remaining out in public much longer.

"Haven't you heard?"

I whirled around at the voice and saw a thick-lipped woman with a reddish face. A small infant was strapped to her back with a wraparound blanket. "H-heard what?" I asked.

"No one opens the gates these days. A rumor has made the workers afraid, so most have fled."

"What rumor?" My voice cracked.

"Soon, all Catholics will be treated as traitors, and you know what that means. The entire household and servants will be punished—"

Wood creaked, the door opening.

I darted a glance back to see a young lady around my age, peering out from behind the gate. Her silk jacket was crane white, while her shimmering skirt was pink, and decorating the hem was a colorful floral design. She was, from her appearance alone, a high-class lady.

"You must be Seol." Her eyes lifted from the branding on my cheek. "Quick. Come in."

I left behind the reddish-faced woman and followed the stranger inside. The emptiness of the courtyard pressed in around me. The pavilions were swamped in shadows and silence. Only two servants passed us by, unlike my previous visit, when I had seen lines of servants flowing in and out and around Lady Kang's mansion.

"Are you here to speak with my eomeoni?" the young lady asked.

I tried to hide my swollen eyes. "Eomeoni?"

"I am her daughter. Hong Sunhŭi."

It took me a moment to remember that Lady Kang was a divorced woman, so Hong was likely the surname of the girl's father. Hong Sunhŭi certainly did not look like her mother, with her broad forehead and pointed chin, and her ears that stuck out. Not at all similar to Lady Kang's long and angular face.

"A pleasure to meet you, agasshi," I whispered.

"This way."

We stepped through the inner gate into a separate quarter. It was the women's quarter; the space that was closed off to the world by a gate, bolted at night. I had snuck into this courtyard on my first visit and had witnessed Woorim secretly peering in at a mysterious male guest in the middle pavilion, which Sunhŭi and I now approached.

"My mother is inside," Sunhŭi said.

Taking off my sandals, I followed Sunhŭi into the chamber of hanji screens. There was no one else present but Lady Kang, who lounged on a silk mat, a book open before her. She set it aside upon seeing me, then unfolded both hands, palms out. "Come closer."

Lowering my head, I crawled into her shadow.

"What brings you here, child?" she asked.

"Woorim," I whispered. "I have come because of her, mistress."

A shadow passed over her face. "She might have gone to visit home, as she sometimes does."

"But she would have told us, eomeoni," Sunhŭi interjected.

"She was kidnapped," my voice rasped.

"Kidnapped?" A note of disbelief rang in Lady Kang's voice. "How did you learn of this?"

"I . . . I saw it happen myself. And I think . . ." I wrung my hands. "I think she was taken by the same man who killed Lady O and Scholar Ahn."

As the two ladies blanched, I was drawn to a question I'd had no space in my heart to ponder before. I had spent most of the day crouched in the alley, reading Inspector Han's letter over and over, sobbing until my uniform was wet with my tears. But now I wondered . . . What was the killer's incentive for taking Woorim?

Lady Kang's voice was deadly calm as she asked, "How did this happen?"

"I wished to see Inspector Han's former residence, the haunted mansion," I replied, my ears burning with shame. "Woorim offered to accompany me."

"What time did she disappear?"

"Yesterday morning. I've searched for her everywhere," I added, as though this would absolve me of my guilt.

"You ought to have come to me right away," Lady Kang snapped. "I was wondering all day where she had gone. I could have helped you."

I remained still with my head lowered and fingers intertwined, accepting her scorn. It was all my fault, indeed; I deserved this. But then something stirred beneath my silence. First a molten bubbling, then an erupting sense of unfairness. I looked up at Lady Kang, remembering the red scratch I'd left on the inspector's face. "I could not come right away, mistress. How could I?" I asked, my voice trembling. "I visited your residence only to be caught and dragged away by the police. I came again only to be told you were away. I *tried*!"

"Hmm . . ." was her only response, deep and solemn, absorbing my words. At length, she asked, "Why did the police take you?"

"Inspector Han—" The memory of his gentle letter rose up, burning at the hilt of my throat. I swallowed hard, yet my voice still trembled. "He is behind it all. He sent the man to steal Woorim, so I went up to Inspector Han and I demanded that he return Woorim."

All fell still, as though time itself had stopped.

At length, Sunhŭi whispered, "You confronted a military official."

Lady Kang's frown remained. "What do you mean, the inspector has taken Woorim?"

I felt that I must tell Lady Kang everything, and so I told her all I knew about the night of Lady O's murder.

"Lady O had knowledge of the priest's whereabouts. Scholar Ahn did, too." My voice was weak, my soul too drained. "So the inspector targeted them. He had motive."

"How do you know she had knowledge of this?" Lady Kang asked.

"The police officers found out that the victim had been baptized by the priest himself," I explained, and I was about to add that the police also knew Lady Kang had converted Lady O herself when it clicked.

My lips parted and shock set in. The priest had baptized Lady O, so someone must have introduced him to her, someone with authority in the Catholic community and with enough power to protect the priest. Lady Kang. It had to be her. Leader of the Heretical Virgin

Troupe, and furthermore, an aristocratic lady immune to police attention. Woorim had disappeared because, as a servant living in Lady O's household, she must have possessed valuable information about the person hidden there.

"You look as though you've seen a ghost." Lady Kang watched me steadily, and I felt that she'd witnessed her secret unfold before my eyes. There was a strained caution to her voice as she said, "Seol, remain here with my daughter, and do not leave the premises. It is safer for you within."

Sunhŭi rose with her mother. "Where are you going, eomeoni?"

"We cannot lose Woorim," she whispered.

●

Alone in the middle pavilion, I looked again at the crack in the screen, the hole through which I had once seen the middle-aged gentleman. I remembered his dark hair, tied back, revealing a broad face covered with small scars. It felt bizarre, knowing that in my memory was the face of Priest Zhou Wenmo, the man the entire kingdom was hunting for. As was the killer.

This could mean my death sentence.

I shifted and sat in the spot where I had last seen the priest. Cross-legged, I looked around, wondering if I could find a trace of him. A strand of hair. A shred of fabric. But all I saw was an empty cleanliness, as though Lady Kang had ordered the entire quarter to be swept and scrubbed. The priest must have been sent away to hide elsewhere, perhaps when the rumor of the anti-Catholic edict had first circulated. Where was his new hiding place?

Maybe Woorim knew the answer.

●

"You can sleep here tonight," Sunhǔi said. "For however long you need."

We arrived before a humble pavilion where four screen doors lined the veranda, its tiled roof held up by beams of timbers. A fishy scent drifted around, rising from the squid left to dry on pegs hammered to the wall outside. A bamboo broom lay abandoned, resting against the stone steps. A typical quarter in which servants slept, but there were no servants occupying the space, only shadows cast by the darkened sky.

Following Sunhǔi, I stepped into a room. There were two mats and a stack of folded blankets. Setting the paper lamp down, Sunhǔi gestured around. "Whatever you need from outside, do tell me, and I will find a way to retrieve it for you. It will be wise of you to stay hidden." Her eyes then landed on my cheek. "All the police officers will recognize your scar too easily."

"Your mother once said I could burn it off," I remarked. "I don't intend to ever return to the police bureau."

"For now, should you feel compelled to go beyond the mansion walls, it will be better to conceal it. I have the perfect idea for you!"

Sunhǔi left the room, returning with a tray of little porcelain pots. "First you must clean your face." Like a sister, she helped me wash the grime off, even cleaning the corners of my eyes, crusted with dried tears. She ground peach-toned powder into a thick consistency, then painted several layers over my cheek.

"There," she said, gesturing at the little mirror propped up before me. "This will do."

In the mirror, next to the flickering lantern, was the face of a girl unmarked, unscarred, free. But something had changed. She did not look like the Seol I knew from Inchon Prefecture; her eyes had seen too much. Death had blown out the lights, the shimmer of childhood. I had grown out of myself and into a stranger, just like my brother.

"I don't like change," I whispered. "I despise it."

"Hmm?"

"I do not like change," I repeated, forgetting momentarily our difference in status. Perhaps it was the way she was looking at me, so open and accepting, or the fact that she was touching me, adding more layers of paint onto my branding. "Change in people, in circumstances, in anything."

She smiled. "We must learn to embrace the new seasons in our lives. There is a season to gain, a season to lose; a season for peace, a season for war; a season to laugh, a season to mourn, and to betray. As for me, I long for change," she added in a whisper. "I will soon be sent to a better place—my real home."

"Home." I thought of the home once glowing in my mind, an echo from a dream, now a gaunt shell. "Where is that?"

Our conversation halted when footsteps crunched over the dirt yard. Sunhŭi leapt to her feet and peeked out of the door. Her eyes gleamed in the moonlight as she looked over her shoulder at me. "Eomeoni has returned."

●

I joined Sunhŭi outside the servants' quarter and saw Lady Kang standing in the courtyard, her back to us. The moon illuminated the silk dress that flowed down from her waist, glowing like the underside of a seashell, and the long pin that secured her braided coil twinkled. She stared up at the three-horned peaks of Mount Samgak, a jagged silhouette protruding into the sky.

"'Gosan,' they called the traitor's son," she said. "I sensed it from the start that his ending would not be good. He accumulated too much hatred." Then she looked sideways, only enough for me to catch a glimpse of her cheekbone, so sharp my finger would likely bleed if I touched it. "You have made a mountain fall. Inspector Han is under arrest."

I had somehow expected Inspector Han to escape with his cunning. He was supposed to be invincible.

"After speaking with an acquaintance of mine," Lady Kang continued, "I visited the bureau and I learned that he is being detained in his office until the end of the inquisition, after which he will be placed under house arrest."

Sunhŭi must have sensed that something was wrong with me, for she placed a hand on my shoulder. "What is the evidence against him?" she asked her mother.

"His uniform covered in dried blood, a gisaeng, and a maid—as well as an officer. This officer was kneeling in the courtyard, and in a loud voice, he said he would not refuse to die ten thousand times for the crime he had committed, and even asked to be punished with execution tools."

"What crime did he commit?" Sunhŭi asked.

"He gave false witness."

I only managed to whisper, so quietly that I could barely hear myself, "Was his name Shim?"

"That was his name. Shim Jaedeok. He confessed that at around dawn, after the murder, he had received a message from Madam Yeonok, begging him to come quickly to the House of Bright Flowers. He arrived and found Inspector Han half-conscious, and he kept saying, 'She is dead.'"

I bowed my head. This was the same testimony given to me by Maid Misu.

"Shim offered to be Inspector Han's alibi—not only out of loyalty, but because he genuinely believed Han's account to be true. The account was that Inspector Han had a few drinks, for it was the anniversary of his father's execution. A little after midnight, he rode toward the South Gate—his father was executed there."

I closed my eyes, feeling my heart pound against my chest. Inspector Han had left the House at around midnight. This was so close to the hour of Lady O's murder.

"That is when Inspector Han discovered the body of Lady O. He was intoxicated, and thus he claimed he'd mistaken Lady O for his dead mother."

A memory crept into my mind and lingered, as fine as mist, of Older Brother climbing down a cliff, a rope around his waist. He reached down to touch Mother. Crabs scattered from a pile of splintered bones and flesh. Had this moment stamped itself permanently on his mind, making him see Mother when it was another woman?

Lady Kang placed her hand over her throat to steady her voice. "When he discovered the victim, she was dead. What could have followed next? No one seems to know, and Inspector Han claimed he could not recall the following hours. Shim believed this, for the inspector has an illness . . . seizures sometimes triggered by blood and the sight of murdered women, which had been suppressed over the years. It was under control until that night. Perhaps it was the alcohol."

"Inspector Han, afraid of death?" Sunhŭi said. "It cannot be."

I frowned, concentrating on a sensation in my chest that coiled into a tight, painful knot. A memory that made me say, "It is true."

"What do you mean?"

"I don't know," I said. "I just feel that his fear is true."

The silence that followed unpacked the sharpness I'd felt,

unfolding before me something I must have forgotten, which returned to me now. I remembered finding a wild dog too wounded to run away from us, and later Older Sister fighting with Brother, telling him we needed meat for the winter. He had kept refusing to stoop so low.

My sister had pretended to back down, and without him knowing, she dragged the wild beast to the backyard. The creature whimpered, as though sensing its end, right before Older Sister knocked it unconscious. She used a large blade to make an incision along its jaw, severing arteries and veins, cutting across the throat, until I heard the blade scrape its spine. The still-pumping heart squirted blood all over the snow, and I made sure to crouch far away while watching the blood drain.

"How could you . . . ," a voice had said behind me. I looked over my shoulder, and there he stood, my brother, frozen and staring at us.

"Orabeoni!" I'd called out, clueless, and as though my voice had broken the spell, he turned and stumbled away. At the back of the hut, I later found him curled up into a ball, breathing hard and sweating like he'd run for a hundred li in distance. His fingers had frightened me the most, all cramped up.

Several more incidents came to mind. Times when I had found my brother crippled by fear after a bloody incident, of which there had been many while living on the unforgiving island of Heuksan. Blood made him panic, the death of women made him faint. And now Officer Shim had confessed that the inspector also feared these things, after keeping this truth a secret for so many years.

"Officer Shim confessed all this?" I shook my head. "His loyalty to Inspector Han was unshakable. What made him confess now?"

"He learned of how you'd attacked Inspector Han and of your accusation that he had abducted Maid Woorim. This news weakened him, and then Officer Kyŏn confronted him and told him that

Commander Yi had summoned Madam Yeonok and a maid named Misu to the police court. Shim realized that he had been blinded by loyalty."

"So Shim too will be under arrest," I said.

A pause, and Lady Kang murmured, "That is what I found odd." She paced around before us, concern knitting her brows. "Councillor Ch'oi joined in and convinced Commander Yi to show Officer Shim leniency. Shim will be spared punishment if he is able to use Inspector Han's investigation to capture the priest. For everyone knows that there is no one more capable of finding the priest than Han, and if not Han, better to make use of his closest ally."

"What . . . ?" Confusion whirled in my head. "Commander Yi would never overlook an offense of that magnitude. It makes no sense."

"You do not understand the turmoil our kingdom is in." Lady Kang moved to sit down on the veranda. "Already there is word about a Silk Letter."

I waited for an explanation, but she kept silent. Sunhŭi stepped closer and whispered to me, "It is rumored that this letter will be smuggled to China, demanding military help to protect us . . . Catholics . . . from being murdered by the queen regent. But, mind you," she quickly added, "we think this Silk Letter is dangerous."

Military intervention. Did this mean the West would invade Joseon? All this caused by a priest who was spreading heretical teaching. I touched my forehead, feeling feverish. I had followed the thread connecting Lady O's death to Priest Zhou Wenmo, and never would I have thought it'd lead me into a web of conspiracy and rebellion among heretics, as well as to so much suffering. I remembered that Inspector Han's father had been beheaded, his corpse later laid out in the open. A father bewitched by the priest's teaching.

This priest had wrecked so much.

How often, I wondered, had Inspector Han woken at night with unthinkable memories alive in his mind? Was he so wrong in wanting the priest dead? All because of him I had lost my home and family, and I could not even mourn my loss, for I had been deprived of everything at so young an age.

"Priest Zhou Wenmo is a troublesome man," I said, words I knew I ought not to say aloud, yet they brimmed over. "So troublesome."

Lady Kang looked at me. "You think you know about the priest, when in fact, you know naught at all," she said in a sorrowful tone. "The story you know is only one strand of a vast tapestry."

I remained quiet, wondering what else I had yet to understand; I felt I understood all. Those who did wrong should pay for their crime.

"But let us not concern ourselves with the priest. Let it not divide us," she added. "We are here because we share a common concern for Woorim's safety."

Help me, Woorim had called to me with bloodshot eyes, the veins protruding from her forehead. Her hand slipping out from mine as the killer dragged her away, wrenching her hair. There was no time to be wondering who was right and who was wrong.

"And what is going to happen to Inspector Han if he is charged with murder?" I asked. "Lady O and Scholar Ahn were both aristocrats from influential families."

"Perhaps he will be poisoned. The gentle way to execute an official." Lady Kang did not look at me but at the mountain peak again. "This is the consequence of the clash of old and new. We must prepare our hearts, all of us. No matter which side wins, we will all be heartbroken."

I lay in the room with no one else but the whispers from my past, filling the space like the fluttering of a thousand wings. I pressed my palms against my ears, burying my face into the pillow, yet I could not escape.

We can't fight, Older Sister said. *It's just the three of us. We must stick together.*

There had been three of us—her, Brother, and myself—but because of my choice to betray Inspector Han, now there would be only two. My sister would have made a different choice. She would have moved heaven and earth to protect her brother, even if he were a murderer, and perhaps I would have gone far to protect him too. Only, Inspector Han would never be my brother.

Older Brother was supposed to be gentle and deeply kind. He had told me stories about home, promising that we would one day sit around a table and eat together, shoulder to shoulder. He had promised to write me a warm poem. He had made so many promises while counting the moons, waiting for our banishment to end in Heuksan, and these promises had sung me to sleep for years afterward. Just for him, I had kept myself from running away again and had stayed in the capital to look for him, for the brother who had promised me a home bursting with the warmth of reunion. But instead I had found a cold and distant superior, a military official who had told the bandit to let me die.

Unable to sleep, I rolled out of the blanket and wandered out of the room. A single black cloud hung in the moonlit sky. As I paced about in restlessness, a fistful of dread churned in my stomach, and I remembered Lady Kang's words. Inspector Han might die because of what I had discovered, his bloody robe. Was I my brother's killer?

I pulled out Inspector Han's letter to the dead. I couldn't make myself read it again; it was enough just to see the crumpled paper. Enough to remind me that I could not stop now. I'd come too far.

The ground scraped beneath my feet as I walked, and with each step, there was a growing sensation in me that nothing would be the same again. Setting my palm on the wooden double doors, I pushed them open. I ran through the alleys and pathways, then arrived at Jongno Street, a broad road illuminated by women holding lanterns that could easily expose my face. I still had my branding painted over, but most patrolmen would recognize me nevertheless.

Shadows beneath the tiled eaves and narrow alleys cloaked me as I journeyed toward the Capital Police Bureau. My heart pounded so hard in my chest that someone could have heard its echoing beat. Soon, I glimpsed the establishment built on its stone foundation, the roofline flaring out at the ends. The entrance gate, capped with an imposing pagoda, was protected by guards with spears. I had almost forgotten how frightening the police bureau appeared.

I remained hidden in the alley, far enough that the guards wouldn't see me, but close enough to observe the bustling through the opened gates. Roundsmen stepped out of the bureau, accompanying a man garbed in a blue silk robe, his shoulders drawn back, standing tall and shameless. The silver embroidery on his robe glinted in the moonlight. Inspector Han.

Over the bureau, the moon was bright, and clouds flowed across the spread-out sky. Senior Officer Shim then stepped out of the main gate to stand by Inspector Han's side, soon joined by Commander Yi on horseback. The horse let out an echoing neigh.

The autumn wind howled; paper lamps hanging from eaves swayed.

Hooves clopping, and again, the loud, echoing cry of the horse.

Horse. I frowned at this word, paced around it in my mind, until another creature appeared by its side. *Dragon.*

And suddenly scattered pieces shifted into place.

The necklace discovered in Lady O's hand. The wooden horse-dragon pendant discovered near the place of her death, the same in design as Councillor Ch'oi's jade piece. All a mere coincidence, possibly. But there was one point that bothered me.

I edged along the wall, closer to the corner. I looked across the dirt path and watched the shadows cast by torchlight stretch and shudder in the wind. Officer Shim, his cheeks so drawn, his eyes like black hollows under the brim of his police hat. All I knew was that he was an illegitimate son, and now also a friend who had betrayed Inspector Han—for what? Had Shim really exposed his comrade merely because he felt bad? Soldiers were known to cover each other's most heinous crimes in the name of loyalty. So what else had pushed Shim into confessing? It had to do with Councillor Ch'oi somehow. There *had* to be a connection there—a reason as to why the councillor, of all people, had stepped in and convinced Commander Yi to release Shim. They must have formed a deal . . . but over what?

I retreated into the shadows and pressed my back against the wall, wondering wildly what could have lured Senior Officer Shim and the councillor into one scheme. Then it hit me. Shim was illegitimate, and I remembered being told that his father had adopted a nephew as his heir, just as Councillor Ch'oi had done. What if this was not a coincidence? What if they were related by blood, and the councillor had known of their ties? How would he have used this to his advantage?

Muscles tightened in my shoulders as I pressed my knuckle to my lips, to keep myself from cursing aloud as emotions roared; of panic, bewilderment, though mostly waves of trepidation that left me edgy.

Seol-ah, came my sister's reproachful voice. *This kind of suspicion will kill you.*

A cold prickling sensation warned me that Sister was right; this path would lead me onto a mountain ridged with crumbling, skull-crushing cliffs and ankle-breaking burrows. Not only was a police officer possibly involved in the killings, but a government official, too. Yet I had no intention of backing away, and this left me with only one question.

What should I do next?

NINETEEN

ONCE, ROYAL SOLDIERS docked on Heuksan Island and marched to my neighbor's hut. His sentence had changed from banishment to execution. Without weeping or trembling, he changed into his best robe, then bowed four times to the east in the direction of Changdeok Palace, expressing gratitude to the king for not shamefully beheading him. Then he sipped the bowl of arsenic poison, melting his innards into a mouthful of blood, which he coughed out, dying a painful death.

Was it possible for Inspector Han to die in such a way? Would he permit his life to end? The man I'd feared had always been just that—a man. Not a god. Commander Yi could crush him like a worm if he so wished.

Following the sound of murmuring voices, I arrived at the east side of the wall enclosing Inspector Han's residence. The wall was only two heads higher than me. With a leap, I managed to grab onto the ledge, which was capped with black tiles. I hoisted myself up onto my elbows and peered into what looked to be the men's quarter—the place where men discussed social matters, wrote poems, played instruments like the geomungo—for it was located near the outer wing of the compound. At the center was a pavilion guarded by officers, positioned in all four directions.

My muscles burned, struggling to hold up my weight, but I couldn't let myself look away. Something bad was going to happen to the inspector. At any moment a soldier might arrive with poison in a porcelain bowl, and I would have to yell out "Stop!" for I was no longer certain of Inspector Han's guilt.

She is dead, she is dead, Inspector Han had wept on the night of Lady O's death. *She* is dead—I'd thought he had been referring to Lady O, but I wondered again. What if, in his terror and intoxication, Inspector Han had indeed mistaken Lady O for his mother? Rain pouring in sheets, a woman bleeding at the neck, blood oozing out from the gash like a mother who had jumped only to land on to the craggy shore. Had he held Lady O in his arms? Hence, the blood on the sleeve and the torso of his robe? *Mother is dead, Mother is dead.*

A movement caught my attention. A woman's silhouette crept along the shadowy wall opposite from me. The guards seemed oblivious, standing still. What was a woman doing inside the men's quarter? Seeing her disappear through the side gate, I leapt off the wall to follow, and soon I heard her footsteps scrambling down the street. The woman had a cotton robe draped over her head and flapping behind her.

"Excuse me?" I called out.

The woman hiked up her skirt and ran faster. My suspicion spiked. Breathing fast, I chased after her, surprised by the woman's speed. Even in the village when I had raced other girls, I had always won. Pushing myself faster, I managed to latch my hand onto the woman's shoulder, whipping her around. Her robe came flying off, and I saw not a woman but a young man, his coarse black hair falling over his eyes. It was Ryun, the inspector's manservant. I gaped at him in confusion.

"Curses. It's you." He reached down and threw the robe over himself again, allowing only his face to peek out. "Don't stare at me like that. Disguise is the only way for me to wander the streets during curfew."

At length, when my nerves settled, I asked, "Where were you going in such a hurry?"

"You must know what happened. My master got arrested. Not that you would care. You wounded his face, didn't you?"

"I can explain—"

"No time. I can't stand around talking to you when his innocence needs to be proved."

"You don't think he is guilty of murder?"

"Of course not!" Ryun shook his head, a frown crinkling his thick brows. "Councillor Ch'oi is involved somehow. Only a few days ago, His Lordship summoned Senior Officer Shim to his residence and must have convinced him to betray the inspector. He must have used Officer Shim's weakness somehow."

Realization dawned on me. "I think I know how Councillor Ch'oi convinced Shim."

In the distance, I heard footsteps and the low murmuring of male voices. Patrolmen, perhaps. I couldn't risk getting caught.

I grabbed Ryun's cloak. "Come. There is a safe place nearby where we can talk without being seen."

I led him toward the haunted mansion, the last place I wanted to be, yet its presence—only a few winding alleys away from us—tugged at me with an inhuman force. The mansion, though swamped in shadows and the coldness of death, was still the place where everything had begun for me.

●

We sat on the veranda, staring at the empty courtyard of dirt and weeds. Not wanting to disturb the haunting stillness, I spoke in low murmurs, telling Ryun about Councillor Ch'oi, Madam Byeol, and the bastard son who had been thrown into a well. I also told him about the jade and the wooden horse-dragon pendants, as well as the "Mighty Infant" tale that Senior Officer Shim had mentioned.

"This was a startling coincidence," I said. "Among the many tales Officer Shim could have chosen from to describe the mythical horse-dragon, he chose the story that was related to Councillor Ch'oi's bastard son."

"So what are you suggesting?" Ryun asked.

"Madam Byeol's son fell into the well at the age of thirteen. This was seventeen years ago; so if the boy had lived, he should be around thirty. And the bastard son would have come to the capital, to the place where his father lives."

"Thirty . . ." Ryun stood up and rubbed his chin, the frown never leaving his brows. "That is Officer Shim's age."

I nodded and licked my dry lips, my throat parched from talking so much. "You said Councillor Ch'oi must have discovered Officer Shim's weakness. Perhaps their blood connection became Shim's downfall. Surrendering a friend to gain his father's approval."

"You are making quite the leap . . . All you're basing this on is the fact that Shim chose the 'Mighty Infant' tale, and nothing else. We don't have enough information."

"But I heard there are *many* horse-dragon legends. Why that one?"

"It is the only horse-dragon legend that belongs to Joseon, not to China. Even when I was young my mother would tell me this tale to frighten me. To keep me from being peculiar."

I tapped my finger against the veranda, thinking. "Then what about Councillor Ch'oi? You said His Lordship summoned Shim to his residence—you have no idea what they talked about?"

"No. I wish I could be of help, but as close as Officer Shim was to Inspector Han, I know little about him. Besides the fact of his illegitimacy, he is a mystery."

"I also know that Myeonmok village is his—" My heartbeat

suspended in midair as my attention shifted to the village's name. Myeon-mok. Names in our kingdom were packed with meaning. I didn't know what *myeon* meant, but the word *mok* sounded familiar. We called the field where ranchers tended to horses *mok-jang*.

"Do you know where Myeonmok village is?" I whispered.

A pause, and then Ryun said, "I do."

"Does the village have anything to do with stables?"

"The village is famous for its horses."

"Why do they raise horses there?"

"The village is located at the base of Mount Yongma in the town of Goyang, and that is where it came from, the legend you told me about. They believe the yongma horse-dragon spirit descends upon the stables every New Year, and that is why their horses are so strong and fast."

I clutched my skirt, knuckles white. "Myeonmok village. This is Officer Shim's hometown, and this must also be where Madam Byeol conceived Councillor Ch'oi's illegitimate son. I was told this, that Madam Byeol was from a town close to Mount Yongma. Her father was a rancher."

Ryun's eyes widened and his brows rose high. "I think you are right," he said. "There has to be more to these coincidences."

"What will you do now?"

"I need to question servants," he replied. "I am acquainted with a few in Councillor Ch'oi's household. One of them might have heard what went on between the two."

"I hope so . . ." There was still a sinking weight in me that Inspector Han might have been involved in the killing. The possibility of Shim's connection to Councillor Ch'oi did not prove Inspector Han's innocence.

But I hoped Ryun would prove me wrong.

I looked around, noticing my surroundings again. The broken screen door creaked on its hinges, swaying back and forth in the wind. And ahead of me, I saw the pine tree with its sharp green needles, and there seemed to be something there. I rubbed my eyes, wondering if exhaustion was fogging my vision, for I could see a white haze watching me from beneath the branches.

"You know this place."

Ryun's voice startled me; it took a moment to gather my thoughts to reply. "I came here once out of curiosity. I heard this mansion was haunted."

"I mean, you *know* this place," he repeated, and when I met his solemn gaze, I sensed that he knew something. "I was ordered to follow your trail before, Seol."

"Ordered? By whom?"

"Inspector Han, after you left a mark on his face and he heard you say, 'Never my brother,' I followed you all the way to Madam Song's inn. I wanted to find out why you've been digging into my master's past, and through her, I learned that you were looking for your brother, a boy named Jeong Inho. I know that name. I know who it is, and I know the new name he goes by."

Shock jabbed at the tender spot right under my ribs. Breathing was painful as I waited for the questions, questions about why I had kept silent about my connection to Inspector Han, about why I had betrayed someone related to me by blood.

Instead, Ryun kicked the ground, and said, "You shouldn't have come back for him."

"What?"

He raised his hands at me. "The inspector told me that. He said you shouldn't have looked for him. There is an old saying that before a man embarks on a journey of revenge, he ought to dig two graves. He said his life has reduced itself to only that. Two graves."

Inspector Han's life had no room for me.

Ryun said no more. Some concern had sewn his lips together, or perhaps it was the expression on my face. I realized that my jaws were locked, teeth clenched, my eyes wide, and from the light-headedness, I imagined I must look frightfully pale. And I was holding my breath, resisting life so I could resist change from happening.

I had so much fear in me.

Fear that in this change my home would disappear. I had grown up under the memory of my brother's stories of home, and in the twelve years that had passed without him, I realized that I had been waiting, that I had never truly left Heuksan Island. The home Brother had told me about, I had dreamed of arriving there one day. A home where there was no more sorrow or tears, no more deaths or farewells.

A place of togetherness.

But now this place would change into a haunted mansion full of strangers and ghosts. How could I embrace them? What did family mean when family had gone away and returned, scarred to the point of being unrecognizable? How could you embrace a stranger with haunted eyes that looked right through you?

"After speaking with Madam Song yesterday afternoon," Ryun continued, speaking slowly and timidly at first, testing to see how I'd respond, "Inspector Han reviewed your record, then journeyed for half a day to a government office in Inchon Prefecture. He interviewed the officers there that night and this morning, and returned to the capital hours ago . . . just in time for his arrest."

I swallowed hard, but the ball of pain wouldn't ease. "What did he find out in Inchon?"

"He found out why you were transferred to the Capital Police Bureau."

I knew why. My registration in the local government had transferred to the capital, all because of a passing remark, which I shared with Ryun now. "An officer told his superior that I was strong, that damos like me would help him regain Commander Yi's favor."

"Did you overhear the discussion yourself?"

"No . . . my sister told me."

Ryun shook his head. "That is not the story the inspector heard."

"What?"

"Apparently, your sister was the one who cunningly convinced the government official. She is the one who told stories of your strength and courage. She did not tell you, did she, that Commander Yi was the closest friend of your father's? She was probably afraid to let you know, lest you make obvious your association with a traitor. That is why she changed your name too, isn't it? To keep you in the dark about your family's past."

My heart hammered in my chest and I managed to say in a trembling voice, "Ridiculous . . ."

"After so many years, and after your father's treason, how could she know whether Commander Yi was friend or foe? But she must have known that sending you close to him would be sending you close to information about your brother."

Something like laughter shook me, leaping out of my mouth with twisting notes of madness. "My *sister* sent me to the capital?" I touched my scarred cheek, fingertips burning against the memory of humiliation. "My own sister . . ."

"Do not blame her so much. What would you have done to bring family together? What is done is done, and right now, we need to help my master."

It was entirely like my sister to make such decisions, just like the cruel choice she had made long ago, refusing to follow our brother to Hanyang. Rejecting him. Then the bitterness winding my muscles loosened. But I . . . I had delivered my brother over to the police bureau, without trying to ask for his side of the story, too afraid to face him at all. I could not say who had made the crueler decision this time—my sister or myself.

"Yes," I whispered. "We must help him."

Ryun ran a hand over his face. "I was already concerned about my master overworking himself with this case. The physician kept telling him to rest, but he wouldn't listen. And now this! I looked into his room earlier and saw him sitting in the darkness, so still. Frozen, almost. He's unable to sleep, and whenever he tries eating, nothing stays down. I think he is afraid, and I have never seen my master so helpless."

Everything made sense now. Why I was here in Hanyang. Everything fit together.

Almost of their own accord, my eyes turned up to the night sky, as though I were the dancing waves reaching for the full moon. I was reminded of the story my brother had told me long ago. Brother Moon and Sister Sun. It had left the deepest impression on me, the tale of two children who had tried to escape a tiger and so had climbed up a rope into the sky. The brother had chosen to lock himself within darkness so that his sister might not be scared.

I didn't know why, but I could feel my eyes light with fire.

I would be the moon for my brother now. I would save the one whom I had once called orabeoni—Older Brother—whether it was to prove his innocence or to save him from his own darkness.

"Ryun," I said. "I am going to Myeonmok village."

TWENTY

"TAKE CARE OF yourself," Lady Kang said, and behind her, Sunhŭi stood and smiled at me. "Be brave and do what is right. For the weary and the frightened, create a paradise on the cold bones of this earth."

Clasping my hands, I bowed deeply and bid them farewell. I wondered if this would be the last time I'd see them, for soon they would be called traitors and condemned to death.

Drawing myself back up, I tried to memorize their gentle countenances and smiles. They had fed me and had shared tea with me last night. Generosity and gratitude had filled every plate and bowl served to me.

I did not believe in their Western God, but I knew that Lady Kang and her daughter must have been an aunt and a cousin who had loved me very well in a previous life.

Lady Kang stepped forward. "Right now, the darkness before us is all we see, but the bright morning is sure to come." Her large and bony hands then wrapped around my rough fingers. "I pray many blessings over your life, Seol. Wherever you go, may you be shown kindness after kindness."

●

I lowered the brim of my satgat over my face as I made my way toward the soldier guarding the East Gate. I presented to the guard the identification tag lent to me by Lady Kang, which belonged to one of her manservants. He cast a cursory glance over me, and I knew that what he saw was a gray robe, ragged and dusty, secured by a black sash belt.

The topknot all men wore, I wore too, hidden beneath my conical straw hat. I was to him a harmless, lanky young man.

The guard gestured at me with his chin. *Get going.*

I stepped out of the capital and took the road that wended east to where Mount Yongma, Mount Acha, and the Han River met. Even from where I stood, I could see the shadow of the mountains silhouetted against the early morning sky, painted purple. A shiver rippled down my limbs. The air was cold, and I was relieved that Lady Kang had thought to line my robe with cotton padding to keep the heat in. Overnight snow had fallen unusually early for autumn, layering the fields and mountains, white as bare bone.

The sound of footsteps behind made me wary. It was a water carrier with pails hanging from a yoke, splashing their contents. His large eyes protruded from his burnt face, and our gazes met, only for a moment. I quickened my steps until he was but a spot in the distance.

I no longer felt safe anywhere. No one could be trusted.

The wind grew fiercer as I drew closer to the mountains. Their towering peaks blocked out the sunlight, leaving me in an icy sea of shadows. Strands of my hair escaped from beneath my hat, flicking across my face, obscuring my vision. Sometimes I saw only my streaming hair, sometimes glimpses of the purple sky and giant mountains. Holding back the strands, I paused now and then to look behind me, to make sure no one was following, before feeling safe enough to push forward.

The journey was not meant to take too long, yet it felt endless, like the seemingly endless journey I had taken with my brother and sister toward the port after the end of our three years of banishment.

I love Older Sister. I love the sky. I love the sea. I love the fishes in it. I'd listed all these things while running my fingers through the long grass. *But best of all, I love you, orabeoni.*

Best of all.

My fingers numb, I reached into my robe, and it took a while for me to feel the crinkled paper I was looking for. I slipped it out and unfolded the sheet on which I had drawn my brother's face. His lightly shaded eyes, his round face, his timid smile.

He belonged to the past, a place he would never leave, not even to come looking for me.

I kissed the sheet and then tore it in half, then in half again, the paper hissing with each motion. I opened my fingers and let the torn pieces be swept away like moths on the wind.

●

Several hills protruded from the land, and Mount Yongma rose like the high storm waves, as though a gigantic dragon swam underneath. With every passing hour, more people appeared on the road, evidence that I was nearing a village of sorts. A farmer leading a string of ponies loaded with salt, a woman with a basket of country produce resting on her head, and another water carrier. I stopped each passerby to ask where Myeonmok village was located. They pointed, and their bony fingers led me to the southern base of Mount Yongma. My legs, which had carried me for surely more than five hours, trembled beneath my heavy heart.

I had arrived.

The scents of pine and snow filled my nostrils as I approached a village of rickety stables and thatched-roof huts. Horses with thickly lashed eyes watched me, nodding their heads while standing in their stalls. The first person I encountered inside this quiet village was an old man in a bulky white robe, sitting outside on a wooden stool as he brushed out his long, long black hair.

He looked me up and down. "A stranger! Now, I have not seen a stranger since a month ago! He snuck into the village at night then was gone by the morning. Perhaps it was you?"

My brows twitched. "No."

"I see, I see. Then what brings a young man like you to Myeonmok?"

I cleared my throat and lowered my voice to sound like a man. "Questions."

"Mmm." He continued to brush his hair, and I wondered if I was speaking to the wrong person, for the man looked rather ridiculous with his hair hanging down his shoulders. He also had an old man's smell to him—strong, spicy herbs and ginseng.

"Do you know Councillor Ch'oi?" I asked casually.

"*Councillor* Ch'oi?" He laughed. "We know nothing about lords and ladies in these parts."

"How about an Officer Shim?"

"Officer?" He pursed his lips and shook his head.

"I am told a woman by the name of Byeol used to live here."

"No—" Then his cracked lips formed into a silent O. "You mean the ghost of Myeonmok village."

"Ghost?"

"A few days ago, a man was drinking in the forest and heard cries coming from an abandoned well. He shone a lamp over but saw no one. He swears it was the ghost of Byeol. She threw her son into that particular well many years ago."

A boy thrown into a well. This matched Madam Song's story.

"Ghosts roam this world because they are kept here by too much anger," I said. "So what made her accumulate so much pain and resentment?"

Lowering his gaze, he continued to brush his hair. "The shaman comes down from the mountain every full moon and tries to resolve Byeol's accumulated han. The shaman says collective repentance is the only way we'll sleep peacefully at night."

"Collective repentance," I repeated. "So you think the reason why Byeol roams this earth is because of the villagers?"

He kept avoiding my gaze. One thing I had learned in the capital was how many dark secrets an individual had, layers and layers—like Soyi, who had taken days to confess her last secret, and I'd finally witnessed her release a few days ago, her mind and legs crippled by torture. *This* was what it took to find the truth, sometimes. But I did not have time to peel each layer off to examine them. I needed to speak with someone who would answer my questions, not clam up. "Where might I find the shaman?"

He set his comb down and waved at me. "I will take you to her. All I've got is time."

I followed him down the dirt path, through the village and its silent alleys, and at last we arrived before the forest entrance into Mount Yongma. A little to the side was a hut covered in strips of fluttering charm paper. The resident had left the door wide open, gesturing for any and all to enter without hesitation.

"Go on." The old man nodded. "I will follow in behind you."

I stepped in, and my nose was assaulted by the strong scent of herbs and oil and smoke from the incense that filled the dark room. Behind a low-legged table sat a woman smoking her pipe. Her face was rectangular, with deep pouches beneath her drooping eyes, her lips pressed together and pursed as though she found the entire world a great disappointment. Her hair, parted sharply in the middle and drawn tightly back, made her look severe and cruel.

"A boy with yin energy." Her voice was quiet and mischievous, the way one would speak when telling a secret. She took in a deep puff on her copper pipe and let the smoke seep slowly out of her lips. "How strange."

I squirmed. Was it that obvious to her that I was a girl dressed in men's clothing? Women had yin energy, and men had yang.

I cleared my throat, and in a deep voice, I said, "I have come here to ask about Madam Byeol. I would like to know more about her."

"Mmm. She is a stubborn, angry ghost. She has much han accumulated here on this earth . . ." Her eyes skimmed over to the man kneeling behind me. "Before she died, we all knew her to be the most beautiful woman in our region. But her beauty was her curse."

"Why?" I asked.

"An unsightly servant might become the wife of a lowborn man, but a beautiful servant will become a concubine, later discarded when she grows old. That is what happened to Byeol when she encountered a passing traveler; he was staying at our inn for three lunar months."

"Why so long if he was only passing by?"

"She bragged that he was a secret royal investigator, come to survey this province."

Around three decades ago, how old would Councillor Ch'oi have been? I assumed somewhere in his thirties, surely. Young enough to have received such a royal appointment.

"Byeol was impregnated by the man," the shaman continued in her scratchy, whispery voice, "and when the child was born, she named him Ji-Won. Not the 'ji' that means wisdom, but the character that stands for ugliness. So that was the meaning of his name. Ugly Origin. A not-so-very-subtle name, but then, everyone knew of her disgrace. She was dismissed from her employment and became the village whore." The shaman again looked at the man behind me, who was picking his ears. "Used and rejected, used and rejected by all the men here."

I shifted away from the old man. He must have been involved

in Byeol's accumulated resentment. Returning my attention to the shaman, I asked, "And no one knows who the father of the bastard is?"

The shaman shook her head.

"And what happened to Ji-Won?"

"When he turned thirteen, perhaps thinking his future too bleak, or perhaps merely despising him, she strangled him and then dumped him into the well."

The shaman took another puff from her pipe, and as the smoke unfurled from her lips, she shook her head, looking deeply puzzled. "I saw her that day, perhaps moments after she had returned from the well. She was standing under a tree, smiling and laughing, telling me that she was waiting for her son. Then at night, there she was, hanging by the neck from a rope. The townspeople buried her, and for many years after that, I have held a ritual there to comfort her spirit."

"And her son's corpse?" I asked.

The shaman shook her head. "A street urchin witnessed his death, from the strangling to the dumping of his corpse. She was too afraid to tell anyone until the next day. But when we went to the well, we couldn't find Ji-Won's corpse. Never did. We only discovered Byeol's corpse, and no one wanted to bury her at first, knowing she had murdered her own son. But we did in the end."

"Show me to the grave," I said, my voice low. I did not know where else to begin searching for the truth.

Both the shaman and man, perhaps curious to know the reason behind my insistence, rose to their feet and led me out of the hut. We traveled along the base of the mountain, and as we ventured through a thicket of trees, I noticed three trunks, each of which had white charm paper tied around them. They were meant to contain evil spirits from wandering into the village. I was led past these trees and into an eerily quiet open field sprinkled with snow.

"This is the place." The shaman gestured with her hand, and the raglike robe she wore over her dress billowed behind her, appearing as though a ghost was hanging on to her. "Her grave."

A lump protruded from the ground, no higher than my knees; a burial mound where the casket would be buried below. I didn't know what I'd meant to find by visiting Madam Byeol's grave, but then I noticed something strange. Madam Byeol had been buried seventeen years ago, so the burial mound ought to have been covered in snowy grass and weeds. Instead, the mound looked freshly disturbed, the grassy soil overturned.

I walked around the site, bewildered, and right behind the mound lay a hoe, the angled blade thick with dried soil.

"Are you certain this is Madam Byeol's grave?" I asked.

"Of course!" the shaman said, her voice screeching. Fear had widened her eyes. "I came here on the previous full moon to cast out her han . . . and it was covered in weeds!"

The man wiped strands of his hair away from his face. "Perhaps Madam Byeol woke up and went searching for her son."

●

After managing to shake off my two companions, I returned to the burial site. Large shadows, reflections of clouds, glided across the barren land. The brooks rolling over the rugged slopes murmured. I heard the occasional rush of a wing as a bird swept by. Otherwise, an oppressive silence hovered over the land.

I was alone.

Crouching, I reached out and touched the overturned soil, hardened from the cold. The snowflakes melted beneath my palm.

I worried my lower lip. I knew with complete certainty that someone had disturbed this grave. But why? To hide or retrieve something? I picked up the hoe, telling myself there was no choice but to find out for myself. I swung the hoe, and the blade hit the mound, dirt spattering onto my robe. Another swing, and chunks of soil tumbled to my feet. I continued this repetitive motion—the *thwack* of the blade, the *shhh* of falling dirt.

Then came a hollow thump. The sound of blade hitting wood.

With shaking hands, I dug some more until a wooden casket lay before my eyes. Fear filled me up, so thick and prickly in my chest.

Taking in deep breaths, I held in a scream and threw the lid open.

Inside there was nothing but bones and a small plaster box. The raised hair on my skin settled, my heart relieved. Fear clearing from my mind, I picked up the box; it was an ancient practice to leave articles for the dead, that they might see them in their afterlife. I opened it and found a letter. Was this why someone had dug up the grave? So that this box could be placed within?

I opened the letter and saw words drawn out in ink. I struggled with the words for a moment, but I managed to decipher the contents.

Dearest Mother,

I did you no wrong, yet you accumulated so much hate against me. I lived embracing your fury, bound to the vile name you had given me. I consulted a shaman and got myself a new name. Jae, "to slaughter, to rule." Deok, "ethics, morality, virtue." I think if Father had listened to me when I cried out for help, matters would have been different.

There it was. The suspect's name. Jae Deok.

And then the rest of the truth rushed in upon me like a wave: Officer Shim Jaedeok had killed the victims. Shim Jaedeok the seoja, the bastard. Shim Jaedeok the insignificant, the shadow.

He must have gone to Hanyang to reclaim his honor. And his father, Councillor Ch'oi, had given him the perfect opportunity, perhaps telling him, *Find the priest and bring him before me, even if that means betraying Inspector Han.* Then *you will be a worthy son.*

Perhaps Shim was the one who had received the anonymous tip to the police, the one containing information about Lady O's Catholic faith and her association with the priest. Seeing his opportunity to please his father, Shim had gathered information about Lady O, and in the process, he must have discovered her secret affair with Scholar Ahn. So he had lured Lady O out with a love letter, had waited to follow her to the lovers' meeting spot, a place that would surely be somewhere isolated. At some point, he must have accosted her, but she had fought against him. And before she could call out for help, Shim had slammed his hand over her mouth. In her struggle she must have ripped off his wooden horse-dragon pendant. Perhaps the scarf covering the lower half of his face had fallen off, too. I could almost hear her muffled cry, the fierce longing to live. Desperate, Shim had grabbed her suicide knife and sliced her throat, silencing her forever. But why had he taken the time to cut off her nose?

Scholar Ahn, after being lured out of his home with a letter, had been kidnapped, stolen away in a palanquin. In the desolation of Mount Nam, Officer Shim had tortured Ahn for information about the priest, for the secrets Lady O had left with him. Whether Officer Shim had collected the information he'd needed or not, he must have known that it would've been too dangerous to let Ahn live. So Shim had let Ahn drown. His nose, too, had been sliced off.

I pressed my hand to the earth to steady myself. At least I knew now who the true killer was, when for all these weeks I had believed Inspector Han guilty of the killings. How dreadful he must have felt when I had accused him of such an evil deed—

"I see you've dug up a grave," said someone behind me.

At the sound of his voice, my blood ran cold. I spun round and found myself face-to-face with Shim Jaedeok.

TWENTY-ONE

SHIM JAEDEOK DID not look like a killer. His eyes were full of luster and changing lights, and when I looked closer, there was a shade of melancholy lurking deep within.

"Good afternoon, Seol." He took a single step toward me. "I never expected you to come this far."

"Afternoon," I croaked.

"I visited the inspector's residence to speak with him . . . to apologize, and that was when I overheard a manservant telling him that you were coming here, so I thought to visit myself." His eyes dropped to my hand. "What did you find?"

My fingers tightened over the letter, and one thought succeeded in breaking through the haze of panic: *He mustn't know that I read it.*

"A piece of paper," I said.

He stretched out his hand, his long fingers uncurling.

I placed the letter into his hands. "I do not know how to read," I assured him. My fingers trembled and my expression likely did a poor job of hiding my fear. "I wish I did. I—I wonder what's on it?"

"Do you know who wrote this letter?"

"It is Madam Byeol's grave, so p-perhaps her son, sir?"

"I think so too," he replied. "I pity the boy. Sometimes monsters are born, but sometimes they are made by an accumulation of hurt."

"I hear he lived a very harsh life here in Myeonmok village . . ." My lips formed words while my mind searched frantically for a way to escape. "A very h-harsh life . . ." The words dwindled away as Shim took a few more steps forward and picked up the hoe. It looked deadly in his grip.

I wiped my forehead, drenched in cold sweat. "I just . . ." I cleared my throat upon hearing my voice shake. "I just found that lying here too. That hoe."

He used the hoe to pile the soil back over the exposed casket, and his voice was menacingly calm as he asked, "You disrespected the dead. For what reason?"

"He was Councillor Ch'oi's illegitimate son, so I thought I might find . . . something to prove Young Master Ch'oi's guilt." My mind went blank with fear; I could not think of a more clever response. "It was clear to me that someone had dug up the mound recently. So I thought something important was hidden inside, but I couldn't understand what was written . . ."

Now. I needed a way to escape *now*. Out of the corner of my eye, I saw the dirt path that wound its way toward the shaman's hut. I could run to her, but Shim would likely grab me before I reached safety. There was the entrance into the wooded mountain nearby, and there was a chance that I might be able to seek refuge in the thicket, but the isolation of the mountains warned me that I would most likely be butchered alive.

"The evidence you found," he said quietly, "the bloody robe. You ought to have hidden it better." Again, he struck the dirt, the blade slicing deep. "Better yet, you ought to have burned it."

He thought I had lost the robe to Kyŏn; he did not know that I had handed it over to him myself.

"You left me with no choice but to betray Inspector Han. Do you think I found delight in that?" There was real emotion in his voice now, the deepest shade of pain. He raised the hoe and slammed the blade into the soil. "It was like feeding my own brother to the tigers. Now things cannot be undone."

Now. The word pulsed through me. *Run away. Now.*

So engrossed as he was in reburying his mother's casket, I wondered whether taking him by surprise would be the best tactic. I could creep forward and—what? Push him? He would instantly grab and tackle me to the ground. Throw dirt at his face, then run? That still would not give me enough time to outrun him. If I did not run now, I might lose my chance. I took a step back, the soil crunching beneath my step, and he looked up.

I froze.

"I saw you enter Lady Kang's home yesterday afternoon. An acquaintance?"

I blinked. "She rescued me the day I got lost on Mount Inwang. I do not know her too well."

"Tell me what kind of conversations you had with her."

"We only spoke about . . . about . . . I cannot remember, sir. It must not have been important."

"You never asked her what the cargo was?"

"Cargo, sir?"

"On the night you disappeared on Mount Inwang, we crossed paths with Lady Kang. She was disguised as a gentleman, but we recognized her, the notorious Catholic rogue that she is. She had cargo, and as she was a noblewoman, we could not order a search. You do not know what it was?"

"No. No, not at all."

"Not suspicious at all? You did not see what was inside?"

"No . . ."

"Perhaps you did."

I kept quiet.

"Catholic books were in there. Perhaps you did see them but chose not to report the matter to the authorities and instead chose to keep quiet. Are you a Catholic, Damo Seol?"

"I am not!"

"Then are you sympathetic toward them?"

"I . . ."

"In which case, you will not easily tell me what I want to know."

"What is it you wish to know? Of course I will tell you, sir!"

"Did you see a man inside her mansion?"

"I did," I blurted out, "but just a glimpse. He is gone now."

"Good, you admit it. All I want is information, Seol, and nothing more. What did he look like? What was unique about his appearance? Did he speak our language well?"

"He . . . he . . . He had long, long white hair," I lied. "His face was that of a very old man. I believe the man was Lady Kang's relative—"

"It is getting late." Officer Shim tossed the hoe aside and looked up at the sky, the light fading, and for a long moment, he seemed interested only in admiring the colors of the sunset. At length, he lowered his eyes to me. "I already know the priest was within, but it seems he was moved elsewhere. I also know that he is no old man. You are fooling no one, Seol."

Deadly silence strangled me. Had Woorim told him that Priest Zhou Wenmo had been moved elsewhere? Shim might even think I knew the secrets of the priest's whereabouts, and if he discovered that I truly knew nothing, he would dispose of me. Scrambling through my thoughts, I searched for a way to pique Shim's interest, a reason to keep me alive even a moment longer. All I could think of was the truth. "You are Councillor Ch'oi's son, are you not?"

This seemed to catch him unawares. "What makes you think that?"

"Because of Councillor Ch'oi's horse-dragon pendant, and . . . and because you were born in this village, right next to Mount Yongma."

"You're a very clever girl," he said, almost regretfully. "Though perhaps you would have come to the truth much quicker had both you and Inspector Han worked together."

I had to keep him talking. "And the noses? Why did you slice them off?"

"You continue to surprise me with your boldness, Seol. You seem to have come to a firm conclusion that I am the killer." He unraveled a coil of rope hanging by his side, slowly and with heavy hands. "Seeing a dead person continues to be difficult, but with their nose removed . . . it reminds me that they were heretics. Wicked people."

Cold sweat dripped into my eyes. I took a step back, and now I was five paces away from the man who clearly did not expect me to live. That was why he was telling me the truth. I knew too much now for him to let me go.

"And all this," I said, my voice tight with fear, "did Councillor Ch'oi order it of you?"

His eyes flashed. "Councillor Ch'oi had nothing to do with this. It was me, all me. I am the one that approached him first. I swore I'd find the priest for him. He was confused by my offer, but a man whose neck is on the line knows not to ask too many questions, and I'd promised to explain everything in due time. Once I catch the priest, that is when I will tell him who I am." He sounded eager to share his wretched story with me. It seemed the weight of his unspoken life had become unbearable, and he had chosen me to be his confidante. "I will save Father from the Catholic purge and make him call me his son. Someone he would not be ashamed to call his true son."

"So it is shame that drove you," I whispered.

"It was justice," he corrected. "Justice stamps out evil."

"And you stamped out the lives of Lady O and Scholar Ahn—" I froze, remembering Woorim's hand gripping mine, her plea for help. My voice shook as I asked, "Did you kill Maid Woorim too?"

A menacing stillness followed. Something about his face changed, as if a shadowy veil had drawn across it. There was a sudden chill in the air. He continued to unravel the rope slowly.

"She is dead," I whispered. Grief choked me and panic swelled up in my chest, making it hard to speak on, but I did. The horrible question prickled up my throat. "You killed three people?"

"There was another, long before Lady O."

I knew I shouldn't look, but he was gazing intently at something behind me, his eyes growing so red. I took another step back, creating more space between us, then cast the quickest glance over my shoulder and saw what Shim was staring at: the grave. His mother. She hadn't committed suicide by hanging herself: her own son had killed her.

Now, a panicked voice in me urged. I had to run *now*—

Suddenly I felt a roughness tighten around my own throat. A rope. Pressure built in my temple, my skull about to crack as blood filled it to bursting, and a hazy darkness closed in around my vision. Then I saw no more.

●

Seol, Seol, I told myself. *Wake up!*

Ignore the painful ripping sensation in your throat. Ignore the confusing stabbing pricks in your eyes, the squeezing of your brain.

You mustn't sleep forever.

●

In the darkness, I heard a voice speak, muffled, as though I lay underwater. "He said to get rid of her quick."

A beam of hazy light shone through; someone had pried my eye open, holding up a torch. The faces of two men, grimy like peasants, floated before me.

"I think she's dead."

Their faces faded away again.

●

A dragging sensation woke me up. A tug, and my entire body shifted forward, then another tug, and I realized four hands were pulling at my arms, the earth passing by under me. I tried to move but could not, weakness tingling in my arms and legs, making me want to never move again. I was aware, on some level, that I should be alarmed.

The two men dragged me as if I were a sack of rice, talking with a dialect used by those from the eastern coast. "Abooji, Abooji." A young man's whispered call for his father, tense with fear and uneasiness. "Her pulse, it's beating still."

"I told you, she's dead. And that is what you tell Officer Shim too, do you understand me?"

"But I don't trust him, Abooji."

"What do you mean?" Panic and fury contorted the older man's voice.

"The shaman, she recognized Officer Shim as Madam Byeol's son earlier today. She called him a killer. What kind of man murders his own mother?"

"We do what we are told to do. It's not our business to know these things."

"He looked ready to beat me for calling him 'Officer' in front of that shaman. What if he murders me too?"

"If you keep on spewing nonsense, he *will* kill us both! Now pull harder!"

The odor that clung to their rags drifted into my nostrils. The gamy smell of lamb and blood. Only baekjeongs, the outcast group, butchered living things—whether animals or criminals. Through my dizziness, a realization pushed through, like a figure stepping out from the fog. The police bureau had hired baekjeongs to execute criminals. Had Officer Shim taken advantage of them from the capital, luring them with promises of acceptance and respect, if only they helped him?

It seemed entirely possible. I remembered Young Master Ch'oi's words: *Evil comes from the unfulfilled need for significance.*

As I weighed the possibility, my body was hoisted off the ground, my head lolling in the air. How strange.

I blinked against the darkness of night, trying to clear the painful confusion beating in my head, but before I could figure out what was happening, I felt a rushing sensation. My entire body falling in cold air. My stomach leaving me. Weightless.

A loud splash fractured the silence.

Water filled my mouth and nose, rough against my blinking eyes. I grabbed onto something as I thrashed in the panic of pitch black. Whatever it was lifted me upward, and soon I broke the surface, gasping. Only when I caught my breath did I notice the complete stillness, save for the water lapping against the stone wall encircling me. My mind startled awake.

I had been thrown into a well.

High above me was a circle of night sky powdered with stars, illuminating the grimy wall and the ripples around me. And then I looked down at what I was holding. It was stiff and covered in fabric, slimy in places. I ran my fingers around until I felt tangles of hair.

Human hair.

My heart rammed against my chest. I pushed away from the

corpse, which was floating facedown, rotating now in the small waves. I struggled to tread water, my robe wrapping around my legs, then managed to dig my nails into the crevices of the rocky wall. *Please no, please no.* I looked over my shoulder and stared into the shaman's gray-filmed eyes, a hole where her nose ought to be, her lips a dark O. She started screaming; or rather, it was *me* screaming. In my panic I could not say which.

"She's still alive!" the young man shouted somewhere outside the well. "Abooji, I told you!"

"Too late! We need to get back to Madam Byeol's house before sunup. He told us to meet him there. Then we can relocate to somewhere safer and pretend all this never happened. Let's go. Now!"

"But, Abooji!"

"Hush!" the father cried, his voice full of tremors. "Th-think. Just think! We'll never have to shed blood again. He promised us. Promised!"

"But—!"

"She knows too much. You think we'll survive if she lives? We'll not only lose our fortune, we'll lose our heads as well. Hurry, let's go!"

Staring at the shaman's missing nose, I reached for my own, and the moment I touched it, I felt pain. It was still there, but blood oozed from a deep cut. Shim had had every intention of slicing my nose off, but perhaps the sound of approaching people had stopped him.

I faced the wall and tried to climb up, but the rocks were so slippery I plunged back into the water, the ripples pushing the corpse up against me. I screamed again, a raspy sound, even though my throat and head pounded with pain.

I was trapped. Fear as I had never felt before gripped me. My teeth chattering, I remained still, my back to the corpse, clinging onto the wall. I dared not move, afraid that the corpse would awake, that her slimy hand would touch me, that her loosened black hair would creep around my throat.

"Orabeoni," I sobbed. "*Orabeoni!*"

Sometimes we must cease feeling, he had once said, when we had lost our way in the rain, *and think instead.*

I took in a few deep breaths, trying to calm the shuddering in me. Then reason reached into me, asking questions to keep me sane.

Is the body dead? Yes.

So it is not moving? No.

Is there something holding your ankles? Yes.

Could it be your robe? Yes.

I became aware that so long as I did not move, my robe did not wrap around my legs, and the corpse remained still, not reaching out for me as I had imagined it was.

Breathing came easier.

I forced myself to look over my shoulder. The corpse floated, staring up unblinkingly at the sky. I had encountered drowned corpses before. Hyeyeon had explained why they were floating: *When people suffocate to death, they remain floating for a while and then sink under.* The fact that the corpse was still floating, after only a few hours since I'd last seen the shaman, told me she had suffocated either from the water or from being strangled.

Fear subsided, and I no longer saw a haunted corpse, but rather an innocent woman, killed because she had lived too long. She had known Officer Shim as a child, had recognized him still after so many years, and so Shim had had to silence her. Otherwise, her gossip would have traveled fast and could have reached Councillor Ch'oi in no time.

"I'm sorry," I whispered.

Craning my head back, I gazed back up at the sky. I would join the shaman in death if I did not find a way to escape. Already my fingers trembled, exhausted and cramped from digging into the crevices.

"I'm here!" Pain strangled my throat, like a blade jammed in. "Help!"

Only the distant fluttering of a wing answered. The hushing of leaves in the mountain wind. The water lapping against the stone wall. The unending and indifferent silence terrified me. There was no one out there.

I dug my nails into a higher rock, tried scrambling against the wall and pushing my weight up, but I slipped. Gurgling, I went under, my mouth filled with tainted water, waves closing over my topknot. I flailed until I managed to reach the surface, even more drained of strength as my entire life clung again onto the crevices.

I couldn't give up now, so I tried climbing up again. It didn't seem impossible, for the wall was rugged. But I only managed to barely lift myself out of the water with each attempt. By the time the circle of sky deepened into the darkest shade of ebony, I was trembling from exhaustion and cold. A haziness crept into my mind, and I wanted to let go and fall asleep.

I pinched my cheek hard.

I couldn't die like this. Not after all that I had gone through. I had to tell Inspector Han that I knew who the real killer was. I'd never even had a chance to tell him, "Orabeoni, do not be scared."

I struggled around the wall, desperate to find an easier way up. I needed more jutting rocks and deeper crevices. I pushed myself from one side to the other, and right then, I froze. My hands and feet, spread-eagled, touched the opposite walls. Moving one foot, then the next, quickly up, I braced myself with my hands pressed against the stones as I pushed myself farther up toward the opening. With my soaked robe and my already trembling arms, I felt as though I was hoisting up a sack of rocks with me, but it was working, the water releasing me from its icy embrace. Water from my drenched hair slid into my eyes, blurring my vision, but I could see it. The circle of sky above me was growing closer.

And even closer.

With every ounce of my remaining strength, I pushed myself higher, and I was so close to the ledge that I could smell the fresh air, crisp with dried leaves and moss. Then all at once, I felt a popping in my shoulder, a bone twisted out from its socket. Sharp pain ripped down my arm, rendering it useless. Only my wobbly legs held me up now, and already, I could feel myself slipping. The sky was getting farther. Soon I would sink under.

A surge of sorrow replaced my panic. I was going to die, and one day a peasant was going to fish me out, a corpse bloated and unrecognizable.

A hand shot down and grasped me by the collar.

"Keep climbing, Seol-ah," came a deep voice. "Take my hand."

I looked up. Torchlight funneled down the well, illuminating the grimy wall, my blood-soaked hands. Inspector Han stared down at me with frightened eyes. For the first time in twelve years, I touched his hand, and his fingers wrapped around mine.

"Don't worry. I won't let you go. You're almost there."

Fresh air greeted my damp face. Relief soared in my heart as, with a final lurch, I flopped forward onto the ground. I couldn't believe it; I was safe now. Hearing footsteps rustle through the frozen leaves, I barely managed to turn and look.

Torches encircled me, the officers and Commander Yi all watching me with wide eyes.

"What?" Officer Goh cried. "Isn't that Seol?"

"The scrambling noise was her?" another officer said.

"Who threw you in?" Goh demanded. "Was it Officer Shim?"

"H-he ordered it." My right shoulder continued to burn as I weakly pointed at the well's opening. "Th-there is one more p-p-person. Dead."

Goh rushed forward and peered down, his torch raised high. "It's true," he called out over his shoulder. "A corpse, I see it. Who is it?"

"A shaman who dwells on the mountain—"

A startled sound escaped from the crowd. It was the old man, one of those who had used and abused Madam Byeol, who had shown me to the shaman's hut earlier. He must have also offered to be the officers' guide when they had ridden into the village.

"So Officer Shim has killed in total three victims," Inspector Han said.

"There was a f-f-fourth." My teeth chattered. "His mother. I know he k-killed her."

Another stranger watched me. A man of regal stature, garbed in his silk riding robe of purple, stood among the officers. The darkness did not hide his features, which held the handsomeness of a soldier; brave, chiseled, and with honorable eyes. It was Councillor Ch'oi, and at the news of how his former mistress had died, he placed his hand over those eyes. "His *own* mother . . . You are certain Officer Shim is the killer?"

"There is no doubt about his connection to the murders," Inspector Han said, and he looked my way. The scratch I'd left on his cheek looked red and raw in the torchlight.

Woorim. He hadn't mentioned her name. My pulse quickened, beating hard against my right temple.

"When was the last time you saw Senior Officer Shim?" Inspector Han asked me.

The beating in my head grew stronger, making it difficult to think, but I still managed to reply, "Around midafternoon, sir."

"Hours have passed since then." He gazed up at the gray-blue sky, the moon still hanging over a cloud. "Shim wouldn't have returned to the capital. He told a guard he'd come to speak with me, and he must have overheard my manservant through the hanji screens. The accusations against him. Wherever he went, he might already be too far for us . . ."

As the officers speculated, and as others dragged the shaman's corpse out from the well, I stood still, unable to move. Woorim's grip on my thoughts tightened, her fingers wrapping around mine in desperation, cold and sticky with blood. *Seol, please help me, please, please help me.* Her plea echoed and sent a ripple of bumps down my spine, her voice growing louder and louder until it was all I could hear.

"What is the matter?"

My attention snapped back to Inspector Han, and a light sparked in my mind. "Officer Shim . . . he might not be too far away."

"What do you mean?"

"Dead woman Byeol's house," I whispered, my eyes widening. "Officer Shim's helpers, they mentioned that place, that they must return there. Woorim could be there as well."

Once, my words would have fallen upon deaf ears. But at this moment, perhaps only ever this moment, my voice was like a torchlight raised against the darkness of night. There were no eyebrows raised, no rebukes flying my way for speaking out of turn. There were only men watching and listening.

"And where is this dead woman Byeol's hut, Damo Seol?" Commander Yi asked gently.

"I . . . I don't know, sir." We would have to go from hut to hut, asking for directions, but we didn't have time—

My panic stilled at the sight of the old man. "*He* must know."

The old man stared at me, pointing his finger at himself.

"Yes," I said. "That man."

A soldier pushed the old man, and he came stumbling forward into Commander Yi's periphery. He flicked a nervous glance toward the near mountain and said, "It is up there on Mount Yongma!"

"Well then," Commander Yi said. "Lead the way."

"*Me*, sir?"

"You offered to be our guide. Now lead."

The officers, around twelve of them, mounted their horses and gathered into a line. As for me, horseless as I was, I fell behind, far from Inspector Han, far from the possibility of being stopped and told that my lips were too blue, that I ought to stay behind and search for shelter. He would be *right* to suggest this. And it did occur to me, as I gazed up at the jagged shadows of Mount Yongma's peak, that I might not survive the icy journey if I followed.

Still, my feet moved forward, one step after the next.

Not because of fearlessness—no, my stomach ached with terror. I followed the officers because the moment I'd grabbed onto Woorim's hand, trying to pull her out of danger, her destiny had bound itself to mine. I had seen desperation gleam in her eyes and I had touched her wound.

How could I forget? How could I turn away?

●

We traveled into the forest that covered the mountain, trees rising like the hackles of wolves. My damp robe had frozen stiff under the spare blanket offered to me, and strands of my once-dripping hair now hung on either side of my face like black icicles. With each step, I could feel my limbs less and less, the cold piercing so deep into the marrow of my bones that tears rolled down my numb cheeks.

As I wiped the wetness from my face, Inspector Han—who was riding ahead of us—slowed and looked over his shoulder. He said something to Commander Yi, then tugged at the reins and steered his horse around. Hooves tramped down the slope, and soon the creature came to a prancing halt a few feet away from me.

"Go back down to the village. I'll send an officer with you," he said. "The cold might kill you."

I shook my head and gritted my teeth hard, to still their chattering. "N-no."

He observed me, and for a moment I could imagine what he saw, a girl garbed in a frozen robe, whose fingers and toes would likely be lost to frostbite, but a girl who had risked her life by going against *him*—an inspector of the Capital Police Bureau, a military official of the fifth rank. He knew I would not change my mind so easily.

"Very well then, I won't ask you again . . ." I followed his gaze, trailing past the trees and through the mist. "Can you manage?"

"I c-can, sir."

He swung off his horse and the forest floor crunched beneath his feet. "Then get on."

I accepted his hand and slipped my foot into the stirrup. He hoisted me up into the air with surprising strength, like I was his four-year-old sister again, and the next moment I sat perched on the horse's back with one hand holding on to the saddle horn, and the other hanging uselessly, my shoulder burning after Officer Goh had forced the bone back into its socket earlier. As for Inspector Han, he continued on foot, holding the creature's reins as he led the way.

Venturing farther up the mountain, the servant ahead of us held up a blazing torch that illuminated the crystallized forest. The freezing cold had arrived so early this year, it seemed a spell had been cast over the land. Icicles gleamed orange. Snow-dusted pine trees soared high. Everything was still, too still. Even the glow of torchlight, which stretched across the frozen land, seemed painted there—never shifting, never flickering. Somewhere beyond the serene facade of the woodlands, surely a vile darkness awaited us.

My only wish was that Woorim still lived.

"There is s-something I do not understand, sir. H-h-h—" I gritted my teeth and tried again. "How did Officer Shim s-suspect that she knew something about the p-p-priest's whereabouts?"

"Suspect whom?"

"Maid Woorim."

Inspector Han let out a breath, a cloud of steam forming before his lips, and a heaviness weighed his voice as he said, "The safest place for the priest would have been the residence of a woman immune to police attention. I suspected Lady Kang, and so I asked Woorim why she was seen purchasing gentlemen's clothes and shoes."

"W-what did she say, sir?"

"She claimed they had a guest, her mistress's father-in-law . . ." He held aside a branch of sharp needles, letting me pass without being whipped. "Yet I later learned that the father-in-law had never left the province, and I shared this with Shim. This must have led him to think that the maid knew the priest was inside."

"And now the priest is m-m-missing again," I said. "Officer Shim said so."

"Then Woorim is more valuable to him now. She may still be alive."

A burst of hope fluttered warm against my rib cage. "P-perhaps, sir."

Silence settled between us, emphasizing the woodland noises—the hardened layer of snow cracking underfoot as officers pressed upward, the trees creaking like old bones.

"You know," Inspector Han said quietly, glancing at me over his shoulder, "I am impressed with all you've done for this case. With your determination, you can be anything you want."

I whispered my gratitude, yet the delight I might have felt withered at the sight of his pale face, the pallor of a man trapped in an unending nightmare. *Orabeoni.* A tenderness in me wanted to reach out . . . and do what? What could I do or say to wake my once-brother from whatever it was haunting him? *I am here. You aren't alone anymore, orabeoni.* But all I managed to say was, "It has been a difficult case, sir."

"It began as a simple case of jealousy," he murmured, "then turned into one that I was hardly prepared for."

It was easier talking about the investigation, the only thing we had in common. Sadness pinched me at the realization that we'd spent more years as strangers than as siblings . . .

"How did you know it was Senior Officer Shim, sir?"

"After Ryun told me of your discoveries, from Councillor Ch'oi's true son to the horse-dragon pendants, I informed Commander Yi of all this, and he had officers search Shim's house. The bloody palanquin and his journal were found, which was enough to confirm his guilt, and that is why I was released from house arrest. But I also had another piece of evidence against Shim."

"E-evidence?"

"Calligraphy reflects a person's character, and an erroneous but habitual brushstroke order serves as a person's signature." He raised a finger, and as though he were painting the sky, he traced out a slash, followed by an angular slash, then he closed the box with one last stroke. "The way the character 'meum' was written in the criminal's letter stood out most to me. Its brushstroke order was peculiar, and this distinguishing characteristic repeated itself throughout the letter."

"How was it p-peculiar, s-s-sir?"

"It was written in one stroke, when it ought to have been written in two strokes, or three or more by the unlearned. But just one stroke? Very rare. No such errors existed in Ahn's writing. Oddly enough, it was identical to Shim's handwriting."

His words reopened a gash. The stinging resentment returned, though duller this time, less intrusive. Why had it taken the inspector so long to notice the similarities in an obvious brushstroke mistake? Officer Shim had shared his written reports with the inspector several times.

"W-why did you not second-guess Officer Shim right away, sir?" I asked, and withheld myself from adding, *If you had, this investigation might have ended long, long ago.*

"Whenever a murder occurred in the past, I'd never had to suspect one of my own. It was always others who were culprits."

One of his own . . . I would never understand this. The bureau was home to Inspector Han and to the other officers, who would face knife-wielding killers together, who would spend nights without sleep while tracking down a criminal, sharing their life stories in whispers over rice wine. They had chosen to walk the same path that twisted through no-man's-land, and most likely, they would reach the very end together. Always together.

"I could not sleep, I could not eat, consumed by the cases of Lady O and the priest," Inspector Han continued. "I relied even more on Shim to keep me sane."

I nodded my head while my brows remained crumpled together. This answer would have to do—

A distant whistle looped and twirled, piercing the stillness.

For a moment I thought the whistle had come from our team, but by the way Inspector Han froze, as did the entire line of officers ahead, I knew the sound had come from somewhere beyond. Tension tightened the air around us, and officers were already reaching behind for arrows.

"Spread out," Commander Yi's rasping whisper echoed. "Do *not* let Officer Shim escape."

The quick-footed officers scattered in all directions, leaving Inspector Han and me swallowed up in isolation. Dread gouging into my chest, I tried holding tighter on to the saddle horn, afraid that at any moment, something might leap out and knock me off the horse. Instead, my fingers would not move, trembling with exhaustion. Cracks had formed in my red skin, strength draining out in quick waves.

Inspector Han's warning drifted into my ears. *The cold might kill you.*

With the back of my hand, I rubbed my eyes as a dreamlike haze edged the corners of my vision. It cast a fog so thick over Inspector Han, blurring him into a shadow even though he walked near me. I looked around. The sharp lines of the ancient trees were also blurred, bleeding like ink with too much water.

Then I heard it.

A growl reverberating from deep within the chest of a gigantic beast, a rumbling noise that shook the branches and sent tremors though me. But every time I turned to look, the echoing growl came from a different direction—from the mist lurking ahead, from the rock right next to me, from the sky high above. Panic clutched my heart. "D-did you hear that, sir?"

"Hear what?"

"A tiger."

"Seol-ah . . ." A note of concern edged Inspector Han's voice, and I realized that my mind was tipping into delirium. "There are no tigers here—" The rest of his words froze in midair. Stretching out his arm, he gestured at me to be still.

It took a moment of squinting and rubbing my cloudy vision to see a figure stepping out from behind a tree. The forest was barely illuminated by the moonlight that streamed through the gnarled branches, revealing a crescent of Officer Shim's face and the blue-white gleam of his blade, drawn partially out from the scabbard.

"Why is it you?" came Officer Shim's strained voice. "Why did you come this way, Inspector?"

"To arrest you."

"I do not know what Damo Seol told you, but she is a liar. She's the one who betrayed you."

"No. She's the only one who chose to do what was right. Now put down your weapon, Shim. You can fight me, but you will not escape."

The blade rang as Shim withdrew it entirely, and yet a shadow of reluctance weighed his brows and blunted the sharpness of his gaze. "So be it . . . So be it then . . . ," he repeated, as though he needed to convince himself.

Inspector Han reached for his own sword as he took a step back, and I thought he would dash through the trees for safety. But instead he turned his head, ever so slightly, and whispered to his horse, "Get her away from here." Then he slapped its rear flank.

Everything happened so quickly I couldn't tell what was occurring. The glint of the inspector's own blade, flashing bright. The neighing horse, eyes wide. The whirring of leaves and the landscape passing quickly by me.

Exhaustion lay thick in my mind, making it difficult to think, but whatever sense remained swam through and clung to a steadying thought: it was not the inspector alone in the woods, but my brother. The boy who had carried me on his back through the eastern torrent, the boy who had spent most of his days memorizing Confucian classics or writing poems. *He* was determined to fight Officer Shim, an expert swordsman.

I slapped my cheek. "Wake up, Seol. Wake up." Another slap, firmer this time, and the pain struck awake a moment's clarity. I swung myself forward and reached for the reins, nearly falling off, having barely any strength left to hold on to the saddle horn. I tried again, and once the reins touched my fingertips, I held them tight and then dragged myself upright.

We steered around and tore through the blue mist, and the wind gathered around me. Grief wailed and echoed off the peaks of the soaring trees. Snow lining the pines shook and fell to the ground. The forest parted for me, the fog parted for me.

I would not lose my brother. I would not lose him a second time.

"Wait for me," I whispered through my clenched teeth. "Please, wait for me."

The moment I neared the sound of clashing blades, I climbed off the horse and fell onto all fours. My left shoulder throbbed as I crawled, my feet too frozen to walk, and all the while, I searched for anything—a stick, a stone, *anything*—to fight with. But nothing solid touched my searching hands.

"Did our friendship mean *nothing*?"

At the sound of Officer Shim's voice, I peered through the

swaying branches and saw Inspector Han lunge forward, his sword striking Shim's with a resounding clang that turned into a grinding noise as blade pushed against blade. Shim managed to parry away, yet Inspector Han was faster, dashing forward and gaining enough momentum to leap and turn, wielding his sword in an orbit that slashed across Shim's arm. A ribbon of blood arced into the sky.

For the longest moment afterward, the two men stood opposite each other, puffs of clouds forming before their lips like smoke.

Shim touched his wounded arm, then looked up. "I used to think of you as a brother."

"I still think of you as my friend, my only friend for more than a decade." Sweat trickled down Inspector Han's wrist as he gripped his sword tighter, his eyes glistening bright. "But while I will follow a friend when he is good, if he chooses evil, I will abandon him."

"Good and evil depends on which side you are on." With this, Officer Shim lunged into the darkness. Something had uncoiled in him, letting loose the ruthlessness that had slit a woman's throat, drowned a man, and strangled his own mother. His sword swung, but Inspector Han dodged, spinning away as his robe billowed around his legs. A breath of relief escaped me, seeing the inspector safe now, anchored on his feet with his sword at the ready.

"Just like your father," Shim hissed. "A traitor."

He came whirling back, swinging his sword with the force of an ax striking a log, a swing that knocked the sword out of Inspector Han's grasp and sent him hurtling into a tree. A loud thud, and chips of bark flew off.

Get up, Inspector. The plea pounded in me as I wondered what to do—me, a weaponless girl against a sword-wielding tiger. *Please, Inspector.*

Inspector Han grabbed his sword and leaned his weight on the hilt as he struggled back upright. But he wasn't quick enough. Officer Shim's blade gleamed as it slashed through the air and swiped the inspector's side.

Time slowed. Every expression that moved across Inspector Han's face—disbelief, hurt, dawning realization—passed slowly. He reached down and held his side. A rivulet of blood streamed down his knuckles, the flow nearly black in the fading moonlight. The pain weakened his legs and he collapsed to the ground, only to be met with a blade pointed at his throat.

"You were dying long before tonight," Shim whispered. "If we meet again in the afterlife, do not blame me for your death."

Inspector Han kept his chin raised, and the moonlight gleamed off the blade, casting a white slash across his face and twinkling against the silver pin of his topknot.

"But . . . ," Shim added. "I'll give you another chance. Run away."

"Why would you let me go?"

"Remember when I tried to meet my own father?" Shim's voice rasped. "He hadn't recognized me, called me a thief, and had his men beat me. Remember your promise—that one day you would help me rise from my status? Keep your word and let me go."

"I would rather you be quick and kill me," Inspector Han said calmly. "Add to your shame."

His words sent a shock through me, and through Officer Shim as well, for he stood frozen. Perhaps the thirteen-year-old boy in him, the one thrown into the well by his own mother, beaten by his own father, did not have enough greed and fury left in him to drag the blade across the throat of his longtime friend—and possibly the only human being who cared for him.

As hesitation gripped Shim, I knew I had to move. This was my only chance, and they were but a few paces away. Like a calf with wobbly legs, I stumbled forward. My arm moved of its own accord, reaching behind and grabbing hold of the steel pin that held up my own topknot. I jerked it out, the end gleaming fang-sharp.

With all my might, I raised it high and then plunged the end into Officer Shim's upper back, feeling flesh rip and the tip scraping across bone.

A roar exploded from his throat, a sound so full of rage that I startled back, falling to the ground. He swung around, the pin still protruding from his back. "You again," he growled, brandishing his sword, the blade whooshing through the air. "I thought I'd killed you!"

I closed my eyes. *Enough,* I thought, *I have done enough in this life.*

And I waited to feel the burning slice of death.

But it never came.

I opened one eye, then the other. Waves of shock reeled through me at the sight of Commander Yi on horseback, as well as officers, around a dozen of them, in a circle around us with arrows nocked and drawn.

"Halt!" the commander's voice thundered. "Lower your sword, Senior Officer Shim."

For a moment, the briefest moment, Officer Shim's eyes darted from one side to the other, as though he was calculating his escape. But he was surrounded.

"Lower. Your. Sword!"

The moment the blade dropped to the ground, two officers hurried forward. They held Shim Jaedeok in a painful grip, his arms twisted behind, making him stagger with his back bent forward. At the sight of his sword, left on the snow right before me, my body shook uncontrollably. I had been too close to death. The inspector had been, too.

I looked over to see Inspector Han struggling on the forest floor, one arm slung over Officer Goh's shoulder. I moved forward to help, but stopped at the sound of Officer Kyŏn's voice.

"I knew it was him all along." Kyŏn stood a few paces away, whispering to a fellow officer, a red flush burning the panes of his cheeks. He wouldn't look my way. "I knew it must have been someone close to the inspector—"

"Silence!" Commander Yi snapped. "If you stir disorder again in the police court, I will cut out your tongue myself."

"But, yeonggam, anyone would have misunderstood the evidence I'd discovered—"

The officers elbowed Kyŏn, gesturing at him to be silent. And the thorny memories in me also fell still as Councillor Ch'oi stepped through the row of officers, arriving before the seoja, his bastard son, who stood with his torso and wrists bound in rope.

"You are Madam Byeol's son?" Councillor Ch'oi demanded. His gaze was sharp and firm, his jaw locked, and his shoulders drew back as though he were king. "The son of the woman you killed?"

Officer Shim's face was white and his lips bloodless. He spoke without emotion and did not meet anyone's eyes. "I am he. The boy named Ji-Won."

"You were her disgrace."

"I . . . I did not ask to be born."

"But you were, and you caused chaos in the capital." Councillor Ch'oi gathered his hands behind his back and stared over his son's head, like he could not bear to spare him another glance. "Tell the commander. How many did you kill?"

Shim remained silent, only breathing in and out the cold night air, a night that was coming to an end. With anyone else, he would likely have withheld the truth, but before the man who had haunted his life for years, the word slipped out.

"Four."

Lady O, Scholar Ahn, the shaman, his mother. That was four.

"Is Woorim still alive?" I blurted out.

"Councillor," Shim said, ignoring my question, his gaze still fixed upon his father. "Please. My crimes were indeed dreadful, but I thought to myself, perhaps this path I walk is neither black nor white, perhaps it is gray—"

"Answer the girl!" Councillor Ch'oi bellowed.

Officer Shim flinched as a boy did under his father's raised hand, and in a hoarse whisper, he said, "She may still be alive."

●

A narrow path wound through the mountain. To one side was a thickly wooded slope that fell away steeply for about five hundred cheok in distance, and to the other side a cliff wall with plant life sprouting from its cracks.

No one seemed to know where Senior Officer Shim was leading the whole team, which included Councillor Ch'oi, and I wondered if Shim even knew himself. The forest stretched on and on, an endless landscape of trees after more trees, so unchanging that I paused at one point, wondering if we had not crossed this path before.

The uneasy sensation that we were being led in circles coiled tight in my stomach several more times before Officer Shim finally stopped in his tracks. His stare drifted down the trail, which wound around granite slabs, down toward a small crevice in the plateau. "Here" was all he said.

Inspector Han cautiously descended with a limp, along with two other officers. In a few moments' time, he returned and signaled for the rest of his officers to join him. He hadn't looked my way, hadn't signaled me, but I followed anyway.

Woorim, please be alive, please, I begged with each step down the trail and into the crevice, with each hollow thump of my heart. *Please.*

"Why did you lead us here," Inspector Han demanded, "and not to Madam Byeol's house?"

Shim kept his gaze lowered as he replied, "Her house was our meeting point, but this cave was where I intended to hide for the night."

"So your helpers are inside?" The inspector's lips were as pale as a dead man's, his jaws clenched against the excruciating pain I imagined he was in. The strip of fabric bound tightly around his waist was already wet with blood. "Then order them to come out."

"Come—" Shim's voice cracked. He tried again, his voice this time loud and clear and strained with a grief-stricken note of defeat. "Come out!"

At first there was silence, the air within the cave so still. Then there came a timid scraping of footsteps, and soon our torchlight illuminated two figures. One was a grime-covered youth, and the other a deeply wrinkled and deeply familiar man. It was the executioner, the one I had often seen washing blood off himself in the backyard of the police bureau. And today, even today, his hands and ragged garment were stained with streaks of dried blood.

"Whose blood is that?" I demanded, panic rising to my throat. "Wh-where is Woorim?"

The executioner hung his head. Repeatedly, he sobbed, "I'm sorry, I'm sorry!"

My knees went weak. As the police arrested the two rogues, I grabbed the torch from a manservant and rushed into the cave. The orange glow of light illuminated the walls, black from woodsmoke, and I flinched as memories swept into my mind—of Woorim hurtling into the stone wall, struck so hard her bones snapped. Lying there on the ground, mouth open, eyes staring at me.

The day seemed to repeat itself right before my eyes, for I found myself standing before a girl curled up on the floor. The torch shook in my grip as I drew the flame closer. Blood from her head covered half her face, dried and crusted down the side of her neck, staining the collar of her hanbok.

"Woorim," I whispered.

She did not move.

Then the torchlight shifted, exposing a different angle to this horror. The blood had flowed not only from her head, but from the gaping wound where her nose had once been—and was no longer.

"No . . . no, no, no." I shook my head, darkness pulsing through my veins. I wanted to crush something and scream. Guilt clawed at my chest. Woorim was dead because *I* had asked her to show me to the haunted mansion. *I* had made sure that her heart would never beat again.

"Seol?"

The sound of her voice drew me back, sending a surge of tremors through me. Woorim couldn't move, tied up as she was, but she managed to lift her head ever so slightly to look my way. Her forehead crinkled, her tiny lips opened as trembling words wobbled out. "Seol, is that you?"

"I-i-it is." I couldn't believe it: she was alive. "Woorim!"

Panic widened her eyes, and words rushed out from her. "We don't have time. They will come back soon!"

"Shh, shh." I crouched before her, so relieved my head swirled with lightness. "The police have come. You are safe."

Her eyes remained wide as I untied her wrists and her ankles.

Then I held her arm, and with whatever strength remained in me, I gritted my teeth against the burning pain in my shoulder and hoisted her up onto her feet. I kept her steady as we both staggered through the tunnel. We squinted as we neared the mouth, the pitch darkness of the cave chased back by the skylight. It was almost dawn now.

"Seol-ah," Woorim whispered, tears dribbling down her cheeks, showing streaks of skin beneath the blood. "I thought the morning would never come."

The fragile beauty of the sky-lit forest yawned around us, the beams of light streaming in through the branches touching my face and reaching their arms into my soul. Never had I imagined this day would come—the end to darkness. I had succumbed to a hopelessness that had colored my world in storm-cloud gray, a hopelessness that swore the end would always remain unreachable, like home, like all my dreams, a distant land I knew of only from its faraway echoes. But it was over. The investigation was over.

I let out a breath and whispered, "Finally."

At the sound of crunching snow, I glanced over to see Councillor Ch'oi weaving through the crowd, and I was not surprised. Every moment possible, the councillor had made his way back to his bastard son, as though pulled toward him by their blood ties, but also by shame. This time, the councillor's face was pale, and he appeared a decade older as he stopped before the monster he'd created through neglect.

"You mutilated a living girl. You killed four others," Councillor Ch'oi said, his brows knitted over eyes wide with disbelief. "Compassion, sympathy, and empathy. Could you not feel them when you were hurting your poor victims?"

Officer Shim remained still, kneeling on the forest floor. It took him an entire minute to muster enough strength to speak, and even then, his voice shook. "You . . . you begged Inspector Han to deliver the priest to you, but he wanted to kill the priest himself. So I did what the inspector refused to do: I offered to help you catch the priest." All the confusion in the world seemed to cram into the dark pool of his eyes as he looked up at Councillor Ch'oi. "Is that not what sons are for?"

Silence stretched as Councillor Ch'oi continued to stare down at his son. Shim turned away; he must have seen pity in His Lordship's gaze. Pity from one's father was the worst humiliation.

"Suicide." Everyone's attention snapped back to Councillor Ch'oi as he spoke. "It is an accepted practice according to the customs of Joseon. A military officer who has served the Capital Police Bureau for years should be permitted to end his life honorably."

Above us, the trees hushed, as though a ripple of dread had passed through the forest. The snow crunched as officers shifted on their feet, uneasy, while Shim stared at the gleaming object in the councillor's hand, a dagger drawn out. Perhaps Shim was wondering whether a little blade could truly empty the blood from his body, and how fast the blood would drip. As he looked up at the spectators, a flurry of emotions seemed to cross his pale countenance—his realization and horror at what had been done, his feelings of personal guilt, his wish for death and yet fear of execution, the shame of being spared.

Before I could even close my eyes, Shim scrambled toward his father, taking the soldiers off guard. It seemed the fear of shame was greatest, the fear of being called Ji-Won again. His bound wrists moved and his fingers strained for the knife, but just then, Inspector Han swept forward, grabbed his old friend by the shoulder, and threw him down to the frozen ground.

"You murdered to escape shame," the inspector rasped, as though he dared not speak any louder lest his voice fall apart. "Now pay the price. Endure a public trial."

Shim's breath escaped him like the wind on a wild night, and then at long last, he crumpled forward with his face to the earth, curling up into a ball like a boy after a beating.

●

None of the remaining spectators moved after Officer Shim was dragged away. No one had been prepared for what they saw. Then the sound of a twig cracked as I stepped forward and whispered, "Inspector."

His silk robe rustled as he turned. Without a word, he donned his police hat, the black beads falling around his chin. Then he accepted his sword from a manservant and secured it to his sash belt. All this he did moving at the pace of a snail, burdened by an immense load upon his mind and body. Then at last he looked at me and said, "What is it?"

So accustomed to my role as a damo, I made sure to bow to him in the position of submission—hands clasped before me, head lowered. "You are still bleeding, sir."

"Do not worry about me." He then did something unusual. He reached out and patted my shoulder, and when I glanced up, I saw the rims of his eyes slowly redden. "Investigating with you . . . it was quite the experience, Damo Seol."

Without another word, he moved away, leaving my shoulder cold. He staggered past the officers, his hands hanging down by his sides. I took a step toward him again, but Commander Yi said, "Let him go."

I watched him walk through the pines, heading into the shadows cast by the first light of dawn. All on his own. He had done his best, and with the memory of the dead drenching the forest floor, the smell of their blood was so thick in the air it was hard to breathe.

Unmindful of the killings, a lone bird called out a blissful song, the welcoming of a new day.

TWENTY-TWO

SISTER.

A departing whisper echoed into my ear, startling me awake.

Little Sister.

I lay among the other damos, all of them curled up under their blankets. As they breathed in and out with the slow steadiness of those in deep slumber, I rolled off my mat and struggled to my feet. Exhaustion pulsed with a dizzying force against my skull.

"You're still weak from the cold," Aejung had warned me yesterday. "You need to rest."

But I could not.

Just as I had done the past three days, I bundled myself in my cotton-padded uniform, the norigae pendant Inspector Han had given me tied to the inside string of my dress. The norigae meant for his little sister; for me. The cold air bit my skin when I stepped outside. Falling snow, flickers of light against the clouded morning sky, drifted slowly down onto the black-tiled roofs and empty courtyards.

It was over. The truth had been exposed and Senior Officer Shim was awaiting his trial. Inspector Han was alive and needed more rest to recover. There was no reason to feel as I did. No reason for dread to be crawling over me like a thousand tiny spiders. But something felt so very *wrong*.

Frowning over this loose thread, I let my feet carry me to the western courtyard and into the under-floor ondol furnace beneath the Officer of the Inspector. I lit a fire, still lost in my thoughts as I fanned the flames to heat up the pavilion, in case Inspector Han should arrive.

Once the furnace was kindled enough, I shuffled out of the space and out into the cold again. My exhaustion was infecting my mind. All was well. I sucked in a breath of the crisp air—

Little Sister.

My heart leapt at the whisper, and I looked over my shoulder toward the gate that led into the main courtyard. I'd left the door ajar, and so the gate opened onto a scene of the gray sky, the thin blanket of snow, and the unchanging emptiness. The scenery was as it had been a few moments ago, and yet a tug of dread, fierce and relentless, dragged at my guts.

With hurried steps, I returned to the main courtyard, turning on my heel to find the source of my uneasiness. A shadow caught the corner of my eye, and as I whirled around, the shadow sharpened into a familiar figure.

Our gazes met across the courtyard, mine wide and his half-lidded.

It almost felt like any other day from the past four and a half months: I'd be sweeping the pavilion and Inspector Han would stride in—the military official capable of shooting two hundred arrows a day in rain, snow, or sleet; the soldier who could slip silently through the grass with scarcely a ripple, like a speedy leopard.

But today, Inspector Han stopped by the gate of the police bureau, leaning against the wooden beam with a book clutched against his chest. He had thinned so much that I could see the sharp lines of his cheekbones and jaw. He breathed so slowly, and it took a few more breaths before he dragged one foot forward, then the other. Yet on his third step, as though struck from behind, he swayed.

"Inspector!" I broke into a run. But no matter how fast I ran, the space swallowed up my steps and expanded, stretching into an enormous distance between me and Inspector Han, now collapsed on the ground, not moving. My heartbeat hammered against my chest, blood roaring in my ears. I nearly missed a step, stumbling in my haste.

"Inspector, Inspector!" My knees hit the ground at last. I shook his shoulder, and when his eyes opened, just a slit, it was as though he were staring up at me from deep under the waves. "Wake up, sir!"

I touched his pulse—weak, but beating steadily. His skin was icy cold. I pulled his arm around my shoulder, and pushing all my strength into my legs, I tried to rise. His deadweight dragged me back down.

"Help!" I shouted over my shoulder. "Someone help!"

The heavy hand of silence did not move from the bureau, nor did the shadows sleeping under the pavilion eaves stir. It was just me, the inspector, and his book. My attention darted onto the latter, its spine bound with five red stitches. Someone had written on the paper cover, *Officer Shim's Secret Investigation Records*, and the sight of this book slid a thorn into my chest. It was the journal with information regarding the whereabouts of the priest. The man whom Inspector Han, despite his torn mind and body, had poured every ounce of his life into finding.

You must kill Priest Zhou Wenmo were Mother's last words to Older Brother in her suicide note. I remembered now. The day Brother and Sister had fought, he'd recited the note, reminding her of our duty to return to the capital, where the priest was rumored to be. I had overheard everything. *Avenge the downfall of our family so that the sorrows of your dead parents might be appeased and that the living might find peace.*

The living . . . that was me. Yet I had never asked for vengeance. All I had ever wanted was a home and a family. A burning emotion swelled in my chest, stinging the corner of my eyes, but there was no time to grieve.

My voice cracked as I yelled out again, "Please, someone help!" I gripped the inspector's arm and heaved. I had not gotten him beyond the gates when I heard the crunching of hurried footsteps. In the white distance outside the bureau, a dark figure grew into a person I immediately recognized.

"Ryun!" I cried the moment he was near, and through my shuddering breath, I managed to say, "What are you doing here?"

"I'll tell you later. Let me help bring the inspector to his office!"

Ryun panted, still out of breath from running, and with his help, we managed to haul Inspector Han up. His feet dragged and staggered as we led him forward. His head lolled. His lips were so pale they blended in with his blanched face.

"Once we get him to shelter," Ryun said, "I'll go find Commander Yi and the physician as well."

"The physician? Do you know what happened?"

"My master has pushed his health to its limit, and with his infected wound . . ." Ryun shook his head. "He thinks himself invincible, but he is not. The physician warned him!"

Specks of snow caught on my lashes and dissolved into my burning eyes. "Of what?"

"For three days straight, he told my master to rest, that his health was failing him. But instead he didn't even sleep and spent his time examining records, searching for that priest. And then last night, he heard Woorim had apostatized to avoid being executed. She hasn't yet confessed Priest Zhou Wenmo's whereabouts, so the inspector told me he'd return to the bureau to interview her. So when I couldn't find him this morning, I *knew* I'd find him here . . ." Ryun's voice wavered, and grief gleamed in his eyes. "His obsession is killing him, Seol. It's *killing* him."

The ondol floor beneath where I knelt grew warm as I waited inside the office, hoping a hint of color would return to Inspector Han's cheeks.

Once he regains consciousness, Ryun had told me earlier, *talk to him, try to keep him awake until the physician arrives.*

I dug my nails into my skirt, bunching it into a tight ball until my knuckles turned white. I waited, but the ghostly pallor clung to his skin and would not leave.

●

Memories flickered in the cavern of my mind. The radiant moonlight filtering in through the brushwood door. A sputtering candle and its dancing shadows. My brother's hands over my ears; muffled voices seeping in through his fingers, *Catholic demons! They'll bring a curse on us!* His eyes, steady and silent as a sunlit meadow, the corners crinkling as he smiled at me.

All will be well, he'd whispered. *I promise you.*

My finger hovered as it traced the contours of Inspector Han's face, his stern brows, the curve of his eyelids, and the straight line of his nose. Was he still there, this brother of mine? My hand jerked back as his eyes half-opened.

There was an odd fogginess still swimming in his gaze, like he was somewhere else, and wherever that was, it was a place where I did not exist. But he was awake, finally! Heartbeat racing, I took in a deep breath to call out for Ryun, for he might have returned by now. But before I could, Inspector Han whispered, "Those letters . . ."

"Letters, sir?" I waited for something more, but he drifted in and out of consciousness.

I looked around. There was the low-legged table that Inspector Han had always sat behind during my visits. The floor-to-ceiling bookshelves on either side of us. And an object I'd always observed from afar: the black-lacquered document box with gold-painted decoration, mother-of-pearl inlay, and metal fittings. Folded sheets were piled inside, with the lid resting on the table next to it.

"Those letters," Inspector Han's voice resurfaced. "Give them to Ryun."

"I will," I promised, and when silence followed, I could hear only the pounding of my frightened heart. "Inspector, please, talk to me. Ask me anything."

"Your older sister . . . she is well?"

He made himself sound even more like a stranger, and I had to restrain myself from correcting him. *Our sister.*

I instead played along. "I believe so. She got married many years ago."

"And your sister . . . when she asks one day, tell her I am well."

"Won't you see her and tell her yourself, sir?"

In the quiet that followed, I realized that it was hopeless. I thought he would want to get to know me and my family, the mystery now solved and my identity revealed. All this time, I must have really thought he would come back as my brother, ready to live in Inchon, perhaps by taking up a humble position in the government office nearby and living a small life.

Small, I thought bitterly. No, Inspector Han was meant for a different life. He would not, could not change back into my brother.

"Too much time has passed," he said, echoing my own thoughts, "for things to go back to the way they were. It has been too long."

It was too late for things to go back, especially after what I had done to him. "I'm sorry," I whispered. "I betrayed you, sir."

"Do not be. Sometimes betrayal is the deepest expression of love."

For a long time I stayed still, watching his chest rise and fall as he breathed. His eyes were open, the dim flickering of light in them growing even dimmer. It was like watching an eclipse slowly shut out the sun.

Then the pace of his breathing slowed, saliva slipping down the side of his mouth.

"Inspector?"

His eyelids flinched. A sign, perhaps, that he'd heard me.

I was running out of time, yet I had so much to say. "In those letters," I blurted out, "did you ever write about me?" I knew he had, but I wanted him to speak openly, to share more about what he thought about me. It was my only way of asking him, *Do you even care?*

The slightest smile tugged at his lips, like a rare ripple in the calm sea. "Tomorrow, Seol."

Just then I heard approaching footsteps and male voices. I rose from the floor and hurried to the door, struggling to breathe through the swelling of mingled panic and hope. But just as I reached the door, I heard it.

A deep sigh escaped his lips. The sigh of a weary traveler at the end of a long journey.

I looked over my shoulder, and it took seconds before I mustered up enough courage to lower my eyes. Inspector Han's gaze stared out like windows opened onto a dark and empty expanse.

I fell onto my knees and dragged my fingers across the floor until I touched the tips of his. Cold and still.

The outside wind burst into the office as the physician, along with Commander Yi, rushed in. There was no more space for me now to remain. Through the blurring of my vision, I turned to look at Inspector Han one last time and I smiled—twisted and crooked, but a smile all the same.

His little sister, Jeong Jeong-yun, had been loyal to him in the end.

TWENTY-THREE

FIVE MONTHS HAD gone by.

I could still remember the way Inspector Han had said those two words to me: *Tomorrow, Seol.* His tone had reminded me of a near-ripe persimmon, bitter and yet slightly sweet. Had I known that he would pass away before sending me home to Inchon, perhaps I would have encouraged him to speak more during our time in Mount Yongma—about our history together. Perhaps I would have been less afraid of what he might have said. Less afraid to know him.

"The inspector's request to send you home was granted," Ryun had explained to me, after telling me to pack my belongings. "The days will grow dark here—men, women, and children will run to the mountains during the Catholic purge. And the inspector knew that you have sympathy for those rogues. He didn't have the heart for you to remain, Seol."

Winter in Inchon was freezing when it came, the scent of snow and pine carried always in the wind. The snow fell until we were knee-deep.

Then the sun melted it away and I saw sprouts of withered green grass. The spring rain drizzled, the dried plants soaking it up. The pathway outside our hut was muddy now. Sandals squished. Carts got trapped. Oxen loaded with brushwood slogged heavily by, their hooves splattering muck from rain puddles. Nothing like the sound I would have woken up to in the great capital.

Life here in the province was slower, one of labor and tranquility. The work was toilsome, for I worked in the rice paddy with Older Sister and her husband, our backs bent and aching from planting seeds. And yet I was ever surrounded by the azure water flooding the paddy, the bright sun winking in the sky.

These calm days sedated my grief. And never did my soul shudder before the sight of murder victims.

On days when there was little to do, I kept my mind occupied by practicing my writing and reading, or visiting the stream where women rolled and beat their laundry. There, I would sit with my friends on a rock and dip a finger into the chilly flow and listen to the daily gossip.

This is the life I wanted, I told myself every day. *I ought to be thankful.*

And yet I missed the capital, something I was ashamed to confess to Older Sister. She would have shaken her head, saying, "Not even a year ago you tried running away and ended up with that terrifying mark on your cheek. Now you wish to go back?"

I missed the capital, the center of power, where the people were organized like the land, with its high mountains and low valleys, never a dull day when the air was tense with conspiracy. There in Hanyang, I had been more than an ordinary girl. The capital made me brave and useful.

But more than anything, I missed it because it was where Inspector Han had once been, and where the others I'd come to care for dwelled. Lady Kang and her daughter. Woorim. Madam Song. Even the lying Maid Soyi. What were they up to now?

●

More and more these days, my mind and my limbs groaned with restlessness.

I rose early one day, earlier than even the farmers, and made my way through the silent, dawn-lit paths up to Mount Gyeyang. I collected wood for fire; a reason to venture out alone. The repetitive motion of reaching and loading the birchwood onto the wooden A-frame was a peaceful distraction.

That night, I wandered off again to collect some more wood, returning home only when it was late and my tired limbs were trembling. I arrived at the hut only to discover that Older Sister was not sleeping, but sewing by candlelight. Waiting for me.

"You're home," was all she said.

Home. Yes, this was home. Pressing my fingers into my eyelids, I told myself this must stop. This restlessness. If I could not be happy, then for my sister's sake, I ought at least to be content. But I could not stop hearing Inspector Han's voice in my head.

You can be anything you want.

●

"Did you hear what Merchant Hong said?" my sister's husband, Mr. Palbok, sat on the veranda of our hut, puffing on his tobacco pipe. He blew out a cloud of smoke that was hurled backward in the spring wind. His head turned sideways, just enough for me to see the irises of his eyes, ever watchful of my sister's fragile mood. "A new edict has been passed by Queen Regent Jeongsun."

I paused in my sewing and shifted my gaze to my sister. She sat cross-legged on a mat, rubbing her large stomach. She was seven months pregnant. "I heard," she said.

"Catholics are being arrested, one after another," he continued, shaking his head. "Commander Yi used torture to make the Catholics confess the whereabouts of the priest. Had Inspector Han lived, he would have led this purge."

I knew why Mr. Palbok was telling her about this. He thought it abnormal, as did I, that Older Sister had stopped asking about Inspector Han. On the first day of my return to Inchon, I had explained the entire story about Inspector Han to her, our blood ties to him, his death. She had asked so many questions, her eyes wide and bright, but when she'd learned that before his passing, he had refused to visit home, her mouth had clamped shut.

"The inspector's dream was to find the priest," I whispered. "But perhaps it is better that he is not found."

"He has been found," Mr. Palbok said.

A heavy weight dropped down into my stomach.

"Apparently the priest was hiding in the Defunct Palace. The two banished royals, Princess Song and Princess Sin, converted to Catholicism long ago and chose to be his last guardians. But the police took their palace maid and interrogated her until she confessed. I hear Priest Zhou Wenmo could have escaped again, but he knew the Catholics were being killed because of him, so he surrendered himself to the police bureau."

Older Sister sighed, then muttered, "It was our brother's dream to kill the priest? When did he become so ambitious and hard-hearted?" She rubbed her belly in wide circles, as though trying to warm the child curled within her. "Father always told him, 'We must not harm others, or we will harm ourselves.' And this I do know—our brother wasted away in the capital."

A few days after learning about the priest's capture, I learned that he had been put to death and not deported. The queen regent had changed her mind—inspired by cunning advice to disguise the priest's death as an "accident." Her Majesty had therefore sent a special envoy to China to present evidence to the Chinese court, a statement claiming that the Joseon authorities had not known Priest Zhou Wenmo was Chinese at the time of his execution, for he looked like a Joseon person, dressed like a Joseon person, and had spoken the Joseon language.

His death was all anyone talked about. I learned by listening to them that his execution had taken place outside the West Gate at Saenamteo, near the Han River. People had struggled to watch the beheading due to the heavy rain shower, but they had clearly heard his voice. It was said that before his execution, he'd said, "The only reason I came to Joseon, despite dangers I may face at the border, was because I love the Joseon people. The teaching of Jesus is not evil. But I no longer wish to do harm to the people or the kingdom of Joseon."

I had seen his face before, so clear before my mind's eye now, the little scars marking his tanned face, his hair tied back into a queue. And now as I repeated in my mind what he had said to the crowd, I imagined I heard his voice waver, as though he were about to weep. It was strange how sadness reached so deeply into my chest for a man I had never spoken to.

As for Lady Kang, I'd never learned whether she lived or died. I did hear that the Heretical Virgin Troupe she'd led had all been decapitated, beaten to death in prison, strangled, or poisoned for refusing to apostatize. A part of me hoped that she had fled her mansion to the mountains and was hiding somewhere safely.

But I knew she was gone. She was no coward.

●

I decided to write to Aejung one day, asking about how her life fared in the police bureau, and if she'd learned anything new about Inspector Han after his passing. Every day afterward I took to the habit of sliding open the screen door, peering past the brushwood gate surrounding our hut and out at the road. I waited to see dust rise into the air. I waited to see a messenger approaching with a letter addressed to me. But whenever the dust rose, only a farmer with his oxcart passed by, or a group of middle-aged women came to gossip with Older Sister.

Soon, dried leaves blew into the yard, and no matter how often I'd sweep them out, they would return in piles.

Mid-autumn, five months after I'd written to Aejung, I paced around the veranda, my socks quieting my steps as I piggybacked my sleeping nephew in a wraparound blanket. I'd promised to watch him while Sister and her husband went to sell vegetables in the village. Then I heard hoofbeats pounding on the hard road. A sound rare to hear in the province, for only nobles could afford horses, and there were not too many nobles in these parts.

I shaded my eyes and saw a young man garbed in a white tunic and trousers, strands of his black hair flying over his sunburnt face. The horse came to a prancing halt a few feet away from me, startling me to take a few steps back. My nephew awoke, his piercing cry sharp in my ears, and yet I was too stunned at the sight of Ryun to notice.

"It's been a long time," Ryun said, leaping down from his horse. "You look the same."

I observed the young man before me, and as he swept his hair aside, I noticed his drawn cheeks and the shadows beneath his eyes. "You look beat up."

"Heh." He walked past me, and as he tethered the reins to a nearby tree, I told him I would return shortly.

Hurrying off to the kitchen, my nephew still bawling in my ears, I pulled down an earthenware jar from the shelf, then poured rice wine into a bowl. I brought it out on a tray to find Ryun pacing the yard, kicking the ground now and then. He stopped when he saw me.

"Thank you," he said, and gulped down the drink in two swallows.

I waited for him to pull out a letter.

"What have you been up to?" he asked instead, wiping his mouth with the back of his sleeve.

"I help around the home and take care of my nephew."

"That is all you have been doing these past months?"

"I help in other ways."

Ryun placed his hands on either side of his waist as he looked around, his gaze taking in the mountain burnished gold, the blue sky above. "A very tranquil life you seem to be living here."

"Tranquil enough."

"Dull?"

I kept quiet.

"Do you have a sweetheart?"

I scrunched my face, confused and wary. "No."

"Your sister has her husband, and now a son, too. You have no sweetheart. You're not much needed here, it seems. There's nothing holding you down. Commander Yi wishes you to return to work at the police bureau. He came and asked me specifically, as he knows we are acquainted."

"Me? He *wishes* for my return?"

"Well, he cannot *demand* it of you. His respect for Inspector Han is too deep to do so. He is aware of your blood ties to the inspector."

"But why does he want me back?"

"He has lost most of the capable damos. Hyeyeon and a few others passed the medical exam and have become palace nurses again."

I bit my lower lip as I rocked my nephew back and forth on my back. To say that I had not thought of returning to the capital would have been a lie, and now the idea of chasing after another mystery skipped in my pulse. But that skipping beat slowed and turned into a heavy weight, remembering that Inspector Han was gone.

"It will be different. A new inspector, a new case," Ryun said. "Inspector Han told the commander that detectives are born, not made. A good detective is one who is inquisitive and full of fight, which you are—he said so, these precise words. This is the main reason why Commander Yi wishes for your return, though he seemed reluctant to admit it. No military official will openly admit that they need the help of a *girl*."

I almost smiled, but it was difficult to feel complete joy these days. "A new inspector . . ."

"Yes, a new one." Ryun swallowed hard and a shade of gloom passed over his countenance. "Sometimes I forget that Inspector Han is really gone. But he is, Seol. And he would have wanted you to move on. Don't look back for him too long."

●

I lived a walkable distance to the sea.

I inched cautiously alongside the edge of a cliff, the sea spray soaking my face and ragged dress, until I found the trail that descended all the way down. The pebbles crunched beneath my steps as I landed on the shore, and I stumbled across and crawled onto the rocks that reached far into the waters. I stretched out my arms on either side of me, and after a few cautious steps, my balance grew steadier. The mist lifted and I stood before the sea, which lapped against the rock where starfish and clams clung. A black crab skittered by.

I unclenched my fist and stared at the crumpled letter in my hand. Ryun had given me a black-lacquered document box, the one I'd seen before in Inspector Han's office. "*My master must have felt vulnerable,*" Ryun had explained when I'd asked him why the inspector hadn't given the box to me himself, for he'd had the chance to do so. "*The letters within, they are his heart, and he has never been good at sharing his innermost being.*"

I had brought with me the most recent page Inspector Han had left behind. As I stared at it, I wondered if my memories of the capital were all a dream. I wondered if I had ever known the inspector, or if I had even found the haunted mansion where our history had met in the form of an old pine tree bent into the shape of a river.

I waited. It took a while for him to appear in my mind, and when he did, I saw his long and thin face, his high nose, his brown eyes that were filled with light. What were his eyes seeing and witnessing now?

I looked out at the expanse and knew where he had gone.

He had sunk into the sea of rebirth, into the rushing of ten thousand rivers. Closing my eyes, I prayed to the heavens that in his next life, orabeoni would be surrounded by people whose hearts brimmed with kindness. And I would brim with kindness to those around me, because my brother could be anywhere. His life could be hidden in the form of a child, an ant, or a blind turtle adrift in the waters.

Perhaps, if I listened closely, I might even hear his heartbeat come from the depth of the sea.

TWENTY-FOUR

INSPECTOR HAN'S LAST LETTER TO THE DEAD

The great rainy season continues. I traveled through the mire and went to Inchon Prefecture to speak with Older Sister, to see where you had grown up, but I turned back at the gate of her hut, deciding that I could not face our past. You want and need from me what I do not know how to provide. I can do so through my imagination by writing this letter to you, but not in person. I would not know how to be the brother you long for.

I turned to travel back to the capital, where I am wanted. On the way, I looked to the east, and can you imagine what I saw, Little Sister? I saw the memory of you during our journey to Suwon, laughing and shaking as you rode through the overflowing grassland. I was glad to see you so amused and grateful to see how you had grown.

Older Sister and I did not think you would live past your tenth winter. When you were a child, every time I left to collect wood, you fell ill. You were so weak and your stomach so sensitive.

It bewilders me how you returned so capable and clever. Now you are taller than most men in the bureau. Your bones still look brittle enough to break, except you know how to protect others. It is hard to believe, but you are not a child anymore. You grew up and now you are strong without me.

Perhaps much later when Older Sister is sixty and you are forty-seven, we will greet each other again and our hearts will brim with fullness.

Until then, I will be on my way home.

AUTHOR'S NOTE

The first major persecution of Catholics in Joseon Korea was the Shinyu Bakhae of 1801, when approximately three hundred Catholics were beheaded. Thousands of others were arrested, tortured, and sent into exile.

When I first learned about this time in Korean history, there were two women who stood out to me: Queen Jeongsun, the regent with the fierceness of a general, and Lady Kang Wansuk, the noblewoman who moved beyond the domestic sphere and became a highly respected leader in a male-dominated Catholic community.

However, in order to understand these women, it's important to know the political context of that time, which greatly shaped their lives.

In nineteenth-century Joseon Korea, there were four major factions, also referred to as the Four Colors: Southerners, Northerners, Old Doctrine, and Young Doctrine. Party affiliations were formed over generations, tied by family and teacher-disciple–based loyalty, and political power was monopolized as factions destroyed their rivals through imprisonment, exile, and even death.

During this period, the Old Doctrine was most powerful. They strongly supported the rigid, classical social structure that emphasized the importance of bloodline purity and the preservation of tradition. As a result, they were determined to prevent foreign influences from entering the royal court. In contrast, the Southerners were barely surviving and turned to new influences in their attempt to regain political power. They were therefore associated with Western ideas of philosophy, religion, and science. As Southerners brought Western teachings from China into Joseon, the Old Doctrine accordingly hardened their stance, and the contention between the two factions increased over time.

The factional strife made palace life difficult for Queen Jeongsun. At the young age of fourteen, she married the elderly King Yeongjo and strove to maintain her Old Doctrine family's power in court. While the Old Doctrine faction held the most power, they were responsible for influencing King Yeongjo to kill his own son—the reform-minded Crown Prince Sado—and this move would ultimately backfire on them. Because once the elderly king passed away, the new king to ascend the throne was Chŏngjo, the son of the murdered crown prince. He locked arms with the Southerner faction, and together, they punished Queen Jeongsun's Old Doctrine family members and stripped her of power.

For the next twenty years, her resentment toward King Chŏngjo and the Southerners grew. Then suddenly, after Chŏngjo's unexpected death, she rose as regent, wielding enormous power over the government. Jeongsun immediately set about taking her revenge. She joined forces with the Old Doctrine faction and decided to use the persecution of Catholics as a means of eliminating the Southerners, for many of them were Catholic converts. By coming down hard on her political rivals, she would finally be able to vent her rage after the years spent powerless and in isolation.

Outside the palace walls, there was another woman who defied the gender ideology of the Joseon period, where women were expected to be completely hidden from the outer world. Lady Kang Wansuk took on a public career as a leader in the Catholic community. She was involved in the project of smuggling Priest Zhou Wenmo into Hanyang (now called

Seoul) in 1795. When the government learned of the priest's arrival, the intense hunt for him began, which was when Lady Kang decided to take Priest Zhou Wenmo into the protection of her home.

During this time, her home became the center of Catholic activity and propagation. But Lady Kang was not only an active teacher of the gospel; she was also known for inviting illiterate servants and maids into her home, where she would teach them how to read.

When the Shinyu Bakhae broke out in 1801, the persecution was spearheaded by the queen regent's political offensive against the Southerners, but even those who had no ties to the factional strife were affected by it. Lady Kang was immediately arrested and was taken to the Capital Police Bureau, where she was tortured for the purpose of extracting information about the whereabouts of Priest Zhou Wenmo. Even then, her priority to protect the priest did not waver, and the torture continued until Priest Zhou Wenmo decided to hand himself over.

Soon after, Lady Kang and the priest, along with many others, were condemned to death. She was beheaded outside the West Gate in Hanyang on July 2, 1801 (May 22, by the lunar calendar). She was forty years old.

ACKNOWLEDGMENTS

As I think of all those who supported my writing dream, it has never been clearer to me than now that the publication of a book is not a solitary achievement. I am deeply grateful to my editor, Emily Settle, for tirelessly helping me turn this manuscript into a novel.

A special thank-you to my production editor, Alexei Esikoff; my copy editor, Valerie Shea; my designer, Katie Klimowicz; my cover artist, Kasiq Jungwoo; and everyone at the wonderful Feiwel and Friends for bringing this book to life. Many thanks to my agent, Amy Elizabeth Bishop, for championing my work and patiently replying to all my anxious emails!

To my critique partners, early readers, and supporters, this writing journey would have been so lonely and despair-filled without you all: Kim S., Clariza, Mina, Kerrie, Maybelle, Tatiana, Matthew, Mado, Evan, and especially Shaylin, who believed in this book even when I doubted it. To my small group ladies and Cristina: the way you listened so patiently and lovingly to all my writing woes kept me going. To Joan He and Roselle, thank you for being there for me, especially when I have questions about publishing! Also, a big thank-you to Rebecca, Francesca, Maria D, Amélie, Katie, Kathleen, Grace, Eunice, Liz, Nafiza, Adele, Rachel, Patrice, and Tanya, among many others, who advocated for this book on Twitter. And a humongous thank-you to Julie Dao for encouraging me when I was stuck in the Query Trenches and for being a role model to so many writers.

I'd also like to thank all the critique partners from back when I first began writing, who helped me become a stronger writer: Rowenna,

Cassie, Priscilla, Becca K, Flore, Grace V, Val-Rae, Rika, Sarah Dill, and Brenna. I hope I didn't miss anyone, but it's possible that I did (forgive me!), because so many people helped me along the way.

All my love to everyone in the Toronto Writers Crew: Kess, Fallon, Elora, Kelly, Sarena, Sasha, Liselle, Deborah, Joanna, Louisa, and Maggie. Thank you for being so supportive and for being a source of never-ending inspiration. Having dinner and cocktails with you lovely people, and chatting for hours about writing and publishing, is something I always look forward to.

And, of course, my eternal gratitude to my family. To my parents, who encouraged me to pursue writing, never pressuring me to do anything other than what I love. To my sister, for always being my greatest ally and never doubting that I could make something of my writing. To my brother, for believing I'll one day make enough book money to buy him a house and a car (that day's still far, far, far away). And to my husband, Bosco, for his unwavering love and consideration. Life is so much richer with a best friend like you by my side.

A towering pile of books and articles helped me bring Joseon Korea to life, but the resources I turned to the most were Jahyun Kim Haboush's *Epistolary Korea: Letters in the Communicative Space of the Chosŏn, 1392–1910*; Sun Joo Kim and Jungwon Kim's *Wrongful Deaths: Selected Inquest Records from Nineteenth-Century Korea*; Yungchung Kim's *Women of Korea: A History from Ancient Times to 1945*; Peter H. Lee's *Sources of Korean Tradition, Vol. 2*; Key P. Yang and Gregory Henderson's *An Outline History of Korean Confucianism: Part I: The Early Period and Yi Factionalism*; and Moo-Sook Hanh's *Encounter: A Novel of Nineteenth-Century Korea*.

One last thing: I thank Jesus, my Lord and Savior, for guiding me through the darkest moments in life and for putting up with all my bad moods.